The Far Northern Land Saga Book III
Finnish Legends Come to Life

The Queen of Pohjola

David Allen Schlaefer

Printed in the United States of America
Paperback ISBN: 978-1-953910-81-3
Ebook ISBN: 978-1-953910-82-0
Library of Congress Control Number: 2023934385

DartFrog Plus
A division of DartFrog Books
4697 Main Street
Manchester Center, VT 05255

The Far Northern Land Saga

Synopsis of Book I: The Mark of the Bear Clan

ULLA, a seven-year old girl, lives in a poor village of rye farmers near the cold wastelands. One day a bear badly mauls her, leaving her for dead. The wizard **VÄINÄMÖINEN** discovers Ulla by chance and heals her. The old wizard notices something strange; the scars on her back form the perfect shape of a bear's claw, the clan-mark and totem of her people. He at once recalls an old prophecy of a child who will unite the Seven Clans against the Witch, **LÖHI**, but the old man is unsure about Ulla. Soon afterward, Ulla's village is attacked by the savage Easterners. Her family dead, her village in ruins, Ulla escapes and meets another scatterling, a red-haired girl covered from head to toe with freckles, **KIRSIKKA**. Famished and exhausted, the girls are rescued improbably by Väinämöinen, who takes them to his home deep in the forest.

Hundreds of miles away, the precocious Prince **EGAN** of the Swan Folk is thrust into power when his father the king is slain by **LOVĚATAR** a hideous ghost from Hell unleashed by Löhi. Väinämöinen sees something in Egan akin to what he sees in Ulla: purity of spirit, steadfastness of purpose, and hope. He champions Egan and gives him a precious gift—the famous Sword of Legend used to defeat Löhi in ancient times. Meanwhile, Ulla discovers that she possesses the power to work magic and secretly learns several spells. The girl loves Väinämöinen by now, seeing him as a father-figure offering home and belonging, and hopes that in becoming what everyone seems to want her to be—the Child of the Prophecy and Löhi's enemy—she can bind the old man to her and never be alone again.

Väinämöinen and Ulla visit the old **SEER**, a mortal witch alone in her tower with a crystal ball. The old woman tells the wizard that the captain of Löhi's army bears an enchanted crystal that he uses to spy on the Seven Clans. Väinämöinen sends Ulla away and prepares for a desperate defense. Terrified of being alone again and wanting to prove her worth to him, she weaves a magic spell, slips into the enemy camp, and steals the magic crystal. The old wizard sets a trap for their enemies, but despite his trick, the Witch's men and goblins are on the cusp of victory when Egan finally arrives and slays the Witch's captain with the legendary sword. The battle is won and Löhi's first invasion blunted. The wizard embraces the little girl, finally accepting her destiny as a wizard and promising never to leave her. Egan is hailed as a hero and steels himself to lead the Seven Clans in great battles to come. Returning to the old Seer's tower, Väinämöinen, Ulla, and Egan discover a miraculous thing. Compelled by vivid dreams, dozens of people from all the Seven Clans are gathering to learn the old magic.

Synopsis of Book II: The Heir of Lemminkäinen

Seven years has passed since Ulla stole the precious crystal and Egan became king. War rages; the Seven Clans battle Löhi's legions, and dozens of men and women study magic with Väinämöinen. The old man finally relents and allows Ulla to go on her "hunt," a spiritual quest to kill her totem—the bear—and become a true wizard. She succeeds, but not before encountering Löhi in spirit form and barely escaping with her life. Egan and Ulla fall in love, although the girl seems more terrified of happiness—and the prospect of its loss—than of death in battle. Väinämöinen and Ulla discover that an ancient hero, the great smith **ILMARINEN**, is still alive. They convince him to reforge the mighty **SAMPO**, a magical object that Löhi stole long ago and which was later destroyed.

The old Seer convinces Egan that his destiny is to become the High King of the Far Northern Land, the first high king since the days of the hero

Lemminkäinen. Uniting the Seven Clans, Egan leads a great army into the wastelands, hoping to end the war with one stroke, one battle; but he was tricked. In a final tragic battle, Egan is slain by Löhi, the army destroyed, and the new wizards scattered. At the same time, faraway, Ilmarinen the smith is betrayed by **SIITSA**, a servant of the Seer whom Löhi secretly seduced; the Sampo is lost forever. Väinämöinen and a shattered Ulla lead a small group of broken survivors back from the battle to their homelands to carry on the struggle—with or without hope.

Acknowledgments

I first became interested in Finland and its heroic tales as a child. I owe this interest to my parents, Dan and Jeanie, who collected an odd assortment of amazing books on all sorts of subjects. One such book was a *Reader's Digest* special on folklore of the world, which introduced me to Väinämöinen and the Kalevala. The other was part of a Time Life series on World War II and battles in Scandinavia. My interest whetted, I read everything about Finland I could get my hands on. Many years later, I had the opportunity to serve in Finland as an American diplomat, fulfilling a life-long dream and setting the stage for the Far Northern Land Saga.

My Finnish teachers, Anuliinna Santry and Anna-Mari Barrineau, provided inspiration and amazing instruction. The staff at the Gallen-Kallela Museum in Espoo, Finland generously gave their time and patiently answered the strange American's many questions. I was encouraged throughout the writing process by many friends, but Heikki Hämäläinen, Vera Stah, Marja Sevón, and Ulla Anttila stand out among them; I thank them profusely.

The gorgeous map of the Far Northern Land that accompanies this volume was created by Misty Beee, as was the map of Pohjola found only in this volume. The creative process that led to the final versions was one of the most rewarding experiences of my artistic career, and I encourage those interested in fantasy cartography and design to visit her website.

Although written over the course of many years, I found myself caught up in the war in Ukraine in 2022 when working on the final edit for the Queen of Pohjola. The raw emotions I experienced during my initial evacuation from Kyiv, subsequent return, and observation of so much suffering and loss informed my last revisions of the book's critical passages. I feel indebted to the people of Ukraine for teaching me so much about strength and resilience.

Finally, no author worth their salt can fail to acknowledge the support of their family, and I'm no exception. My incredible wife, Raluca, and children helped me in so many ways and I am grateful to all of them. Gaddison, Christian, Anastasia, Viktoria, Maria, and Klara, I thank you all, with love.

Notes on Names and Language

The stories that appear in the Far Northern Land saga are inspired by Finnish folklore, especially the famous work *Kalevala* by the great compiler of Finnish oral poetry, Elias Lönnrot. In addition to his expertise in medicine, ethnography, and many other fields, Lönnrot was a philologist and loved language. Having had the unique opportunity (for a foreigner, at least) of studying Finnish full-time for an entire year and then living in Finland for almost half a decade, I naturally incorporated Finnish into my work when I set out to write the series. Beautiful in phonology and structure, it is not an easy language for non-native speakers to acquire and I beg patience of readers who find themselves confronted by pages of unfamiliar words and letters with no mentor like Väinämöinen to guide them as they journey.

The chief peculiarity, at least to English speakers, is the extensive use in Finnish of diacritics: the letters ä and ö. These letters represent distinct sounds and their use is governed by the process of "vowel harmony." This, and the multisyllabic, compound structure that encourages long words with lots of double consonants, can be a challenge. But the recompense is that readers will catch a glimpse, however dim, of the sounds that Ulla, Egan, Väinämöinen, and the peoples of Iron Age Finland actually used and heard and which they bequeathed down the centuries to their contemporary descendants. I believe this glimpse is worth the challenge.

By necessity, I have been inconsistent throughout my stories. For any violence done to the Finnish language, I can only offer sincere regret. Most words in the Far Northern Land saga used to represent the speech of its inhabitants at the time the events occurred are contemporary Finnish. But I have "antiqued" some to better match the feel of the age in question. In a few instances, I have purposefully dropped diacritics, which Finns will quickly notice (*Etela* vice *Etelä*). Perversely, I have added them to one word. Most egregiously, in a very few instances, I have used incorrect case, a cardinal sin. I can offer only apologies and the feeble justification that as Väinämöinen taught Ulla, balance in all things is ideal, and to strike a balance between fidelity to the language and accessibility to non-native speakers was my intent. Undoubtedly, I sometimes failed, but I hope the sincerity of effort warrants forgiveness.

Finally, to assist the reader, I decided to spell out a few phonetic pronunciations of some of the chief characters and places, and a glossary of some key words here at the onset of the book. The proto-Finns who lived in the Far Northern Land at the time of this saga were divided into many clans and kinship groups. The chief groups each had its own totem, which often appeared in the clan's name or the name of its homeland. There are exceptions. The great kingdom of the south was *Etelamaa* and its people were the *Etelalaiset*, which literally translates as "Southland" and "Southerners." However, their totem was the swan (*joutsen*) and they were colloquially called the Swan-Folk by the other clans. Since these names can be confusing at first (and second and third, etc.) encounter, I set them out below and encourage readers interested in such things to thumb back whenever needed to this page to refresh their memory of who was what and lived where. The maps will also offer assistance.

<u>Proper Names</u>

Väinämöinen—VĪ-na-MOY-nen—(the great singer)

Lemminkäinen—LĔM-min-KĪ-nen—(ancient hero and high king)

Löhi—LŌ-hee—(the Witch of the North)

Länsimaa—LĂN-si-maw—('Westland')

Ulla—OOL-la—(the girl who bears the Mark of the Clan)

Egan—Ā-gun—(King of the Swan Folk)

Kaukomieli—KOW-ko-MEE-e-lee—(wizard of the Singing Valley and Ulla's companion)

Kirsikka—KEER-sik-ka—(Ulla's friend)

Mielikki—MEE-e-LĬK-kee—(the Lady of the Forest)

Tulikki—TOO-li-kee—(Mielikki's daughter)

Pohjola—PŌ-ho-YŌ-la—('Northland')

Kuupää—KOO-pă—(the 'Moonface,' Löhi's captain)

Sariola—SAW-ree-Ō-la—('place of sickness,' the Witch's Keep in Pohjola)

Lovêatar—LŌ-vee-a-tar—(ghost from Hell that spreads disease and death)

Tuonela—TŪ-Ō-ne-la—(the underworld, abode of the Dead)

Peiko—PĀ-ko—(troll who befriends Ulla and her companions)

<u>Homelands and Clans of the Far Northern Land</u>

Karelia—Karelialaiset—(the Reindeer Folk)

High Länsimaa—Karhulaiset—(the Bear Folk)

Deep Länsimaa—Hirvilaiset—(the Elk Folk)

Etelamaa—Etelalaiset—(the Swan Folk)

Tavastia—Tavastialaiset—(the Hare Folk)

Akkala—Kotkalaiset—(the Eagle Folk)

Susila—Susilaiset—(the Wolf Folk or Lost Clan)

Erilaiset—(the immortal race of heroes, Väinämöinen's people)

____

Pohjola—Pohjolaiset—(the Northerners or Löhi's Folk)

Itäläiset—(the Easterners)
Hiisia—(the goblins)

<u>Weapons and Things in the Far Northern Land</u>
Pitkälehti—('Long-leaf,' Ulla's dagger)
Pojhanpiikki—('North-thorn,' first Tyë's then Ulla's sword)
Jääpuikko—('Icicle,' Väinämöinen's sword)
Runolaulaja—('Poem or Spell-singer,' Kaukomieli's sword)
Tarunmiekka—('Sword of Legend,' first Lemminkäinen's then Egan's sword)
Arrow of Tuonetar—(magical arrow made of stone from the Isle of the Dead in Tuonela)
Kantele—(traditional Finnish stringed instrument played by Väinämöinen)
Bloodrock—(ore-bearing rock used to forge high-quality iron and steel)
Winterfast—(secret technique used to keep swords and other weapons from becoming brittle in extreme cold)
Tietäjää—('one-who-knows,' the wizards of the Far Northern Land)
Metsävartija—('forest-guard,' the March Wardens of the Seven Clans)
Sampo—(magical object forged by Ilmarinen the Smith to ensure prosperity in the Far Northern Land)
Loitsu—(song or spell used by the Erilaiset)
Kalma—(song or spell used by Löhi, black magic)
Etianen—('frontwalker,' a spirit-like form that wizards could project to travel great distances)
Taivaantappi—('nail of the heavens,' the North Star)
Pirtti—(traditional timber and sod cabin built by villagers in the Far Northern Land)
Seidi-stone—(rock with a spirit trapped within)
Colorless Woods—(the spirit-world, the border between the material world and death)
Reiki—(traditional large sled, pulled by reindeer or ponies)

TABLE OF CONTENTS

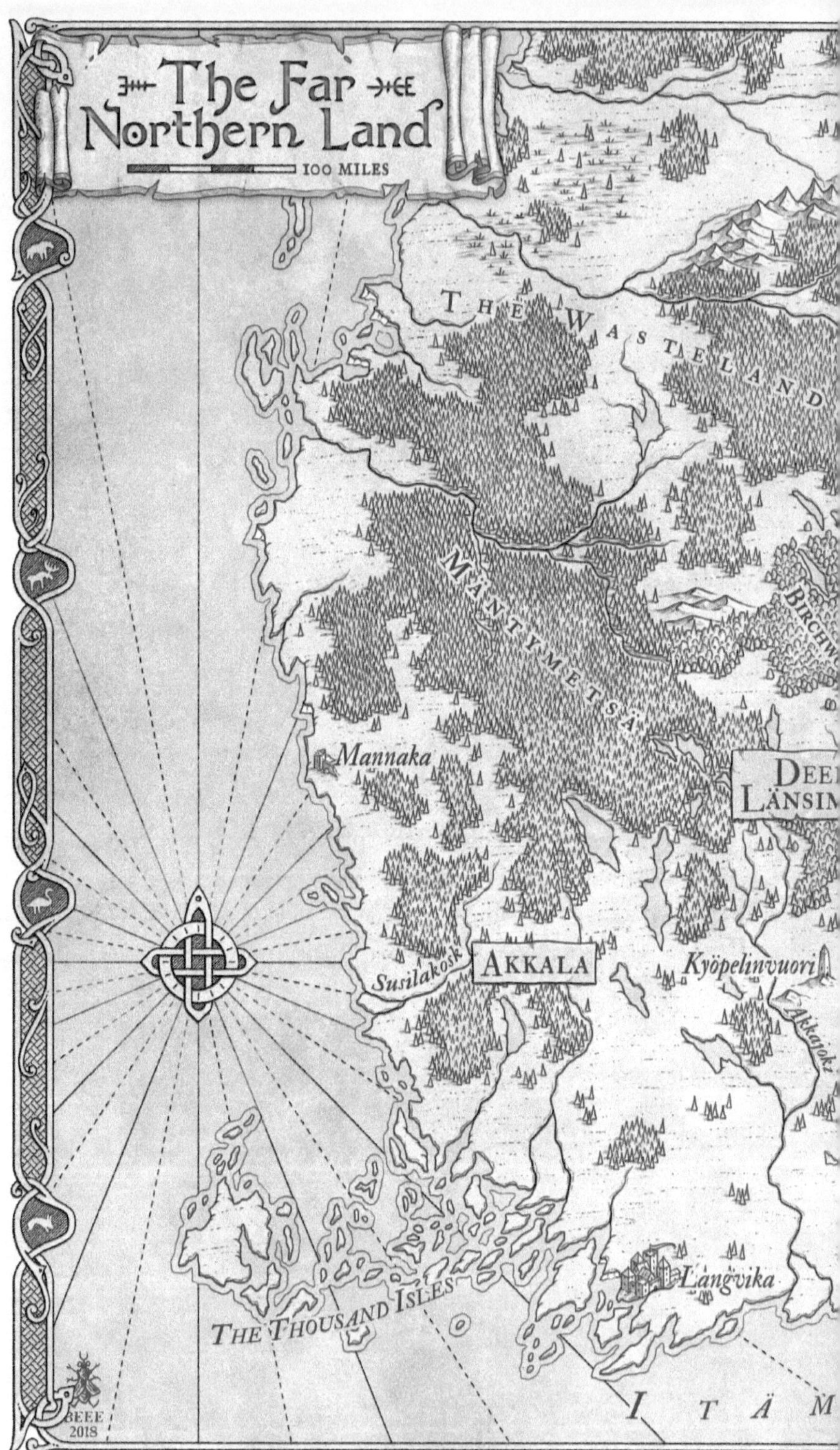

The Far Northern Land
100 MILES
THE WASTELAND
MÄNTYMETSÄ
BIRCHW
DEE
LÄNSIN
Mannaka
AKKALA
Kyöpelinvuori
Susilakoshi
Akkarjoki
Längvika
THE THOUSAND ISLES
ITÄM
BEEE
2018

NORTH MARCHES
Gränkulta
Gamla
LAKE SUURIJÄRVI
Metsäposti
KARELIA
Vainöla
ENCHANTED VALLEY
Joukri
HIGH LÄNSIMAA
Keskimaa
Valkeakosk
Siinesaare
innavuori
ANISKITA
THE WALL OF THE GIANTS
GREEN VALES
NECK
Kotanrannta
Rajavesi
ETELAMAA
LAKE ETELAJÄRVI
Tapiola
Haamerouku
AVASTIA
Stone City
E.rannta Harmaaniemi
Sepällä
SEA

The Land of Pohjola
50 MILES
JÄÄVUORI
WHI
To the
Kääpiövuri
POH
PO
Pimentola
Candlestick Forest
KAMAL
BEEE
2021

WILDERNESS
MOUNTAINS OF POHJOLA
N
O
L
A
KUUN PUSIKKO
Kipuvuori
Sariola
The Witch's Keep
Hiitola
Way Station and Cabin
Dwarves' Road
KEMIJÄRVI
Kemi
Saami Reindeer Trail

Chapter One

The Gates of Tapiola

The hooded rider all in black looked down at the ragged crew. A hunchback and a one-armed man with an ill-favored face, scarred as if cut by a blade, had just dug a long, shallow trench by the roadside, piling the earth beside it. Behind them lay several prostrate figures wrapped in dirty shrouds, bare feet sticking out: men, women, and children, one scarcely more than a bundle of rags. They had died from plague or starvation in winter's dearth, miserable persons now released from torment and dispatched to Tuonela.

The gravediggers paused their foul work; the hunchback bowed, cautiously extending a filthy hand, palm up.

"Pity, my lord, pity," he mumbled, hoping for some small coin rather than the sharp lash of a horsewhip. The one-armed man said nothing, his bleary eyes retaining a sullen pride as if they remembered a time before inescapable shame and disgrace.

The rider made no sign and kicked the horse to a quick pace, leaving the gravediggers behind with the corpses and half-frozen earth. Few folk traveled the road winding around the nearest of Tapiola's Seven Hills, the Hill of the Wolf Folk. The north wind blew cold, and the rider shivered. Sledges and sleds still sat in barns and sheds as there was little snow. However, the animals were already sequestered in their winter homes. They'd stand in thick straw throughout the long, dark months until the farmers swept the stalls in spring and carried the manure to the rye fields.

The black-cloaked rider approached Tapiola's great southern tower and gate where some folk moved about on their business. Dozens of thin trails of black smoke wafted slowly upward, filling the air with a bitter, acrid scent.

The town's white stone walls, built of *valkoinen marmori* and enchanted by the magic of old, remained beautiful. Neither flaw nor blemish marred their perfect design. But within the white walls, things were otherwise. Like all the Far Northern Land, Tapiola had suffered greatly in the seven years since the disaster at Sumuvuori.

Plague and illness had repeatedly visited the town. Lovêatar, the ghost from hell who spread death throughout the Seven Lands, had paid special attention to Tapiola. Many people had died, especially children, grievously reducing the townsfolk. Others fled into the countryside, believing it safer, and now dwelt in villages to the south. But during the past year, some refugees had arrived from the North, slowly increasing its numbers. Men had built towers and hillforts in the Neck of Tavastia, since Löhi's servants harassed the Hare Folk in those parts, ruining their villages and fields.

In the second summer after the Battle of Sumuvuori, the Witch had launched a great invasion with what strength was left to her. The Easterners had overrun High Länsimaa and taken Keskimaa. The Bear Folk who did not flee became their slaves or serfs. Still worse was to come. The following summer, Deep Länsimaa fell and Valkeakosk was burned; Teemu and the Elk Folk held out only at Siinesaare, the great island within the Blue Lake that had become a fortress. The Witch now struck across the Wall of the Giants. She attacked the Hare and Swan Folk in their homelands, roaming ever southward, though she had yet to find the power to break the failing strength of the Seven Clans.

The rider reached the open gate and passed within. The guards wore fine mail that bore the livery of Tavastia, a yellow sun against red and white. They said nothing, either knowing or guessing the shadowy figure's identity. A crowd of beggars gathered in the paved square just within: the poor and infirm, the lame and scrofulous, and the mad. The Tavastian crown permitted them to beg of those who entered the town.

An older boy, blind, with two dark holes where his eyes should have been, laid his hands on the black horse's flank; other beggars crowded around, imploring. But the rider in the dark hood pushed through the gaggle, giving no alms, but taking the broad lane running north toward that part of the town wherein the most beautiful buildings of white stone could be found. Behind, in the stone-flagged square, a madman cackled, romping about with a broken stick between his legs as if he, too, rode a horse.

The lane climbed steadily upward. Passing crossroads and intersections, the rider came to a circular commons set about with trees. Hawkers stood behind shop stalls selling food, drink, and needful things. A fountain stood in the commons, surrounded by a greensward. Silent now, in spring and summer, water splashed down over an argent rock face into clear blue pools filled with flower blossoms. People looked darkly at the rider, noting the black mail, the iron spurs, and the long sword in its leather scabbard strapped to the horse.

Something else about the hooded figure made them uneasy, some hidden power, shrouded yet terribly present, putting them ill at ease. The townsfolk looked around for their own guards to stop and question the stranger, but no one dared utter a word; they were glad when the black-garbed figure passed by.

The rider continued up the lane, which was the main way of Tapiola leading to the beautiful palace where Asikkas had been king. Asikkas had died several years earlier, however. Wounded at Sumuvuori and wracked with grief over the loss of his son Pekka in the battle, the king had thrown himself from a height, ending his own life. Since his only surviving son was half-witted, his cousin, Aslo, had taken the crown. A young man full of promise, he had profited greatly from the trade in bloodrock before the battle. He lived in the palace now with his wife. The dark rider clattered into the palace's fair courtyard and dismounted.

Stiff and weary, the rider gingerly swung to the ground, took a bag from the horse's saddle, and whispered into the mare's ear, stroking its flank until the jittery animal calmed. Hoisting up the bag, the hooded stranger strode up the white marble steps to the palace's main doors.

The door guards, who had watched the strange figure ride up, now sprang to block the path; their captain drew his sword.

"Stay," he commanded in a stern voice. "Who are you and what is your business?"

The cloaked figure raised a mailed arm, the shiny, black vambrace glinting dimly. Speaking a few words in a soft, singsong voice, the stranger cast a quick backward glance at the horse steaming in the courtyard, then strode past the guards into the palace. The men stared blankly ahead, swords and spears loose in their hands.

The palace of the king of the Hare Folk was not small. Many halls, chambers, and courts lay within, beautifully designed and well-appointed as befitted the ruler of proud Tavastia. The strange figure seemed familiar with the palace, expertly navigating the halls, bag still in hand, stopping only once to inquire of a servant where the king might be. The man answered without hesitation.

The rider came at last to a long gallery brightly illuminated by torchlight. Recesses cut into the gallery's paneled walls contained beautiful things of glass and amber. Works of silver by the Smiths of Seppälä and carved stone images of past kings of the Hare Folk stood there. No image of Asikkas sat in that gallery, but there was one of Lemminkäinen, fashioned of flawless *valkoinen marmori* by the craftsmen of old. At the end of the long gallery stood two dark doors with two tall guards on either side of them.

The men wore the devices of the king's royal guard: a silver hauberk on which was painted a shield, red and argent, made of some precious enamel from afar. Red cloaks hung down their backs. Silver thread entwined their forked, plaited beards, and ancient bronze helms sat upon their heads. The rise and fall of the rider's heavy boots echoed down the hallway. Not so tall as the guards was the rider, not so fair the stranger's devices, but the knights drew their swords at the dark figure's approach and barred the way.

Without breaking stride, the rider threw back the black hood and tore off the visored helmet, releasing a torrent of long, dark hair and revealing a young woman's pale face, sprinkled with freckles. She stared back at them.

"Lady Ulla!" exclaimed one of the guards. "How came you here? But the king is in private chambers within and—Lady Ulla!"

Ulla walked past them, pushing through the doors.

The chamber within, large and fair, felt cold with only a single small hearth in the corner. Shuttered windows stretched across its far wall around a single door, the very door that opened onto the courtyard where perched the Hare Folk's totem. There, seven years earlier, the chiefs of the Seven Clans had made their League and sworn to follow Egan to victory beyond the faraway Marches. Opposite the windows, stools and chairs surrounded a large oak table. Several men stood nearby. Ulla recognized Isku, the Master of the Shipwrights Guild, grown fat now and leaning on a stick. King Aslo sat behind the table. An older man, his counselor, sat next to him, poring over some documents. On Aslo's other side stood a woman, slight of build, a slip of a girl richly dressed in the courtly fashion of Tavastia with golden thread twined about her flaxen hair. In her wan face, even paler than Ulla's, her blue eyes flashed with displeasure. They all started in surprise at Ulla's entrance.

"You!" cried the slight woman, who was indeed Aslo's wife, Vara, the Queen of the Hare Folk. She came from behind the table to bar Ulla's way.

"You!" she said again. "What are you doing here? How dare you come into the chamber of the King of Tavastia unannounced and uninvited? Who do you think you are, witch-child?"

Ulla ignored her, walked up to the king, and tossed the bag onto the table with a thud. The startled man jumped to his feet.

"For you, my lord," she said, shaking her unbraided hair and brushing the wild strands from her face. "The last one. Open it."

"This is unacceptable," said Vara, glaring at the two guards who had trailed Ulla into the room, seemingly uncertain of what to do.

"Take her out of here *now*. And do not allow her back until we call for her."

Before the guards could act, Aslo held up a hand and shook his head. The pox had scarred his face with a hundred pits as a child, but he remained a handsome man and pleasantly disposed.

"No, my dearest. Stay your anger. Ulla Karhulainen is always welcome here, though the manner of her coming and going may seem strange to us of different folk and custom. But what is this thing? The last, you say; the last of what?"

Ulla nodded toward the bag, reaching for a bronze ewer of water that sat nearby. As she drank, the king opened the dirty sack. Out rolled a misshapen head onto the table.

"Great Thunder!" cried the king. Vara shrieked. Several others recoiled from the hideous, stinking thing.

"What is that?!" said Aslo.

"*That* is Maanavilja," she answered. "The Tavastian, the last of the three Tornilaiset who betrayed us to Löhi." She put the empty ewer on the table beside the severed head.

"I found him in Akkala, filthy and miserable, skulking in a hole and trying to hide from me with his feeble enchantments. He cried, begging for his life like a child. But before I slew him, I read his mind. He was the one who went to Akkala with Siitsa and raised rebellion against Airikki. And it was he, along with Tappi, his confederate, who marched with the Host to Sumuvuori and betrayed our every move to the Witch. So be it. Now he is with Tappi in Tuonela, and the Tornilaiset are no more."

Aslo flushed deeply. One of his men ran up and threw a cloth over the rotting skull.

"What am I to do with this?" Aslo stammered.

Ulla shrugged. "You set a price on his head, did you not? So here it is. Do with it what you will. It is a proof that Maanavilja is dead, nothing more."

"It was Asikkas who set the price," said the white-haired counselor in a thickly accented voice that reminded Ulla of the Seer. "Asikkas, who in his madness set the price at one hundred gold Tavastian crowns—a king's ransom. Doubtless he was thinking of his son, Pekka, who was slain at Sumuvuori. Is that what you seek?"

Ulla laughed. "I don't need your gold, my lord. Keep it. Or, better yet, use it to arm your men. I passed south of Kyöpelinvuori on my journey here. Your soldiers in those parts are ill-equipped. They have few horses and few swords that are *winterfast* or made from bloodrock. This is what I came to report to you and your captain."

"There is no rock," said Aslo. His tone changed, stern and defensive. "Nothing comes south now and the stores are depleted. We cannot replace what was lost at Sumuvuori or two years ago at Jääkeko. But the men who guard the watchtowers in the north do not want for mail or arms, nor do the knights and soldiers of Tapiola. The smaller garrisons must make do with what they have."

"You know your own business best," she replied. "But those men may still be called upon to march if the enemy attacks. Soon there may even be raids out of Akkala. The north of that land is in turmoil and enemies now creep about it."

"Tavastia is safe," said the older man. "As safe as may be amid such times of strife. More we cannot do with what strength is left us. But what was ill-ordered in the past, in the days of Asikkas and the great disaster, has been put right."

"Ill-ordered?" answered Ulla, her hazel-green eyes flickering with anger. "Nothing was left to chance in the days of Egan Dragonslayer; treachery and black magic brought disaster upon us all. Look again, if need be, at what lies before you: Maanavilja Tavastialainen, the servant of your Seer."

The dark-haired young woman picked up a leather-covered bottle.

"Yes, well . . ." stammered Aslo. "Let us speak about this with our captains. Tomorrow or perhaps the next day they should return for the north and— look, will you not take some refreshment? Lady Ulla is thirsty and tired, bring us warm and cold drink and something to eat."

"No thank you, my lord," she said, draining the bottle. "Water is enough. I must see to my horse now, who is also weary and waits in your courtyard. But I'm glad to hear that your captains are returning; to speak with them was my errand here—that and bringing Maanavilja back to his home."

Ulla bowed as best she could in mail, then turned to leave as quickly as she had come. Yet Vara, recovered from her fright, stood before her. The tiny queen put her hands on her hips, glaring defiantly at the wizard and warrior.

"Water may be acceptable for you, but you don't have enough of it," she said sharply. "You stink of horse and of the field and forest. Do not ever again presume to come so before the King of the Tavastia. And if, strangely, you were made a princess of our land by virtue of your ties to Väinämöinen, you would do well to remember it and look the part."

The king and his men started, fearing Ulla's anger, but the dark-haired young woman's face was cold and impassive. She reached out a gloved hand to touch a strand of Vara's hair that escaped the gossamer veil atop her head. The queen tensed.

"One does what one must," said Ulla. Switching to the courtly fashion of Tavastia and Etelamaa, which she despised yet had grown adept at, she added, "On a time, mayhap even thou shalt find thyself in such straits; but let us hope not, my queen."

Vara flushed deeply, a beet-red stain creeping over her face like the bloom of an early morning. At her side, her fists clenched, but she said nothing. Ulla stiffly bowed again and left the room, helm in hand. In the hallway, she passed the captain and his men whom she had enchanted at the palace door. Now they rushed to the king's chamber to see what was amiss. But none dared to stop or gainsay her—she, Ulla Karhulainen, Löhi's enemy and *tietäjää* of the Singing Valley who bore the Mark of the Clan.

Still, they were glad to see her go. After the Battle of Sumuvuori where Egan fell and the League was destroyed, everything had changed and Ulla had changed too. She became grim, fell, and suspicious of all save the Erilaiset and her closest friends. Her power had grown apace with her stature. Now a full-grown woman, she was tall for her folk, her limbs and long face almost Erilaisen in appearance. Her great strength wrapped about her like a mantle, visible to the world. Indeed, she had become the most powerful wizard in all the Far Northern Land, more powerful than any other save old Väinämöinen, perhaps.

After checking on Midnight, the black mare that had been her horse for many years and survived the long march home from Sumuvuori, Ulla went to a small lodging close by the stables. The simple room in a modest building held bed, basin, and table with a small courtyard behind enclosing a single elm. The room was always kept ready for her on the rare times she came to Tapiola. Not far away stood another room, the room in which Egan had declared his love to her.

The Hare Folk had offered it to her, but she refused. She would not enter it. If that door was never opened, if the dust that lay upon the white marble lay undisturbed, perhaps that lost world might still exist. Within those walls, perhaps she and Egan yet embraced, gentle shades of what might have been. The elves believed such things were possible. She would not enter that room, but ensured that it remained locked, even as she kept her father and brother locked away within her heart as the years slipped by. And none dared question her; she was Ulla, Ulla Karhulainen.

Tired, the young woman quickly fell asleep. She awoke famished in the frosty morn. There was no food in her room; she had not bothered to eat or buy food the day before. Ulla washed in the basin's freezing water, the cold shock exciting her pale skin and setting it a-tingle. She dressed in a rich, warm cape lined with fur, identical to Väinämöinen's, and stitched leather boots encased her feet. Her armor and stained traveling clothes sat tossed in the corner.

Sword, dagger, staff—all three lay on the table. She left the sword and staff, but picked up Longleaf, fixing the short, sharp blade to her belt. Grabbing a leather pouch that held a few silver coins, she walked out into the sunlight.

Ulla sought two things, food and news, and she knew where to find both. Hawkers and merchants sold their goods in an open space beneath the east gate's shadow: Itäkauppa, the East Market, men called it. The dark-haired young woman bought cold sour milk, sausage, and blood bread from a fat man with a splotched face. He begged her to cure his blemished skin with a word or charm, but she shook her head at him; pine tar worked better.

The milk, soured in Tavastian style, was delicious. The distinctive taste of her favorite drink immediately transported her to the Singing Valley and the *pirtti* that she and Kirsikka had shared for so long. The serfs of Kyöpelinvuori had sent barrels of the stuff to the Valley each month. *Sour milk. Songs and spells. The fire that always burned in the long hall by the rowan trees.* As these things flashed through Ulla's mind, she lost herself, as she often did, in a reverie so deep that she was almost deaf to the sounds around her—almost.

A horse whinnied as it clapped through the gate, bringing her back to the present. The Singing Valley was silent and empty now. Far away in the Stone City, Kirsikka mourned for the husband who would never return. Reality was war on the marches, war unceasing, and that, not sour milk, had brought Ulla to Tapiola.

Finishing her meal, Ulla set out to achieve her second goal. She needed news, specifically news of the Wardens. She heard what she hoped to hear. Ilkka, Lord Captain of the March Wardens of the Far Northern Land, had arrived in Tapiola during the night. Moreover, Teemu of the Elk Folk was with him, escaped from his fortress on the island of Siinesaare. Ulla made straightaway for the Warden House, reaching it just as Ilkka and Teemu were setting out for Aslo's palace.

She paused, observing the two men from a distance. Ilkka's close-cropped hair was grey, his beard clipped and short after the Wardens' fashion. Tall and spare he was, grim-faced after his many ordeals. The pressure and responsibilities of being Lord Captain and commanding the men who held the borders against the Witch were etched upon his face. Ulla, however, saw the merry eyes of her old friend, the one who had found her in High Länsimaa so long ago.

Teemu was of a different sort. Shorter than Ilkka, the Lord of the Hirvilaiset, the Elk Folk, wore his light brown hair long and braided, and his dark beard full. A man in the prime of life, he had done much to save as many of his people as possible. Ulla remembered the first time that she had seen him, at Linnavuori, just before the battle, just before she had sung the spell that made her invisible while she stole Tyë's precious glass. Teemu had been young then, scarcely older than Egan. He still looked younger than his years or troubles.

And troubles he had. Teemu and Ilkka had survived the disaster at Sumuvuori, together leading thousands of men out of the wild and back to their homelands. The strong bonds between them had been forged in a fire that only those who have gone to war together, risking life and limb side by side, can ever know. Now Valkeakosk was gone, taken by the enemy, and all the Hirvilaiset not enslaved had fled deep into the woods or across the borders to Tavastia or Akkala. But Teemu had gathered many of his folk and fallen back to the tree-covered isle within the Blue Lake. Twice now he had slipped Löhi's nets and escaped to Tavastia to consult with the Wardens in Tapiola. He never stayed long, however. No matter the danger, he was resolved to return to Siinesaare and his people who endured the Witch's siege.

Even as Ulla watched the two men, Ilkka noticed her. The Warden's stern expression melted, transformed into a broad smile.

"Ulla!" he cried.

Returning the smile, Ulla came and embraced him.

"I hadn't heard that you were in Tapiola," Ilkka continued. "But it is good to see you, my young lady."

"And for me," said Teemu. "Indeed, I'd hoped to find you here."

"Find me you have," answered Ulla. "And here I am—I only arrived yesterday myself."

"We were on our way to see Aslo," said Ilkka. "But perhaps we should go back inside."

Ulla sniffed the air. "It's a fine morning," she said. "It will be full winter soon enough. Let's talk as we walk together. It's a ways to the palace and Midnight is stabled nearby. I need to see her. But I don't believe Aslo or the queen will wish to see me again so soon."

Ilkka signaled to the three Wardens accompanying him to remain at the House, then he, Teemu, and Ulla set out across the White City. The Warden hadn't seen her since summer. As they walked, she told him about her search for Maanavilja and their final encounter in the woods of Akkala.

"It wasn't much of a battle," she said matter-of-factly. "He was weak, half-starved, and cowardly. I don't know why Löhi sent him back. Perhaps as a trap for me, but I was wary."

"How did you find him?"

"The jewel," she replied. "I made a finding spell, the strongest I could, and used the jewel to focus it. It was hard to do, the jewel is not made for such *sight*, but I made it work all the same. I've discovered a lot about that glass over the past few years, but it's dangerous to use. Löhi is somehow connected to it. I feel like she can see me when I look into it."

"Then don't use it!" said Ilkka. "You know there's a price on your head, higher than any other in the Far Northern Land. Don't make it easy for the Witch to find you."

"I passed by Kyöpelinvuori on my way back," said Ulla. "The men there were anxious. How did it go on the Marches?"

Before Sumuvuori, Ulla had never raised a blade in battle; afterward, she never sheathed her sword. With sword and staff, spear and spell, the dark-haired woman with the pale, freckled face had fought along the Marches unceasingly. From High to Deep Länsimaa, and from Tavastia to Etelamaa, she lent aid to the people of the Seven Clans in their desperate fight against the Witch, pitting her power against Pohjola's and doing whatever she could to upset Löhi's plans, though it seemed a losing battle as their strength ebbed.

All who bore arms welcomed Ulla, though she was no queen and commanded no army, particularly since so few *tietäjää*, the mortal wizards trained in Laulavalaakso, remained. People feared the woman warrior who bore the Mark of the Clan upon her shoulder, but when battle came to them or evil spirits wailed on the wind, they turned to her. She had become the most famous hero in all the Seven Lands.

"After you left us," Ilkka continued, "There were a few more skirmishes. The Easterners raided the villages that still stood south of the *lansikita*. The people fled. But word came later of a larger attack in Etelamaa, even on the borders of Kotanrannta. The Pohjolaiset have never been so bold or struck so deep. The Swan Folk are panicked. They seek to build a line of towers straight across Etelamaa, but who knows if it will be too late?"

"And around the Wall?" she asked, referring to the Wall of the Giants, the stony ridge that separated what used to be Lansimää from the lands to the south.

"Ever worse. Evil things, unclean things, creep about it. Goblins, trolls, and horrors from Tuonela. People flee in fear for their lives while the rye rots in the field uncut. Always when it seems it could become no worse, it does."

The lane opened into a square where women surrounded them, begging for alms. Ilkka gave out several pennies.

"Dark days have come to Tapiola, too," said Teemu. "Or so it seems. The city is much changed since last I was here."

"And how are your folk, my lord?" asked Ulla.

Teemu sighed.

"We hold out," he finally said, as they left the square and took the street leading to the palace. "For now, we hold out. But if help does not come, from the Hare Folk or elsewhere, then I have little hope.

"The isle of Siinesaare is fair. I made my summer home there in my youth. Two villages sprang up among its trees. But when the north of our land was destroyed, many thousands came to the isle—men, women, children, all who could be saved. We brought as great a store of food and weapons as possible and built strong places at the landings. Twice the Pohjolaiset attacked in great numbers, once across the water and once across the ice. Both times we drove them back with loss. Now all the land about the Blue Lake is despoiled and we are surrounded.

"An inlet winds its way into the island's heart. Fish spawn there and we have no lack of food from the water, but little else. The grain is almost gone. We have felled most of the trees for shelter or fuel, save for the wood at the island's crown. And a sickness, a black pestilence from Löhi, rose among us, killing children especially and most of our animals. My men are battle-hardened and brave—many fought at Sumuvuori—but we will not last beyond winter if help does not come to us."

Teemu's voice faltered as he spoke. Ulla was taken aback. She had not known that the Elk Folk were in such straits.

"I did not know your plight was so evil, my lord," she said.

"Our strength fails," said Ilkka. "Our will must be harder. The Wardens do not have the numbers to come to Teemu's rescue and still man the hillforts that hold back the enemy elsewhere. I had hoped that Juvari and the Swan Folk might send men this coming summer, but the threat to Kotanrannta may prevent this. Always the Witch remains one move ahead of us. And it seems that something more is at work. Sickness and plague afflict us; crops fail. The very earth, sea, and sky seem poisoned. The Witch's season is upon us.

"At least some good news awaited me here in Tapiola. More men have volunteered for the Wardens; two hundred from Akkala alone and others from the coasts. We will have three new companies next summer to replace those who fell in battle."

"If the Marches are strengthened," said Teemu, "Perhaps Aslo will send his army to break the siege, allowing my people to escape. It would be a bold stroke, but no other kind will suffice in such times. Such is my plea."

They reached the palace courtyard, where a cold wind blew through the open space. Ulla wrapped her cape tightly about her. A company of Tavastian guards assembled on the cobble-stoned square.

"One other plea I have, my lady," said Teemu, looking straight into Ulla's hazel-green eyes. "Where is Väinämöinen? Can he not help us? Ever has he been a friend to the Elk Folk since this war began. A single singer we have at Siinesaare, not a true *tietäjää*, and, while he has some skill in healing, it is not enough. On the journey from Länsimaa, I asked this question of those I met;

all told the same tale—he is gone and none have seen him in these parts for some time. Tell me, Ulla, is he in Etelamaa or Karelia?"

Ilkka looked keenly at Ulla. For a moment, she was at a loss.

"He is in Karelia," she said at last. "Or, at least, he was when last I heard from him. But wherever he is now, I fear he will not return in time to answer your call, my lord."

Teemu nodded. "So Ilkka guessed," he said sadly. "And what about you, my lady? Or Turi the Changer? Will you not come to our aid? They say you have grown to become the most powerful wizard in the Far Northern Land, as powerful as the Witch of Pohjola. Can you not help us?"

His last words were lost on the wind as a cold gust whistled through the courtyard, snapping the guards' red and white banners, but Ulla knew what he asked.

"I do not know what I can do to help the Elk Folk of Siinesaare, Lord Teemu. But whatever may be possible, I will try it."

She stood silent for a moment, looking at the two men she had known almost all of her short life. It pained her to see the earnestness in Teemu's face and Ilkka's stony resolve. Something was slipping away, fading. They were losing their faith, their hope. But she, Ulla, had long since put such things behind her.

"Will you come with us to see the king, Ulla?" asked Ilkka.

"Not now. I must see to Midnight; she is very weary. But I will come to the Warden House later, or at any time you call me."

Ilkka smiled and touched her shoulder.

"Very well, little one," he said, echoing Väinämöinen. "See to Midnight. Any horse that made it back from Sumuvuori deserves no less."

He clasped his hand across his breast in the Warden's salute. Teemu bowed. The two men mounted the steps leading up to the palace doors, but Ilkka suddenly turned and called to her.

"Ulla!" he cried. "More news, lest I forget. Kaukomieli was on the Marches with us; he is still there, hunting trolls. He wishes to see you. Send word to him if you are not going north!"

She watched them climb the steps and greet the guards, the same guards she had enchanted yesterday in her impatience to see Aslo. Then she turned and left the chilly courtyard for the nearby stables where Midnight waited.

Midnight, happy to see Ulla, whinnied in excitement. The stabler had given her a snug stall with plenty of straw on the ground and hay and oats to eat. Ulla stroked the black mare's flank, checking the wound on her foreleg. Ulla had closed it with a song; now it had healed. Midnight nuzzled Ulla's face and neck, her warm breath tickling the girl, who hummed a little tune into the horse's ear to calm her. But soon Ulla fell silent, lost again in her own thoughts—thoughts of Kaukomieli.

Chapter Two

Kaukomieli

It was cold. The north wind whistled in the pine tops. The dim winter sunlight filtered through the branches like candlelight through a keyhole, reflecting here and there off patches of snow. One hundred feet below the knoll, a path ran through a gully surrounded by woods. It was hidden from sight at ground level, but clearly visible from the height above where Kaukomieli crouched. The young wizard sat uncomfortably in a shallow hole, half-propped against an outcropping of black stone. He fixed his eyes on the path and tried to pay attention; it was hard to stay awake. No matter. He had woven spells of warning all along the path and his wizardly sense, the sense of a singer and mage, would wake him at once if any trolls came near.

Kaukomieli had been tracking the monsters for three weeks. He had spent most of the summer with the Wardens in their hillfort at Kanervakenttä, built to protect the approaches to the Tavastian heartland. First Ulla had left, and later Turi, leaving Kaukomieli alone, the only wizard—mortal or Erilainen— remaining in those parts.

Although most of the Hare Folk had fled the land just below the gap of the *lansikita*, some still remained in scattered villages, and refugees from the Elk Folk in Deep Länsimaa came among them, seeking shelter. Here, north of Kanervakenttä, people lived mostly undisturbed by the Itäläiset since there were few paths for horses. Worse things were on the loose, however. Wolves howled during the dark night. Black shapes prowled by day. Löhi's goblins might never again march in great legions, but more than enough remained to gather into bands to trouble the poor folk of the north.

Kaukomieli wasn't hunting goblins, however; he was hunting trolls. Word had reached Kanervakenttä that trolls were about, a group of several dim-witted oafs, scarcely more than dumb beasts, yet filled with an evil cunning by the Witch of the North. The trolls had burned isolated cottages, killed their inhabitants, and spread terror all throughout the district. It was too late in the season for the Wardens to give chase, but Kaukomieli had set out to find the monsters and kill or chase them away.

Now he had discovered them. The young man had twice spotted trolls shambling through the woods; he heard their cries. He had read the signs and knew they were close by. Finally, he had found the path in the gully below, which they used to move quickly through the trees round the hillside. So, he had set a trap for the trolls, weaving nets of sorcery along the trail to ensnare them when they passed by. Lying in ambush atop the knoll, he waited. It wouldn't be long. He felt their presence—not so near, but not so far—and knew that it was only a matter of time before the creatures stumbled into the trap to their doom.

Kaukomieli yawned. He shifted his cold, aching legs. Reaching for the badger-skin pack that the Wardens had given him, he rummaged inside. There wasn't much left by now, only hard blood bread, fish, and his last dried apple. The Wardens had given him half a dozen apples, but he had eaten them quickly. He decided to save the apple for after the ambush.

With a sigh, the wizard tightened his cloak. He thought about the Wardens of Kanervakenttä with whom he had spent the last summer, Pekka, Janni, Vile, and the rest. Most of them were his own age or only a little older. He enjoyed their friendship and good-natured, if sometimes rough, comradery. They had been put off at first, of course—abashed by a *tietäjää* from the Singing Valley, none other than the Last Wizard, the final mortal to make a hunt and win a staff before the great disaster. They became accustomed to him soon enough, however. He more than earned his place among them with healing spells, finding spells, and words of ward and protection.

They recognized another bond too. Most of the men were Hirvilaisen, Elk Folk, men from Deep Länsimaa who had joined the March Wardens to fight Löhi. *Hirvilaisen, just as I am.* It was true that none of them came from the far western reaches of Deep Länsimaa as he did; his home region was sparsely populated, with more elk, deer, and beaver than people. Yet Hirvilaisen they were just the same, sharing the impotence and frustrated rage that came from watching the destruction of their homeland.

Kaukomieli had been born in a *pirtii* beside a still lake filled with fish. Like Ulla, his mother had died soon afterward, joining the three children who had gone before her, none of whom had lived more than a few months. He had a sister, though. Perhaps ten years old at the time, she was the family's firstborn. He would have died, too, had she not cared for him. His father, a grim, silent fisher and forester, paid him little attention as a baby and not much more as he grew older. But Kaukomieli's grandmother lived nearby and, when he didn't die and began to thrive, she finally took him in.

His grandmother wasn't like the district's other women. She was a singer. Not a wizard or witch like the mortal *tietäjää* who would soon return to the Far Northern Land, but a singer nonetheless. She knew hundreds of old songs and tales about ancient heroes like Lemminkäinen, Enkeli, and the mighty Väinämöinen. She sang and chanted in a strange voice, sometimes almost toneless, sometimes keening, and she was always singing. She sang when she fed her scrawny goats. She sang when she stirred the pot. She sang when she brushed the old straw out the cottage door and when she built the fire up as the cold wind blew outside. In those parts, a few people still lived who knew the old songs and stories, passing them down from generation to generation.

It was his grandmother who finally named him. Among the Elk Folk, children, especially boys, might be renamed around the age of five, usually after some unique trait or characteristic became apparent. The boy's father had named him Paavo after one of his dead brothers. But his grandmother woke him up one bright spring morning, took him to the lake, and told him, "You are not Paavo any longer; don't ever let me hear that name again. From now on, you are Kaukomieli."

He knew the name, had heard it many times before. One of his grandmother's favorite tales was about a wizard called Kaukomieli—the Far-Sighted One—and so she named her little grandson after this ancient hero.

"Remember what I teach you," she told him. "There's something different about you. You're not like your drunken father. You see the wonder that's all around us and know that things aren't always what they seem.

"There's another world, there is. Its spirits are all about. If you listen closely, you'll hear them. Some are good, some are bad, and some aren't concerned with you at all. They're in the woods, the streams, up in the clouds, behind the stars where the great bear, *karhu*, comes from. I'll be dead soon and pass to the other side, but you remember what I've taught you and keep your wits about you. Maybe you'll wake up a power inside yourself like the old songs tell of."

She had not died so soon after all, but had lived several more years. Kaukomieli listened and remembered what she taught him. And she was right. The fair-haired little boy *was* different. Kaukomieli could sometimes feel Ilmatar's power when the wind swept over him, standing his hair on end. When he waded through the water with fishing nets, Ahti's own strength would sometimes well up around him.

Moreover, from an early age, Kaukomieli perceived nature's wild and restless spirits. A playful spirit, though still dangerous, bubbled in a brook's little fall. The gnarled pine by the lakeside housed a kind spirit, gentle and sleepy, always whispering of pleasant dreams. The black stone on the hilltop held a spirit of a different sort. Like the seidi-stone in the Singing Valley, it had a spirit locked within, only this black stone's spirit was angry, vengeful, longing for freedom, and promising sinister wisdom to anyone who might release it. Though just a boy, Kaukomieli understood the stone's message and avoided the hilltop.

Eventually, the old woman did die, of course, peacefully. Kaukomieli and his old uncle, the woman's brother, buried her in the forest as she had wished. Not long afterward, his dreams had started, vivid and terrifying. He could find no rest or respite, night or day. His sister had long since married and gone away, and his cold, distant father had little for him but hard words and a harder hand. So, he had left his homeland and, with no clear idea of what to do or where to go, walked east.

Two months later, famished and exhausted, he had met Unaja on a little trail north of Kyöpelinvuori. That was the moment for him. Nothing would ever again be the same.

Kaukomieli shook himself. His reverie had almost become a dream while the sky above clouded over. His wizardly sense buzzed; he instantly became alert.

He peered down into the draw. *Nothing.* Next, he pushed his *sight* down the path. His webs were untouched. The spells held fast. Whatever it was, it wasn't the trolls.

The young man stood up, brushing snow off his thick cloak. He stomped around a bit for warmth, flapping his arms like a bird, then jumping back and forth over his staff a few times. He felt better after that, life creeping back into his cold, aching limbs. With a sigh and a shake of his head, he slouched back into his hole, resigned to the lonely vigil.

The Last Wizard. Kaukomieli of the Valley. That was what they called him now and, so far, he had lived up to the lofty title. One of the last mortals to come to the Singing Valley before the great disaster, his time there had been short. He was also the youngest, scarcely come of age in the reckoning of his clan, and almost the same age as Ulla, though he couldn't really be sure. No one ever doubted that he was a wizard born, however. He learned swiftly, never needing any lesson twice. His power grew. Väinämöinen and Turi were well pleased with the young Hirvilainen and an elf from the Enchanted Valley had taken him on his hunt.

It had been in the woods of Akkala just after harvest. The spirit-elk tried to elude him, leading him into a marshy dreamscape fraught with peril. But he had trapped it in the end. And he had seen *karhu* prowling about the edges of the waking world.

Kaukomieli had returned a wizard, proudly holding his new staff high when he rode back to Laulavalaakso. But they were all gone by then. Väinämöinen, Turi, Ulla—all gone away, gone to war north of the Marches to fight Löhi. There had been no homecoming, no celebration, only anxious waiting with the few others who had also been left behind.

As Kaukomieli sat in the frozen earth musing on the strange, lonely time he had spent in the Valley after the Erilaiset marched away, he suddenly thought of Siitsa. Not long after Väinämöinen rode to war, a message came to him from Kyöpelinvuori. It was not from the Seer, however, but from Siitsa, the chief of the Tornilaiset, who was busy in those days on errands for her mistress. Siitsa sent greetings and congratulations to him, asking him to meet her, not at the old tower, but in a little meadow near one of the serfs' villages. Kaukomieli thought back to that day, picturing Siitsa in his mind's eye as he had seen her then.

She had braided her hair after the fashion of the Tavastialaiset, with silver thread entwined about her curls. As always, she wore black. She waited for him in the middle of the meadow, the grass freshly cut and gathered into sheaves by the Seer's serfs. She looked all the world like a silent scarecrow. Oddly, she bore a strange staff. Not the short staff of Kyöpelinvuori, which the Seer gave to all of her servants, but a tall staff made of ash, carved differently than those borne by the *tietäjää*.

Siitsa had praised his skill and cleverness at winning his staff. She questioned him intently about his hunt, stroking his pride and ego. He remembered how satisfied he had felt at the time. Yet before she dismissed him, Siitsa's manner had changed, her words puzzling him.

"It must be hard for one so clever to be left all alone," said Siitsa. "Does it bother you?"

"What do you mean?" he asked in surprise.

"They left you behind, did they not?" she replied. "All gone, gone to the Marches and to deeds of glory. But you'll be left out of all that, won't you?"

"I had not yet made my hunt when they marched away," he answered lamely. "I have only been in Laulavalaakso one year."

"Ah, yes," she said. "I forgot. So quickly did you become a *tietäjää*. You must be very powerful, indeed. It is too bad that you did not come here sooner. Everything will change after this battle, you know. Everything will be different."

"The war will be over," said Kaukomieli. "And the Sampo will be raised in the spring."

Siitsa had laughed then, a queer laugh. Kaukomieli remembered well the gleam in her eye and the faintest hint of mockery in her voice.

"Will it?" she asked. "Do you really believe the Witch so weak that one lost battle will end her reign or send her back to Pohjola forever? The war will not end, lord wizard. Yet all will be changed nonetheless. And there will still be deeds to do for those who would do them."

Siitsa had then asked him to perform some small errand for her in Laulavalaakso and they parted. Before she left, though, she told him that she would call for him again, wishing to discuss magic and wizardry with him. She never did. In those busy days at Kyöpelinvuori, Siitsa had much to attend to. Kaukomieli never saw her again.

Long afterwards, he learned of her treachery and fate. He often pondered their strange encounter. What had Siitsa intended? Why had she sent for him? To sound him out, to seduce him to the Witch's service, or to gauge his strength so as to kill him the next time they met? She had never sent for him a second time. If she had, would he have survived the encounter? He had told Ulla about it and seen one of the rare instances when the girl with the Mark of the Clan betrayed her emotion.

"Let her rot in Tuonela," Ulla had said sharply. "The nothingness of oblivion will be her eternal reward."

Another twinge, this time sharper, shocked Kaukomieli back to the present. He grasped his staff. His eyes narrowed. The path was empty. He listened to the forest's music. It was calm and tranquil, a gentle harmony that anyone born in the Far Northern Land knew deep within their soul. A cuckoo started in the pine boughs, trilling like a warrior sounding his horn before battle. The bird took off with a rustle, passing near to Kaukomieli before settling again somewhere in the trees below. As suddenly as it had come, the sense of warning was gone. Nothing was amiss.

A thief thinks all others a thief, even when the wind blows from the south.

He settled back down, eyes on the path, and forgot Siitsa for the moment. His thoughts turned instead to the one who filled them most often, Ulla.

Ulla had seldom noticed Kaukomieli when he first arrived in the Valley, though he had noticed her. He had heard of her in Deep Länsimaa, of course. Rumors came to his district about the witch-child from Karelia who bore the Clan-Mark and who had killed Löhi's champion at the Battle of Linnavuori. He had not seen Ulla much that first year, though she was the only singer in Laulavalaakso his own age. He spent most of his time with Unaja, Turi, and the elves. That had changed after Sumuvuori.

The long vigil of waiting ended abruptly. First, Kyöpelinvuori had burned. He had watched the flames from afar, listening to the eerie wails on the bitter wind. They found the Seer dead soon afterward. Next, a messenger from Tapiola arrived with word of Ilmarinen's murder in Seppälä. Finally, a golden eagle came to the Valley, the largest Kaukomieli had ever seen. Three times it circled before lighting upon the roof of the great hall. Opening its beak, it spoke with the voice of a mortal man. This was no wizard changed to eagle form, however, but a real bird, spell-enchanted to deliver a message across the length of the Far Northern Land.

"Woe is come upon us all," said the eagle. "The battle is lost and our men return as beggars from the wild. The king is dead and Löhi victorious. Look now to your own defenses and prepare for the Witch's assault lest you be o'erwhelmed. Woe is come upon us all!"

Thrice the eagle delivered its warning and then it died.

When the survivors finally returned, Kaukomieli learned the whole story of all that had happened. The tragedy's full extent became apparent.

Väinämöinen took him aside one day and walked with the young man through the woods. *The Last Wizard.* During that walk, Väinämöinen became the first to use the name. No more mortals came to the Singing Valley. Löhi was ascendant. The dreams had stopped. The old man told Kaukomieli that if he stayed with them, nothing awaited him save toil, struggle, and battle, with or without hope. The choice was his to make.

He did not hesitate. Kaukomieli's power grew by the day and, with it, his passion. He vowed to serve his folk and fight Pohjola with all the strength that he had.

One day soon afterward, he was sent to find Ulla. The girl had recently returned to the Valley with her cousin, Siria, whom Kaukomieli would come to know well. He walked through the little birch wood searching for her, finally finding her atop the seidi-stone.

Ulla lay sprawled on the stone, her long, dark hair tousled about her face, her staff on the ground. She cried, sobbing like a lost child abandoned by her parents, sobbing like the maiden in the tale whose unceasing tears cried a river that carried her away to the sea. Kaukomieli hid behind a tree and watched.

He knew why she cried. All knew the story of Ulla's love for Egan by now—how they had plighted their troth before the battle, how they hoped to marry and rule over the Far Northern Land as king and queen. But Ulla didn't cry for thrones, crowns, or titles. She cried like a maiden for her lover, lost now forever, and for the joy she had so briefly known and would never know again.

Kaukomieli had seen Egan only once. A novice and newcomer, he had turned out with the folk of the Singing Valley on the morning that the king's party rode to Kirsikka's wedding. Egan was newly returned from battle then; the tale of his fight with the dragon was on everyone's lips. His white horse passed directly in front of Kaukomieli. Kaukomieli remembered his flowing cape and fine clothes, finer than anything he had ever seen or imagined. A long, sharp tooth—the dragon's tooth—hung from a chain about his neck.

"Dragonslayer! Dragonslayer!" Kaukomieli had cried alongside all the others. Egan looked down at him and smiled. For a brief moment, their eyes met. The sandy-haired king was only a few years older than Kaukomieli, but to the boy from Deep Länsimaa, he looked much older. The scars from the dragon were fresh on his face, his arm in a sling. Etched on his expression were battle and care. Egan rode on, the Swan Knights behind him, and Kaukomieli never saw him again.

Watching Ulla cry atop the seidi-stone, Kaukomieli's heart filled with pity. He thought of rushing to her, comforting her, doing anything he could to stop the tears. But what could he do or say? Singer though he had become, what was he to her but an unlettered foundling from the wilds, the latest *tietäjää* to come to the Valley, one who had not even fought in the battle? After a while, he felt guilty for spying on her. He carefully crept away, telling no one what he had witnessed.

Väinämöinen had promised him toil, struggle, and battle. He came to know all in full measure. He also came to know Ulla. Sent to help his own people, the Elk Folk, Kaukomieli put the sword-spell that Turi had taught him to good use. Though he had never seen combat before, he proved a natural in battle. He did for his folk all that he could and, when Teemu was defeated and Deep Länsimaa overrun, Kaukomieli had helped lead a great part of the Elk Folk to safety in Tavastia.

He fought alongside Ulla after that, up and down the Marches. His magic grew apace until all acknowledged him to be one of the greatest *tietäjää*. He secretly fancied himself Ulla's equal. Many singers had been killed at Sumuvuori; others had been slain or vanished in the following years. Few now remained, the Valley abandoned. Kaukomieli's people saw him as a ray of hope. Not only did he work the spells he had been taught, but, like Unaja before him, the young man proved adept at designing his own, weaving the power of the spirits he discovered all around him into his songs.

He carried another secret within his heart, an unspoken desire; Kaukomieli had fallen in love with Ulla, perhaps from the very first time that he saw her.

Long were the days and weeks they spent together from Tavastia to Etelamaa. He learned much of Ulla's mind, though she seldom shared her thoughts. She respected his strength and power, but treated him like a wayward apprentice, urging him to be wary and distrustful of others, hardening him to the hopeless war that carried on. A certain awkwardness lay between them, no matter the hours and perils they shared. He never declared his feelings or spoke to her about her love for Egan and its tragic end. Still, his feelings grew until his heart could scarcely contain them.

Ulla certainly knew this. For that reason, he supposed, the distance between them remained. The young man had no idea what to do with his love or how he might, beyond all hope, win Ulla over.

Ulla Karhulainen. Kaukomieli shook his head, throwing back his hood so that his fair locks fell free. Another day of waiting hastened toward its end. Snow was in the air. He could not stay awake another night nor keep the spells up in his sleep. If the trolls failed to appear soon, he would have to begin again in the morning.

Kaukomieli's eyes glanced at his pack. The apple—why not? Now was as good a time as any. He needed something special after the trying day. He rummaged through the pack and drew out the Tavastian apple, all sweetness and juice inside, even when dried.

He took a bite, savoring the rich flavor and letting the cold fruit melt in his mouth. As he swallowed, he felt a seed between his teeth; he leaned forward to spit it out. A flash of pain shot through his arm. He dropped the apple. A roar like a giant's bellow shattered the forest's calm. Twisting around, he saw a wooden club drive into the frozen earth inches from his face. On his back now, boots kicking in the air, he saw his attacker: a troll. His prey had caught *him*, after all.

The troll, at least eight feet tall, stooped over him. Thin as a rail, it raised the club high with its knotted, muscular arms. The creature's carrot-like nose stuck out from its ugly face; its tiny eyes blazed red with hatred. It struck again. Kaukomieli ducked in the nick of time, and the club just missed his head.

The young man scrambled to his feet, jumping out of the hole. The troll bellowed. Flying spittle struck Kaukomieli's face.

His staff lay just out of reach. As the troll swung its club a third time, the wizard thrust out a bleeding hand and cried, "*Pysäyttää!*" The monster staggered back, arms and neck twitching wildly like the mad dance of some crazed creature.

Kaukomieli's breath grew ragged. He had no time to recover. Several other trolls moved about the clearing. One charged. Shorter than the first, round and squat, it carried a long pole. Before Kaukomieli could react, the troll thrust the pole into the pit of his stomach. Had it been a spear, that would have been the end of Kaukomieli, skewered like a hog on a spit. It knocked his breath out all the same. He fell over, grabbed at a standing stone, and toppled backwards off the knoll.

The world turned upside down. Amidst panic and pain, he saw trees, leaves, and sky wheel overhead. Even as he fell, he grasped at a stunted pine that clung to the hillside. Catching a branch, he stopped abruptly. Kaukomieli dangled over a sheer drop to the gully far below.

Kaukomieli's right hand trembled. He struggled to hang on. He couldn't breathe, fading in and out of consciousness. Another scream filled his ears; he looked up. He dangled just below the knoll's lip. Above, the troll peered down at him.

Its face was horribly clear. The troll's black lips were open, fangs protruding, and slaver dripping down. The creature's mottled visage was ghastly, like some terrible mask or nightmare vision brought to life. Kaukomieli slipped lower, his strength failing. The troll straightened. Kaukomieli waited for it to make an end of him, to knock him off or send a stone hurtling down. A final thought flashed through his mind: maybe better to let go and fall to a swift death than be crushed from above.

But the troll didn't move. A riot of jabbering cries broke out. The monster stood on the precipice, staring blankly with beady eyes. It swayed. Suddenly, without warning, it rocked one way, then the other, then tumbled headfirst off the knoll. It nearly took him with it as it fell, but he held on. The crash of its heavy body echoed from below.

Everything faded to black. Kaukomieli closed his eyes. He lost his grasp. At the same instant, a gloved hand grabbed his arm. He heard a voice cry out for strength in the Old Speech. *Voimaa!* He opened his eyes, looking up. It was no troll; it was Ulla.

With a jerk, Ulla hauled Kaukomieli up. He tumbled on top of her as they fell together into the shallow hole at the gully's edge.

The young man, beyond all wonder, sprawled on top of her, gasping for air. Ulla brought her boots up, pushing him away.

"Get off me," she said.

Ulla scrambled up, pulling him to his feet. He dropped back to his knees, sick and retching. Shaking her head, she crossed her arms.

"This is how you lay in wait for enemies? If this is the best you can do, you had better stay in the hillforts and leave hunting to the Wardens."

At length, Kaukomieli could breathe again. He slowly stood up and looked around. His first attacker lay on its back, arms stretched above its head. Another troll lay nearby, a sword sticking straight up from its belly. Ulla approached it. With a boot on the creature's chest, she thrust the sword deeper, twisting; the troll arched once, then collapsed. Its dying breath rattled in the frosty air. Ulla pulled the sword out. Dark green blood dripped onto the snow.

"There," she said. "That's better."

Slack-jawed, the young man stared at Ulla with a dazed expression.

"You're welcome," she said. The rebuke brought him back to the present. He bowed clumsily.

"I'm sorry. Thank you."

Ulla sighed, cleaning her sword in the snow.

"Where are the others?" asked Kaukomieli. "There were more of them, weren't there?"

"Can't you hear them? Running for their lives. Two of them, at least.

They are lucky. If I hadn't needed to save your neck, they would be dead now, too."

Still shaking her head, she retrieved her staff, pack, and water skins, which had been set beside a tree just outside the clearing.

"You're also lucky. If I hadn't followed them, they would have killed you. After everything we've taught you, I would think that you'd be more careful."

"I don't understand it," he said. "I wove warning spells all about this place. They never should have gotten so close."

"Spells don't work if you're dreaming," she replied. "And some spells don't work on trolls in any case. They may be dumb as nails, but there's a magic to them all the same. A strange *väki*. These were clever enough to track and find you. How is your hand?"

He had forgotten in his surprise. He looked down at his bloody right hand, which had been smashed by the troll's club. It was already turning blue, but he could move his fingers; it wasn't broken.

"It's all right. It hurts, but I think it will be fine."

"Put snow on it and wrap it," said Ulla. "It will swell if you don't."

Kaukomieli did as she instructed, then gingerly lowered himself to the ground.

"Let me rest a bit," he said, "I'm spent."

"And I'm not? Really, it's as if you have no training at all. We rest later. We just fought a battle here. Who knows what else might be nearby or who might be watching? Do you want to stay here and find out? When we've put some miles between us and this place, then we rest."

The young man rose, making a move toward the pinewood. He turned. Ulla stood stock still.

"Your staff?" she asked.

He sighed. "Sorry. I'm not thinking straight."

"When did that ever stop you? Come on now, let's go. I'll help you."

They climbed down the slope into the thicker woods, picking their way through fallen trees and matted litter. A measure of strength returned to

Kaukomieli. He felt foolish, knowing that he had embarrassed himself in Ulla's eyes. Her tone was unusually sharp. Had he not rescued her just the year before in similar circumstances?

"How did you find me?" he asked, his curiosity getting the better of him.

"Pure chance," Ulla replied. She pulled a blue cowl up over her head as the evening's cold came on. "I searched for seven days, coming upon the trolls just south of here. They were obviously tracking something, so I followed to see what it was.

"It was my mistake," she said, more gently. "If they had tapped you on the head, it would have been my fault. I should have acted quicker."

"You saved my life," he replied. "I'm in your debt. But why were you searching for me in the first place, Ulla? Who told you I was here?"

"Ilkka, of course. Did you not tell him you wanted to see me?"

While they walked, Ulla told him about her journey to Akkala, the fight with Maanavilja, and her visit to Tapiola. She soon fell into the easy tone she sometimes enjoyed with him, the distance between them almost gone. They were two wizards, friends, discussing the tools and toils of their trade. Kaukomieli knew Ulla well enough not to cross the invisible, unspoken barrier, however. At the first sign of unwarranted familiarity, she would draw back like a tortoise into its shell.

"How goes it in Tapiola?"

"Bad," she answered. "They have men enough for their own defenses, at least now that so many Bear and Elk Folk have joined them. But the Tavastians will not come to Teemu's aid. He says that Siinesaare cannot hold out long, maybe another winter. After that, who knows?"

She saw the pain in his face. It was Kaukomieli's own clan that suffered at Siinesaare.

"And in the city itself there is sickness, disease. The shadow of Lovêatar has grown longer. It lingers even when she has gone elsewhere. She is Löhi's greatest weapon now, more dangerous even than the Moonface. Sickness and famine may rot strongholds from within even when walls remain strong."

"There is something else," said Kaukomieli. "A sickness not of the body, but of the spirit. Whether it comes from Lovêatar or the Witch herself, I don't know. But I felt it in the spring. I felt it in the summer, before you left. It was growing throughout Tavastia, throughout the whole Far Northern Land, I'll wager."

They reached level ground. The going became easier. Kaukomieli's pain subsided.

"And what about Väinämöinen?" he asked at last.

Ulla stopped.

"I thought to ask you," she said, heavily. "So he has sent no word, no message?"

"Nothing."

"Then you know as much as I do. He is still in the Enchanted Valley, I suppose. It is too far for me; my *sight* is not that strong. I tried to use the glass, but it was not made for such long distances."

The sun had fallen well below the tree line. Shadows faded into the dusk. The young man blinked. Ulla's blue cape looked black in the winter twilight. Snow crunched beneath their boots as they walked.

"Where are we going?"

"Midnight is about a mile away, in a little glade. We can stay there tonight. We will have to take turns riding tomorrow, one on Midnight while the other walks. The going will be slow. It may be several days before we reach the Wardens."

Suddenly Kaukomieli stopped. Ulla went on a few paces, then turned about.

"What's wrong?" she asked.

Kaukomieli gazed at a tree, a strangely shaped Tavastian pine. Rooted in a mossy tussock, the twisted pine wrapped itself around a southward facing boulder and reached for the sun through an impossible opening amidst its taller neighbors. The grey-green bark was scored and split. He reached out with his wounded hand, touching the old, weathered trunk.

"There's a spirit within this tree," he said slowly, almost as if to himself.

"Sleepy it is, ready to hibernate for the winter like a bear in its den, but aware of us just the same. Can you hear it talking?"

Ulla came beside him. She touched the tree with her staff.

"Yes, I think so. Yes, now I can feel it, but I cannot understand such speech. What is it saying?"

Kaukomieli hesitated.

"Winter is here. More snow is coming. Now is the time for rest. What are two mortals doing alone in the forest when the Witch's voice sings on the wind?"

"A good question," said Ulla. "And the answer is that we shouldn't be here. Let's go."

They continued toward the glade where Midnight waited. Quietly now, each wrapped in their own thought, they plowed along. Kaukomieli eventually broke the silence.

"I've been considering something," he said. "Thinking about it quite a lot these past few weeks while I've been out here alone."

"Well, what is it?"

"I've a plan I want to tell you about, Ulla."

Chapter Three

Spirits of the Dead

His hair was wet, damp from fever. Towheaded, this one was, like so many other children in the Far Northern Land, his hair so fair that it was more white than yellow. His deep blue eyes shone like the gleam of a lake in Old Talvimaa at twilight. The little boy's chest rose and fell, his breathing irregular and shallow. Inside, the pitter-patter of his tiny heart beat like a hummingbird's wings, frenzied and wild. He was leaving, that's what he was doing, leaving his mother behind to chase after his dead father's soul, whose body, covered with homespun cloth, lay in the corner of the cottage. No mortal healer could stop it; the child lay dying. But the old man who sat beside the little boy was no mortal healer; he was *Erilaisen* and a wizard.

The old man's eyes were moist. No matter that he had lived centuries, that his memory reached back to the earliest of days—it was still hard to watch a child die, carried off to Tuonela before ever having a chance to truly live. He stroked his forked and plaited beard, then sighed. The old man's eyes strayed to the bedside. His staff lay against the wall. The child's mother sat on a stool at the *pirtti's* single table, her face as pale as her son's, her eyes red and stinging. More a child herself than a grown woman, she had perhaps seen all of sixteen years. Girls often married young among the Swan Folk.

He looked at her with pity. How could she begin to understand what was happening to her? A girl so young had lived her whole life beneath the Witch's shadow, but the Marches were far away. Men might sometimes leave the village for battles far from home, at least in the days of the king, but what did that mean to her? The seasons came and went, snow fell and melted, rye grew and was cut; such was the rhythm of life for peasants in the Kingdom of Etelamaa. Not so long ago, the girl had danced at her wedding feast, flowers in her braided hair and bronze chains spinning round about her neck. Now the young man who she had called husband lay dead with his old mother as well, and her little boy lay dying. Evil voices wailed on the wind at night and frightful things crept through the woods. Ghosts had come among them. How could one so young begin to understand?

The old man turned back to the boy, stroking his fine, fair hair. The blue eyes glittered, shaking with a faint tremor. The wizard knew what they saw: the forest with no colors. The little boy was already wandering in those woods on the borders of Tuonela.

"Do something!" the mother screamed suddenly. "Save him if you are a wizard!"

Startled, the old man jerked his head. Breathing heavily, he took the child's little hand in his and closed his eyes. It wasn't easy, even for one of the great among the Erilaiset, to induce a trance in such circumstances. There was no smoke, no fire, and no drum, but he had done it before, saved children not much older than this from Tuone's kingdom. The old man let his senses wander, letting go of all focus, feeling nothing but living energy all around him. No sight, no sound, only the familiar sensation of his spirit-self, his very soul, leaving his body. He knew the sensation well, perhaps better than any other in the Far Northern Land.

He came back to himself soon enough. The trees rustled. His sharp ears caught the soft splash of water. The old man opened his eyes. The cottage's four walls were gone, the crying woman vanished. He stood still, alone among the trees, alone in the spirit world on the marches of death's kingdom.

He blinked. His hand grasped his staff; he had brought it with him! Now that was something, a rarity even for the most powerful singers. He had no time to ponder this, however. Somewhere in the colorless woods was the child, and he had to find the boy before he reached the river.

The wizard moved sluggishly at first, as he always did. The thick, heavy air felt oppressive. Brown, dun, grey—the muted colors made it hard to guess distance and discern shape in the unnatural light. Moving more quickly now, he raised his hands to his mouth and called out the little boy's name.

"Pekka!" he cried, a common enough name for boys throughout the Far Northern Land. "Pekka, listen to me! Come back, my lad. Don't go on just yet. Pekka!"

The old man cocked his head to one side; at first he heard nothing. Then, almost imperceptibly, he caught a rustle in the bramble ahead. He hurried forward. At last, he caught a glimpse of something rushing through the pines, something small and white like a rabbit hopping over fallen logs.

"Pekka!"

The little boy turned and looked back. Only a tiny child in the waking world, tottering about with uncertain steps, his spirit ran swift and sure here on the borders of life and death. He smiled a quick, mischievous smile, then, laughing, ran on, naked, his skin shining like a lamp amidst the gloom. Leaping over another fallen tree, he raced ahead.

"Stay, Pekka!" commanded the wizard, drawing on his power for the first time. Stomping through the marshy ground, he quickly gained on the boy. The child hesitated, staring up at the darkling sky. The soft sound of lapping water carried to the old man's ears.

"Pekka, lad," he said, out of breath as he finally caught up to the child. "Come back with me, son. Don't go to the river, not yet."

"Why not, *Turi?*"

The cracked, sinister voice came from behind. Turi spun round, instinctively raising his staff. There, in front of him, stood Löhi.

"Why not?" she repeated mockingly. "He's already dead. His little heart stopped just moments ago. Who do you think you are to call him back? Is that power given to you? Only I command the paths in and out of Tuonela.

Or do you wish to go with him to the other side? I can take you to the cold maiden who will carry you across. I can hear the splash of her little boat even now. Foolish Turi. You might have hidden away with Väinämöinen and stayed alive a little longer. But you always wish to be the hero, don't you?"

The Witch wore the aspect of the old crone of Pohjola, a gap-toothed hag with a long, pointed nose. Her black, peaked hat and dark robes were in tatters, but the light in her spiraled eyes shone red with fire.

The little boy, who had been gazing up at Löhi, made off toward the water as if suddenly summoned. The Witch cackled, spitting on the ground.

"He's getting away," she said gleefully. "Don't you want to go after him? Or have you lost your appetite for excursions into the realm of the dead? Perhaps I should help send you across."

Turi was frozen to the spot, planted like a tree in the ground. So powerful was Löhi that her spirit, her *etianen*, could work strong magic when she walked through the woods without color, using his own name against him to enchant him unawares. Yet even Löhi had her limits. To weave so strong a spell, the Witch's incarnate self must not be far from where his own body sat beside the dead boy in the cottage.

"Do you wonder what brought me here?" she asked, guessing his mind. "The same as you. To check on the handiwork of my servant. Lovêatar has been steadfast in her efforts, but she's prone to distraction, poor thing. Still, I admit that I had other motives.

"I had hoped to find Ulla nearby. Chasing around the Marches on her fool's errands is one thing, but I'm disappointed in her. I thought that the ruin of her precious Etelamaa might draw her hither. Perhaps I expect too much of her. One of these days, she'll learn that her luck's run out, shot down by a goblin's arrow or some other mundane end. You know all about goblins' arrows, don't you, Turi? Tell me, where is she now? Skulking with Väinämöinen in Karelia?"

His mouth was suddenly unstopped. The force of the Witch's compulsion fell upon him, but he tried to remain calm. Whatever happened, he would not betray his friends.

"Wherever she is, you'll never find her," he struggled to say. "But someday she'll find you. You do not know how strong she has become. She's the sign of your ultimate failure, Löhi. Your ultimate doom."

Pain burned through his mind like a shooting star.

"Oh, she'll find me, all right. Ulla will always return to me in some fashion. And when she does, I'll take her with me to Pohjola. Unless..." The old crone licked the spittle from her thin lips. "Unless Kuupää finds her first. He's always searching for her. It's very personal."

"The Moonface will never catch her," the wizard hissed in anger. "She's the hope of the Far Northern Land. Tapio's instrument. That's why you fear her so much; you have no power over her. Why else have you not already found her? *When the cold hand reaches southward, reaches with its frozen fingers, comes a child into the Northland, all—*"

"*Ka*," cried Löhi, angrily, cutting him off. She spat again. Her voice changed, now proud and regal.

"I *am* the Far Northern Land. Lookest thou not at the night sky, Turi? Seeth thou not my star ascendant? It is already over, thou fool. The reaping alone remains." Laughing, the Witch continued in her cracked, heckling tone.

"Foolish, foolish Turi. I had thought to take you with me, perhaps, to return you to your body and take you with me to Sariola. Not Ulla, but a worthwhile substitute and reward for my long journey south. After all, I have always been overly sentimental about such things. But now I don't think so; your companionship might prove far too irksome. No, I believe that this is where it ends for you, Turi. All the years, all the struggles—it all comes down to this. Strange, is it not? Now listen well!"

The Witch came close to him, even grasping his staff and looking him straight into the eye.

"Remember this as you die, Turi. The Far Northern Land is mine. No hope, no possibility, no future: all is in ruins for you. And after you are gone, one by one, all the others you love will fall to me until not a soul is left."

All the while Löhi spoke, Turi tried desperately to break the enchantment that bound him or think of some way out of the trap. There was no telling what Löhi might do to him. She could destroy his spirit-body and send him flying over the river or she might bind him, helpless, while his body in the waking world withered and died. He had seen the sad fate of singers whose spirits became lost or trapped, lingering in a half-life, witless and dumb, until their desiccated bodies finally expired. If only he could break free—then what? Flee to the cottage where his body waited? Or attack Löhi, trap her in turn? Was that not the chance that they all had been waiting for? Seldom did the Witch leave the safety of Pohjola, seldom was she as unprotected as she might be now, if he could only discover a way to turn it to his advantage.

Smiling, the Witch stepped back, her hand still on his staff. He felt her power contesting his own, like a stone dam holding back white water. If only he could work a change here on the other side—a snake, a bird, or even a bear to challenge her, like *karhu*.

Just then, as if in answer to his thought, he felt another power nearby, neither his nor Löhi's. The Witch felt it too. She turned, peering through the dusky woods. Bracken snapped. A brown figure shambled among the shadows. Turi heard a low growl in the distance.

That gave him all the opening he needed. Löhi's spell wavered for a moment and, distracted, her hand slipped off the staff. With a final effort, Turi summoned all his strength and broke the spell. Falling backwards, he scrambled into the trees, jumped up, and ran. Behind him, Löhi cursed.

All thoughts of challenge forgotten, Turi sped away, both from the Witch and the creature prowling the woods. Expecting an attack from behind at any moment, he leapt over trees, stones, and mossy holes. Finally, he stumbled through a thicket of thorny bushes, coming up short.

Before him ran the Dead River. Beyond lay Tuonela, the Kingdom of the Dead.

Slow and silent flowed the river; sad and lonely streamed the flood. Into the Dark Land it wandered, where all feeling dulled and all passion died. Dark, dark was its water, and dark the shadows on the other shore where cool mists curled about trees, trailing beards into the shoals. Sound was silenced here, the past forgotten; the river told no tale nor held any promise, yet still it beckoned to all who beheld it. For most, it marked the beginning of their final journey.

Turi had seen it before, had passed over that current and walked in Tuone's kingdom. Long ago, he had found stepping stones, black as jet, with which to cross the flood. The river still enchanted him. Within his heart, he heard a sad voice calling to him, irresistibly: *Come to us. Come now.*

With an effort, he shook himself free and turned away from the sullen water. Dimly, as if at a great distance, he heard a muffled commotion in the woods from whence he had fled. *Karhu!* How the Witch feared the great bear of the spirit world, the creature from heaven over which she held no power! Only *karhu's* coming had saved him; prowling the margins between life and death as it always did, drawn, perhaps, by their great magical power.

Raising his staff, he cried, "Me to my body, my body to me!" Then again, louder, "Me to my body, my body to me!"

Like an arrow, his mind sped back through a swirling vision of forest, sky, and stars. Then, with a *whump*, he fell off the ramshackle little bed onto the earthen floor.

He was whole again, back in the humble *pirtti*.

The wizard was unsure how long he had wandered through the colorless woods. It seemed only a brief time, less than an hour, but he knew well how deceptive such perception could be. Here in the mortal world, hours might have passed, even days.

He picked himself up. Some time had certainly passed. Little Pekka no longer lay on the bed. His mother sat on a stump in the corner, holding a small bundle wrapped in homespun cloth. She said nothing.

Turi grabbed his tall hat, placing it on his head.

"He had gone too far," the wizard said, plainly. "I'm sorry. There was nothing to be done. And there was an enemy too, who accosted me; her spirit almost trapped me."

"Lovêatar?" asked the girl, dully.

"Not she," he replied, "But another even worse. Be comforted, child. Pekka is innocent. The stain of the world is not upon him. He shall pass through Tuonela swiftly. Only his shade will remain there, no more meaningful than the clothes we wrap around ourselves. You will see him again, and his father too."

The woman made no reply.

"Now listen to me. Leave this farm now and do not return. Bury your child in the woods at once; I will see to your husband. Take only what little you need and go swiftly to your own folk, your own parents. Do not come back. There is sickness here, and if you remain, you will catch it."

Hoisting his pack, he carried the dead man's body as best he could. Weary and shaken as he was from the day's events, he half-expected to see Löhi at any moment. He knew she might be nearby, in the flesh. If *karhu* had not wandered by, Turi knew that he might be as dead as the unfortunate villager. The great bear was drawn to magic and power, to anything that disturbed the twilight woods where his spirit prowled. *Karhu* was also drawn to Löhi. She feared him, no matter her bluster. Of all creatures in the world, over *karhu* alone the Witch held no power. It was too much to hope that she had been taken unawares, however. Löhi knew the pale woods better than any Erilainen and passed in and out of Tuonela at will.

The wizard didn't have far to go. Many people of nearby villages who perished in the plague were buried together in a glade beside a little lake. Turi soon found two men, villagers, making the rounds with their sled. He gave them his charge, speaking what words he could over the young man. The villagers had news—Wardens were in the area, searching for him. Word was out that he had come to the upper reaches of Etelamaa just beneath the Wall.

Turi had actually been in Alamuuri district for several weeks. After the summer's skirmishes in Tavastia, he had set out for the Karelian Forest to see Mielikki and Väinämöinen. He hadn't made it very far.

Easterners rode through the region, sacking villages and farms. Their curved swords did not trouble Alamuuri the most, however. Lovêatar haunted village streets and lonely homesteads, communicating sickness and death. The people in those parts had been spared the war's ravages until this year, but now it seemed that the Witch was in a hurry to make up for lost time.

Turi spent the night at a nearby farm. He slept with his ear half-cocked for any sound of trouble, but all was quiet. Falling into deep slumber, he awoke at noon, when dim sunlight leaked into the *kota* where he sheltered. He heard voices outside, the voices of friends, not enemies. Mikko and Gerlag, two March Wardens, stood there.

"Aha," cried Turi, popping out of the *kota*. "Hei, my lads! I heard you were looking for me and now you've found me! I hope I was not so easy to track."

Mikko smiled. "*A friend appears in full daylight, but an enemy remains hidden.* So of course it was easy to find you. But Gerlag and I have scouted these parts for years. In need, I dare say, we could track you down anywhere, so long as you didn't turn into a bird or some such and fly away."

"Yes, well, that hasn't turned out so well for me of late. What brings you here? Sit down with me and rest a spell. I'll have hot drink for you both if you give me a minute."

The Wardens sat in the lee of the *kota* as Turi prepared the drinks. Mikko, a typical Karhulainen, was short and stocky, with a potato-like nose and a scraggly beard. Gerlag was Kotkalaisen, however. Tall and spare, he had fought with Airikki at Sumuvuori where more than half of the Eagle Folk's army had perished. Gerlag escaped with Ilkka back to the Marches. He went for a Warden then, serving in Etelamaa for several years.

"Here you go, lads," said Turi, passing them a steaming bowl of herb tea that all three could share. "Now, on with your tale. What are you doing in these parts?"

"Gathering news, mostly," answered Mikko. "We were sent north before heavy snow comes. Rumor of Lovêatar's presence in Alamuuri has spread across the kingdom. We met many people fleeing south as we approached the district. Where will they go so late in the season, I wonder?

"An ill choice is upon them, to stay in this place of sickness or take their chances on the open road. If they do not have friends or family elsewhere, death may still find them."

"None whom we met had seen Lovêatar," said Gerlag, "Although ghostly cries echo on the night's wind."

"Lovêatar does not linger," answered Turi. "Winter is her season, just like her mistress, Löhi. The ghost moves from place to place, village to village, while her sickness stays behind and works its evil. Fell spirits are indeed all around. I hear them and feel them. Alamuuri has become an unwholesome place."

A gust of cold wind blew over them. Turi's small fire crackled and popped.

"This plague will be the death of us," said Mikko. "The death of us all and the end of the Far Northern Land. The Easterners' swords are one thing, but at least a man can fight back against them. This evil magic is something else. I never thought that Etelamaa could fall; it is so large and strong. Now I do not know."

"Can the *tietäjää* do nothing to stop the plague?" asked Gerlag. "Can the Erilaiset not slay Lovêatar or send her back to Tuonela?"

"It is not so easy," sighed Turi. "Some have tried and failed. How do you slay a thing already dead, even with magic? And if you *could* send her back to Tuonela, what then? Unless her father, Tuone, catches her, she will only return to this world again. That is Löhi's doing, a spell she has created to convey Lovêatar to the Far Northern Land whenever she wishes. A dark magic that must be—and a powerful one.

"Truly I've thought about it, lads; many times over the past few years, I've pondered ways to craft a spell to defeat Lovêatar. Some healing power I have to help the afflicted. That, at least, some of the Great Ones among the Erilaiset may still do."

"The Great Ones," mused Gerlag. "Like Mielikki, the lady they say lives deep within the forest among the trees. Or Väinämöinen. I've only seen him once since the battle. There are rumors about him too. They say that he has disappeared, vanished from the Far Northern Land, gone on some quest from which there's no return. Do you know where Väinämöinen is, Turi?"

The wizard hesitated. The men's blue eyes looked searchingly at him. Turi had been asked the question many times before, wherever he went.

"Väinämöinen is in Karelia. He hasn't disappeared. He will return. I'm on my way there now. Many things happen in the world that the Erilaiset must attend to. He will soon be back."

The Wardens dropped their heads, staring at the crackling fire and sharing the warm brew while dark clouds gathered in the sky above.

All three men stayed at the farm that night, but Turi left his friends sleeping in the early dawn. Taking an uncertain path to the northwest, he soon left the village far behind. Although known as a lone wolf, a solitary singer who often travelled without companions, he felt lonely now. He usually liked journeying by himself, listening to nature's song and watching animals in the woods and fields. Now he would have welcomed the Wardens' company, but he would not endanger them, not with Löhi so near. If the Witch still lingered in the area, she surely knew that he was close by.

Throughout Alamuuri, folk told stories of ghosts and unclean spirits wailing in the tumbled wilderness. Turi was not sure what to do next; should he continue to the Enchanted Valley or hunt for Lovêatar? If he found her, what then? Did he have any hope of defeating her or at least chasing her from the district? He decided to search the wilderness first and discover, if he could, what manner of spirits might haunt the place.

As Turi walked down the seldom used country path, wrapped in a thick cloak and hood against the cold, he thought about Väinämöinen. The look in his friends' eyes when they asked about the old singer haunted Turi more than the prospect of meeting ghosts in the woods at night. He had chosen his words carefully so as to give them no cause for despair; whatever hope they had left was fragile enough. The truth was that Turi himself was in doubt.

Väinämöinen! If the great singer, the oldest Erilainen alive in the Far Northern Land save Löhi herself had given up, what hope was there for anyone? And yet, as the months passed and the moon and stars raced over-heard in their heavenly courses, Turi's suspicions grew stronger that things were amiss with his friend.

Väinämöinen and Turi had led a large part of the survivors of Sumuvuori through the Wastes and back to the North Marches. In the terrible time that followed, Väinämöinen fought relentlessly against the Pohjolaiset, rallying men wherever he could and counseling all against despair. He seemed to be everywhere and, if not for him and Ulla, perhaps the folk of the Seven Clans would have been overwhelmed that year by the wave of the Witch's assaults.

Nonetheless, defeat followed defeat. High Länsimaa fell, the Bear Folk enslaved. The lands of the Elk Folk were laid waste. After Airikki's death, the Eagle Folk turned against the Erilaiset as they had done before, and the Heroes were again outlaws in Akkala while lords and chiefs fought one another for the throne in Langvika. Unless they went as Wardens, no Kotkalainen fought alongside their kinsmen. The Seven Clans were fractured. The unity that the League had achieved had dissolved in fear and mistrust. Finally, even the Singing Valley had been abandoned.

Something changed in Väinämöinen then. The old man had a melan-choly streak like any good forester and, throughout his long life, had at times sought silence and solitude. However, he had never left his friends.

Two summers ago, as grim and despondent as Turi had ever seen him, Väinämöinen had journeyed to the Enchanted Valley to take counsel with Mielikki. He never came back. Turi's *sight* was long and well-attuned to Väinämöinen's. At first, they often communicated as *tietäjää* might do. Always Väinämöinen asked for news of Ulla and her deeds; always he had little news of himself. Less often he reached out to Turi and, as the Witch's power waxed, it grew more difficult for the Erilaiset to use *sight* over great distances.

Many months had passed since he last had word from Väinämöinen. If not for a brief message from Mielikki, the Changer would not even be sure that his friend was still in the Enchanted Valley. Turi almost expected Väinämöinen to set out for Pohjola alone and unaided.

The path diminished into an uncertain trail meandering through thin woods. No men lived nearby. Darkness enveloped the land. Snow would soon fall. Were it not for the danger, Turi would have enjoyed such a walk. Scurrying sounds caught the wizard's ear—badgers, not yet nestled in their winter's den. Somewhere in the distance, a wolf howled mournfully, strange since few wolves lived in this part of Etelamaa.

Turi reached an open space where the trail failed altogether. Fallen birches lay here and there; the white trunks of trees still standing appeared to glow softly with their own luminescence. Lonely snowflakes began to fall.

All at once, Turi felt a disturbance, a power and magic coursing through the woods around him. It was strong, stronger than anything he had ever felt before. *Did something happen at this place, something that left its imprint upon the woods for all eternity?* He stopped in his tracks.

A new sensation crept over him. Coils rose from the ground, wrapping around him like a curling mist, a binding spell, different than any he had ever encountered. He flung his staff wide as if violently casting off some clinging thing. The coils withdrew.

The he saw them.

Three figures stood in the little clearing. One faced him, no more than twenty feet away; the others flanked him on either side. White they were, pale as moon sheen. The snow blew straight through their translucent bodies, twinkling like little stars. They would have looked beautiful if not for the scent of evil borne on the cold north wind. The wizard's vison cleared and a chill passed through him, for he knew them.

Closer they came, ghosts that hovered over the broken ground. The shade directly before him had long braided locks. A tall helm sat upon its head, rent and shattered. Tattered robes blew in the breeze. It raised an ephemeral hand, but the hand was broken, three fingers missing. Long had it been since Turi had seen that elf, for an elf's ghost it was, and well the singer knew him. His name was Tursas, Lord of the Dark Elves of Pohjola, slain at the Great Battle hundreds of years before. Turi descried that within the soft glow, his face was twisted and rotten.

To Tursas's left, another shade, no less dreadful than the first, held a chain in its dead hand. Snow blew past its head like a crown of frost. The spirit smiled, cold and mocking. Faint laughter came not to Turi's ears, but to his mind. The ghost was Saarelon, whom Lúven had slain at Sumuvuori. Upon his ethereal breast was battered mail, which bore his device, a ghastly death's head.

The third spirit did not laugh. The putrid, mottled face was set in an expression of hatred so intense that it struck a blow to Turi's heart even as he gazed upon it, for it was Tyë, the great Haltia and Löhi's captain. A hole there was in the elf's armor, and red blood still seemed to drip from a gaping wound. But Tyë's hand was empty; no sword lay in its grasp.

Turi was terrified, wizard though he was. Fear swept over him. So strong had Löhi now become that not only did she command lesser spirits, but also the very ghosts of her dead champions returned from Hell. And as he blinked in horror at their hollow, empty eyes, the elves spoke in unison with deadly voices: "Turi."

A vise gripped his throat; his voice had been taken. He had hesitated a moment only, for one instant of panic and fear, but that was all it had taken. His enemies had stopped his voice and taken his songs.

He turned to run, tripping over a mossy tussock. Twisting round, he saw the spirit of Tursas race toward him. The ghosts wailed like banshees; the wind blew strong. Struggling to speak, Turi used the only weapon he had. He thrust his staff toward the flying specter. The oak wood blazed with yellow light. The ghost came within a few feet and stopped short, recoiling as if from an invisible barrier. Its companions assailed Turi from both sides. The wizard had just enough time to scramble to his feet before they were on him.

The spirits whirled about like a cyclone, a spinning white tornado with Turi trapped in its spout. Their evil voices cried out in the tongue of Pohjola. Turi turned in circles, waving his staff, a mad dance that filled the woods with electric light. Thunder boomed and the snow fell harder.

More from panic than strength, at last Turi shrieked, breaking the dreadful spell. Before they could silence him again, he cried, "*Tuli*! Catch Fire!"

Sheets of flame sprang from his staff. A birch tree ignited, blazing into the sky. The cyclone dispersed, the elvish ghosts cursing. Round and round turned Turi, sending flaming bolts in all directions. His enemies flew madly about like shooting stars descended to earth.

It's now or never, he thought. With a final burst of flame toward Saarelon, swooping down from above with his chain, Turi turned and ran back up the trail, his breath ragged. Fire had singed his beard. The smoking staff felt hot in his hand. The wizard heard Saarelon's mad cackling just behind him. The ghosts gave chase, racing through the darkling woods.

For at least a quarter of a mile, the race was on. The old man ran as fast as he could with his enemies behind him, turning now and again to blast them with wizardly power. He knew that he had no hope of outrunning them; there was no way that he could escape on foot or defeat all three at once.

Tyë's voice suddenly sounded in his ear. "Turi!" he shouted.

"Come back!" the others cackled with fell voices. "Come back with us to Tuonela!"

A ghostly hand touched his shoulder, burning like ice.

At that moment, Turi stopped and ducked. Tyë passed overhead, wheeling around with a snarl. The wizard dropped to one knee. The shades came at him from all directions. Even as they converged, Turi cried out in a great voice, "*Lintu!*"

He disappeared in a flash; the spirits passed through one another, crackling and sparking. A grey pigeon took flight from the glimmer.

Never had Turi worked a change with only a single word of power, never had any wizard. The bird climbed swiftly above the birches despite the storm. The ghosts screamed, wailed, and cursed in such dreadful cacophony that the very terrors of Tuonela seemed unleashed into the waking world. So much power had Turi put into the spell that already he was losing himself, forgetting who he was and knowing only the bird's instinct and fear. At first, it seemed that the shades were right behind him, a spectral claw grabbing at his tail feathers. The bird's wings beat violently. Skimming the tree tops, it sped away.

The caterwauling receded. Spirits from Hell they might be, but either the ghosts could not fly so fast or else they could not pass beyond the spell's set bounds. The pigeon came to a lake already half-covered in snow and dropped low. Patches of open water loomed large in the mist.

A village lay on the lake's far side. The ghosts had been left behind. As if in a fevered dream, Turi dimly realized where and what he was. He flew a short way into the wood, planning to find a *pirtti*, but, exhausted, landed in a birch tree's upper branches instead. No sooner had the bird landed than the snow-covered branches snapped under the wizard's weight, and he tumbled to the ground. For just the second time in his long life, Turi had grown so weak that his changing spell had failed before he intended.

Turi hit the ground hard, staff still in hand. The hot oak wood sizzled in the snow. Groaning, the wizard tried to rise, but slipped back, not a drop of power left to him.

"*Oi Ukko Ylijumala! Suojaa tietäjää tuholta, vapauta vainon väeltää!*" he prayed, then added to himself, "I've got to stop doing that."

For some time he lay on his back, too tired to move, staring up at the night sky and falling snow. Then, with a grunt, he crawled into a bracken of fern and brush, burrowing within. He closed his eyes and knew no more.

***

Turi awoke to the muffled sounds of the forest. A strange translucent light shone all about. He felt very cold. Sitting up, he broke through the layer of snow covering him and breathed in the open air. The sun was shining. Snow lay thick upon the ground. If the old man hadn't crawled under the fern, then been covered with snow, he might well have frozen to death during the night. Still, he felt chilled to the bone and famished.

Turi rose and set off, hobbling through the woods, leaning heavily on his staff. He knew there must be cottages nearby and possibly even his friends, the Wardens. The wizard considered what the cottagers must have heard last night and what they must be thinking right now—that an army of demons had come in on the north wind's wings. *If the ghosts were sent by the Witch to find him, if Löhi herself was near, was he not putting his friends and all the folk nearby in even greater danger by lingering in the area? Even if Lovêatar remained in the district, should he not flee?*

The wizard decided to set out for the Enchanted Valley at once, as soon as he had found food, rest, and shelter for another night, and either a horse or sled to speed him on his way. He calculated how long it would take him to reach Taikalaakso with snow already falling. The possibility of a heavy fall was real. It was late, very late in the season to start such a journey. Even a wizard might come to grief in the Far Northern Land's bitter winter. He needed to reach the great river Jouksi as soon as possible, in less than a week if he could find a mount. From the Jouksi, the forest was not so far away and the going would be easier.

Something crashed out of the woods, interrupting his rumination and spraying snow all about. Turi swung his staff up instinctively. A small golden-brown deer ran by, leaping over fallen trees and disappearing into the bramble beyond. Turi shook his head. After his fright the previous evening, such surprises were most unwelcome.

"*Ka!*" cried a voice from behind. A sharp, stabbing pain pierced his leg; he stumbled forward. Before he could react, a blow to the head sent him reeling. His staff was torn from his hand. Strong arms grasped him, turning him over.

Goblins stood there, several white-eyed goblins clad in black. Sharp spears pointed at his breast; leering faces mocked him. At the direction of the goblin leader, two Hiisia hauled Turi to his knees while another cast an iron chain about him. He felt the chain's enchantment immediately. Wizard or not, he could cast no spell while that chain held him. But there was something else, another presence more malevolent than any Hiisi.

"He is bound, my lady," hissed the goblin leader in the tongue of Pohjola.

"Excellent," said Löhi. "Be gentle with your charge. He has a long journey before him. Do not damage him overmuch."

The Witch leaned forward, coming close to Turi's face.

"Do not worry, Turi. We will make sure you have good company on the long road north. I will be there in Sariola, waiting for you when you arrive and, trust me, my friend, I will have a very special welcome prepared for you. Very special, indeed."

Chapter Four

Among the Downtrodden Folk

The Wall of the Giants stretched hundreds of miles across the Far Northern Land. From the high fells along the border of Karelia, it descended to the southwest, neatly bisecting the Seven Lands, trapping the lakes above. At its highest peaks, the stony ridge rose hundreds of feet above the plain of Etelamaa. Lower and lower it dropped as it stretched into Tavastia, as if the giants who built it had tired of their task and hurried to finish the job before winter came. The tumbled hills north of the Neck of Tavastia marked its end where it petered out in uncertain dales and valleys ringed by little heights. All the way to Akkala, however, rose occasional outliers, such as the hill at Kyöpelinvuori where the Seer had dwelt: lonely outposts that commanded the surrounding fields where birds, beasts, and sometimes men came to survey the lands.

In High Länsimaa, villages stood in some places atop the ridge. Good land could often be found there, fertile for rye and excellent for slashing and burning. Now the Witch had come and High Länsimaa was no more, but the villages remained. Not all the Karhulaiset had fled south. Many Bear Folk stayed on their farms.

The Itäläiset came among them as conquerors then, taking what they wanted for spoils and making serfs and slaves of the folk of the

Seven Clans. More recently, great wagons arrived from the East carrying Itäläisen women and children, the families of their chieftains and champions to whom Löhi showed special favor. They held the land in her name, worshipping her as queen, even if they bore her little love. But the people who remained, the dispossessed of the Bear Folk, worked the fields as thralls, living in fear.

Kuupää stood in front of the *pirtti* he had taken as his own. Several other *pirttis* stood nearby; a large wooden roundhouse built by the Easterners sat across the way. Smoke rose from stone-piled hearths. The farm atop the ridge had once been called *Kiviselkä* in the language of the Kaamoslaiset; now it was *Zemyayuri*, Yuri's land, Yuri being the Itäläinen who had taken it for his home. Yuri himself was a vassal to Bor, the chief of the Crooked-Tooth Clan, which held the land along the Wall for twenty miles to either side of *Zemyayuri*.

The farm buzzed with activity. Sleds skated over new fallen snow, carrying straw to the stables. Maidens carried water in wooden pails fixed to long poles slung across their shoulders. Children ran and played in the fallow rye field. The farm was as full of life as ever, but it was definitely not the same as before. The laughing children were Easterners. The peasants' faces looked dour, the glum visages of dispossessed serfs. The buzz of preparation for the deeper winter to come was not for the Bear Folk's benefit; the Itäläiset had come now and were determined to make Länsimaa their own.

Kuupää surveyed the scene, which would have appeared peaceful from a distance. His own camp, from where he directed the summer's raids, was close to Keskimaa. Instead of returning to Pohjola for the winter, he had ridden south to visit the Easterners and gather news. So far, he was displeased. The Easterners were becoming complacent, satisfied to live off the lands they had taken, exploiting their slaves. That was not Löhi's desire. She had brought the Itäläiset to the Far Northern Land to destroy the Seven Clans, not rule over broken Länsimaa while the Hare and Swan Folk lived free. Let the Easterners beware! Löhi gave to her servants, and she could also take away; and the Moonface was the Witch's captain and instrument of her dominion.

Two goblins from the Moonface's guard appeared, dragging a man through the snow. The goblins, taller than most and wrapped in black hoods, tossed the man at the Moonface's feet. An Easterner in heavy boats walked beside them—not Yuri, but his chief overseer.

The Karhulaisen man, though beaten and bloodied, was still very much alive. He had helped others escape into Etelamaa and been caught spreading news among the Bear Folk. The Moonface had ordered the man brought before him.

The frightened serf stared up at the Moonface. The ghastly silver mask he always wore stared back, leering with its permanent, evil smile. From the hollow eye slits flashed a pair of hazel-green eyes.

"What is your name?" asked the Moonface in the tongue of the Seven Clans.

"Tero," the man stammered.

"Are you frightened, Tero?"

"Yes, my lord," he answered. "Please, sir, I did nothing, I swear it. I was only—"

Before the man could finish his sentence, the Moonface savagely kicked him in the face. Blood poured from a shattered nose. Kuupää's sorcery was strong; he knew much black magic from Löhi. It would be easy to enchant this beast and compel him to tell all he really knew. It was much more pleasurable to hurt him, however.

At a signal from the Moonface, one of the goblins kicked Tero again, spitting on his bloody face. The poor man groveled, choking on his own spittle. The goblin's white eyes shone with malice and delight. Excited by the slave's terror, it hit him again. Its companion joined in the assault.

"He belongs to this place?" asked Kuupää, addressing the Easterner in his own language while the Hiisia continued the beating.

"Yes," came the reply. "One of the serfs who lives in the barns yonder. They slash and burn in summer."

The Moonface considered this for a moment, then raised his gloved hand. "Stop."

Immediately the goblins drew back, breathing hard with excitement. The slave sprawled in the bloodstained snow.

"That's enough. Take him back to his hovel. I want him alive. Let him recover before you send him out to chop wood again."

"The punishment for rebellion is death," said the Easterner.

"Do you not need his hands at harvest time?"

"We have no shortage. But if rebels are not made example of, it will encourage others. It is dangerous, my lord. They will raise their hands against us."

The Moonface laughed.

"Have you become so fearful in your abundance? You are afraid of *this*?" He gestured dismissively toward the Karhulaisen serf.

"At least we should cut out his tongue," said the overseer.

"No, I don't think so. I want him alive. And I want his tongue in his mouth. It will serve *our* purposes now."

At another sign from Kuupää, the green-skinned goblins picked the man up off the ground.

The Moonface lifted his head by the chin. The sorcerer's power could be felt by all, rippling outward like circles upon troubled water.

"How is it that you dare to defy your master? Defy the queen? Do you not know your life is forfeit for such deeds?"

The man coughed, a racking cough that left him gasping for breath.

"I'm sorry," he gasped. "I'm sorry. Please, lord, I'm a good worker, strong. I've always worked hard, I'll work even harder. I'll never talk to a runaway again, I swear it."

The Moonface cocked his mask oddly, considering his prey.

"I daresay. Yet, why should we believe you, Tero? Why shouldn't we slay you here and now?"

"Please don't kill me, lord. I have a family, a wife, children. They need my share, lord. Have mercy."

"Family?"

"Yes. My wife, Anni. Two sons. We... We belong to Master Yuri. Please let me live, lord."

The goblins cackled wickedly, waiting for their captain's command.

"Pitiful Karhulainen," the Moonface said at length, his voice dripping with mock compassion. "You will live, Tero. Yes, you will live. But your oldest son will not. His heart will be cut out, his blood spilt on this very spot. And think not of revenge or betrayal. If you should escape these lands, help runaways ever again, or spread rumors among the downtrodden folk, your other son shall die. I will take him to Pohjola, where the queen will hang him in a gibbet from the towers of Sariola while your wife looks on. Yet still you will live, blinded and bound, so that you may think on this for all eternity."

At first there was silence. Then the serf, eyes wide with horror, began to howl, a plaintive cry like the wail of some lonely animal in the wastes, wounded and desperate as night closes in around it.

The Moonface turned away. The Hiisia dragged the man off, still babbling like a beast.

"Take the oldest child's head and put it on a stake," said Kuupää to the overseer. "Place it at the crossroads. This fool's testimony is all the example we require. Does this satisfy your needs?" The Moonface's tone was faintly mocking and the Easterner answered carefully.

"Our needs are satisfied, my lord. I will tell Yuri what has been done."

"See to my instructions first. The Hiisia have a habit of getting carried away in their enthusiasm. I hold *you* responsible. Yuri is returning today with the scouts. I will tell him about this myself."

Expressionless, the overseer bowed, walking away down the slope. The serf's wailing wafted on the distant wind.

Too soft. Too greedy. Löhi gave, and Löhi could take away. Even among the Itäläiset there were rumors, grumblings. The first clans who came east years ago had suffered heavy losses; few remained alive after Sumuvuori. New clans came from further east. The pickings were easier now, the Karhulaiset and Hirvilaiset all but ruined. Yet the job was unfinished, final victory still to come. Let the Easterners remember who they served and worshiped as a goddess; for when Löhi's victory was complete and her power once again ran throughout the land as its lifeblood, she would have ample time to attend to her servants, both good and bad.

Kuupää tramped through the soft snow toward the roundhouse. The people nearby, Easterner and serf alike, avoided the silver mask's fixed gaze. He stopped, summoning his black horse from the stable with a silent command. The beast, saddled and harnessed, waited for him. As he swung up, another Hiisi appeared, handing Kuupää his black iron staff. The horse shuddered at the goblin's approach, but Kuupää instantly calmed it. With a word, he set off down the path, past the cottages and outbuildings, and took the white road that led to Löhi's Fence.

In the sparse woods here, scattered pines and white birch grew, pruned from the roadside so that one could see quite a way in either direction. As his horse loped along, the Moonface cut a strange figure, a figure visible to eyes for miles around. But what did the Moonface care? Sorcerer, captain, servant of Löhi, he was strong beyond the reckoning of the simpleminded folk. He feared no serf's arrow or slave's knife in the back. Only the Erilaiset might threaten him, and they were far away. What was there to fear if he did ride alone?

The queen might not yet have the power to finish off the Seven Clans. She needed more men, more spears, and after Sumuvuori, these were hard to come by. The day of reckoning was still approaching. Lovêatar was busier than ever. Etelamaa and Tavastia slowly faded. Akkala's turn would come. The Karelialaiset hardly mattered. And when the time came, Löhi herself would deal with Taikalaakso. That did not concern him. He was the destroyer of the Kaamoslaiset, and his task was to subdue the Seven Lands, deliver them to his mistress, and then rule over all of them in her name.

The Moonface smiled beneath the silver mask as he considered this. Their would-be king was dead; he had slain the counterfeit himself, putting an end to the legend that Lemminkäinen lived again. The power of the *tietäjää* was broken. One by one they would be hunted down, one by one exterminated. Even the so-called Great Ones would be found, unless they fled and hid themselves as some said Väinämöinen had done. Yet still there was one he wanted more than any other Erilainen, more than any other mortal *tietäjää*, more than all of them put together: Ulla Karhulainen.

The smile died beneath the silver mask. He gripped the reins tighter.

How he hated her! The one, the only one, that they must fear, the queen said. Her power had grown apace with his own over the years. Always she was there, rallying their enemies. No trap would hold her, no dart pierce her. He had put a price on her head above a king's ransom and still none dared the challenge. *Ulla!* Even Löhi's magic failed where Ulla was concerned, though always the Witch sought her. And Kuupää knew something more. The queen harbored strange notions about the girl; dangerous notions.

She must be stopped. There was no longer any alternative. And if his spies and assassins could not do the job, he would do it himself, whatever the cost.

His mood now turned foul at the thought of his enemy, the dark captain continued down the road until he approached the ridge, the very edge of the Fence. An uncertain trail cut across its face, leading treacherously to the fields of Etelamaa below. Snow-clad trees marked the ridgeline. The Moonface checked his horse and waited. The beast's breath steamed in the chilly air.

Finally, he spied something rising over the ridge; figures in the creeping mist moved toward him over the fell: one horseman; two others on foot. Kuupää's horse snorted.

"I am waiting," he called out as the three figures sensed his looming presence in the grey fog and hesitated. "Hasten!"

The rider was an Easterner— Yuri, who held the farm. So was another man, dressed in tattered red and black, his beard and drooping mustaches frozen in the cold. The third companion was no Itäläinen, however. Clad in green and brown, he looked like a March Warden except for his wild beard; indeed, the man was Karhulaisen, one of the Bear Folk, a scout and spy in Löhi's pay, one of dozens who roamed south of the Fence betraying their own folk for promises of power, gold, or whatever other strange desire led them to treachery.

The Karhulainen stopped short at the side of Kuupää. The mist obscured the mask's fixed expression. From the gloom it seemed featureless, a glowing, frosty disk.

"Are these the only ones?" asked the Moonface tonelessly.

"All there are today," answered Yuri, just as flatly. The Easterner was bundled warmly against the cold. "I met them just beyond the gap."

"Where have you been and what is your report?"

The tattered Itäläisen scout spoke first.

"I was in Etelamaa. The Swan Folk are in their winter garrisons. Heavy snow came early to the south. They have stopped building their towers; they will not be finished until next summer. There is panic among the people not far from here, just below the Fence; the ghost was there. Many died and the rest were fleeing wildly into the snow."

"And the harvest?"

"Poor. There will be hunger in some places, but no great famine throughout the kingdom. Not yet."

"What of Kotanrannta?"

"I did not go that far south. My kinsman, Voji, did so."

"And where is he?"

"He did not return."

"This man knows the roads among the new towers," said Yuri. "He can tell you the numbers the Wardens keep in their hill forts."

"Later," said the Moonface. "That is enough for now." He turned to the brown and green clad man shivering in the snow. "And you?"

"It was a hard journey, lord," he began animatedly, using the Easterner's tongue with a heavy Karhulaisen accent. "I come from Tavastia. Straight across the Neck I've been, chased most of the way too. More Wardens than ever and they'll hang me if they catch me. And goblins below the Wall, and worse than goblins. They don't know friend from foe and don't care anyways."

"There is always room for you in Yuri's stables. Dost thou prefer that?"

"Eh, no, lord. But a hard journey it was, nonetheless."

"The gold that awaits will remedy your ills. Take care thou dost not create new ones. Now then. Your report?"

"Well," the scout said, more subdued, "Things go poorly for the Hare Folk, especially in the north. The harvest's bad; they're starving. More people flee south all the time. This new king they have isn't much for fighting and people are grumbling against him. He keeps most of his men around the White City. Lots o' knights and men in armor and such, but not so many in the Neck anymore—nor in that old tower. I heard folk say that the king will go north himself in spring, if it ever comes. Try to calm the folk down and see things for himself."

"What of the *tietäjää*?"

"Eh, beg pardon, your lord?"

"The wizards."

"Ah, I was coming to that. You see, I was in Tapiola myself no more than a month ago. I saw her with my own eyes."

"Who?"

"Ulla. The witch-child, though she's no child no longer. Tall and dark she's become, dressed all in black. It hurt my eyes even to look at her."

The Moonface tensed. The Karhulainen heard a low hiss like that of a wary cat.

"Four weeks ago?"

"Yes, lord. They say she'd been in Akkala and brought back the head of Maanavilja, the one who used to serve that old Seer, to Tapiola. She's killed 'em. Didn't stay long in the city, though. Right back to the Marches. I was afraid I'd run afoul of her. I met some Itäläiset on my way back through the Neck and they had word of her. Some of your people tried to lay a trap for her with those trolls, those big monsters. But she killed 'em, too, and got away. They said that young Hirvilainen, that young wizard out of the Elk land, was with her." The man paused. "A hard journey it was to bring this news to you, lord, a hard journey indeed."

Wind whistled through the treetops. A shower of fine snow fell upon them.

"*Ka!*" screamed the Moonface suddenly, wheeling his horse so that the mask's leering face was finally visible. "Tuonela take you and your journey! What else of Ulla Karhulainen?"

"Nothing, lord," the frightened scout stammered. "That's all. I, uh, I saw the Elk lord, Teemu, in Tapiola too and—" But the Moonface had already turned, galloping back up the road, his anger wrapped around him like a cloak.

So she was still alive! Maanavilja, the weak fool, had failed. He had been good bait and she had taken it, but again she had slipped the noose. And the troll raid had failed as well. Another winter come, another season, and his plans once more fell flat. "*Ka!*" he cursed again.

Despite the snow and ice, he spurred his steed, riding off his anger in a wild chase through the gathering darkness back to the farm.

When he returned to the camp, his wrath cooled by the mad race, the Moonface went straightaway to his *pirtti*. It was dark night outside, but the fire had been tended, red coals glowing amidst fragrant wood.

The Moonface flung off his wet gear. He took off the silver mask and set it aside, a fall of dark hair spilling out. He shook his head like a dog, snow-spray flying everywhere. Seldom did he take it off now, never in the company of others. Few had seen his naked face and most of those were in Pohjola. *Naked.* Indeed, that was how he felt without it. When Löhi first gave it to him, it had been a symbol of strength, power, a talisman to awaken the magic that lurked within him.

She had taken him to the pinnacle of the Kipuvuori, the Mountain of Pain, on which the towers of Sariola were built. In the clear winter sky, a full moon bathed Pohjola in silvery shadow.

"Take now thy inheritance," she said, her aspect cold and beautiful. "Look at *Kuu*, who fills the night sky. She is attendant on Taivaantappi, the North Star, the nail of the heavens. Great magic lies within *Kuu*, the magic of night everlasting, the magic that lies within me and upon which all Pohjola draws. This shall be thy token, then, and from this day forth shalt thou grow in my purpose."

So spoke the queen. She gave him the mask she had forged and placed it upon his head. A change took hold from that moment on. Nothing was ever the same again.

Many years had now passed, and to the Moonface it was no mere talisman, no mask of war to stir despair in his enemies' hearts. It had become his face, his real face, and he was not complete without it. And when he saw himself in his mind's eye, he saw the silver mask upon his head.

Kuupää sat down beside the fire with a little drum. Strange images danced about the circumference of its taut black skin: skeletons, demons, and goblins. He began to tap, slowly and rhythmically, and then to sing in the tongue of old Talvimaa, the queen's first land that in time became Pohjola. He did not try to invoke a trance or seek to make a sorcerer's journey to the colorless woods. He sang a song of invocation. Fire leapt, smoke hissed, and, all at once, she appeared with a flash, hovering as if on the edge of a dream: Löhi!

So attuned were they that she might find him quickly, anywhere, unless he turned his mind and will elsewhere. She waited his call and swiftly came, her *etianen*—her spirit—clad in the same fair aspect with which she had first found him long ago.

Löhi turned her gaze from side to side, then fixed her eyes upon her servant. The Moonface knelt and bowed his head.

"Rise," she said to her servant. "No such ceremony is needed between us. Anxiously have I awaited thy report. How dost thou fare, my captain?"

The Moonface stood up, meeting her steady gaze.

"I am well, my queen, but my report is middling."

"I expected as much. Hard tasks lie before us. Setbacks are inevitable. Tell me what thou hast learned and do not shy away from ill news."

"The Itäläiset grow soft off the fat of the land and backs of the serfs. But I have reminded them of their place."

"That is well. My plans are full wrought, yet half done."

"They will fall into line," said the Moonface. "Their necks may be stretched as easily as the slaves'. I will show them as much, if need be.

"But the folk of the Seven Lands are weakening. Disease is everywhere. Many still believe that their strongholds are safe, but some have begun to doubt. If not for the Wardens, they would already have come to ruin. I deem it is time for a harder blow."

"Which land is ripe for such a blow?"

"Tavastia and Etelamaa are both ripe, but I deem the blow should fall upon Tavastia first."

"And the Hirvilaiset at Siinesaare?"

"Let them wither on the vine. They are of small account. Or send Lovêatar among them to finish what hunger has started."

Löhi's spirit moved about the *pirtti*, seeming to look at this and that with curiosity until she came to Kuupää's silver mask atop its stand. She reached out and touched it while he watched.

"What is middling in thy report I cannot guess," she said slowly. "All thy news pleases my ears. Yet thou hast not spoken of our greatest enemies. Hast thou no news of them, Lord Kuupää?"

The Moonface's expression turned dark. The fire's red glow flickered against the mask. For some reason, he felt loathe to see Löhi touch it.

"She lives," he said bitterly. "Maanavilja is dead. The other traps failed. She lives and wherever she goes the enemy is emboldened and our own strength lessened. And she teaches new wizards, training them in Väinämöinen's crooked ways even though Laulavalaakso is deserted."

"The young Hirvilainen?"

"More besides. She is a threat that can no longer be ignored."

Löhi looked hard at her captain. Her stern countenance shifted, as it often did when she grew angry; for a moment, the Moonface saw her aspect change, a gap-toothed crone with red eyes.

"I searched in Etelamaa myself," she said. "Not so far from this place, in fact. I went not to find her, but rather Lovêatar. Tuone's daughter has grown reckless and wayward. I ordered her to go to Tapiola. I, too, sense that the Hare Folk are ripe for a fall. But Lovêatar seems to have taken a liking to the Swan Folk and their white maidens. She's still there somewhere, I believe. A pity that so useful a servant is so unreliable.

"I sought Ulla afterward, but she hides herself from me and seldom uses *sight*. I found someone else, though—Turi. Come to challenge Lovêatar, I believe. Had he found her, the fool would have died. I almost had him on the edges of the spirit world, but he slipped away. The cursed demon in the colorless woods spoiled my attack. *Ka*! As reckless as Lovêatar is that damned beast. So thou art not alone in thy disappointment, Lord Kuupää. My traps, too, failed at first."

"Where is Turi now?" asked the Moonface.

Löhi laughed.

"On the long road to Pohjola," she answered. "I said my traps failed *at first*. Persistence will always win out. I set the elvish ghosts to find him. Though not so strong as Lovêatar, they are useful nonetheless. They flushed him from his lurking place, straight into my arms. So ends one of our chief worries, my friend. Turi the Changer will no longer trouble our counsels."

Kuupää nodded. He welcomed the unexpected good news, but it did not allay his concerns. Ulla Karhulainen was the greatest threat; Ulla alone stymied his inexorable march to victory.

The Witch read his thought in his face. Smiling, she said, "Let not her elusiveness vex thee, Lord Kuupää. All yet goes according to my design. The Karhulainen will be ours soon, one way or another. And that shall spell our enemies' doom."

The Moonface took up his staff. His pale complexion looked scarlet as dancing shadows played across his face.

"She gives them strength," he said, flatly.

"No," replied Löhi. "She gives them hope. And this is what makes her so dangerous."

Löhi put out her hand to the fire, seeming to touch the flame.

"Vepsa is on his way to thee. He will reach Keskimaa in one week, perhaps. He brings thee three precious gifts, three chains forged by the dwarves in Kääpiövuori of iron unbreakable. Great magic I have put into them; a mighty spell to capture an Erilainen.

"They are for our enemies, one for Ulla, one for Mielikki, and one for Väinämöinen. Thou shalt spare no effort to find the Karhulaisen girl. Vepsa and his folk will help thee. I have been too patient in waiting for her to come to me or come to ruin. No longer.

"Thou shalt find Ulla now—thou alone, if need be. And when she is in thy power, bind her with the chain and bring her to me."

The Moonface bowed his head.

"If that be your will, my Queen."

"Oh, but it is," answered Löhi. "That is precisely my will."

CHAPTER FIVE

THE HANDMAIDEN OF MISERY

Snow whistled over the broken sled. The freezing north wind hit Ulla and Kaukomieli like a hammer, pelting their faces with tiny darts of ice so cold, they burned. Pulling her fur hat over her eyes, Ulla tightened the scarf around her neck. Beside her, Kaukomieli stomped his feet, his black boots digging holes in the snow.

The sled, a real Karelian *reiki*, lay pitched to one side. The left runner had snapped and stuck out at an odd angle. Though it was half buried in a snowbank, they could see that the joint between the runner and frame was loose. Children of the far north, the two young wizards had ridden sleds all their lives, yet neither had any idea of how to fix it.

"I cannot do this," mumbled Ulla beneath the scarf. "The spell didn't take. Look at it—it didn't even move."

Kaukomieli struggled to work his mouth.

"Try a binding spell," he finally said. "Make it whole, all one piece."

"That *was* a binding spell," Ulla said sharply. "And that's not how the sled is made. It's fitted together, can't you see? I don't know how it's done and, if I don't know how it's really made, I can't sing the right song to fix it. If only Väinämöinen were here; he knows the song for everything."

A mournful howl echoed in the distance, but there was no telling if it was a wolf or the north wind's plaintive cry.

"Wonderful," said Kaukomieli. "That's all we need." He raised his staff. Yellow light illuminated the sled, making a bright circle in the dark night and blowing snow.

"I thought you said your father was a cartwright!" he spit out.

"And yours was a hunter, but you couldn't even call an animal to us last night."

"It's winter, for the love of Ilmatar! Exactly what do you think is roaming around here, except for wolves?"

They stood silently while the light from Kaukomieli's staff slowly faded. Another gust blew darts at them.

"This is ridiculous," he said at last. "It's too dark, anyway. We can't see anything in this snow. Let's make a fire and shelter for the night. We can try again in the morning light."

"If there is any morning light," said Ulla, turning and tramping toward the thicker woods to where Midnight patiently stood, rooting for moss in thinner snow.

Bred for work in winter, the shaggy black horse could withstand much worse as long she was protected from the wind. It felt warmer here in the shelter of the firs and pines; the darts couldn't find them. Kaukomieli scrounged for fallen pine branches while Ulla made a meager meal from what was left in their packs. After gathering a likely pile of pinewood, Kaukomieli thrust his staff into it and spoke a word of power, but nothing happened. Shaking his head, he chanted the full fire *loitsu*.

> *Light from heaven, stars, and sun,*
> *Down to the earth as gold shall run.*
> *Strike the flint, spark the flame,*
> *Let the blaze be seen again!*

The wet wood hissed, but no flame struck.

"Tuonela!" he cursed.

Ulla thrust her staff beside his. Together they cried, "*Tuli!*" At once, the bracken sputtered and burst into flame. As the smoky pine fire popped and sizzled, Kaukomieli threw several large logs into the middle of the blaze. "This is a good spot," he said. "There are friendly spirits in these trees, even if they're sleeping now."

After spreading blankets atop the snow, they sat near the fire, wrapped in thick fur, while the slush melted. It grew much warmer now. They both felt life returning to their frozen limbs. Ulla passed Kaukomieli a hunk of hard rye bread, Tavastian bread, baked in Tapiola's ovens weeks earlier and kept fresh by a magic spell.

"Blood bread's better," she said, chewing determinedly. "But this is all that's left. Rye and some dried fish."

"Are there any apples?" he asked, a little too eagerly. Ulla shot him a withering glance and Kaukomieli dropped his head, gazing at the sputtering fire.

The young man sighed.

"Here we are, half-frozen, south of the Wall in Etelamaa. Foolish, foolish striking out in deep winter. Wizard or not, a man could die out here."

"We can always find a *pirtti* if need be," said Ulla. "We are in Etelamaa, not in the wilds of Länsimaa. Besides, this was your idea, remember. The new spell? Lovêatar?"

"I know," he replied. "I know. What choice did we have, anyway?"

"None," said Ulla. "We've been over this all before; you were right. There's a sickness growing, spreading into the very earth itself. Crops fail, woods wither, rivers freeze. All things done are ill done. The Season of the Witch is upon us."

"One by one, the *tietäjää* are hunted down."

"Yes. Now they say Borger of Etelamaa has disappeared and he was the wizard of Kotanrannta. I'm even afraid for Turi. He was supposed to meet us. It isn't right."

"But worst of all is Lovêatar," said Kaukomieli, dully.

The fire popped.

"Yes," replied Ulla, softly. "Worst of all is Lovêatar."

The destruction wrought by Tuone's daughter increased as Löhi's power grew. Disease spread everywhere. Whole villages perished or were abandoned. Ulla realized that, even more than the Easterners' curved swords or the goblins' terror, Lovêatar's sickness was the Witch's greatest weapon. She'd come to believe that unless it was stopped, all the Seven Clans would succumb to the foul pestilence.

In past years, Lovêatar moved from place to place, lingering for a time in Akkala, perhaps, before next appearing in Karelia. That had changed. Misery's stepchild had taken a liking to the northern plain of Etelamaa. She had stayed in the region for months, though it was not densely populated. So Kaukomieli hit upon the plan to catch her unawares before she disappeared again.

"Is the water warm?" he asked. Ulla handed him the skin that had been sitting near the fire. The young man drank half and handed it back.

"Do you think we are too late?" he said.

"You heard the villagers," answered Ulla. "She is still here or, at least, she was last week. We must be close to the place they described. Whether we fix the *reiki* or not, Midnight will carry us if need be; we've taken turns with her before. It cannot be far."

"I'm not sure what to hope for," he said, poking at the fire's leading edge with his copper-shod staff. "To find her or to find her gone."

"Do you doubt your spell?" asked Ulla, irritated and almost mocking.

"You know the answer," he replied angrily. "Who can say what might happen? I'm not afraid to try.

"I'm a good spell-crafter," he continued in a matter-of-fact way, almost to himself. "I put a lot of thought into the *loitsu*. If I'm right...maybe, just maybe there's a chance."

The wind rustled in the tall pines above, sending a dusting of snow down upon them. "A chance," Ulla said, more softly now. "So be it. You've done your best; more than I could have. Still, it's strange to think that it will all be over soon. We are probably going to die, you know, horribly."

"So be it," echoed Kaukomieli, laughing out loud. Ulla smiled despite herself.

"Are you afraid to die?" he asked.

"Of course not. Are you?"

"If we fail, better to die anyway. I'd rather not know what comes after."

Ulla nodded in agreement, her frosty breath lingering like a tiny yellow cloud in the firelight.

"I feel bad about one thing, though," Kaukomieli said.

"What's that?"

"My people, the Elk Folk. Teemu begged me to come to Deep Länsimaa."

Ulla sighed.

"I promised him too," she said. "I told him that I would go to Siinesaare and do whatever I could. They are desperate. But what could we have done, even the two of us together? Raise the siege by ourselves? If Lovêatar is not stopped, there is no hope anywhere."

"Maybe," said Kaukomieli. "My mind tells me you are right. My heart speaks otherwise. They are my folk, Ulla, my clan, my kinsmen. Fighting. Dying. My heart tells me my place is with them. It was a hard, hard choice."

"True choices always are." Ulla peered at the boy from under her cap. He looked very young and very sad. She thought of her own folk, the Bear Clan, scattered and homeless, slaves to the Easterners or already dead. She knew how he felt, maybe better than anyone. *To have so much power, but to be helpless at the same time...*

"Tell me one of your stories," she said suddenly.

"Stories?" he said, surprised.

"One of the Hirvilaisen tales. They are different from the ones in Karelia and High Länsimaa. Even the Tavastian tales I heard in the Valley of Song were more or less the same ones that my father and Väinämöinen told. But yours are different."

"I was born in the west, far from Karelia and the other Clans."

"So tell me one now."

Kaukomieli thought for a moment and then began.

"In the Elk Land, in Deep Länsimaa, they tell a tale about a boy who lived near to the western sea, as far from the lands of other settled folk as might be in those times. He lived nigh to the old ruined city where the Wolf Folk once dwelt and where ghosts now walk. The boy was poor, but quick-witted and strong, and likely to become a leader among the little villages clustered together in the deep wood.

"One day, the boy, whose name was Matti, set out alone into the forest. He hoped to find a bear's den and kill the inhabitant. He knew that if he came back home with a bear-kill, his reputation would soar and his luck would turn good from the dead bear's magic. He walked deeper and deeper into the woods until he was far from his village and quite lost. He slept on the forest floor rolled up in his simple cloak, wondering if he had not made a huge mistake. Would he starve, alone and forgotten?

"Just as he decided to turn back and attempt to find his home, Matti heard a noise in the bramble like animals fighting. Gripping his spear, he readied himself for a wolf, boar, or badger. Suddenly, out of nowhere, a woman burst from the bracken, crying in pain. Her wounded legs dripped blood onto the forest floor, her clothes in tatters. Before Matti could say anything, three other figures appeared behind her, green-skinned and white-eyed. Matti knew that they were goblins, even though he had never actually seen one before.

"With a swift thrust, he skewered the first goblin, who died before he even had time to be surprised. Matti wheeled round with his spear and knocked the second goblin to the ground, spitting him as he lay cursing. The third goblin was not so easy to deal with. It had a long knife and fought hard, but Matti was big and strong, and a good fighter to boot. In the end, Matti caught him in the leg and the goblin howled in pain. He ran off and was never seen again.

"Now Matti turned to the woman. Despite her unfortunate state, she was beautiful. Matti could see at once that she was no mortal. Her spiraled eyes, long face, and leaf-shaped ears betrayed her: she was an elf. Matti calmed her, bandaged her wounds as best he could, and gave her what little food and clean water he had left. She quickly recovered and told him her tale. She was the daughter of one of the last families of elves to live in those parts since the Witch came, living an unsettled life like the wandering folk of the clans, moving from place to place each season. But disaster had come upon them. A troop of goblins had discovered them one night, killing everyone—everyone except for her, that was. She had run away, run as far and as fast as she could, while the three goblins pursued her for miles and miles until they finally caught up with her. She would have died had she not stumbled into him unexpectedly.

"'I'm glad you found me,' said Matti, 'Though I'm far from home myself. No one lives in these deep woods anymore. But I'll help you back to your home, if I may, and if any more of these goblins bother you, they'll have me to deal with.'

"'Thank you,' said the elf, 'But I have no home now and all my folk are dead. I am the last of my clan and I owe you the Life Debt. I will go with you and pay you back for my life as I may.'

"There wasn't much Matti could say to that. Together, they journeyed back to his home, avoiding the goblins. The villagers welcomed the strange woman in their midst and Matti soon fell in love with her. He had never seen so beautiful, kind, and gentle a woman before. Moreover, she worked magic, so his fortunes began to prosper. He asked her to be his wife and she readily agreed, elf though she was and he a mortal man. They were happy enough, though they had no children. And Matti became the chief of that entire district, poor and isolated though it might be.

"Of course, all was not happy forever, for Matti was a short-lived mortal and she an Erilainen. The years went by swiftly, and the young, strong Matti grew old, but no stain of time could be seen on his beautiful wife's face. Some envied his fortune, but Matti grew sad. He knew no young woman wished to be chained to an old man, condemned to wait on doddering feet. Eventually he fell ill; he felt his life slipping away and darkness approaching.

"Lying in their simple *pirtti*, Matti looked up at his elvish wife who sat beside him patiently, caring for him. 'I am sorry, my dearest,' he said at last. 'This parting is bitter. I should not have married you, for you have only been condemned to watch me wither and rot. Better you had sought your own folk in the far north.'

"At that very moment, Matti noticed a grey lock twined in his wife's hair. He reached out to touch it.

"'Have no regret,' she said, gently. 'Indeed, I, too, am now aging, albeit more slowly. Our lives are intertwined. No Erilainen may form such a bond and yet remain immortal. When you are gone, it shall quicken even more, and I, too, shall pass even as you.' Then Matti grew even more distraught.

"'I have truly brought ruin upon you, then. Such was not my wish.'

"'No,' she answered. 'Had you not saved me that day in the woods, I would already have died. Every day of my life with you has been a gift, as will be all the days that yet remain. Be at peace! And I shall pass through Tuonela and find you again in the life that lies beyond. Wait for me again as you did in the forest so long ago!'

"Then the old man smiled, for he was at peace, and he passed away gently. And when the elvish woman's time came, she, too, died with grace, never regretting her choice, but rejoicing for the gift of life Matti had given her."

"And that, Ulla, is a tale of the Hirvilaiset."

Ulla considered the tale for a while, her brow furrowed.

"It is a sad tale," she said at last. "As melancholy as that forest you lived in."

"I think it is a happy tale," he replied. "Or, at least, one full of hope, no matter the circumstance. It was very popular among the Elk Folk in my parts. I told that old story many times in the Singing Valley, though you don't recall it. Only Unaja had ever heard it before, in her home village. She smiled when she heard it again."

* * *

Ulla's eyes opened on daylight. The clouds had broken. It was clear and cold. The fire had died, leaving black ashes mixed with slush, but she felt warm beneath her furs. She lay on her back, looking up through the trees. Then she noticed a lock of blond hair on her arm. Turning, she saw that Kaukomieli's head lay upon her shoulder. He was asleep.

"Get off me," she said.

Stumbling up, they stood blinking in the morning light.

"It's late," she said. "We slept too long. Why did you not wake up sooner?"

"Me?" Kaukomieli said, groggily. "What about you?"

"You're the one that always wakes early, remember?"

Picking up their things, Ulla packed the bags while Kaukomieli saw to Midnight, brushing her shaggy mane with his fur-lined gloves. The horse had cut a wide swath all around them, rooting out wet grass and moss from the forest floor. The *reiki* still lay toppled over in the snowbank, but in the morning light, with yellow sun shining down and no wind, things didn't seem as hopeless.

Ulla considered the sled with her hands on her hips.

"I have an idea."

She told Kaukomieli to chop off the ends of the tapered, curved runners with a hand ax. Meanwhile, Ulla knelt by the sled, running her hands over the fitted wood. Singing a binding spell again—this time, only for the basket—she fused the broken joint and mended the splintered wood into an empty shell. Short runners remained fixed underneath.

"There," she said. "I made a barrel or, at least, half of one. Turi showed me that trick once, for mending leaky beer barrels, of course."

They hitched Midnight to the stumpy sled. To their relief, it still ran smoothly, although it was difficult to steer. With the packs piled on top, they huddled together and set off again, heading northeast toward the Wall of the Giants.

The short day passed rapidly. Even in Etelamaa, the sun shone for only a few hours in deep winter. As it set, it hung in the western sky for a long time, a huge red orb slowly sinking behind the trees, streaking the sky with pink, saffron, and purple. The going was slow. The sled ran true, but they couldn't pick up speed without risking another tumble. Ulla held the reins for the most part, needing no whip to drive Midnight on. The horse had been with her for years now. The girl who bore the Mark of the Clan had only to reach out her mind to urge the black mare forward.

Toward nightfall, they came out of the woods and struck a road, a country cart path bordered here and there by low stone walls that marked a dike. Rattling across a sturdy wooden bridge, they saw a few *pirttis* in the distance. Several people trudged toward them, pulling hand sledges. They were peasants, Swan Folk, bundled against the cold, their children piled on sledges, dogs at their heels.

Ulla stopped Midnight, pulling herself from the sled with her staff. The Etelalaiset looked askance at her and her strange contraption.

"Where you going?" she asked. "It will be dark soon and very cold."

The peasants seemed frightened, as if unsure whether she was a living mortal or apparition.

"Don't be afraid," said Kaukomieli, coming up beside her. "This is Ulla, Ulla Karhulainen, the daughter of Väinämöinen. I am Kaukomieli, a wizard of the Valley."

An old man wrapped in a great blue cloak stepped forward, threw back his hood, and peered at them in the gloaming.

"Ulla?" He said uncertainly. "Ulla, the friend of the king?"

Ulla brought her staff down; light blazed from the tip. The old man's blue eyes glittered.

"Lady Ulla," he whispered, almost reverently.

"What are you fleeing?" she asked. "You'll freeze to death on the road at night."

"Better that than what waits behind," he answered, jerking his head back toward the path. "Don't go any farther! Save us, Lady, and yourselves too. Only madness and death wait down that road."

"Lovêatar?" asked Kaukomieli.

The old man winced as if the name hurt his ears.

"Aye," he said. "The Plague Mistress. All about these parts, she's been. We heard her wailing in the night. The villages are on fire. Every day she comes a little closer. Back there, the folk are all dead or dying. Save us and save yourselves! But don't go any farther—there's naught even a singer can do against a ghost from Tuonela."

The dogs sniffed at Midnight. The mare stamped and whinnied, sending them running back to their masters.

"The woods are your best hope," said Ulla. "Get off the road and make a fire, if you can. There might be some *kotas* nearby, hidden among the trees. You need shelter for the night."

"How close is she?" asked Kaukomieli.

"We came from yonder," the old man said, pointing back toward the *pirttis*. "But there is a village, Talomäki, some ways back, three, four miles, maybe. That's where she is now, I'll wager. Her voice flies on the night wind."

"Let's go," said Ulla.

They climbed back into the makeshift *reiki* while the peasants stood aside.

"Take shelter," said Ulla one last time as she moved past them. But the old man put his hands to his mouth as she drove off, crying, "It's the end of the world! The end of the world!"

Ulla and Kaukomieli didn't drive far. Midnight was tired; the sky clouded over. It grew very dark. Turning off the road, they found an empty *pirtti*, a work-cabin, fitted with simple tools and lathes, and decided to stop for the night. They needed warmth, rest, and a chance to go over their plan one last time. If they faced Lovêatar the next day, in the village or on the road, they would need to act fast. There would be no time for reflection.

When the little cabin warmed up, they fell asleep by the fire while

Midnight sheltered in the cabin's lee. Ulla dozed on and off, her ears half-cocked for the cries of Lovêatar, but nothing disturbed the peaceful northern night. Even the wind died down and the pine tops stilled. All the countryside waited expectantly for the morning, as if anticipating some fateful stroke. The long night slowly passed.

Daybreak brought a slate-grey sky, heavy with the promise of snow. The thin, watery sun flickered white above the eastern horizon. Kaukomieli piled the packs on the sled while Ulla tightened her leather boots around her calves. *Pitkälehti*, her dagger, nested in a short scabbard lashed to her left arm. The sword *Pohjanpiikki* hung from her belt. Kaukomieli's sword, *Runolaulaja*, lay loose in its sheath. Fully-armed, they knew there was little chance any blade or weapon would bite Lovêatar's undead flesh; only a strong magic might suffice, if any magic in the waking world was strong enough to assault the spawn of the Lord of the Dead.

They had just eaten the last of the dried fish, their only food, when the first sign of trouble appeared. Midnight grew restless, rearing up when Kaukomieli tried to harness her to the sled. The black mare stamped nervously in the snow.

"Calm, calm," said Ulla, stroking her nuzzle. "It's all right, girl. The journey is almost over. Just a little further." She reached into the badger-skin pouch at her belt, pulling out a wrinkled green apple, which the horse gratefully accepted.

"I thought there weren't any more apples!" cried Kaukomieli.

"I saved that one for Midnight," said Ulla. "Do you need something to calm you down too?"

"I would have preferred something besides safta-fish for my last meal, but no matter. Let's go. I'm tired of waiting, I need to move."

Ulla gently harnessed Midnight to the sled; the horse took off almost at once. They chased it, jumping into the sled as it pulled away, pushing and shoving to find a secure position. Kaukomieli wound up in front with the reins while Ulla clutched him from behind.

Midnight sped down the slope to the road. Unable to control the nervous beast, they turned the wrong way at first, back toward the bridge. Kaukomieli pulled hard on the reins and slowly brought Midnight around, describing a circle in the snow until they once more headed toward Talomäki.

"Have you ever driven a sled before?" yelled Ulla over the bustle, pinching the boy's shoulder. "Slow down!"

"Be quiet!" he replied. "It's all I can do to control this beast of yours. Speak a word to her, won't you?"

"No magic, not now. The ghost will feel it."

Bouncing along, snow flying, they drove toward the village where the old man of the Swan Folk believed Lovêatar to be. Pine and fir wood stood a ways off on either side, but ahead, they spied cleared fields where the villagers grew rye and barley. If the day had been fair, they might have seen the Wall of the Giants looming in the distance, the great ridge that ran from Karelia to Tavastia, neatly bisecting what used to be the Seven Lands of the Kaamoslaiset. No longer. The Wall marked the border of their lands now that Löhi had taken everything to the north for herself and her servants.

Without warning, they came to a sharp bend where the trees marched all the way to the roadside. With a whinny, Midnight bolted, racing around the bend. Kaukomieli lost the reins. The harness snapped and the sled rolled violently. Thrown into the snow, the two wizards tumbled into a heap. Midnight ran on toward the woods.

"By the vaulted heavens, get off me!" cried Ulla. "My neck's almost broken. Are you all right?" She started to curse, but stopped short.

A line of *pirttis* stretched down the snowy lane. Black smoke rose from behind the cabins. They were in the village of Talomäki and, as the old man had said, nothing awaited but madness and death.

Ulla scrambled to her feet, extended her hand, and pulled Kaukomieli up behind her. Plucking their staffs from the snow, they walked warily down the road.

A high-pitched crying filled the air, animal-like, but horrible to human ears. They soon found its source.

In the middle of the road sat a child. Only a toddler, the tow-haired little girl spluttered and wailed. As they came closer, Ulla saw that the girl's face was streaked red with sores, her eyes matted. She inhaled deeply with a gurgling wheeze, then coughed, and wailed again. Beside her lay a woman, face down on the ice. Blonde hair spilled from her veil. Her bare feet were blue.

Ulla raised her staff, as if to put the dying child out of her misery, but Kaukomieli stopped her with a hand on her shoulder. He shook his head.

Skirting the crying child, they saw another body slumped in a *pirtti's* doorway. The two young singers continued down the lane.

"Steady, Ulla," said Kaukomieli. She was shaking. "Hold steady."

A man's voice suddenly called out from behind the cabins, a madman's laughter, hooting like an owl.

Kaukomieli walked behind the *pirttis* toward the voice. Two more bodies were laid out beside a dung pile. Scattered *kotas* and sheds clustered behind the cabins. One was on fire, red flame blending with black smoke. A figure ran from one *kota* to another.

"Stop!" shouted Kaukomieli. The man poked his head from behind the *kota* and stared back.

"Boo!" he shouted, laughing, his face distorted in a leering grin. Sticking out his tongue, the madman wiggled back and forth, then darted behind a charred sled. He clutched a bundle tightly to his chest.

Returning to the road, Kaukomieli took Ulla's hand. They both felt a spell oppressing them, enveloping the entire village. A sense of horror and of sickness bore down upon them, inviting despair.

"There is no one left alive here," said Ulla. "No one whole or sane. This isn't the waking world, it's Tuonela."

"We have to keep searching," answered Kaukomieli. "We—"

A flickering movement caught their eyes. They turned to face it.

A shadow crept toward them in the distance. Now crawling on the snow, now creeping across a *pirtti*, the dim silhouette came closer. A noisome stench wafted on the breeze. Ulla, transfixed by the apparition, did not move. The putrid smell grew so strong that Kaukomieli doubled over, throwing up the little food in his stomach. Ulla, sick herself, pulled him back up.

Then they saw her.

The shadow disappeared. In its place, no more than thirty feet away, stood a tall woman. Raven hair flowed down her shoulders. Her expressionless face shone like flawless alabaster. A black mantle covered her body. Her right arm remained hidden within, but, to their horror, the left slowly withdrew, revealing a whip in her bone white hand. Nine tails it had, undulating slowly like snakes. As she raised it, Ulla perceived that each tail ended in a ghastly head, writhing in misery, the mouths from which issued the nine deadly afflictions that Lovêatar spread to the ruin of mankind.

"Kaukomieli!" Ulla cried.

"Steady, Ulla," he said, though his own voice shook. "Steady! Wait until I give the signal."

They separated, Kaukomieli moving swiftly toward the *pirttis* while Ulla headed toward the woods, slowly backtracking, never taking their eyes off Lovêatar.

The ghost stood unmoving for a moment, her hand held high. Then lightning flashed, briefly blinding them. The cold maiden of death vanished. In her place stood another aspect: a gibbering crone, gap-toothed and mottled, clad in filthy rags that stank of the graveyard. Her empty eye sockets stared blankly into nothingness, but she had other senses to find her prey. Life itself drew her, wracked with torment and misery as she was, lusting only to infect and destroy, and to dispatch all she could to her father's kingdom.

Lovêatar laughed, a hideous cackle. Viscous spittle dribbled down her splotched chin, hissing in the snow. She came forward slowly, leaving bloody prints where her rotting feet had trodden.

She could feel the power in these two—wizards. Strong they were, stronger than any others who had dared to face her. But what did Lovêatar care! Other wizards had sought her out, mortal and Erilainen alike, and she had slain them cruelly. Their spells and swords were powerless against her. She killed when she liked and feared none. Not even Löhi, her mistress, could send her back to Tuonela now, so great had she become as she fed off of the very pain and torment she inflicted upon her victims.

Twisting her head from side to side, Lovêatar drew nearer. She paused for a moment, uncertain; something felt strange here. Then, making up her mind, she turned toward Ulla. *This one should surely die first.*

"Pathetic deformity!" cried Kaukomieli suddenly, drawing *Runolaulaja* with one hand, his staff in the other. "Slave of Pohjola! You have no power over us. Your stink and pus-filled face may frighten peasants, but we are *tietäjää* of the Singing Valley!"

Lovêatar stopped only a few paces from Ulla, turning to look at him. A maniacal smile played across her ghastly face.

"Afraid of me?" mocked Kaukomieli. "No wonder. I've heard that you won't face men. *Ka!* Bitch of Tuonela! The sword I bear was blessed by Tapio himself, forged to send you straight back to Hell. No wonder you run from me, miserable hag. What's wrong with you? Feeling ill today?"

Lovêatar cackled insanely, spittle flying from her lips. Turning away from Ulla, who stood stock-still with staff in hand, the hag approached Kaukomieli.

The boy pulled his cap off, his yellow hair falling free. He began chanting in a shaky voice, but the song grew in strength as he mastered himself. He worked the spell he had slowly prepared, the *loitsu* that he had thought about all winter long. A second time he sang it, and then a third, and the air around him crackled with electricity.

Lovêatar came on. She raised her bony hands, fingers working, still chortling with demented glee.

"Let me show you how I feel," she gasped, her cracked voice thin and threatening. Even as she reached out to lay hold of him with her deadly clutch, Kaukomieli broke off his song and yelled, "Ulla, now!"

Springing forward, Ulla raced to Lovêatar, drawing something from beneath her cloak as she ran. It was the star-shaped glass that she had stolen from Tyë. She held it aloft. The saffron glass blazed with light. Twisting about with a speed that surprised them, Lovêatar faced the girl, ready to lunge.

Summoning all her power, Ulla shouted, "Lovêatar, Lovêatar, *Lovêatar!* You to the jewel, the jewel to you!"

Lovêatar stopped in her tracks. A ray of yellow light shot from the glass. A voice, not the hag's, but one wild and fair, cried out, then quickly faded into the distance.

Beset with lightnings, Lovêatar's body snapped and twitched in a ghoulish chorea. The ghost gave one final howl. With a thunderous boom, she was sucked into the jewel. The explosive force threw Ulla and Kaukomieli to the ground. All was silent.

Simultaneously, the singers lifted their heads and looked at one another. They scrambled up. The glass lay in the snow between them. No longer saffron, a black shadow darted about madly within. Lovêatar was trapped inside.

"We did it," mumbled Ulla. "We actually did it. It worked, Kaukomieli. We actually did it!"

"I knew you could do it!" he exclaimed. "Nobody else but you!"

"It was your spell!" she cried.

"It was your power," he replied.

They embraced, dancing around in the snow, then looking wildly about as if expecting a crowd of grateful spectators to rush out and congratulate them. There was no crowd, however; it was absolutely still. The child had vanished, the madman's laughter fallen silent. The village was still deserted, the dead bodies still frozen in the snow, but the oppressive cloud had dissipated. The spell of sickness and despair was broken.

Ulla impulsively pulled Kaukomieli to her and kissed him. His eyes widened, more shocked by this unexpected gesture than by Lovêatar's capture. She quickly pulled away.

"So, what do we do now?" she asked, trying to sound nonchalant. Kaukomieli looked stunned. "Are you exhausted?"

"What? Uh, yes, I suppose. I'm tired, Ulla, and my power's low, but I still feel better than before. You?"

"I feel wonderful. I feel like I could fight the whole army of Pohjola. But it won't last. We'll both be exhausted, absolutely spent, by nightfall, and we've got to find some food."

They gazed at the glass in the snow.

"How did you know there was a spirit trapped inside the jewel?" she asked, shaking her head.

"I told you," he replied. "I heard a tale about such a thing where I grew up in Deep Länsimaa. I could feel it from the very first time you let me hold it. That was Seppo's secret, the smith who made these jewels; he learned how to imprison these spirits in glass. The *sight* it gave you was the spirit's *sight*. But even spirits can be tricked and deceived.

"Did you hear it? So happy to be free. It was an air spirit of Ilmatar, I'll wager. It took flight on the wind. Once I understood the secret, it was easy enough to craft a spell to release it, but the glass belonged to you, not me. Only you could turn the key and unlock it."

"And the transfer spell to capture Lovêatar?"

"I didn't know if it would work. What choice did we have but to try? If anyone could do it, it had to be you. You bear the Mark of the Clan, Ulla. You are the Child of the Prophecy. It was *karhu's* tooth that set the spell, one of the teeth that you brought back from your Hunt. If there's any hope left, it's in you."

Ulla smiled. Reaching for her staff, she said, "Glad you remember that; don't forget it."

"Don't get a big head," he said. "If anyone else could have done it, it would have been me."

The dark-haired young woman looked around.

"Midnight," she said. "I can feel her in the woods. Let's find her and leave this place."

"Yes, it's still unwholesome. We should leave as quickly as possible."

Ulla picked up the jewel. The black shadow inside it slunk around like ink. She shuddered.

"Here, why don't you take it?" she said.

"No, it's yours; this victory is yours. You should keep it."

"Really, I want you to have it. You discovered its secret. I give it to you now, Kaukomieli."

"No, I couldn't. It's yours."

"This thing has Lovêatar inside it! I don't want it!" she cried.

"And I do? I'm not sleeping with that thing next to me."

And so they walked toward the wood where Midnight waited, still arguing over who deserved the honor of wearing the daughter of Tuone around their neck.

Chapter Six

Princess Cherry Red

I t would have been impossible to keep Lovêatar's demise secret even if Ulla had wished to. Trapped inside the jewel, the ghost's power vanished at once. The Winter Plague burned out; no new victims fell ill. The sense of despair that afflicted Etelamaa's northern plain dispelled. The Swan Folk rejoiced, publishing the news however they could. Soon the few remaining *tietäjää* spread word of Ulla's deed as far as Tapiola and Langvika. The story of how Ulla Karhulainen, Väinämöinen's daughter who bore the Mark of the Clan, fought Lovêatar to the death was on everyone's tongue. However, Kaukomieli's role was mostly forgotten.

So much the better, thought Ulla. *Better for Löhi to focus her anger on me and leave Kaukomieli alone. Better still for the Witch to know that Lovêatar has been defeated and wonder how, becoming uncertain about my power.*

Famine, curved swords, monsters, and magic—these things the Witch still had aplenty. Yet the defeat of her greatest servant, one who alone might have destroyed the Seven Clans, was a bitter pill. All had gone Löhi's way for years, but, for now at least, there was a victory to celebrate.

Ulla had another hope as well. News of Lovêatar's doom might embolden Väinämöinen, drawing him out from the Valley or wherever he had gone. She intended to go to Karelia soon, but wished to see Kirsikka in the Stone City first.

As for Kaukomieli, he had never seen the City of Etelamaa before and greatly desired to go there. He would have followed Ulla anywhere, however. They had never repeated or spoken of the mad, joyful kiss. Ulla had returned to the sometimes friendly, sometimes bickering manner she always used with him. He didn't dare press his suit, but not a word passed between them unmarked—for his part—by his love.

The journey south was easy enough. The grateful peasants of the first village they reached gave them provisions and a swift sled, small but sturdy. With Midnight in the lead, they sped across Etelamaa. They crossed frozen lakes and streams to shorten the way. The sled's runners left telltale signs of their passage. Tall pine and spruce trees groaned with snow, leaning this way and that. In the mornings, when they emerged from the cabin where they sheltered, frost covered everything. The closer they drew to the sea, the damper the air became. At last, they reached the Stone City where an escort awaited them outside the city gates.

A dozen riders, clad in the blue and white of the Royal Guards, had been sent to bring them into the city with honor. Everyone in Etelamaa knew the story of Ulla's ill-fated love for Egan and the city's people loved her. The girl with dark hair had no relish for such a triumphal entry, however. Eschewing the entourage, she chose two men to escort them through one of the lesser gates and on to the Keep.

The way led past the quays and piers where the city's fishing fleet lay. In summertime, many-colored sails streaked the bay with a rainbow of colors, but it was frozen now. Snow fell on the boats sitting on logs, while others sheltered in sheds. Clinker-built and skillfully crafted, the polished, well-made boats were the city's pride. Even coated with ice, the dark hardwood shone in the snow. Graceful prows beckoned. Two war galleys sat nearby. Kaukomieli looked at the beautiful craft with wonder.

No less wonderful to him were the tall, gabled roofs and stone houses. Except for Tapiola, Kaukomieli had never seen one of the great cities of the Seven Lands; even then, he had only known Tapiola in decline, plagued by hunger, sickness, and madness. Much larger than Tapiola, the Stone City, in contrast, projected confidence and strength.

Famine and fear may have reached northern Etelamaa, but the people of the Stone City still thought their town impregnable. The army of the Swan Folk had suffered the greatest loss at Sumuvuori; no more did they fight outside their borders. Juvari had marshaled every man he could to the kingdom's defense, however. Now they built towers, three great war towers upon the central plain where their people could rally in need. The city itself bristled with spears. Trade still brought all they needed, despite battle and fire upon the Itämeri Sea. It seemed impossible that any foe could ever threaten the City of the Swan Folk.

Kaukomieli felt this strength, or its illusion, as they passed through the streets, yet he also knew the truth of what waited along the Marches. And Etelamaa was also a kingdom without a king.

"There is still no king among the Swan Folk?" he asked Ulla, gazing about. "No one was crowned after… after Egan died?"

"There is no king," she replied. "There was a boy—Sampsä, Egan's cousin. After the battle, they made him the heir, the prince presumptive, since he was the last of the Royal House. At least the last male."

"What happened to him?"

"Don't you remember? He was never crowned, since he had not yet come of age. Juvari acted as Regent. But Sampsä was killed in the Green Vales near Lake Etelajärvi when his camp was attacked. They said that ghosts, evil spirits, came upon them at night and panicked their horses, scattering the whole company. Then raiders of the Vartilaiset, the men from across the Itämeri Sea, rode them down. They found Sampsä dead, driven through by a spear."

Kaukomieli considered the news.

"No, I don't remember," he mused. "I don't know much about the Swan Folk. Did you know this Sampsä?"

"I met him only once. I think Väinämöinen knew him better. They said that he was brave, like his cousin. But the Witch bears a special hatred for the Royal House of Etelamaa."

"So who rules the city now?"

"Juvari rules in Etelamaa. He is Löhi's enemy. He was almost killed at Sumuvuori; he left his leg in the Wastes and rides a horse now, but otherwise recovered. Many battles has he fought, many battles."

They came to the Keep and saw that their intended escort had arrived before them. Horsemen lined up on either side of the street. Many other men dressed in the blue and white of Etelamaa stood at attention. A crowd of townsfolk gathered close by, shouting as they passed, "Ulla! Ulla!" and "*Lovêatarin Kuolli*"—Bane of Lovêatar. No one seemed to notice the yellow-haired young wizard beside her.

As the sled passed through the crowd, Kaukomieli watched Ulla. To his surprise, she stood erect, staff raised high. He almost did not recognize her. With stern face and proud mien, she gazed straight ahead, her hazel-green eyes glittering in the gloom while the folk cried out. A sudden thought took him. *She will never give up, never surrender. After all else fails, Ulla will be the last to go and she will go down fighting.*

The sled skated across the bridge and into the old courtyard.

A smaller crowd, the Keep's household, waited within. Vendla the Queen had gone to the Green Vales and seldom returned to the Stone City, but Egan's sister Marjatta stood there with Toiva Merikainen. Various other counselors and servants waited to greet them. Before them all waited a young woman in a sky blue dress and tall, peaked hat, her long, gossamer veil almost touching the ground. Ulla had no sooner climbed out of the sled than the woman ran to her, slipping in the snow.

The red-haired woman embraced Ulla, holding her tight, while Ulla buried her head on Kirsikka's shoulder.

"Lumikki, Lumikki!" cried Kirsikka. "I thought you'd never get here! Oh, how I've missed you for so very long."

Kaukomieli lurched out of the sled, grabbing his staff. He was struck at once by the contrast he and Ulla in their worn, raggedy furs and torn cloaks made with the Swan Folk in their finery. The two of them were filthy. But he forgot that when he saw something astonishing, something that he had seen only once before. Ulla was crying. The stern hero had vanished. She seemed smaller, a young maid clad in ill-fitting clothes, with tears welling in her eyes as she clutched her friend.

"I missed you so much," Ulla said through her tears.

Kirsikka brushed her friend's hair from her face.

"You smell like the forest," she said, laughing. "Or like Midnight here."

"That's what the Tavastian queen told me," said Ulla. "Next time, I'll take her with me and see how she does on the road."

Ulla smiled at her friend, the little girl from the hardscrabble village in the north. Kirsikka had grown even more beautiful. Freckles still covered her pale skin; her luxurious hair still cascaded down her back beneath the veil. Her comely figure made her appear much older than Ulla, who looked thin and wan.

The others stepped forward to greet them. Recovering, Ulla wiped away her tears and introduced Kaukomieli.

"This is the Last Wizard," she said. "Kaukomieli of the Singing Valley. Together we defeated Lovêatar. His spell trapped her in a prison from which there is no escape."

Kaukomieli doffed his cap, smiling awkwardly. With his sun-yellow hair and scant beard, he looked boyish, hardly the image of a powerful *ti-etäjää* taught by Väinämöinen himself. Kirsikka rescued him from his embarrassment.

"Welcome to the Keep, Kaukomieli!" she said cheerily. "I remember you now, the blondie from Deep Länsimaa. My, how you've grown."

"Your Highness," he answered, a little too animatedly, bowing with an exaggerated flourish out of place in sober Etelamaa. He slipped on the ice, catching himself with his staff. Ulla shook her head.

"The blondie from Länsimaa," she muttered. "Maybe that should be your title."

* * *

Ulla spent the first few days in the Keep with Kirsikka, catching up with her friend on all that had happened since they had last seen one another almost three years earlier. Kirsikka was interested in everything from Väinämöinen's strange disappearance, to the changes in Tapiola and the well-being of friends like Ilkka and Turi. The only things she did not wish to discuss were the plight of the Bear Folk and the conditions in northern Etelamaa. She had less to say about her own life in the Stone City. Marjatta sometimes joined their conversations and Kaukomieli trailed along, treated politely by the soldiers and servants, yet largely ignored.

To Ulla's disappointment, Juvari, Regent of Etelamaa, had left the city. He had gone to Harmaaniemi where the lords of the coast were again causing trouble. The Captain of the Swan Folk pressed more men into service each year, demanding that the rich coastal fiefs pay an ever increasing share for the towers and forts being built further north. Rumors were spreading that rebellion was in the works, that one of the lords might rise up to claim the kingship, but Toiva dismissed such talk.

"There is no lord strong enough to unite the southern fiefs against the city," he told Ulla. "Nor could any defeat Juvari if they did. The army is absolutely loyal to him. It is also well-armed. Egan was farsighted. Before he left for Sumuvuori and the great battle, he placed new orders with the Smiths of Seppälä. The last of the great trains of bloodrock was made into a thousand swords and spears."

Egan had demonstrated his farsightedness in another way as well. Kolkka, the *tietäjää* from the Singing Valley, still dwelt in Etelamaa, serving its people. Against Kolkka's wishes, the king had ordered the wizard to remain behind while the great host marched north. Now he told Ulla of the sickness creeping into the heart of the kingdom.

"Lovêatar's demise is good news beyond all hope," said Kolkka. "But I fear it will prove but a respite in the Witch's assault. I can feel her power flowing into the land itself, flowing south. All things are ill done. Rebellion and disquiet grow. If Juvari's spears failed to stem the tide, is there any hope left for mortals in the Far Northern Land?"

"Juvari has done well to marshal the Swan Folk," replied Ulla. "Their strength is needed in other places too. Teemu is besieged in the north. Tapiola is fading. If there is any hope, it is in the union of the Seven Clans. Otherwise, it will be as you already perceive. Like a creeping mist, Löhi's tendrils spread throughout the lands."

"I cannot speak to such things," said Toiva. "I have neither the wisdom nor power of the Erilaiset. But the towers of Etelamaa will be completed within a year and people here trust in their strength. The Swan Folk will not fight outside our borders again. We cannot afford to lose men beyond the Marches, less so now that there is unrest along the coast. The League of the Seven Clans was the king's great achievement, but he is gone now, and that union cannot be remade."

"It is wise to build strong places," replied Ulla. "But not to hide in them. It will only delay the end, not prevent it."

"Then what must be, will be," sighed Toiva. "Juvari will not march north. Yet we will strengthen what we can to weather the storm."

While Ulla took counsel with Kolkka and the royal advisors, Kaukomieli walked about the city. He spent days by himself visiting the squares, docks, and wharfs. Deep winter was passing. In a month, the cycle of melt and freeze would begin. He made friends among the Mariners, fascinated by their many-oared galleys. Carpentry and woodwork were foreign to him, so he strove to understand how the ships were built. For their part, the sailors welcomed a *tietäjää* who could bless their craft with whatever charms he possessed. In truth, he could do little for them. He did not know the songs for the sea. Like Ulla, a child of the wild woods, Kaukomieli knew Tapio's song the best. While he heard Ahti's music in the waters, its harmony was strange to him.

One day the temperature dropped. A cold wind swept across the city. Kaukomieli remained in the Keep, but Ulla went off somewhere with Kirsikka, so he found himself all alone again. Wandering around the old castle, he went up the cold, slippery steps leading to the upper chambers for the first time. He knew that Kirsikka and Marjatta had rooms on the upper floor, but had never visited them.

The dim passage, illuminated by guttering torches, twisted and turned. Kaukomieli passed several doors on his right. A large chamber was closed fast against the cold. Just round the corner, a smaller chamber beckoned; its wooden door sat ajar and scuffling sounds came from within.

Kaukomieli paused. The door opened wider and a shrunken figure shuffled out, a white-haired old man, hunched and leaning on a stick.

His head bowed, the old man almost passed Kaukomieli by without noticing him until, feeling the awkwardness of the situation, the young wizard spoke first.

"Good day to you, sir," he stammered. The old man looked up as if Kaukomieli's words came only dimly to his deaf ears.

"Eh, what's that?" He looked the young man up and down.

"Good day to you," said Kaukomieli, with more confidence.

"'Tis a drear day outside with little good about it," replied the old man in a thick Etelalaisen voice. "But the winters are longer than they used to be. Now, what are you about and what can I do for you?"

Kaukomieli blushed, suddenly feeling that he shouldn't be there.

"Nothing," he replied. "I was just... just wandering about, actually. I still don't know the Keep well."

"Aye, it takes some getting used to. Fifty years I've walked these halls— fifty years old Orvo has been here. I know every nook and cranny. But if you're looking for Princess Marjatta or Cherry Red, they're not here. Eh, who did you say you were again?"

"I didn't."

"What's that?"

"I didn't tell you my name, my apologies. I am Kaukomieli, a guest in these halls. But I don't believe I have met you before, sir."

Orvo shook his white head.

"I've been laid up for some time," he answered. "At my cousin's home out in the farmlands. Or is she my niece? I can't abide the dark months in the castle anymore; my bones ache in the chill."

"Are you a servant here?"

"Indeed, indeed. Fifty years I've walked these halls or stayed in the Vales with the queen. Fifty years. Eh, who did you say you were again?"

"My name is Kaukomieli," the wizard said patiently. "I am a friend of Ulla's. I came here with her from Tavastia."

"Ulla!" the old man said, brightening. "Yes, they told me that she'd come back. Fought the Witch's ghost or some such."

"Or some such," answered Kaukomieli.

"Well, I haven't seen her, all the same. I just came back today myself. Just dusting my young master's chamber, that's all. There's no one else to do it anymore."

"Who is your master?" asked Kaukomieli.

"Why, Egan, of course."

Kaukomieli was confused. "You mean... Egan, Egan the King?"

"I knew him long before that," said Orvo. "He was born right down there in the queen's chamber. Squealed like a piglet, he cried so much. But then they gave him this chamber for his own."

Kaukomieli realized with a sudden, cold thrill that the chamber had been Egan's bedroom. He peered over the old man's head.

"Would it be all right if I, uh...?"

"You want to go inside?" said Orvo, his tone noticeably changing. An uncomfortable silence followed. Kaukomieli thought that he'd offended the old man, but Orvo turned, hobbled back toward the chamber, and motioned him inside.

"This is my young master's room, aye, it is," said Orvo softly.

Kaukomieli stepped inside the small chamber. Daylight filtered in from the shuttered windows, casting dim fingers that stretched across the stone floor. A table and basin sat on one side, a simple bedstead on the other. Several cloaks and blankets were folded neatly across a chair.

"There's no one to dust it anymore," said Orvo, shaking his head. "I take care of it myself. Stay as long as you wish, but shut the door when you leave, if you please."

The old man shuffled out, looking back as he crossed the threshold.

"Eh, who did you say you were again?"

"Kaukomieli."

Still shaking his head, Orvo disappeared down the hallway. His footsteps slowly faded away.

Kaukomieli stood alone in the middle of the chamber. He looked from side to side, corner to corner. *Egan's room. Egan Dragonslayer. The King of the Folk of the Swan.*

Kaukomieli tried to wrap his mind around the fact that Egan had lived in this room, lived in it for years. The old man kept it just as Egan had left it. He thought again of the one and only time he'd seen the king, riding by after the battle while the villagers clapped and cheered. Their eyes had met. What did that mean? *Anything?*

He walked over to the table. Touching the basin, he ran his hand around its shiny lip, noting the simple impression of a swan stamped upon it. He touched the folded clothes and saw that his hand was shaking.

On the wall beside the table hung a small, round looking glass. Like Ulla, he had seen his own reflection in a looking glass only a few times. He positioned himself directly before the mirror, taken aback, as always, to see his reflection looking back at him.

He blinked his right eye; the reflection did the same. He worked his mouth. Yellow hair shone brightly in a ray of sunlight reflected off the glass. He ran his hand over his fair beard, scant and thin, just enough to cover his angular face and cheeks. Drawing himself up to his full height, Kaukomieli looked sternly into the looking glass; his blue eyes sparkled.

A sudden flash of light blinded him. Staggering, he blinked until his vision cleared, still gazing at the blue eyes in the mirror. Then he realized that these blue eyes were not his own. Slowly, as if watching frost creep across a shiny lid in a sudden cold, he saw a face appear in the looking glass, a face other than his own. *Alabaster skin. A cascade of raven hair.* He had never seen it before, but he had no doubt who it belonged to. The face was that of Löhi of Pohjola.

The blue eyes in the mirror came to life; the room shimmered with electric energy.

"You are not the one I expected," said the Witch. "I can feel your power, though. It drew me. I have been waiting for her, waiting for her to visit her shrine. I knew that she would come to the Stone City to celebrate. And why not? Victory deserves a triumph. But you...What is your name?"

But Kaukomieli was not so foolish, even when surprised. He drew away from the mirror in silence.

"Rather young for a *tietäjää*, are you not?" she continued. "And yet across the leagues, I sense your strength. Yes, so very strong. You were there with her, were you not? Tell me, what did you do to my errant servant? How did you send her back to her father in Tuonela? Such a deed deserves to be sung in halls across the Far Northern Land. And if you have robbed me of Lovêatar, surely at the very least you owe me the story. What magic did you use? How did you defeat her? Come now, tell me your tale!"

Kaukomieli felt the compulsion of her voice, felt it winding around him like unseen cords. His heart raced. He tried not to look into the Witch's eyes, focusing instead upon her ruby lips. They were perfect, flawless. Yet he could not tell if she smiled or frowned.

"A silent hero," said Löhi at length. "Or perhaps not one with a gift for words? I do believe I know you now, however. You are the Hirvilainen boy who has become Ulla's companion. The Last Wizard, if I recall correctly. Of course, that is a rather unfortunate title, is it not?

"I can understand your reticence, my young friend. After all, you are standing in *his* chamber. A scatterling from the wilds of Deep Länsimaa who would replace a king!" Löhi laughed, a strange, metallic sound that echoed throughout the chamber.

"Are you surprised? Don't be. Throughout the Far Northern Land, my spirit travels wherever I wish. Indeed, I have watched you from afar, my young friend, even as I watched him in years gone by.

"Well do I know this room! Oft did I visit him here and enter into his dreams. And well may I divine your desire. You wish to replace him in her heart, do you not? But how could that ever be! More hope have the deluded Kaamoslaiset of resisting me than you have of your dream coming true."

Kaukomieli gasped. He made to turn away, but found he could not, though he focused his eyes on the floor, avoiding her steely, hypnotizing stare.

"Unless…" said the Witch very slowly. "Unless we work together, you and I. I am not Ulla's enemy. Nor am I yours. Listen to me! One so strong and clever should grasp and take what he desires. Born to greatness you were, yet born out of place. Let me give you that place! Let me show you true wisdom! And I can give you her heart and release you from his shadow forever.

"Will you not listen to me?" asked Löhi.

With a final effort, Kaukomieli shook himself free.

"No," he said.

And, turning away from the looking glass, he left the chamber, closed the door, and never came back again.

* * *

Kaukomieli never told anyone about Löhi.

The weeks passed. The thaw approached. Ulla spent her time alternating between the stern wizard she had become and the girl from the north she used to be, the one who shared an unbreakable bond with Kirsikka. Juvari did not return, so Ulla made up her mind to leave the Stone City while the lakes were still frozen and sledding possible.

One day, Ulla and Kirsikka met alone in the Hall of the Swan. The hall was bright as ever, the blue and white molding and high ceiling cheerfully lit by the hearth fires. Only the Black Throne, empty since Egan's death, reminded them of the things still amiss throughout the kingdom.

Kirsikka had asked Ulla to come alone and the dark-haired girl noticed her unusual tone. Clad in simple garments of Etelalaisen weave, her long hair braided, Ulla looked like any young woman of the city, but Kirsikka wore a fine mantle over her dress, midnight blue like the pools of the Vales and covered in tiny white swans.

"Have you decided where you're going?" she asked.

Ulla sighed. "To Karelia. I've got to find Väinämöinen. I have tarried too long here. I had hoped to see Siria this year, but it will have to wait. She is safe in the south near Seppälä, as safe as one can be."

"What did you say her husband's name was?" asked Kirsikka.

"Torio," Ulla answered. "He was a farmer near Kyöpelinvuori, but he's become a tinsmith now. I sent his whole family with them, his parents, brother, and sisters, too. Siria was pregnant again when last I heard from her. The child has been born by now. Her second child."

"Well, if she's happy, that's all that matters, right?"

Again, Ulla detected an odd note in her red-haired friend's voice.

"What's wrong?" she asked, in the blunt, frank tone that she used with almost no one else. "Something's troubling you. I don't need to be a *tietäjää* to realize that."

Kirsikka walked behind the Black Throne, running her freckled hands along its smooth, cool surface. A stray lock of copper hair slipped from beneath her veil.

"Lumikki, I have something to tell you," she began. "I've been waiting until the right time, and now you're leaving again and all."

"All right, what is it?" asked Ulla, smiling a bit at her friend's discomfiture. She knew Kirsikka better than anyone in the world; what seemed like an insurmountable problem to her was just as often quickly resolved.

"Lumikki, I am going to be married."

Stunned, Ulla stared blankly, not comprehending what Kirsikka had said. The silence grew deafening.

"I'm going to be married, Ulla."

Ulla took a step toward the throne on its low dais. "What are you talking about?"

"I'm going to be married. I've been waiting to tell you, but everything has been so nice. This year, in the springtime, I will be married. I was afraid it would upset you."

"Upset me?" cried Ulla. "Upset me? I don't even understand what you're talking about."

"I'm talking about getting married, as soon as it's green again."

"To whom?"

"Siuri of Poronlinna. You met him two weeks ago when the Mariners came here."

"Who is he?"

"He's of high blood, very high. Oh, he's a little older," she continued, falling back into her familiar, easy way. "But he's still handsome and very rich. He is the Lord of Poronlinna and owns all the lands about it. It's a very good match."

"A good match! How can you say that? You were married—*are* married—to Eglano!"

Kirsikka shook her head, coming from behind the throne.

"See, I knew that you would be angry," she said. "His wife died two years ago and he's looking for a bride; and I'm not getting any younger myself."

"You are a princess and the wife of the Grand Duke of Etelamaa."

"Oh, come now," said Kirsikka, crossly. "You are being ridiculous. That's over, been over for years. Why should I pine away in this Keep forever while I am still young? Why shouldn't I be happy? You are happy for Siria, aren't you? You sent her and her husband's whole family to the sea just to keep them safe from harm. Do you love me any less?"

Ulla's face hardened. Her eyes flashed green.

"You are betraying Eglano!" she cried. "Betraying your husband and betraying your own child."

"My child!" exclaimed Kirsikka. "He didn't even live two weeks. And you never wanted me to marry Eglano in the first place, don't you remember?"

Ulla turned and walked to the middle of the hall, Kirsikka trailing after her.

"Ulla, listen to me," she said. "You are always saying that there is no hope; maybe there isn't—not in constant fighting and battles along the Marches. Even Väinämöinen has given that up, hasn't he? But there is hope here, hope in the city. Why can't you stay here? Why can't you stay with me in Etelamaa?"

Ulla spun around. "Etelamaa?"

"Yes, Etelamaa. You have defeated Lovêatar now. Everything will be better. Stay here with me. If you go back, if you keep fighting in the north, you're going to be killed. You can be happy here; you should be happy. The people need you. And that boy, this Last Wizard, he loves you."

"Kaukomieli is Löhi's enemy."

"He loves you, anyone can plainly see that. You are both so alike. Why can't you love him back and be happy? Both of you should stay here in the city."

"Don't put your trust in these stone walls!" cried Ulla, pointing her long arm and slender finger at Kirsikka. "When all else is destroyed, Löhi herself will come here. Then you will see what good these paper towers are!"

"The Stone City will never fall!" exclaimed Kirsikka. "This isn't High Länsimaa. We are strong, strong and secure."

The dark-haired young singer laughed.

"You don't know what you're talking about! You sound like the fools in Tapiola. Only the League of the Seven Clans could guarantee Löhi's defeat, but the kings and lords have given way to despair. They turned from the path that Väinämöinen and Egan showed them, the only path where hope remains."

Kirsikka shook her head. "*You* are the fool; you're living in the past!"

"You are betraying Eglano!" shouted Ulla in a stern voice.

"Eglano, Eglano. Eglano is dead. And so is Egan! He's dead, Ulla, dead, and he's never coming back!"

Without a moment's hesitation, Ulla slapped Kirsikka's face with the back of her hand. She struck with such force that the red-haired girl stumbled to her knees. Her face, already flushed and pink, now turned blood red, the mark of Ulla's fingers emblazoned upon it like white scars.

Tears welled up in Kirsikka's eyes, but just as suddenly she steeled herself. A tight smile formed on her pursed lips. She stood up, drawing herself to her full height, and spoke in a proud, bitter voice.

"That's how you handle all your problems, isn't it? Why don't you just enchant me and force me to do as you wish? Would that give you pleasure, Child of the Prophecy?"

Ulla, shaking, continued to stare down at the spot where Kirsikka had fallen. She said nothing.

Kirsikka gathered her skirts and walked across the hall without another word, going out through the main doors and leaving Ulla all alone.

A dry sob wracked her body. She put her hands to her face, standing bent in the middle of the room. Finally, she let them drop and, without thinking, walked to the Black Throne and sat down, slumping to one side, her head resting upon the cold marble.

The image of the White Swan of Etelamaa hung above her. The empty hall seemed cavernous and threatening. The only sound was the crackling of the fire.

Looking out, Ulla had a vision. Men and women filled the hall. Richly dressed, they smiled and bantered with one another. In one corner, people danced a slow, stately dance, the noblemen bowing to their beautiful partners, the women's blue veils sweeping the floor. In another corner, a table groaned with food, apples and yellow fruits from across the sea, white bread and cream, suckling pigs stuffed with greens and sweetmeats. Music came dimly to her ears.

The vision vanished. She was alone again. Straightening, she closed her eyes and drew a deep breath. Slowly, she rose from the throne.

Ulla walked to a side door that led to the sculleries. Just as she was about to open it, Marjatta came to the door.

If she had heard what had transpired, her face betrayed nothing. Slight and shorter than Ulla, she wore her pale, flaxen hair tightly braided and covered with a thin, gossamer veil. Clad in a light blue dress with silver chains and a brooch on her shoulder, Marjatta smiled.

As always, Ulla was momentarily taken aback. Egan's face shone in his sister's.

"You will be leaving soon, won't you?" she said, mildly. Ulla, still quivering, tried to answer in a calm voice.

"Yes. We have to go to Karelia to find Väinämöinen."

Marjatta nodded. "So I thought. And will you be able to?"

"Yes. I will find him."

After an awkward pause Marjatta reached up and brushed a stray strand of hair from Ulla's face.

"I did not see my brother much during those last years," she said, suddenly. "Always he was away, fighting north of the Marches in other lands. There was nothing he would not do for his people."

"Nothing," answered Ulla. "It was only because of Egan that the Seven Clans came together."

Marjatta smiled again.

"He loved you very much, Ulla. More than anyone in the world, I should think. And I know one thing, he wanted you to be happy. Surely if he could see us now, that would still be his dearest wish."

With a slight curtsy, the princess turned and went back up the passage, leaving Ulla all alone again in the Hall of the Swan.

* * *

Cold wind blew ragged clouds swiftly over the city. Dark above, their tattered, saffron fringe below illuminated the eastern sky. The city of Etelamaa, Land of the Swan Folk, still slept at dawn. However, in the Keep's cobblestone courtyard, a small group gathered to bid Ulla and Kaukomieli farewell.

Toiva Merikainen, Kolkka, Orvo, and others of the household stamped uneasily in the dim light. The Princess Marjatta and Cherry Red, wrapped in thick cloaks, stood beside them. Midnight's frosty breath made a dim halo around his nose, expanding and retreating.

Ulla and Kaukomieli were warmly dressed. Ulla wore a black, fur-lined cloak with high boots strapped to her legs and black vambraces on her arms. *Pohjanpiikki* was fixed in the leather scabbard to Midnight's saddle; Longleaf hung at her belt. Clad in the sky-blue of Etelamaa, Kaukomieli wore a silver helm upon his yellow head, a parting gift from Kirsikka and Marjatta. An heirloom of the House of Joutsen, it had been Nigan's in his youth.

"May Ukko's blessings go with you," said Kolkka, moving his staff in a circle as he whispered a prayer of protection over the two riders.

"You will need to ride swiftly to avoid the thaw," said Toiva. "Karelia's far away, if, indeed, that is where you are going. There are good roads until you reach the Green Vales near Lake Etelajärvi, but the ice on the lakes becomes treacherous as spring approaches. Many people fall through the ice in those parts. Be careful if the waters open early."

"They will not open early," replied Ulla. "But that does not make your advice less wise. I have been through the Green Vales twice with Väinämöinen; once when I was just a child, but again only a few years ago. We will not go astray."

A gust of wind blew through the courtyard, scattering the snow like dust.

Kirsikka stepped forward. She reached up and took Ulla's hand.

"*Rakastan sinua, sisku*," she said. "I love you."

Ulla squeezed her hand.

"When will you return?"

Ulla looked at Kaukomieli. "We go to find Väinämöinen. Beyond that, I cannot say. But when I return—if I return—it will be either upon the wings of victory or of defeat. Either way, nothing again will ever be the same. Take care of yourself, sister; know that you are always in my heart."

Kaukomieli's horse pulled, eager to be off.

"It is cold sitting here," he said. "The sun's arc will soon break the horizon and be in our faces. Let us go, Ulla, and part with the city ere it rises. It will be warmer on the road than in this Keep."

He bowed his head to the little crowd. Ulla let Kirsikka's hand slip from her grasp. Kicking his horse with his fine leather boots, Kaukomieli took off from the courtyard, clopping across the bridge. With a last look at her friend, Ulla did the same.

The sound of shouted farewells reached her ears dimly on the wind. Catching up with Kaukomieli, they made for the main gates and soon left the City of the Swan Folk far behind them.

Chapter Seven

The Wizard's Choice

Kaukomieli peered down toward the river. Bright yellow sunlight illuminated the forest. He shielded his eyes with his hand, squinting. A golden glow lay all about the river valley. Cuckoos trilled in the trees as if greeting both the travelers and springtime.

The young man turned to his companion.

"It's more beautiful than I remembered," he said. "The forest seems so much more alive here. I've travelled throughout the Far Northern Land, but have yet to find woods that compare to Karelia."

"And this is only the edge of the Enchanted Valley," answered Ulla. "Remember the woods at Väinölä? And *Isotammi*, the Great Oak? You've never really known springtime until you experience it in Taikalaakso."

Kaukomieli and Ulla walked down the tumbled slope until they came to the lawn beside the banks of the Mustajouki. Green grass ran down to the dark water's edge. Ducklings played along the shore. The Ankkaportti loomed before them; the Enchanted Valley's magic beckoned.

No Näkkia swayed in the slow-flowing river this time, but two figures stood in the middle of the beautiful white bridge. As the wizards drew near, Kaukomieli recognized Tulikki and Janus, the chief of the remaining elves of the Enchanted Valley.

With no need for her somber travelling clothes here, Tulikki wore bright Karelian garb, chiefly red and green. She raised her hand in greeting, calling out in her clear, Erilaisen voice.

"Welcome back," she said, meeting them at the foot of the bridge. "You have been away far too long. And our meeting is the merrier since you arrive on the cusp of spring, though it is late in coming this year. Well met, sister."

Kaukomieli considered the Erilaisen woman as she embraced Ulla. He had met her only once before, during his single visit to Taikalaakso that now seemed so long ago. Turning from Ulla, Tulikki smiled at him, and his thought fled far away.

"Ah, the Last Wizard, the one who mastered Lovêatar," she said. "Mortals may not understand how great your deed was, but your magnificence cannot be hid from the eyes of the Erilaiset. Everyone in the Valley is singing songs about you now." Kaukomieli blushed.

"Well, I had some help," he joked awkwardly, motioning to Ulla. "She's the one most deserving of song."

"Don't let him fool you," replied Ulla. "The spell was all his. But now he makes me wear the cursed thing around my neck, with the hag locked within. Perhaps Mielikki will know what to do with it."

"Perhaps," answered Tulikki.

"And how was your journey from Etelamaa?" asked Janus.

"Long and wearisome," answered Kaukomieli. "I will never become used to such journeys on horseback. I was so sore the first week that I could not bend my legs in the morning and my backside was one great, black bruise."

"We left our horses with the Reindeer Folk," said Ulla. "Starchaser, Väinämöinen's horse, was with them too. They told us that Väinämöinen had not visited him for some time. I thought—well, I thought that he might be here to greet us."

Kaukomieli heard the anxiety in her voice. *What if the old man is not in the Enchanted Valley?* he thought. *What if the journey has been in vain?*

Tulikki looked hard at Ulla.

"He is at Väinölä," said the brown-haired Erilainen. "Seldom does he leave. Nonetheless, he knows you are coming and no doubt awaits you there."

"Indeed," said Janus. "Only last week I visited Väinölä and spoke with him. He certainly waits for you. I do not know if he will be the same Väinämöinen to your eyes or to your heart when you come there, Ulla. Much has passed since Sumuvuori; the changes lie heavy upon his head."

Kaukomieli's eyes met Ulla's. Her expression remained stoic, but Kaukomieli felt her spirit waver.

"Then all the more reason to hasten," said Ulla at length. "It is to find Väinämöinen that we came here. Let us go to Väinölä now."

"Janus and I were sent to greet you in Väinämöinen's stead," said Tulikki. "My mother bid me come, both to greet you and to deliver her message. Go to Kukkatarha first. She waits there for you."

"Yes," said Janus. "Mielikki wishes to speak with you before you go to Väinölä. The way is not much further and the afternoon still fair. Let us pass on to Kukkatarha; there you may rest from weariness and seek the wisdom of Tapio's daughter. Will you not come with us?"

Ulla agreed, though Kaukomieli sensed her reluctance. He knew how eager she was to see the old singer. Janus's strange words made Ulla even more impatient. She had reached out to Väinämöinen many times on the northward journey, but to no avail. Despite their affinity, Ulla could not find him. All was dark. Mielikki she had found, twice, but her words were hardly comforting. *Yes and no*, she had said. *He is here and yet he is not. Come.*

As they walked toward Kukkatarha, Ulla learned more bad news. Turi was missing too. The wizard had been expected months ago, but he had never been heard from again.

"Have you not seen him?" asked Janus. "We hoped that you, who have been in Etelamaa, might know where he is or what has become of him."

"I do not," sighed Ulla, even more despondent. She had also hoped to find Turi in the Valley. "The last time I saw him was in Tapiola, a year ago. I know that he was in the north of Etelamaa after that. Kaukomieli and I did not find him when we went to challenge Lovêatar, however. I know nothing more."

Kaukomieli soon forgot his worries as they walked through the magical land lit by glittering golden sunlight. He told Janus and Tulikki the full tale of the battle with Lovêatar. The Valley and its inhabitants intoxicated the young singer. He wished that he were coming to live there. He would have been happy to dwell in the forest and study magic with the Erilaiset as long as they would have him. Ulla remained pensive, however. She and Tulikki spoke together quietly about the war and how things fared with the Seven Clans. Mostly, she listened to Kaukomieli's tales in silence, tramping along behind the others, sensing the new spring all around her.

They slept one night in a little hamlet where several families of Menninkaiset dwelt. As the next day's noon sun shone down, they reached Kukkatarha.

No matter the season in the outside world, it was always springtime in Mielikki's garden. But when spring, real spring, blossomed throughout the Far Northern Land, Kukkatarha became a special place, the most beautiful in all the Seven Lands. The grass grew green, the flowers blossomed, and the blessings of Tapio's daughter lay richly upon it.

Mielikki greeted Ulla and Kaukomieli warmly. Metsänaiset spread blankets upon the grass. They laid bread, butter, cheese, and cream before their weary guests. After eating and washing in the clear, cold stream, they rested a while in the shade of the trees.

That evening, the tree maidens took Kaukomieli into the surrounding woods, teasing him about his yellow hair and bright blue eyes. The young man was quick to return their jests, sending sparkling illusions of birds and beasts chasing after them among the firs and pines, much to their delight. Tulikki came to Ulla then, bringing her inside her mother's home. Stooping, Ulla passed through the silver door and found Mielikki waiting. Memories came flooding back. Ulla thought of the first time she had entered Mielikki's house long ago, when she was only a wide-eyed little girl trailing behind the old wizard from Väinölä.

Mielikki sat cross-legged next to the fire. Ulla sat down beside her. Yellow candlelight illuminated the room. Ulla peered at Mielikki through the sweet-smelling smoke.

The Lady of the Forest appeared unchanged. Her skin remained flawless; her dark hair cascaded down her smooth shoulders. Among all other women, only Löhi could appear so perfect. Löhi's perfection was unnatural, however. Her beautiful aspect seemed cold, her face like a mask. There was nothing unnatural about Mielikki. Warm, vibrant, she was alive: the personification of nature itself. Smiling, Mielikki brushed aside a stray lock of hair, a gesture so natural and lovely that Ulla smiled too.

Then Ulla caught a glimpse of something that she had never seen before. Mielikki's bright eyes were troubled. Doubt played upon their shimmering surface. Mielikki, the daughter of Tapio and child of the Vanhalaiset, looked frightened.

"The waters of many streams and rivers flow into the Mustajouki," said Mielikki. "They bring tidings from many lands. Already I know your report, daughter. Battle unceasing on the Marches and slow defeat among the Kaamoslaiset."

"Defeat," answered Ulla. "Despair. There are still victories to be won, sometimes, but there is very little hope.

"Yet it is more than defeat in battle. A sickness spreads throughout the Far Northern Land, not a sickness like the Winter Plague, but a pestilence of the very land itself. It is becoming diseased, rotten. All things done are ill done."

"Yes," said Mielikki. "It is the power of the Witch, the power of Pohjola. It flows into the very earth. The Season of the Witch is upon us, Ulla. The Seven Clans are scattered; Löhi's magic grows stronger every day. Her dark *kalma* spreads its curse across the land, making it hers again as it was long ago."

"I thought that when we trapped Lovêatar, things would be better."

"That was a great deed," replied Mielikki. "You saved many lives. Yet I fear your victory only delays Löhi's long march to triumph. Her power waxes and ours fades. There is little hope in this endless war against Pohjola."

Ulla sighed. *Little hope,* she thought. *If even Mielikki despairs, then there is no hope, only death, death in battle, slaying as many of Löhi's servants as possible before the night falls.*

"That is why I came to find him—Väinämöinen. He should have returned to Tavastia long ago. Surely, if anyone can do something, Väinämöinen can."

"Seldom does Väinämöinen leave Väinölä. Lately, he does not even leave the Great Oak save to watch the stars on clear nights."

"Why?"

"He is not the same person that he was before Sumuvuori."

"Nothing is the same as it was before Sumuvuori; everything changed. But Väinämöinen's counsel was to never give up. It is the first and the last thing that he taught me."

"Seven years now," answered Mielikki. "Seven years has he thought about that day. Seven long years of death and defeat. He blames himself for Egan's death, Ulla—Egan, Unaja, Lúven; he blames himself for all of it."

Ulla felt a cold chill at the mention of Egan's name.

"Väinämöinen did not betray Egan," she said flatly.

"No. Siitsa's betrayal determined the fate of many; perhaps even the fate of the Far Northern Land. It can be so sometimes. The choice that one person makes, for good or ill, multiplies like ripples in a pond.

"All the more important then are the choices we make now, each one of us. And many times we need the help of our friends to see clearly and make the right choice. Thus can the balance be restored."

Ulla hung her head, staring at the crackling fire. Mielikki moved closer. The two women faced one another while tiny tongues of flame danced between them. Mielikki took Ulla's face with her hands, looking into her hazel-green eyes.

"Ulla," she said gently. "I have hard words and hard counsel for you. My *sight* is not so clear now, not so far, yet my heart remains true to the song of the Vanhalaiset. There is no hope in war. We must kill Löhi to save the Far Northern Land. And only you can do this deed."

Ulla's heart skipped a beat. Though not unexpected, Mielikki's words still shocked her.

"You bear the Mark of the Clan. You mastered *karhu* in the colorless woods. Löhi's power over you is weak, uncertain. I cannot see how you are to accomplish this thing, but if it can be done, only you can achieve it. It is your quest, Ulla."

The dark-haired Karhulaisen girl trembled.

"I know," she replied at last. "There is no other way. I've known since we trapped Lovêatar within the glass. We must find Löhi and destroy her. But how can I hope to do this without Väinämöinen?"

"Truly, it is his quest too," said Mielikki. "Väinämöinen and Löhi were the same in the beginning. Different paths they took, different choices they made. She became greater than any other Erilainen in the process, but the price was high. Löhi lost herself long ago. What remains is only a pale reflection of what she once was or might have been. They are opposites now, yet their fates are bound together."

"Surely you have spoken with him, Mielikki. If he did not listen to your counsel, how can I ever convince him?"

"I saw him twice this winter," said Mielikki. "Twice he rejected my counsel. But always he thinks of you, Ulla.

"He loves you. He trusts your heart, more than anyone's. You are the Child of the Prophecy. Go to him! Doubt consumes him, doubt, and fear of making the wrong choice. But you can convince him, shake him from his indecision. I love you, too, Ulla, even as I love Tulikki. Still, I would have you make this quest, no matter how hopeless it seems. We must do what is right."

Ulla squeezed Mielikki's hand. The yellow candles flickered. Outside, the faint laughter of the tree maidens carried on the wind.

"I will go to him. I will go to Väinölä this very night."

"Not tonight," answered Mielikki. "Tomorrow is time enough. For this night, at least, I wish for you to stay with me in Kukkatarha. Rest from worry and sleep again in my house even as you did as a child."

* * *

Kaukomieli and Ulla left Kukkatarha the next morning. Väinölä was not far, but they took a longer route through thick woods to enjoy the forest's beauty. It was after midday before they arrived at the village. Väinölä's folk turned out for the homecoming, singing praises for Lovêatar's defeat. The old man did not join the throng, however. Lempi said that he waited for them inside the Great Oak, *Isotammi*.

The little gnome had not changed much. Irrepressibly cheerful, he capered about, delighted to see Ulla again.

"Now, don't you forget," he told Kaukomieli, "That I'm the one who first taught Ulla magic. I knew there was power within her even when she was only this high. Look at her now! The greatest mortal wizard since Lemminkäinen—and that's saying a lot!"

Lempi walked them to the mighty oak. Ulla and Kaukomieli gazed upward at its towering limbs. A fair, southerly wind rustled in its higher branches. Up, up it went into the sky. Kaukomieli felt the great tree's spirit singing in the sunlight.

Turning to Ulla he said, "Best for you to speak with him alone. He's my teacher, but your friend."

Ulla nodded. Glancing back, she saw Lempi and several others watching her. She closed her eyes. With a deep breath, Ulla passed over the threshold.

Steadying herself with her staff, Ulla climbed down the spiral staircase. She thought of the first time that she and Kirsikka had come to the Great Oak. Dreamlike it had been, surreal: the woods, the tree, and the house carved deep within. She had imagined that she had passed into a fairy story, entering another world where everything was possible. Magic ruled in this world, not reason.

But that was then. Ulla was no longer just a little girl with dark hair from Grankulta. It all seemed so normal to her now.

Coming to the bottom of the long stair, she stepped into the soft light of the great lamps. There, sitting at the table, she found Väinämöinen.

His head was back, as if he slept. His long, white beard rested upon his chest. The wizard's ten-stringed kantale lay on the table beside a deep mug of beer, or so she guessed. Ulla took a few steps toward him and half-spoke, half-whispered, "Väinämöinen?"

The old man popped an eye open. He sprang up, knocking over the mug.

"Come here, little one," he cried, a broad smile on his ruddy face. Ulla rushed into his arms. The old man embraced her, kissing the top of her dark head.

"Ah, how I've waited for this moment," he said. "Let me look at you! It's so good to see you again, to finally see you, little one." He took a step back, slowly considering her. His expression turned serious.

"Well and good," he said. "You have grown, Ulla. I see it in your eyes. Almost like an Erilainen's, they have become. You are strong, *very* strong. You stand among the Great Ones now."

Of the dozens of things Ulla had wished to say, not a one remained to her. She stood speechless. Väinämöinen smiled, motioning toward a chair.

"Sit with me, Ulla," he said. "Rest from wandering for a while."

"Why didn't you come to the Ankkaportti to meet us?" she asked, taking the seat beside his. "Why weren't you upstairs, outside under the sun with your folk?"

"Patience," said the wizard. "One question at a time. A thousand years takes its toll; I'm not as young as I used to be. It's a long walk from Väinölä to the Ankkaportti.

"As for your second question, you've tarried. First to Kukkatarha, then a crooked path to Väinölä. I waited outside all morning for you but grew sleepy. The south wind in *Isotammi's* branches will do that to you. So I decided to come back down and give you a little surprise."

"Kaukomieli and I went to see Mielikki. Mielikki has the same questions for you that I do."

"Where is Kaukomieli?" asked Väinämöinen, ignoring Ulla's pointed remark. "Did he not come with you?"

"He's up above, with Lempi."

"Well, there's time enough to visit with him later. Much has happened since last we sat together inside *Isotammi*, child. Tell me all that has transpired with you since we parted!"

The old man made Ulla a little pot of pine-scented tea. Pouring himself another mug of beer, he questioned her about everything she had done and seen. They talked for a long time while the afternoon wore on outside. Väinämöinen seemed to already know most of the news about the battles along the Marches and the policies of the rulers in Tavastia and Etelamaa. He even knew that Ulla had tracked down and slain Maanavilja. The wizard asked eagerly for news about Kirsikka; however, he took Ulla's hand when she told him about their fight and did not reproach her. But his eyes twinkled when she finally told him about the battle with Lovêatar.

"A spirit of Ilmatar, an air spirit!" he said, chuckling. "So that was Seppo's secret. And *karhu's* tooth set the spell! Kaukomieli has quite a gift for divining the nature of things. Unaja recognized that gift; she told me when she first found him that she had a feeling, a foresight. That foresight was well-founded. Unaja was wise."

The mention of Unaja was off-putting and they both felt it. Väinämöinen sighed, momentarily growing reflective. He quickly shook it off, slapping his big hand on the table.

"Show me the glass!" he said. "What a talisman you now possess."

"I don't wear it anymore," answered Ulla, drawing the star-shaped glass from her pouch. "I don't want that thing around my neck. But here it is. I do not know what to do with it. I had thought to give it to you or Mielikki."

She handed the glass to Väinämöinen. He held it up to the light. It was dark, lifeless. Suddenly, the inky cloud within shifted; the pattern changed. The spirit inside was restless.

"Tuone's daughter," mused the old man, shaking his head. "Well, we shall give thought to this thing and what to do with it."

Ulla had been waiting for the right moment to begin the conversation she dreaded. Sensing an opportunity, she seized it.

"We must give thought to many things," she said. "All the Seven Lands ask for you, seeking your counsel. From the Stone City to the Blue Lake, where Teemu is besieged, they all ask the same question: where is Väinämöinen?"

"And what do you tell them?" he asked flatly.

"That I don't know, of course!" she cried, exasperated. "I wasn't even sure if you were here in the Valley. Why didn't you reach your mind out to me or send a message? Why have you forsaken our people?"

"Forsaken our people?" The old man tossed the jewel back to Ulla. Rising, he paced back and forth across the hall.

"Who have I forsaken? Aslo of Tavastia rejected my counsel. The Erilaiset are outlaw again in Akkala. The Old Ways are already abandoned. Who exactly has forsaken whom?"

"Aslo, Akkala—what of the thousands of others who look to you? What of the tens of thousands who need you? What about *me*, Väinämöinen? For two years, you have hidden in the forest. Did you pay no mind to me in all that time?"

It was her strongest card and she knew it. The violence of the old man's reaction still surprised.

"How dare you!" he spluttered, turning scarlet and moving toward her so swiftly that she jumped from her seat and backed away.

"Pay you no mind! Not a day passed that my thought was not upon you, not a night that I did not watch you from afar. All my strength, all my blessing has been wrapped around you, whether you knew it or not. Pay you no mind! Paying you mind has been my chief task now for a long, long time."

Ulla did not relent.

"If so, you had a strange way of showing it," she answered coldly. She moved around the cluttered, almost disheveled room. Amidst the objects of cunningly wrought gold and shapely wood lay empty beer pots, tattered sacks, and scattered clothing. Väinämöinen's sword hung askew on the wall.

"*Jääpuikko* is needed in many places," she said, motioning to the blade. "So are your songs. Löhi's power waxes outside the Forest. Have you forgotten your duty?"

"I spend my time among the Karelialaiset," the old man replied, his voice cold and grim. "The Witch will soon turn her attention to them. I've woven nets throughout Karelia and laid enchantments round every cabin. The Reindeer Folk will survive. The Enchanted Valley will not fall, not even if Löhi comes here herself. We will weather the storm as we did in the days of old."

"Weather the storm?" asked Ulla, incredulously. "Is that all you would do? What happened to the singer who said that he would never bow to Löhi?"

"There are more ways than one to fight the Witch," the old man said. "You are a warrior, Ulla. I never wanted that for you, but destiny will out, looked for or not. You have become the greatest wizard and warrior since Lemminkäinen. But this war is hopeless. The Witch is too powerful, our friends too weak. The swords and spears of the Seven Clans cannot prevail."

"Yes," she said. "Swords will not bring victory. There is no hope in battle everlasting."

Ulla came near to him. She reached up and touched his grey hair.

"*Isäni*," she said, gently. "As a father you have been to me since that day in the woods long ago. All that I am, I owe to you. I love you more than anyone in the world. But now you must listen to your daughter.

"We must go to Pohjola. We must find and kill Löhi. I know not how this thing may be done or if there is hope, yet we must attempt it nonetheless."

It seemed to Ulla that a film covered the old wizard's eyes, as if they filled with tears. He sighed deeply. Pulling away, he strode over to a little table, picked up a golden figure, and ran his hands over its smooth surface.

"There is no hope in that road either, Ulla. I do not have the strength to slay Löhi. Neither do you, not in her own domain, not in Pohjola."

"Yet Mielikki counsels me to try. And it is also in my own heart."

"You will only throw your own life away."

"So it is better to sit here and do nothing?"

"The Witch's Season will pass; it must. Löhi slept before and will sleep again. Lúven was right. We must make strong places and do what we can to preserve all that can be saved. Here, in Etelamaa, in Tavastia...a seed must be preserved, a seed that can blossom again in times to come."

"A seed? If we do nothing, all the Far Northern Land will eventually be overcome."

"I will not send you to your death!" cried Väinämöinen, beating his fist upon the polished wood.

"Pohjola is a trap, just like Sumuvuori. I sent Egan to his death, Egan, Lúven, Unaja, all of them! It is my fault that the League was destroyed. The voices of the slain call out to me in the darkness, reproaching me my choice. It is my fault!"

"Egan made his choice," answered Ulla. "So did we all. Betrayal and the lies of Pohjola paved the path to Sumuvuori and back. How is that your fault?"

"I should have stopped him," said the wizard. "I knew where true hope lay; true hope lay in the Sampo, in the songs. Such was Tapio's rede. Egan looked to me for counsel and I failed him. I did nothing. And when he fought the Moonface upon the cold field, I did not stand beside him. I left him all alone, to die in vain."

"Egan made his own choice!" cried Ulla. Raising her staff, she made a swift, sweeping gesture, almost an invocation. Just as swiftly, the old man struck her staff aside with his arm, knocking it from her grasp. The table shook and the kantale fell to the floor, an eerie, discordant sound echoing throughout the underground hall.

"He made his own choice and it was wrong. I was wrong. But Egan asked no man to take responsibility for him. He accepted the consequences. And he did not shirk his duty. He did not flee the battlefield to save himself; he died a hero. His sacrifice saved us, saved thousands, just as Unaja's did. His sacrifice saved you, saved *me*. He died on that field to give us this last chance, taking a legion of Pohjolaiset with him. Can you not see that, Väinämöinen? Or has the Witch blinded your eyes? It is her words you speak, her *kalma* of despair you channel. Did she enter your dreams, Väinämöinen? Did she bewitch even you?"

Väinämöinen slammed his fist into the table again. The girl and the old man glimmered with electric energy as their wizardly power shone forth, each compelling the other as neither had ever done before.

"No!" shouted Väinämöinen. "You will not go to your death in Pohjola!"

"This path is the right one," said Ulla. "You know it in your heart. For my entire life you have taught me that I am free, free to choose. Victory is not in the outcome; it lies in the choice, come what may. Do you not remember your words to Lúven when you stood before all the Erilaiset? Do you not recall what you said in Airikki's hall? I do.

"You said that, 'In the world of men, of which we are a part, nothing is certain but the sun, wind, sea, and that all things will run on to their appointed end as Ukko set in motion at the Beginning. But that does not make it vain to resist evil or strive for good. The hearts of men are not set in their courses like the stars in heaven. The choices you make govern many things, your own fate not the least.'

"The Seven Clans need you, Väinämöinen. I need you."

Ulla's final plea held so much power that it seemed shadowy wings unfolded behind her; spreading, they darkened the room, obscuring the lamps and candles. The shadow-wings reached out to envelop Väinämöinen and draw him in, but the old man stepped back at the last moment. They closed on nothingness, wavered, and disappeared.

Ulla stood still. Without another word, Väinämöinen sat down in his high-backed chair. He filled his mug. Stooping, he retrieved the kantale and laid it in his lap.

He picked out a few notes, then strummed a simple, melancholy tune, humming along quietly. The old man looked down at the instrument while he played, paying no more heed to the dark-haired young woman.

Ulla closed her eyes; she drew a deep breath. Picking up her staff, she strode to the spiral staircase and mounted the stair. One by one, she climbed the steps back up into the outside world. The echoes of Väinämöinen's kantale faded below.

The sun was westering when she emerged from the Great Oak; its red orb had sunk behind the trees, where it would hang for hours. The western sky glowed yellow, but dusky twilight had already descended upon the east. The moon was out; a few bright stars clustered nearby.

Väinölä's inhabitants were nowhere to be seen, but Kaukomieli lounged beneath a rowan opposite the oak. He stood as Ulla approached, questioning her with his eyes. She shook her head.

"Let's go," she said dully.

Kaukomieli saw the pain in her expression. Instinctively, without thinking, he reached his hand to her face, but she pulled away sharply. In silence, without bidding any farewells, they made for the stone-bordered path that led to Kukkatarha, trudging through the woods as the day slowly faded, leaving behind the colored, twinkling lights of Väinölä.

After a while, Ulla opened up and told him somewhat of what had happened. The young man did not know what to say. Ulla wanted no comfort from him, that much was clear—not from him or anyone else at that moment. But he would not abandon her. Kaukomieli was determined to stay at Ulla's side until the bitter end. If that end came soon, on the road to Pohjola, so be it. At least she would not die alone.

Mielikki and Tulikki were away on some errand when they reached Kukkatarha. The Metsänaiset welcomed them back, drawing them in. Exhausted from waiting, Kaukomieli soon fell asleep. Restless, Ulla left him alone in Mielikki's house while she went outside to breathe in the cool air and watch the stars.

The gentle, southerly wind rustled the treetops. The moon had long since set. A thousand stars gleamed in the clear night sky. The Great Bear had climbed just above the tree line; *karhu* romped through the sky fields. The stars shone so bright in the Enchanted Valley that Ulla cast a dim shadow upon the grass.

The young woman noticed one star to the north, a red star, Löhi's star. Each year, it shone a little brighter. Each year, the Witch sang her spells into the melody of the Far Northern Land. The red star burned like hot iron. How could she, Ulla Karhulainen, ever hope to find a way to stop such power? How could she, alone, find the path to Pohjola? All had gone wrong when Egan died. Ukko's plan had gone awry.

Then Ulla noticed another light almost directly overhead, a star brighter than all the rest, twinkling like a diamond, Taivaantappi, the Nail of the Heavens. The North Star seemed to gather the brilliance of all its companions and reflect it back upon them.

A gust of wind blew her long, dark hair about her face.

"Ulla," said a low voice from behind her.

She spun round. It was Väinämöinen.

"I have chosen, little one; I have chosen."

Chapter Eight

Tuonela

Mielikki returned the next morning. She acted as if she expected to find Väinämöinen at Kukkatarha. The old man said nothing about his conversation with Ulla. Ulla, happy to see him, let all that might lie between them pass. They rested for a while; Ulla finally slept. As the afternoon faded into a fine, golden glow, they gathered again inside Mielikki's home.

Many of the remaining Great Ones among the Erilaiset had come to join them. Satatieto arrived from his home near Loulajärvi. Janus represented the elves. Ulla, Kaukomieli, Mielikki, and Tulikki sat cross-legged on the floor. Viljatoive, the disciple of Akka who had once blessed the Singing Valley with her magic, arrived last. Väinämöinen did most of the talking, however. Having made up his mind, he decided swiftly what must be done.

"Mielikki is right," said the old wizard. "There is no hope in battle, no hope in building strong places and outlasting the Witch. Any such hope ended when Ilmarinen was slain and the Sampo lost forever."

"Such is the fruit of Siitsa's betrayal," said Mielikki. "Immeasurable harm the girl cost us. I knew a black cloud hung over her when first I met her, but never imagined her capable of such foul deeds."

"She paid with her life," answered Väinämöinen. "Small comfort though it may be to those doomed to carry on the fight. Yet she was wise in her own strange way. Siitsa knew much of Löhi's mind and sought to carry out the

Witch's most urgent command, to lure Egan and Ulla, the two whom she most feared, into a hopeless battle far away.

"Egan she slew, despite his heroism, but Ulla escaped. And it is Ulla she now fears more than anything. Indeed, Ulla may be her only fear. She bears the Mark of the Clan; she is the Child of the Prophecy. Löhi will never rest until she finds her. Let the Witch's fear be our guide then, let it illuminate our path. Ulla must find Löhi, find her in Pohjola, and kill her."

"But how can any one person alone slay Löhi?" asked Satatieto.

"She need not go alone," answered Väinämöinen. "I shall certainly go with her. But, whoever makes the journey, I do not doubt that Ulla must strike the fatal blow."

"An assault upon Pohjola," muttered Viljatoive. "If there is no hope in battle along the Marches, what hope is there in attacking the land of the Witch?"

"I did not say *assault*," said Väinämöinen. "Sariola, the Witch's Keep, is far away—a thousand miles, if it's a mile. Even if we could again gather an army as great as Egan's League and march north, what good would it do? Löhi's servants would only waylay us along the road. Should we defeat them, what then? Our army diminished, supplies exhausted, we would arrive at the gates of Sariola as winter descends and die in the snow."

"Väinämöinen speaks the truth," said Mielikki. "This quest must be secret, as secret as possible. I feel the Witch's uncertainty. She ponders Lovêatar's defeat, wondering what it might mean for her own fortunes. All her will bends toward finding Ulla, finding her and killing her. It is a perilous journey, but there is no other way."

"Can you do this deed, Ulla?" asked Janus.

Ulla sighed. Listening to the Erilaiset talk about the hopelessness of the quest, her resolve wavered. She felt frightened and alone.

"I will attempt it," she said at last. "I came back to the Enchanted Valley in order to find Väinämöinen so that he might accompany me on just such a quest. But I do not know what spell or weapon can destroy the Witch."

"What about the jewel?" asked Janus. "Can we not trap Löhi within, even as you trapped her servant?"

They looked at Kaukomieli.

"I do not think so," he replied, shaking his head. "Her spirit is too great and of a different kind."

"Loathsome as Lovêatar is, Löhi is far stronger," said Väinämöinen. "No glass made by mortal smiths, no spell sung by wizards, no blade though forged by Ilmarinen himself can slay her now. Not even the Sword of Legend, wielded by Lemminkäinen, could do so. Perhaps if all the Great Ones of the Erilaiset and the Seven Clans were gathered together, we might destroy her, but Löhi would never face all of us. She would only flee and then attack again as we separated."

"Then what is the point of Ulla going to Pohjola?" asked Kaukomieli. "If no weapon or spell can bite her, is it not a hopeless journey to certain death?"

Väinämöinen's dark gaze swept the room; his voice was grim.

"No weapon of this world will bite her, so we need a weapon from another world. We must seek Tuone, the Lord of the Dead. Only a weapon from Tuonela can assuredly slay the Queen of Pohjola."

All fell silent. Tension filled the room, creeping like mist into its nooks and corners. Ulla's heart beat hard in her chest. Tuonela! Once before, Väinämöinen had spoken of Tuonela, but seemed to reject it. Could this really be the only way to defeat Löhi?

"The Lord of the Dead," said Mielikki at last. "All must make that dark journey one day. But what weapon could you find there to slay the Witch?"

"Tuone does not suffer the living to enter his realm," said Janus. "Few who dare to do so ever return."

"Yet I am one of them," replied Väinämöinen. "I have been to Tuonela and returned to living lands. So has Turi. I cannot say exactly what we are seeking or what we may find there; nonetheless, it is the only path left to us. We must beg Tuone's favor. Any weapon, any token from his cold hand will surely send Löhi straight to his dismal realm. Already she goes there as a living spirit, angering him. When she journeys there in death, Tuone will hold her and never let her ghost trouble the waking world ever again."

"But will Tuone help us?" asked Viljatoive. "Will he not simply hold you as he would the Witch?"

"Who can say?" replied Väinämöinen. "But we must try. Long have I thought on this; I can see no other way." The old man went on, quietly. "Ulla, will you come with me?"

All eyes turned toward the dark-haired young woman. She met Kaukomieli's gaze first, then Väinämöinen's.

"I will come with you," said Ulla. "You agreed to take me to Pohjola. If we must first seek this weapon in the Land of the Dead, so be it. I will come with you. And let us not part again, in this world or any other, until the Witch is slain or else we fail in our task."

Mielikki rose then, green eyes shining.

"As you say, Ulla, so be it. Until the end."

Väinämöinen stayed in Kukkatarha for three days, gathering what news he could. He took Ulla and Kaukomieli aside, explaining his plan to them, such as it was. He recounted all that he could remember of his previous journeys to Tuonela. The old man did not wish to frighten Ulla, but, at the same time, he held nothing back so that she knew what to expect.

One thing greatly disturbed him, however: Turi. No matter how hard he tried, Väinämöinen could not find him with his wizardly *sight*. No news of Turi's whereabouts had reached the Enchanted Valley; the Changer seemed to have disappeared. Janus promised to send out elves to search for him, but Väinämöinen and Ulla could not wait. The wizard intended to go to Tuonela immediately.

To Kaukomieli's dismay, Väinämöinen told the young wizard he could not join them.

"This journey is for Ulla," said the old man. "If we come back, then together we will make the attempt on Pohjola, but it may well be that we will not come back. If so, you will have a hard task before you as our mortal bodies linger in oblivion. And afterward, it will be up to you to carry on with the few who remain. Then *you* will be the last hope, Kaukomieli."

On the evening of the third day, all was ready. Ulla, anxious to end the wait, spoke quietly with Mielikki while Väinämöinen instructed Kaukomieli. The old man and the girl would, of course, leave their bodies behind while their living spirits journeyed to Death's Kingdom. Time passed strangely in the spirit world. To those who entered, it might seem that days or even weeks went by, yet they might return to find only an hour had passed under the sun.

If their spirit-bodies were slain, those who tended them in the waking world might witness their earthly bodies seize and suddenly die. If they became lost or trapped in Tuonela, unable to return, their bodies might linger, sadly, slowly fading while the friends watching over them sat helpless beside them. More than one wizard of the Far Northern Land had suffered such a fate.

Mielikki blessed them both, invoking Ukko's protection. She kissed Ulla atop her dark head. Shadows sprang up across the smoky room.

At last, Väinämöinen sat next to Ulla. His sword hung from his belt; his staff lay across his knees. Ulla, too, kept all her needful things close by. Neither knew what they might still possess when they awoke on the other side.

Mielikki and Kaukomieli took little drums, made of jet black leather, stretched taut, and began the rhythmic beat. *Dum, dum, dum, dom; dum, dum, dum, dom.* Mielikki's melodious voice chanted slowly in the Old Tongue of the Erilaiset. Visions entered Kaukomieli's mind, images floating lazily in a dreamscape. Tall trees climbed upwards toward the heavens. A dark river wound through the forest like a snake. A swan took flight on silver wings. The young man, almost enchanted himself, had to shake free of the spell.

He gazed at Ulla. She held Väinämöinen's hand. Together they rocked back and forth, this way and that, keeping time with Mielikki's chanting. They did this for a long time. Kaukomieli grew sleepier and sleepier. Suddenly Väinämöinen straightened. His eyes fluttered. The old man sighed and, stretching out his legs, lay flat on his back. Straightaway, Ulla did the same.

Mielikki continued chanting for a while, still tapping the drum: *dum, dum, dum, dom.* She stopped. Kaukomieli instantly felt alert again.

The Lady of the Forest rose, gazing down at the two sleeping figures. The trance had worked.

Väinämöinen appeared peaceful, his white beard neatly forked and bound with gold.

Ulla looked young, desperately so; gone was the proud mien and stern visage.

Mielikki sighed. She turned to Kaukomieli.

"They have left us," she said. "They walk in the colorless woods."

"What do we do now?" he asked.

"We wait."

* * *

Ulla opened her eyes. She gripped her staff in her right hand. Her badger-skin pouch was strapped around her waist. Longleaf hung from her belt, but her sword did not.

Väinämöinen stood beside her. He, too, held his staff, but no sword hung at his side; *Jääpuikko* had been left behind. Dun and ash-colored birch trees surrounded them, their sullen leaves painted varying shades of white or grey. No wind rustled the treetops; all was still.

"Listen," said Väinämöinen. "What do you hear?"

At first she heard nothing. Then, faintly, as if from an immeasurable distance, Ulla heard the telltale tinkling of water dripping softly from barren branches.

"This way," said the wizard.

They walked through the colorless woods toward the sound of water. Never before had Ulla sought that river, the dark river that separated the living world from the Land of the Dead. Perilous it was for mortals to come there. On the river's far side lay Tuonela, where the souls of the dead went when they departed. For some, it was but a sojourn until, leaving their shades behind, they journeyed on to whatever fair end Ukko prepared for them. But for others who had done evil, it was their home, a dismal prison within which to lament their failures, or else fall into madness. And the most evil were cast into the pits of oblivion, for the wage of their sins was nothingness.

Then Väinämöinen came out of the woods and before him lay the river. Reed beds and ragged cattails straggled along its sullen shores where marshy turf gave way to the channel. Dark was that river, drear and black, and its inky water flowed so slowly that it seemed almost a pool. Mists curled and crept among the rushes like the ghosts of spindly snakes.

"How can we cross?" asked Ulla. "We have no boat."

"We have only to wait," answered Väinämöinen. "She who brings the souls of the dead to Tuonela will come swiftly if she comes at all. If not, we must find another way or else abandon our quest."

"Who is she? I heard Turi speak once of a ferrywoman, but I recall nothing more."

The old man sighed.

"The White Maiden of Tuonela, one of Tuone's daughters, even as Lovêatar. Her name is Kipu-Tyttö in the Old Speech, that the men of the Seven Clans render as Pain Girl. Why she is so named, I do not know, for they say that she is cold and without feeling."

They stood on the riverbank, peering into the gloom. Both waited silently; the soft lap of water was the only sound to be heard. All else was utterly still. Väinämöinen narrowed his eyes. He could not see the further shore; his wizardly *sight* failed. After some minutes had passed, the old man sighed. Looking up and down the river, he mumbled, "We must find the stones, the stepping stones that Turi found long ago—"

Suddenly an image appeared out of the smoky mists, a long grey shape gliding slowly and silently on the flood's dark current. Soon they could see it was a boat; within stood a maiden, suffused amidst a white light, as white as moon sheen reflected off the glassy surface of a cold northern lake. White too was her raiment, and unbraided hair, and the pallor of her pale skin against the gloom. Only her eyes shone red, as if fiery embers burned within. A long pole she held in her hands. Dipping it in and out of the darkling waters, she wove a path through the overhanging branches and canopy, drawing her boat near to the shore where Väinämöinen and Ulla stood as if enchanted. Then they perceived that her fair face was lined and streaked as if it were a vessel fallen to the ground, shattered, and yet still whole and intact amidst a cobweb of cracks.

And she opened her mouth and said, "I am Pain Girl."

Väinämöinen stirred and shook off the spell. Taking Ulla's hand, he led her into the cold water, wading into the river so as to climb into the boat. But the White Maiden held up her hand and her power surrounded them.

"You cannot cross," she said in a toneless voice as cold as the river water, the very sound of which hurt their ears. "You cannot cross. You are not dead. Go back to living lands while yet you may. You have no coin with which to pay the toll."

"We do not seek merely to cross this water," said Väinämöinen. "We seek your father, the Lord of Tuonela, Pain Girl, whom the wise say yet dwells on his island at the river's end. We must speak with him."

"Do I not know you?" asked Pain Girl, a hint of uncertainty in her flat tone. "Wizards are not welcome here, your magic unavailing. Go back to living lands while yet you may. Else I will take you and bind you in chains that do not break, and here you shall stay in torment and despair forever, even until the world's end, be it your doom or no. You have no coin with which to pay the toll."

"Coin we have," said Ulla. She drew her hand out of her cloak and opened her palm. Upon it lay one of *karhu's* teeth, shining like a diamond within which the light of the stars was imprisoned. "You know whence this came, from the moon's shoulder on a silver string. This is the tooth of *karhu*, whom I slew in yonder woods. Take it as toll for our passage."

Then Pain Girl's red eyes flared as she gazed at the thing in Ulla's hand. It seemed to Väinämöinen that, for an instant, her lips parted and she drew in her breath sharply with a hiss.

Who now can say what the shining thing meant to one such as the Maiden of Tuonela? For the teeth of *karhu* were objects of power, imbued with the essence of the living world itself. Perhaps the girl might make a spell with it to feel, but for an hour, the world's wind on her breast and sun upon her face or else to know and feel hope, or love, or desire, she whose spirit was cold and dead, who felt nothing for all eternity? She reached out her hand to Ulla and took the tooth from her palm; Ulla felt the maiden tremble at her touch. And Pain Girl stood within the little boat and looked upon the totem while the still water softly lapped the sullen shores.

"You may cross," she said at last. The fire in her eyes dimmed. "Step into my boat."

"We do not seek merely to cross the water," said Väinämöinen. "If you would have this thing, you must take us down the river to where your father waits. We must speak with the Lord of Tuonela."

"The river's path is not a straight one," answered Pain Girl. "There are torrents ahead and stony falls that no boat may pass, not even mine. I will take you to the farther shore. But there you must walk through the Dark Land, if you can, and so come once again to the river past darkling woods. More I cannot say."

Then Väinämöinen put his staff into the boat and climbed in, giving his hand to Ulla and pulling her next to him. That boat was rude and unshapen, no more than a dugout like unto that which the Erilaiset used in days of old to float down the lazy rivers or across little lakes when the world was young. Yet it had been fashioned from a tree both mighty and strong. It curved upward at the prow, its wet, dark wood roughly formed into the vague likeness of a skull, a hideous death's head with hollow, unseeing eyes.

They stood together in the boat while the White Maiden drew her pole up and down, the tooth still clutched in her hand. She pushed off from the shallows and into the stream, moving the boat stroke by stroke toward the shadows on the other side. The still air grew colder as they crossed, a chill which entered their very bones, cast a pall upon their souls, and darkened sight and hearing. At last, they gained the shore, and Pain Girl drew the boat up beneath a great, grey tree that reached its sad, trailing branches far out over the water.

"This is Tuonela, the Land of the Dead," said Pain Girl, motioning with her long arm toward the darkness beyond. "You must leave my boat. That which you seek lies within these marches, but do not hope to come through or return ever again to living lands as you are now. No hope lies within this land nor do the Dead return, save as ghosts or shades of what once was."

While Pain Girl steadied the little boat, they climbed out, wading in the stony, shallow flats until they came again to dry land beside the tree. Väinämöinen turned then and raised his staff.

"We may still have need of you, Pain Girl," he said. "Dark as the road may be, we may yet return, seeking passage back to whence we came. Heavy was the toll we paid; it should suffice for the return crossing too. Will you wait for us?"

But the White Maiden with the cobwebbed face made no reply. Her eyes dimmed still further as she stood cold and silent by the dreadful prow, luminous in the night. Then, taking the pole, she pushed off from the shore, trailing boughs brushing her long pallid hair as she slipped back into the current. Mists curled about the little boat as it slid away into the stream, disappearing into the river's foggy gloom. Yet Pain Girl's white light shone on for a bit, a patch of moonglow amidst the murk until at last it, too, vanished and all was black again, black as it had always been and always would be along that river of ultimate sorrow. And the soft splash of the pole as it dipped in and out of the water was swallowed up by the night.

Väinämöinen sighed and shook his head. The old man and the girl looked each other in the eye, reading one another's thought.

"We have crossed," said Ulla, the words falling dully from her mouth.

"So we have," said Väinämöinen. "So we have, child. Well, there is no use standing here, waiting. There's no choice but to trust her, as I do not know the way. Let us go ahead and see what we may find, Ulla." And then, with a last glance back at the slow, winding river, they went on down into Tuonela, Tuone's dark kingdom, the Land of the Dead.

Thick woods soon surrounded them. The river bent away to their right in the direction that Pain Girl had motioned. Väinämöinen hesitated.

"Through darkling woods," he muttered. "So she said. It must be impossible to follow the line of the river to Tuone's isle."

Together they plunged into the forest. Tall oaks and elms clustered in thick stands. Unlike the colorless woods, which marked the margin between life and death, there was color here. No moon shown in the sky, no stars twinkled over Death's Kingdom, but a murky twilight prevailed over all. At times a yellow glow suddenly appeared in one corner of the sky as if the sun sought passage through Tuone's realm, but always it was rejected and the twilight returned, the yellow light fading as swiftly as it had appeared.

Silently they trudged along with no clear idea of where they were going. All the while, terror grew in Ulla's heart. She remembered the first time she had mounted the stairs in the Seer's tower at Kyöpelinvuori. The same feeling of panic had come over her in that closed, dark place. The Seer's stair had its end, however. What end was there to the Forest of Death?

"Väinämöinen," she said suddenly, her voice quivering. She felt the woods closing in around her.

"Be strong, child," he swiftly answered. "You are not alone! I feel it too. Madness, madness and despair. Do not give into it! If you do, we will never leave this place."

On they continued through Tuonela's wood. Still they met no ghost, no soul of the dead departed. The land seemed empty. Ulla began to notice fell things about them, however. Many of the trees had faces, leering and evil. In others, skulls hung from the branches like fruit. Blood oozed like sap from bark. A cold wind broke through the stillness. Within it, voices of loneliness and regret called out to them. Fear enveloped Ulla like a shroud. She would have welcomed any enemy to fight, no matter how strong, rather than face the horror threatening to overthrow her mind.

Whether minutes or hours had passed, neither knew. Suddenly, the woods thinned somewhat. A hill loomed to their left in the distance. Red and yellow lights twinkled upon its shadowy slopes.

"See, child?" said Väinämöinen. "We have come the right way after all. Look at those lights. That is Manala, the City of the Dead. Great is that city, great and always growing, yet still there is always room for more."

They had only walked a short way along Manala's marches when at last they came upon the dead. Paths and trails now cut through the woods, leading to and from the city. Along these paths walked the shades of the departed. Mortal and Erilainen, Easterner and clan folk, master and slave—in Tuone's kingdom, all walked together, no matter their station in life. All riches had been left behind, all glory forgotten. Some were mere shades indeed, shadows left behind of souls who passed through, but others shuffled along mournfully, lamenting their fate for all eternity and desiring nothing but to return to the world of the living.

Ulla saw old people still draped in shrouds, their faces haggard and grey. Warriors walked past them blindly in rent and bloodied armor. Some were yet fair of face, but many were cadaverous, ghastly skeletons clad in rags and jangling chains.

"Do not look at them," said the old man. "Keep moving. They have no power over us save fear."

Yet even as Väinämöinen said this, the dead crowded nearer; the bony fingers of clinking skeletons clawed at them. Drawn to their life and the brightness surrounding them, the dead clutched at the wizards, seeking to feed upon the light. Ghostly voices beckoned, *Come to us.*

Panic gripped them both. They ran, tearing free from the shades and forcing a path through the spectral crowd. Väinämöinen struck down a rotting corpse that barred his way. Swinging her staff, Ulla beat back another, a warrior from some long forgotten folk that called out to her in an ancient tongue, still clutching the tattered remnants of his clan's banner. Climbing now, the wizards spied a copse of trees on the rise above them. The old man pushed aside a final assailant, a gibbering hag clad in rags. At last they reached the height, leaving the ghouls below.

Väinämöinen bent over, gasping. Cold sweat dripped from his face. Ulla shook like a leaf in the wind.

"Let us rest here a bit," he said, in between pants. "I think they will not follow us. Perhaps they must remain near to their city. No paths lead to this hilltop."

At that moment, a figure emerged from the shadow of the trees. An Erilainen it seemed, maybe an elf of some strange *väki*. However, he was dead, his features bloated as if by drowning. Approaching them, the elf came close. He gazed upon them, his swollen face contorted.

Grasping his own long hair, the creature pulled its own head from its neck and held it aloft. Worms and snakes boiled from the neck-stalk, spilling onto the ground. The head broke into a hideous cackle. Slimes pooled about its feet within which maggots crawled. A noisome stench filled the still air.

"Oh, Väinämöinen...," Ulla stammered, her senses reeling.

Transfixed by the horror, slack-jawed, the old man stood unmoving. Then he raised his staff and cried, "*Kadottaa!*" The staff blazed with light, blinding them. When the white light faded, the monstrous thing was gone.

Ulla slumped against the wizard. Breathing deeply, he took her hand.

"We cannot stay here. Let us move on. The heart of the madness is in this place. If we stay, we will be overcome. Praise Ukko that I had at least this much power left to me."

When they passed through the copse, the ground quickly fell again. They descended the hill's blind side, where the slopes of Manala and its horrors were lost to view. The flickering lights disappeared. At once, they felt the sickening despair abate; their panic lessened. Still, a cold fear remained.

Hand in hand, they walked down the hillside, entering yet another wood.

The trees were less close than before. No shades of the dead roamed here; all was still. The darkness deepened.

Recovered somewhat from her fright, Ulla began to contemplate this strange Kingdom of the Dead. No tale that she had ever heard in the Enchanted Valley or Laulavalaakso came close to capturing its loathsomeness. *Was this all that mortals had to look forward to?*

"What is the point of our lives?" she asked the old man. "Why do we struggle, only to journey to this nightmare in the end? The farmer's toil, the mother's care, the sadness and the strife—it seems a pointless, meaningless existence. I do not understand it."

"Do not let the darkness of Tuonela cloud your soul," answered Väinämöinen. "You know the answers to your questions. Toil and strife are the price of freedom, the freedom to choose. Your choices pave your own path through Tuonela. This is Löhi's future, not yours! Löhi's and all those who do evil. Do what your heart tells you is right, no matter the toil. Your path through Tuonela will then be clear, and Ukko's reward awaits on the other side."

"There is no clear path for us now."

"We are not dead," answered Väinämöinen.

Ulla dreamt again even as she walked, strange visions flashing through her mind. Finally, they came out of the wood. The river lay before them. Whether it was the same course that they had previously crossed with Pain Girl or one of its many tributaries, they could not say, yet somehow both knew that this was what they sought.

"We have found it," said Ulla.

"So it seems," Väinämöinen replied.

The dark water was still, a black ribbon meandering through the featureless landscape. No ripple troubled its glassy surface. Väinämöinen explored the bank, but Ulla walked toward an outcrop of stone sticking up from the shallows like a jetty. A small boat had been drawn up beside the rock, its unshaped prow resting upon the shore. She called to Väinämöinen. He joined her.

Like Pain Girl's boat, only smaller, the rough-hewn dugout would navigate the slow-moving flood.

"It could've been left here on purpose," mused Väinämöinen.

"Perhaps it was," said Ulla. The dark-haired young woman sighed. Staring up at the starless sky, a new measure of resolve took hold of her. *We are close, so very close.*

"Come, Väinämöinen. The last leg is before us, let us be swift."

Ulla pushed the boat into the water. Hopping in, she reached out to Väinämöinen and pulled the old man beside her. He held out his staff and cried, "*Kasvaa!*"

The staff doubled in length. Using it as a pole, he thrust the boat away from the bank. To his surprise, he realized the current flowed toward them, issuing from some distant, unknown source. So mild it was, however, that he had no difficulty driving them upstream. Ulla stood in the back of the boat, peering into the gloaming.

In and out slipped the pole, with scarcely a sound save a soft slap. Slowly, slowly they sailed upriver while the tumbled grey lands slid past. Minutes passed, hours—Ulla could no longer judge time's passage. All was dead here, everything forgotten. They journeyed outside the borders of space and time to an uncertain end. Still, Ulla stood erect, all fear left behind in the deathly forest's madness.

At last they came to a place where the banks disappeared, shrouded in mists. The slate grey sky blurred into a dimly guessed horizon. Wisps of cold steam hung in the still, wet air. Vapors crept like serpents across the dark water's surface. Väinämöinen raised the pole up and down. On they glided, blindly.

"We are in the lake," he said, his voice muffled.

So grey it was, so thick the fog, they seemed lost in a sea of cloud. Then Ulla's sharp eyes perceived something solid ahead. The mists parted; the grey clouds rolled back.

An island lay before them, a horn of rock rising up from the lake like a tower of stone. It was the Isle of the Dead, *Kipukivi*, Tuone's home.

High it rose toward the darkling sky. Tiny crystals glittered here and there upon its surface as if it were marble. Two piers of stone stretched out like fingers into the lake. Väinämöinen steered the boat between them, drawing near to the sheer, rocky shore that fell straight into the water, no landing to be seen. The isle seemed barren to Ulla, lifeless and featureless, too, except for two great statues carved from stone that stood upon a shelf.

Tall they were, tall and grey, looming out above the curling mists. The foremost, like a giant, held its long arms at it side. Its left hand held a rod of jet. Dark, hollow eyes stared blankly into nothingness. Behind it stood the image of a woman, perhaps, her stony tresses on her shoulder.

A chill crept into Ulla's heart as she gazed upon the figures. Suddenly, the hollow eyes came alive; the stony robes moved. These were no statues, no carven images of Tuonela's keepers. The wizards gazed upon Tuone, Lord of the Dead, and his consort.

"Who art thou?" said Tuone, his voice as cold as the ice of Pohjola, sharp as *karhu's* claws. "I do not suffer the living to enter my domain. Speak! For thy lives left behind are already forfeit and here in my kingdom shalt thou remain."

The wind blew at the sound of his voice, almost upsetting the boat. The old man steadied himself despite his fear, putting a hand upon Ulla's shoulder, and thus together, they drew strength one from another.

Looking up at the colossus, he answered, "Thou knowest who I am, Lord Tuone: Väinämöinen of Karelia. And this is Ulla of the Karhulaiset, she who bears the Mark of the Clan, chosen of Tapio. Together we have braved thy kingdom in search of you; for our errand is urgent."

"Then thou hast misjudged," said the woman, coming beside her husband. The mighty woman was indeed Tuonetar, Tuone's consort and the mother of his nine daughters whom she had born in Tuonela's darkness. Throughout the ages of the world, she dwelt with her husband in Hell, weaving the ropes and forging the chains that held the dead in thrall. And she was utterly without pity. But if Tuone was as cold as ice, his consort's fiery eyes glittered with malice while venom dripped from her tongue.

"Thy errand hast already failed, wizard," said Tuonetar. "How darest thou return to this land, where thou hast trespassed before? Thinkest thou that I do not remember thee? No grist for the lies that thou call spells shalt thou return with nor counsel to thine profit hear. This time there is no return."

"I do not come willingly," answered Väinämöinen. "But still, a man must do what he must do. And our errand closely concerns you or else we would not risk ourselves in Death's Kingdom."

Tuonetar hissed, a sibilant sound like a snake uncoiling itself ere it strikes. But Tuone said, "What errand of thine could possibly concern me? For I care not what happens in the world of the living nor do I trouble myself over its misfortunes."

"I come to beg your aid, Lord Tuone; we need a weapon with which to defeat Löhi. The Witch has overrun nearly all the Seven Lands and left them in ruins. Thousands have died before their appointed time. Only your power can stop her from making all the Far Northern Land her dominion."

"What is Löhi to me?" answered Tuone. "All souls come to me in due course. Whether they hasten or tarry in the world above is of little consequence. For time does not pass here and my dominion is forever. So, too, shall Löhi come. And thou shalt be here to meet her."

"And yet Löhi has usurped your authority," said Väinämöinen, boldly ignoring the threat behind Tuone's words. "She dispatches multitudes to Tuonela beyond all right. And she would set herself above the Vanhalaiset, becoming a god unto all the world and a blasphemy to Ukko. Are not the Vanhalaiset your brethren, Lord Tuone? Do you not rule by Ukko's will? For I, too, am Ukko's servant."

A red light kindled in Tuone's dark, hollow eyes and he spoke in rising anger.

"Thou darest to instruct the Lord of the Dead? Löhi is no Vanha—nor will she ever rule in my stead."

"But already she defies you. Dost thou not know that the Witch enters Tuonela against thy will, scorning thy command? Dost thou not miss those spirits that she has stolen from you, returning them to the waking world to darken men's hearts? And what of Lovêatar? Your daughter has disobeyed you and is loose upon the world, spreading despair and misery. She worships Löhi as her queen. Do you not wish her return?"

"Speak not of my daughter!" spoke Tuonetar sharply. "Thy insolence shall no longer be suffered. Now I shall bind thee and set thee amidst the frozen pools of oblivion where nothingness will teach thy tongue restraint."

Väinämöinen saw then that, about the Isle, Tuone's servants emerged from the misty shadow as nightmare shapes: vampires, skeletons, and succubae, beautiful to behold yet deadly, with batlike wings outstretched. But before the servants could take hold of them, Ulla stepped forward, speaking for the first time. And a light gathered about her even in that dark place.

"Will you not first answer the question, Tuone? Do you not wish for your daughter's return? You forbade her to seek the living world, yet against your law and Ukko's design, she dwells there. I have seen her."

Tuone leaned over the boat as if to strike it; his wife's fiery eyes flared with fury.

"Born into the Far Northern Land thou mayst be, Karhulainen, to become the Witch's enemy, but the Mark upon thy shoulder is empty in this kingdom. Poorly thou hast chosen and now thou shalt reap thy folly's yield. But as for my daughter, I shall account for her."

"How? She flaunts her freedom and defiance to your very face. Bound by your own law and Ukko's will, you may not enter the living world to seek her. She will never return while the Witch still lives. But if you give us what we seek—a weapon, a token that will surely slay Löhi—then I will deliver Lovêatar unto you and you may punish her as you will. Will you not bargain for your own daughter, Tuone?"

Then Tuone laughed, and the sound of it was like rolling thunder on the wings of the storm. Lightnings flickered in the sky.

"Bargain with thee? Thou hast no power over Lovêatar or any of my kin. Bargain with thee? Tuone does not bargain with mortals! Now thou shalt taste the full measure of thy offense."

Even as Tuone made as if to grasp her, Ulla reached into her pack. Swiftly she withdrew her hand, holding it aloft. And within it lay the jewel! Gleaming now like a star in the night, the jewel that held Lovêatar captive shone brightly, piercing the encircling mists and casting shadows all about that dark place where no brightness ever shone.

Tuone drew back; Tuonetar hissed. The shining glass projected an image like a twisted face, contorted, straining to break free of its bounds, then the image vanished, drawn back inside the magical glass.

And the Lord of the Dead had no doubt that his daughter was imprisoned within.

"How didst thou do this?" said Tuone menacingly.

"With the lies that I call spells," answered Ulla. "How else might a mortal trap Tuone's daughter? But what is that to you?

"Behold! Here is Lovêatar before you! I will deliver her unto you for the bane of Löhi, for a weapon with which to kill the Witch of the North. You may keep her locked within for an age of the world, for all I care. Consider carefully—Lord of Tuonela you may be, but I, Ulla, cast this spell and only I may unlock it. Never will I tell thee the word that can release her, never reveal the secret, unless you bargain. Nor can you torment me to obtain it, for it must be given freely and without press.

"Look into my heart! Until the end of time you may hold me here, but never will I speak. Grant the boon we ask of thee and the secret will be yours, and when we have departed, the power will rest with you. Decide, Tuone. Will you not bargain?"

And Tuone looked into her heart and knew she spoke the truth; for thus is the nature of such spells.

It grew deathly still, utterly silent. Ulla stood with arm upraised, the shining glass in her open palm. Väinämöinen heard the beating of his own heart.

It seemed the fate of the Far Northern Land hung in the balance of that moment. He dared not say a word.

Then the fell light about Tuone dimmed. The press of his thought withdrew. Tuonetar's malice retreated. The ghastly servants withdrew to their lairs.

"So be it," said the Lord of the Dead, his voice now empty and cold. Turning to his consort, he motioned. She reached her hand into the Kipukivi's stony pier as a man reaches into a watery pool. From it, she drew a mass of rock, shaping it like clay in her spectral hands. Handing it to Tuone, she transformed the rock into an arrow. Stone was the tip and stone the fletching, yet there was no doubt that it would speed true from any bow.

"This is the Arrow of Tuonetar," said Tuone. "No hauberk will turn it, no mail withstand it, though made winterfast of silver-steel. If it pierces Löhi's flesh, she will die and swiftly come to me. If even the slightest prick be made in any living creature, it will turn the one it bites to stone; for it comes from the Isle of the Dead. But beware! Only once may the arrow be sped."

Tuone reached out to take the jewel, but Ulla drew back. Slowly, the Lord of the Dead placed the arrow into her empty hand. It shrank to the size of a normal shaft; though made of stone, it felt light to the touch.

And as Ulla delivered the jewel unto Tuone, into his ear she whispered the words that might unlock it.

Then Ulla and Väinämöinen bowed deeply. Stepping back from the prow, Ulla stowed the arrow beneath her cloak. Väinämöinen quickly pushed the boat away with his staff. But as the boat slipped past the outstretched pilings, she called out to Tuonela's master.

"It was a good bargain, Lord Tuone. And I swear by my soul that I shall slay Löhi. Have thy folk keep watch for her; swiftly she comes."

Väinämöinen pushed on. The Isle of the Dead receded into the gloom. The king and queen of the Damned faded from sight until, at last, only Tuonetar's glittering eyes marked where they stood. Then they, too, vanished in the mists.

Coming back into the river, the two companions floated downstream upon the current. The boat seemed to need no guiding hand.

"What was the secret that unlocked the glass?" asked Väinämöinen, breaking their silence. Ulla wrapped her cloak more tightly around her.

"Only her name, spoken thrice."

The old man snorted. "Well and good. But let's make haste to leave this loathsome realm. Cold as he may be, they say that Tuone does not lie. Still, I do not trust him. And I do not wish to meet Lovêatar again should he choose to make trial of the spell ere we depart."

"He will not," answered Ulla, her tone so strangely confident that Väinämöinen peered at her beneath her hood. The girl looked the same, but the old man had senses other than sight. *She is changed*, he thought. *Aye, she is changed.*

On the right bank, trees marched as far as their eyes could see. Somewhere in the distance lay Manala. On the left bank lay a featureless terrain of muddy flats and dimly glimpsed depressions—the Pits of Tuonela. The miles slipped past. Soon they lost all track of time, half-asleep and half-enchanted, each wrapped in their own dark thoughts. Here and there sharp stones broke the water's surface. The hissing breakwater grew white. The current moved more swiftly now.

With a start, Väinämöinen came to his senses, realizing that they were picking up speed and that the land was starting to fall.

"Hei, Ulla," he called. "Take your staff and help me. We must get out of this current and closer to yonder shore."

Even as he spoke these words, the sound of rushing water grew loud in their ears. The creeping mists drew back; a steep drop emerged before them. Before they could act, the boat dropped over the fall and crashed into gurgling whitewater. Racing downstream, the boat twisted this way and that. White spray flew in their faces.

On his knees, clutching the prow, Väinämöinen cried above the sudden tumult, "Tuonenkoski! The Death Rapids! Hold tight, Ulla, and don't let go!"

The boat circled crazily as it rode the rapids. Waterlogged, it sank lower until great foaming waves splashed over the sides. Twice they hit boulders, almost jettisoning them from their perilous perch. Ulla could see nothing save the flying spray. Väinämöinen called out to her, but his voice was lost amidst the tumult.

All at once they shot over another fall and crashed into a boiling whirlpool below. For a moment the boat stood on end, then capsized. Plunging head first into the troubled water, still clutching her staff, Ulla felt herself jerked madly all about. Tumbling like an acrobat, she lost all sense of direction. The icy water gripped her like a vise. *I am drowning*, she thought. *After all this, I am drowning in the Tuonenkoski and will never bring the arrow back to the living world.*

Then, with a final jolt, the whirlpool released her. She popped to the surface.

The river took her, carrying her swiftly downstream. The dark-haired girl struggled to keep her head above its surface. Avoiding the sharp rocks and boulders as best she could, she caught a sudden glimpse of the reedy riverbank. The river took a sharp bend and the current briefly slowed. Lunging toward the reed beds, Ulla lodged her staff between two stones. Using all of her strength, she pulled herself out of the current and into the shallows.

Floating among the reeds, half drowned, Ulla could scarcely move. A hand grabbed her hood. Yanking her upright, Väinämöinen, spluttering and bedraggled, dragged her to the shore.

Ulla coughed for a long while until her lungs cleared of water, then lay dead still. Finally, she sat up, groaning.

Väinämöinen sprawled beside her, shivering.

"Can you walk?" he croaked.

"Yes. Better to walk than sit here freezing. I want to leave this place. And who knows what horror may find us here if we tarry long."

Panicking, Ulla reached suddenly for her belt. The arrow was still there beneath her pack and garments. She sighed.

They rose together, picked up their staffs, and set off. As luck or fate would have it, they had washed up on the shore that led back toward the crossing to the woods without color. The opposite shore lay dark and empty before them. Had they come to it, they would have been lost forever in the fields of oblivion.

Stumbling along, leaning heavily on their staffs, they again held hands. The trees grew thick as they left the rapids behind and set off through the woods. It did not take long for the strange feeling of enchantment to settle again over Ulla. The chill of her wet clothes faded; vivid dreams flashed before her eyes. Then the old man shook her, rousing her from the dream state for a final push. The dark visions vanished.

"Come, little one."

They stood atop a slight rise. In the gloaming below, Väinämöinen could descry the river.

"There it is," he said, his voice ragged. "Can you feel it? Like the sun on your face at noon. We've come the right way and our escape now lies before us, the crossing back to the colorless woods and to the Enchanted Valley where our bodies await us."

Ulla peered toward the riverbank.

"I can feel it," she replied.

Hastening down the rise, they made for the river, the gentle sound of which now came to their ears. Hope arose in Ulla's heart. *We might escape Tuonela after all.* She clutched the stone arrow beneath her belt. *I must carry it back from the spirit world to the land of the living. If not, everything was in vain.*

Passing through a final stand of elm trees, tall and silent, Väinämöinen stopped short. A figure stood there among the trees, barring their way.

A man as tall as Väinämöinen waited there, clad in bronze armor. Ulla immediately thought of pictures that she had seen in Tapiola of the ancient warriors of the Seven Clans. The warrior's breast plate was rent, his helm dented and scoured. Long yellow hair fell upon his shoulders. The scabbard at his belt hung empty and his sword hand was bare, but his left hand held a kite-shaped shield, the image of a bear's claw painted upon it. The warrior's face was burned and bruised, yet still fair; his blue eyes shone brightly in the gloom.

Fearing some horror, Ulla tugged at Väinämöinen, but the old man seemed rooted to the ground. Ulla looked at him. The wizard's eyes were moist; a tear spilled down his ruddy face. He trembled.

"Lemminkäinen," he muttered. "It is Lemminkäinen."

Ulla stared in amazement at the yellow-haired warrior, the High King of the Far Northern Land and greatest hero the Seven Clans had ever known.

"Lemminkäinen," Väinämöinen said again. He took a step toward the bronze-clad figure. Ulla grasped the old man's arm, holding him back.

"No," she said. "What did you teach me? This is only his shade. His mighty spirit passed through this place long ago. Do not touch him; do not go to him. He is only a memory of what once was.

"Come, *Isani*. Come!"

Ulla pulled the old man gently. Slowly, he relented. The dark-haired woman led him away, passing wide round Lemminkäinen's silent shade and walking toward the riverbank. Only once she looked back; nothing followed them.

The dark ribbon of the river looked just as they had left it. Across the way, they sensed rather than saw the colorless woods. Ulla's boots sank into the marshy turf.

"How can we cross?" she asked.

But even as she spoke, a boat appeared out of the fog, angling for the shore. The dreadful prow came closer. Pain Girl stood within, softly luminescent. Her cobweb-cracked face expressionless, her eyes' light extinguished, the White Maiden drew beside them. She motioned with her long arm.

"Step into my boat," said Tuone's daughter, and the man and woman winced at the very sound of her voice.

"Step into my boat and I will carry you across; for so I have been instructed. But hearken well to the words of the Lord of the Dead. If ever again you seek these shores, never will you return to living lands. For we will take you and bind you and here shall you remain with us, even unto the ending of the world."

Then Ulla and Väinämöinen stepped into the ferry. With a push of her pole, Pain Girl turned the little boat. They moved into the current. The pole rose and fell. Slowly, they crossed the river and the mists closed behind them, leaving Tuonela wrapped in eternal shadow.

Chapter Nine

Gathering Leaves

When Ulla opened her eyes, she saw Kaukomieli's yellow hair. He held her head in his hands, brushing back her damp, dark locks.

"Ulla, can you hear me?"

She didn't answer. Eyes fluttering, she turned her head. Across the smoky room, she recognized Mielikki sitting beside Väinämöinen. The wizard lay flat on his back, as if still entranced.

Ulla realized that her mouth felt very dry.

"Water," she said, weakly.

Kaukomieli poured cool water into her mouth from a bronze saucer. Coughing, the young woman lay back.

"Are you all right?"

"Umm," she muttered. Without warning, she shot upright, startling Kaukomieli. Panicked, fumbling about within her clothes, she first felt Longleaf, then something narrower secured next to her skin: the arrow. Squirming, she drew it out. Solid stone it was, barb, fletching, and all, yet light to the touch. Ulla sighed. She had returned the precious thing to the waking world.

"This is the Arrow of Tuonetar," said Ulla. "For this, we braved Death's Kingdom. This arrow will be the bane of Löhi and salvation of the Far Northern Land."

Ulla told Kaukomieli all that happened in Tuonela. As she did so, the horror of the abode of the dead fell away and the heaviness that had afflicted her mind seemed to dissipate. She was whole again, whole and safe, at least for the moment. For the first time in many years, she felt hope stir in her heart.

Kaukomieli listened in wonder to her tale of ghosts, phantoms, and monsters, and the dreadful presence of Tuone and his consort. When Ulla had finished, she took more water and a little bread, then he described what he had seen while watching over her mortal body.

For three days and three nights, Kaukomieli and Mielikki watched over them. Water they gave to them, but a wizard entranced could eat no food. Swiftly, Ulla grew pale and thin.

"No sign did you or Väinämöinen give, in all that time," said Kaukomieli "The hours passed; you lay still and silent. Mielikki said that there was no way to know where your spirit was or whether you would ever return.

"Then in the early hours of the final night, you stirred. You flung your staff, held tight in your sleeping hand, high into the air and cried out. Red lights flickered all about us. Väinämöinen, too, raised his staff and the old man's eyes moved wildly beneath closed lids. I have never seen anything like it. Slowly you settled back; the lights subsided.

"'They have found the one they sought,' said Mielikki. 'Let us hope they survive the encounter. Perhaps we will soon know.'

"It was not much longer, only several hours later, when Väinämöinen awoke and told us all was well. He fell asleep again, waiting for you, and here you are!"

Väinämöinen soon woke again and they talked together quietly in Mielikki's garden beneath the trees. The old man praised Ulla to no end.

"No one else could have done it," he said. "No one could've bargained with Tuone as she did."

"The Child of the Prophecy and Tapiola's chosen one," answered Mielikki. "Not in vain did I recall the old words. Yet there is still another journey before us and little rest for the weary."

Nonetheless, they remained in Kukkatarha several days, regaining their strength. Ulla, veteran of many journeys though she was, had seldom felt so spent. Her body ached and her wizardly power burned low. Väinämöinen, though similarly exhausted, was not content to sit in the Enchanted Valley while spring and summer passed, however. A sense of urgency gripped him.

Leaving Ulla at Kukkatarha, he returned to Väinölä to prepare for their desperate quest. He said little to anyone, even his closest folk and friends, for Löhi's spies might be anywhere. Her ears were always alert for news of Ulla, the only one left whom she truly feared, the only one who might yet mar her plans.

Väinämöinen planned to set out as soon as possible, indeed, that very summer. He thought it best for only a few companions to join Ulla for the dangerous journey north to Sariola, the Witch's Keep. The wizard sent messages far and wide to those he trusted, asking them to come to Karelia for counsel. To the *tietäjää* who still lived, he revealed himself after his long absence, imploring them to remain steadfast and support their people. He could not find the one whose counsel he valued most, however. Turi, his oldest friend, remained hidden from him and Väinämöinen grew ever more anxious for his safety. He spoke little about Turi with the others; it was too painful, but not a moment passed that the old man was not filled with worry.

When he had gathered all the news that he could and made what preparations were possible, the old man sent for Ulla and Kaukomieli. They stayed at Väinölä for several days. Väinämöinen allowed himself that much of a farewell and wanted Ulla with him. They spent time with Lempi and other friends, and Ulla almost felt that she was a child again, romping through the Enchanted Valley's beautiful and mysterious woods with Kirsikka.

After their return from Tuonela and unexpected triumph, Ulla felt an excitement that she had not experienced since Egan's death, but it was not happiness. Rather, she felt a sense of possibility return and, with it, worry. She actually relished it in a strange way. Hope also brought the possibility of loss. She had no illusions about what likely awaited them. Still, after so many years of hopelessness, the feeling was almost intoxicating.

The day before they planned to leave Väinölä, the old wizard disappeared for a long while. Ulla found him some ways away from the Great Oak in a small glade hidden amidst thick rowans and junipers. No Erilaiset lived nearby, but within the glade stood a mossy, grey stone, bare on top, scoured by the wind and rain until it seemed twisted into fantastical form. It was a seidi-stone, like the seidi-stone in the now silent Valley of Song, and one of the old man's favorite places. He had his kantele with him, but wasn't singing. It was a fine, warm day, and he sat atop the stone with the sun on his face, listening to the birdsong.

Ulla dropped her staff, swinging up beside him. The stone felt warm against her bare feet.

"You are too big to sit beside me," said Väinämöinen, without opening his eyes. "Many's the time we sat here when you were young. Would that I could recall those days to the present; but they're gone, so scoot over, and let an old man sun in peace.

"And what have you been doing with yourself, child?"

"The same as you, father. Pretending to be peaceful and forgetting for a while the task that beckons. It is pleasant to do so."

"Well and good. Yet if you pretend to feel peace long enough, be wary; you just might find you aren't pretending. After all, *One's own help is the best help.*"

Ulla laughed.

"So many words of wisdom you taught me here; too many to remember. So many tales. What was that one about the fox and the seidi-stone?"

"Ah, you remember that, do you?"

"Of course. Tell it to me again, just the same."

Then Väinämöinen smiled, thinking about times long past, when Ulla was just a little girl and her white legs dangled over the side of the seidi-stone as she listened in wonder at his stories.

"The fox was ambling through the woods one day when he came upon a shaggy bear sunning itself atop a seidi-stone, maybe the very stone that we're sitting on right now. *It would be nice and warm atop that stone*, thought the fox, who felt cold after the long winter. He knew he had to get the bear to come down first, however.

"'What are you doing up there, honey-paw?' asked the fox, startling the shaggy bear from his pleasant nap. The bear rolled over, peering down at his red-furred friend.

"'I'm taking in the sun,' said the bee-hunter. 'It's nice and warm up here.'

"'*Ka,* how foolish!' said the fox. He rolled about, laughing as if he had heard the funniest thing in the world.

"'What's so funny?' asked the bear, annoyed by the fox's antics.

"'You are!" said the fox, in between laughs. 'It's not warm atop any sei-di-stone; the spirit inside keeps it cool as frost all year long.'

"'It does?' asked the bear, surprised. 'But the breeze is from the south.'

"'No, it's not!" laughed the fox. 'It only seems that way since you're lying upside down. The breeze is chilly. Look how your fur stands on end.'

"'But there's not a cloud in the sky,' said the bear, 'And the sun is warm through the trees.'

"'Rubbish!' said the fox. 'Everyone knows the sun is watery and weak this time of year. It chills your bones from the inside out. You'll catch cold and die if you stay up there much longer. See how you shiver!'

"The bear was thoroughly perplexed. Even though he had felt nice and warm moments earlier, it now seemed cold atop the stone. He had no idea what to do.

"'But how can I get warm?' he asked the fox.

"'Do what I do," said the red-coat. 'There's a lake just down the trail a few miles away The ice is gone. The water warms from the bottom up, so if you jump in and stay there long enough, you'll be heated, too. It may seem cold at first, but after a while, it will feel like a sauna.'

"Straightaway, the shaggy bear jumped down from the stone and ran off down the path since he wanted so badly to be warm. But the fox just laughed, for real this time, and soon was sunning himself atop the seidi-stone and luxuriating in the warmth.

"And the lesson is...?"

"The lesson is to trust your instincts," answered Ulla. "Don't let someone tell you day is night when the sun is staring you right in the face." Laughing, Ulla continued. "Ah, Väinämöinen, now that was just as I remembered it. I daresay not even Kirsikka could tell it better, and she imitates you better than anyone I have ever known."

For a while they sat silently as the yellow sun shone upon them. Then Ulla sighed deeply and began to question the old wizard about their journey.

"So this is quite likely the last time we shall ever sit here together," she said.

"Quite likely," he replied.

"Quite likely the last time either one of us shall see Väinölä."

"Aye, I should think so."

"So you believe our journey hopeless?"

"With you, child, there is always hope."

"You contradict yourself."

"Do I?" the wizard said mildly. "Only mortals think in straight lines. An Erilainen sees the true shape of the world."

"How will we ever find Löhi?" said Ulla, exasperated. "How can we ever hope to avoid being captured by her servants in the very heart of Sariola? Do you really believe the arrow will kill her?"

"Have you been practicing?" asked Väinämöinen.

"You know my aim is true; I'm a good shot."

"Then there is hope."

"But can we really find her? How do we even know she will be in Pohjola?"

"Seldom does Löhi leave Pohjola," answered Väinämöinen. "Her *etianen* roams the Far Northern Land at times—or sneaks into Tuonela—but her living body remains in Sariola, where her power is strongest. Atop the Kipuvuori, the Mountain of Pain, she stands and watches all the world pass by. She is no Vanha! Unlike the Vanhalaiset, she is bound to place and season. We will need luck, aye, we will, but if chance or design favors us, perhaps we shall find her."

Ulla paused, considering the old man's words. It seemed impossible that they could catch the Witch unawares, even if they somehow made it to Pohjola without being caught themselves. Then Ulla thought upon all Väinämöinen had taught her since she had chosen the trail for singers, the trail that the *tietäjää* follow all the days of their lives.

"The hope is in the choice," she said suddenly.

The old man smiled. "So you reminded me, just a few weeks ago. Aye, child; hope is in the choice and victory will be found there, too. Indeed, we have already won, come what may. Take comfort in that!"

Then, suddenly in earnest, the old man took her hand and held it close. Yellow sun spray lit her pale, freckled face and the girl's dark hair shone like jet.

"Ulla, listen to me. You are the mightiest *tietäjää* the Far Northern Land has ever known, mortal or Erilainen. You are mightier than Lemminkäinen of old. Come what may, the victory is already yours. No shadow can darken your spirit or keep you from Ukko's reward. Remember that when things seem darkest or if you find yourself ever alone."

The next day Ulla and Väinämöinen left Väinölä. Bidding farewell to its folk, they took to the path toward the Ankkaportti and soon came to the Mustajouki, the dark, slow stream that marked the Enchanted Valley's border. The sun was shining and the Näkkia did not show themselves, remaining hidden in their murky lair. Mielikki, Tulikki, Janus, and Satatieto waited beside the water. Together, they took to the narrow path that led to the great road of the Karelian Forest and the lands of the Reindeer Folk.

When they reached the standing stone, they found Kaukomieli waiting for them with several Karelialaiset. Mielikki had sent him ahead to gather horses and supplies to speed their journey. Midnight and Starchaser stood there among the other steeds, excited to see their masters after so long. The horses and ponies bore leather packs filled with hard, round loaves and the dried grouse that the Reindeer Folk took on long journeys. All seemed well-prepared, but the woodsmen were ill at ease. They brought bad tidings from beyond the forest and were loath to see the great heroes depart.

"Dark clouds gather outside the forest," they said. "All is amiss with the other clans. The Easterners ride about our borders and come east of the Jouksi, camping where they will without fear. And there are darker things about, evil things from old tales. They have crossed the river and crept within the forest's eaves. We do not wish to see you depart. Soon there may be war and battle within Karelia itself. Why must you go fight in other lands when there is need for you here?"

"We are not all departing," answered Väinämöinen. "The Erilaiset will always come to your aid. But you are right to be wary and remain hidden in the strong places you have prepared. Be vigilant!"

They rode on then, the Erilaiset and Reindeer Folk together, as swiftly as they could through the forest until at last they came to the Green Gate where the totem of the Reindeer Folk stood in its lonely vigil. That was where Väinämöinen had arranged to meet those whom he had summoned. From there, the band would set out on the quest of Pohjola.

To Ulla's delight, Ilkka awaited her. The Wardens' chief had been in Etelamaa that summer, seeing to the building of the great towers that the Swan Folk hoped would stem Löhi's rising tide. Several scouts also arrived, including Taika, the Erilaisen woman who long ago had brought Egan to the rescue of Linnavuori when Ulla was a little girl. But all brought bad tidings, filled with rumor of ruin and defeat. Worst among them was the tale of Sá, who had reached the Green Gate the very day that Väinämöinen and his party arrived.

"Verily, Turi was with me," he told them, sadly. "For he intended to seek out Lovêatar with me as his only companion. This was early winter of last year, when Lovêatar haunted the lands of the Swan Folk. But I had other pressing business with the March Wardens and we parted for that time. I tried to catch up with him afterward, but scarcely had I reached the borderlands that once belonged to the Karhulaiset when I was ambushed by Löhi's servants. Dark elves were there, Haltiatar of Pohjola; I barely escaped with my life. I fled back toward the old lands of the Bear Folk. I do not know what became of Turi. Perhaps he continued to Etelamaa. Perhaps he was slain or taken by the Moonface, who also roams those parts; I do not know. I could not find him again and enemies pursued me.

"A long road I had to escape, for I had no other choice but to flee north while the dark elves chased me. A hard winter it was, but some of the Karhulaiset who remain hidden north of the Fence sheltered me. At last I returned to the lands of the Seven Clans, but no tale did I hear of what became of Turi. Then I hastened here to tell Mielikki and Väinämöinen what I had seen."

Väinämöinen, filled with regret, held himself responsible for Turi's disappearance. Ilkka's news was no better.

"Glad I was to receive your summons, Väinämöinen. But before I left Etelamaa, word reached me of defeat in Tavastia. A strong force came south this summer, the strongest in several years. The Neck is overrun; goblins came as far south as Kyöpelinvuori. The old lands of the Seer are despoiled. King Aslo was ambushed and slain, all his guard defeated. The queen, Vara, escaped to a tower manned by Wardens and rallied the nearby folk to her. My men say that if not for her resolve, Tavastia would be lost. But now even Tapiola is threatened and the Hare Folk believe the end of the world is come."

"And what of the Elk Folk, the Hirvilaiset?" asked Väinämöinen. "Does Teemu still resist the enemy in Deep Länsimaa?"

"Teemu returned to Siinesaare and, last we heard, still held out. But they are cut off now from any hope of succor."

So went the news of Ilkka and the scouts, and all was bad. Tavastia stood upon the precipice and if the Hare Folk fell, what hope could there be for the Seven Clans?

While the others made final preparations, Väinämöinen took a small group into the woods and told them why he had summoned them. He spoke of the journey to Tuonela, Ulla's great deed, and the weapon she carried back. Finally, he told them of their intent to seek out the Witch herself in Pohjola.

None disagreed with his plan, no matter how desperate it seemed. The Arrow of Tuonetar gave them new hope.

Now the scouts reported that all of the Witch's servants sought news of Ulla. The price on her head had swelled beyond the riches of kings, and it would be paid to anyone, of any race, who delivered her to Löhi. So Väinämöinen knew that they would be hunted as soon as they left the forest; speed and secrecy would be their best defense. He proposed that only a small group accompany Ulla to better hide from the Witch's spies.

Väinämöinen, Ulla, and Kaukomieli would go, of course, and Tulikki with them. Mielikki herself wished to go, but the old wizard denied her.

"Trust me in this," he said. "Greatest of the Erilaiset you may be, Lady, but your power is strongest in our lands. You are needed to preserve Karelia should all else fail."

Väinämöinen picked Ilkka, too, for, although he was now the Lord Captain of the March Wardens, he saw no hope of victory in arms unless Löhi herself was defeated. The sixth confederate surprised Ulla, for Väinämöinen chose a Menninkainen whose people came from a distant dell in the far corners of the Enchanted Valley. She had never met Pirtto before, but the stout little man was a powerful wizard, gifted in the arts of illusion and seeming.

Lastly, Väinämöinen thought to take Janus or another of the Haltiatar who knew well the lands north of the Marches. But just then an elf came unexpectedly to the Green Gate with a stranger whom Väinämöinen had sought. The two had journeyed far through dangerous lands to reach Karelia before the company set out. The stranger surprised everyone, however, for he was neither a man from the Seven Clans nor an Erilainen—he was Itäläisen.

Ragnaroskii was his name, or so the men of the Seven Clans reckoned it in their own tongue, but mostly he was called Ragnar. He had ridden into a camp of elvish scouts the year after Sumuvuori, bloodied and beaten. His own clan had disobeyed Löhi's orders and refused to submit to the incomers from the far east, brought in by the Witch to replenish her forces after the battle. He, alone among his kinfolk, escaped the slaughter. Soon after,

Ragnar had met Väinämöinen and served as a scout with the Erilaiset in the east of High Länsimaa. He proved a valuable spy, as he knew all the ways of the Itäläiset and might go among them at times. The man hated Löhi and blamed her alone for the destruction of his people. Väinämöinen had especially sought him out to aid them on the quest.

Neither Ulla nor Kaukomieli had heard tell of Ragnar. They looked askance at the brown-haired Easterner with his long, drooping mustaches and the symbols of his clan etched in color upon his skin. Ilkka adamantly refused to accept the man as a member of their company.

"Whatever good he has done as a scout may purchase his life," said the March Warden. "But an Easterner he is and remains. What is to stop him from betraying us all to his kinfolk the first time chance allows?"

"My kinfolk?" answered Ragnar, his words thick with the Itäläisen accent. "My kinfolk are dead. I have fought alongside these elves for several years now. If you pursue the Witch and seek her ruin, I will help you. No other life is left to me."

But Ilkka would not relent.

"So you say," the Warden replied. "But from the North Marches to Tavastia, I have fought your kind—Raiders, murderers, pillagers of village and farm. The Itäläiset are the scourge of the Far Northern Land, its enemies. I will not ride with one such as this."

"Murderers, pillagers of villages," said Väinämöinen. "Do not the Seven Clans also have these aplenty? Evil is no stranger to any folk, nor good, for that matter."

"Come, Ilkka," said Mielikki. "Judge men by their choices. Ragnar has done much good for the Kaamoslaiset, though you did not know it. His help may prove invaluable on the hard road ahead."

"I would do without such help, though it clears a road to Pohjola before me," answered Ilkka. "Tell me, Easterner; did you fight at Sumuvuori? Did you see the king slain? Did you hear the cries in the woods of the dead and dying as we made our way back to the Marches?"

Ragnar said nothing. The Warden walked away. Ulla, uncertain of her feelings, looked at his face. She saw the eyes of the Easterners who had caught her in the woods near Grankulta. She also saw the faces of those she had herself slain, and these were many.

For a whole day, Väinämöinen debated Ilkka. At last the wizard prevailed; Ilkka grudgingly agreed to Ragnar as a companion since it might help Ulla and since he himself was unwilling to forego the journey.

"You ask much of us," he said to Väinämöinen. "And I wonder at your insistence, but your advice has always been sound. If not for you, Väinämöinen, the Seven Clans would long ago have fallen under Löhi's dominion. I cannot forsake you, Ulla, or the others after so long, nor would I dishonor the memory of all our friends who have fallen. I will do as you ask."

So on a fine, warm day, the little band of mortals and Erilaiset set out from the Green Gate of the Karelian Forest on the quest of Pohjola. The great wooden reindeer stared blankly after them as they moved down the path. Mielikki and several others rode with them for a ways. Ulla, dressed in red and green Karelian garb, much too warm for the season, fidgeted with the long, bronze-clasped cloak draped down her back. She wore her hair braided after the fashion of the reindeer folk. *Pitkälehti* and *Pojhanpiikki* hung from her belt and a bow, finely crafted by the elves of Taikalaakso, was strapped across her shoulder. A quiver filled with arrows came with it, but Ulla kept the weapon of Tuonela hidden away.

Väinämöinen rode upon Starchaser, his great yellow boots thrust into his stirrups. The wizard's fine, crimson tunic was bordered in golden spirals and flecked with bronze. However, it was Ragnar's dress that took Ulla by surprise.

Ragnar had abandoned the green and brown clothes of a border scout for the traditional garb of the Itäläiset. He wore black leather armor over a crimson shirt, his greaves traced with strange designs. A curved sword hung from his belt.

Ilkka's face betrayed his anger, but he said nothing, riding with Tulikki at the back of the line, as far from Ragnar as possible.

They stopped briefly in Metsäposti. Sacked and burned by the Itäläiset, its people had all fled into the forest the previous year. Only a few had recently returned. Osmo, the Master, greeted them.

"I don't know where you are going, Väinämöinen," he said. "But our hope is less without you. I wish you good luck; may you return swiftly to the forest."

"But the forest is great, Osmo," laughed Pirtto, who rode a feisty, shaggy pony with a mind of its own. "It's really only one wood from here to the mountains. We might return to a different spot and you'd never know it."

"The woods are great indeed," said Mielikki. "Tapio's power flows from one end to the other of this Far Northern Land, but the Wizard will always return to its heart, to the Great Oak of Väinölä.

"Farewell, Väinämöinen! Farewell to you all! Fare you well on this journey and may the blessings of the Vanhalaiset go with you. The Erilaiset will await your return. Do not despair, not even when things seem darkest. Through Death's Kingdom you have passed only to bring new hope to all our people. Hearken to the words of my prophecy:

> *When the cold hand reaches southward*
> *Reaches with its frozen fingers*
> *Comes a child into the Northland*
> *All the clans to bring together*

Then Mielikki embraced Tulikki and Ulla, pressing something into Ulla's hands. Smiling, the beautiful Lady of the Forest made a final gesture of farewell to the company, then turned back with Janus, Satatieto, and the others. They rode away toward the woods; only Taika remained with the seven, for she was guiding them to the Fords of the Jouksi.

The horses snorted.

"So here we are," said Väinämöinen at last. "And here we don't need to stay. Let's be off!"

"*Well begun is half done*,' said Kaukomieli. "We have tarried too long already."

"*Iron must be forged while it is hot*," said Ulla. "I feel the need of haste upon me."

Pirtto laughed.

"You taught them well, Väinämöinen. Maybe too well; they sound more like you than you do yourself nowadays, holed up in that big tree and all."

The old man cast a dark eye upon him.

"Do they now? Well and good. Much better than sounding like a gnome from the wrong side of the Valley where the trees are as short as their masters."

With a last look at Metsäposti, they took to the trail heading to the hills and the river. Ulla unwrapped the tiny bundle that Mielikki had pressed into her hands. She had forgotten it at Kukkatarha, but the Lady of the Forest had remembered. Within the soft leather pouch lay two figures, the twins from High Länsimaa that Big Janni had carved so long before.

Chapter Ten

The Lands of the Easterners

The group journeyed northwest through the narrow lands between the forest and the Jouksi river. It was dangerous. The Itäläiset rode at will throughout the North. Moreover, it had become difficult to cross the river on horseback. The Easterners had taken or destroyed the flat-bottomed ferry boats and the only natural ford was far to the south in Etelamaa.

That was where Taika came in. The strange Erilaisen woman had scouted the lands all about the Jouksi. Each year, temporary fords appeared in places where ice had blocked the river in winter, flooding the nearby flatlands. Taika knew where just such a ford had opened. She rode next to Väinämöinen, telling him about her recent experiences in the occupied lands that once belonged to the Karhulaiset. Their luck held and they reached the river without incident. It did not take Taika long to find the ford, a broad fen where the Jouksi ran in many fingers through a reedy bed.

"Well done," the old man said to her. "It is still open. The Witch may watch the southern crossings or look for us to build a great spell-enchanted boat of logs to carry men and beasts across the flood. Such a deed might take many days, leaving us exposed to spying eyes."

"Spying eyes may be anywhere," said Taika. "But less likely here, maybe. The Easterners use the old ferry nigh to Metsäposti. Still, do not tarry; no place is safe any longer."

"You know what to do?" asked Väinämöinen.

"Indeed," replied Taika in her odd, singsong manner. "I will ride south and set phantoms of you dancing about the forest's eaves, then pass into Etelamaa, and spread rumor of Ulla's return to the Stone City."

"It will cause worry in the city when we do not appear," said Ulla.

"So it may," said Väinämöinen. "But that cannot be helped. Better for Löhi's servants to hear that we ride south while we actually make for Pohjola. If we don't surprise her, we've no hope."

Taika bid them farewell, riding swiftly away south along the line of the river. The seven members of the company dismounted, leading their horses through the reeds and into the water, Väinämöinen and Tulikki in front. Pirtto, too short, was obliged to mount his pony while Kaukomieli led it across. The water ran deep, up to their necks at one spot, but they gained the other side without losing their baggage. Wet, bedraggled, and chilled to the bone, they mounted up.

"Let's be off," said the old man, wringing out his beard. "Taika's words were wise; the river is no place to linger. Praise Ukko that the sun is shining and the day is warm!"

Väinämöinen's plan, such as it was, was to pass east of Lake Suurijärvi, striking the North Road above Gamla. The old road to Pohjola, by far the swiftest way to Löhi's Keep in Sariola, was closed to them since the Witch's servants were always upon it. The lands of the Bear Folk where Ulla's people had lived were now largely deserted, however. A few scattered Itäläisen farmsteads lay here and there, but Ragnar advised that large groups of horsemen seldom used the North Road any longer.

"The land is no good so far north," he pronounced, as they rode along. "Farmland and pasture are better close to *Sēdjina*." *Sēdjina* was the Easterners' name for Keskimaa.

"But the Itäläiset always used the North Road," declared Ulla.

"No longer. The *Maizhniki* take the Queen's Road south, then ride along the river. There is little need to journey in the wastelands. Everything north of the Fence is now the Witch's land. She fears no attack."

"So you think we will not meet any of your kinfolk?" asked Väinämöinen.

Ragnar grimaced at Väinämöinen's words.

"My kinfolk," he muttered. "*Btogneya.*"

"I did not say that," he continued. "There will always be some riders north of *Gemla*, that cannot be helped. But fewer go that way now than in the past. Perhaps our luck will hold. We shall see."

"And what of the camp at Sumuvuori?" asked Ilkka, with the edge in his voice that could always be heard when he spoke to Ragnar, which was seldom.

"I do not know. It was no longer needed after the battle. Four winters I lived there with my clan and our herd. Most died during the big fight. I don't think any men live there now, any *Maizhniki*. But Löhi has other slaves."

"Goblins," he hissed, as if the word disgusted him. "*Besov.* The Witch's goblins. Some of them may still be there. They creep about everywhere, especially in winter."

Väinämöinen had feared they would find enemies east of the great lake of Länsimaa, but the land seemed deserted, the miners gone, and the villages abandoned. Marsh encroached upon the trails. Despite the reek from the fens and bogs, the land seemed peaceful, a pleasant place to journey through. Pirtto soon became the group's entertainer. Red-faced, short, and stocky, the jolly gnome constantly told tales and jokes and especially delighted in prodding Tulikki, whom he had once known well. She took his good-natured jests in stride, shaking her head in mock exasperation.

"*Phew*, Väinämöinen," said the Menninkainen. "These marshes stink. Leave it to you to lose us in the middle of a bog. It doesn't seem to bother Tulikki, though, does it? After all, she's accustomed to living in swamps."

"What would you know, Pirtto, about what I am accustomed to?" replied Tulikki.

"Oh, I've heard all about you. Lived for years all alone in the wild when you should have been in your mother's lovely garden. I heard the Näkkia didn't even recognize you when you came back to the Ankkaportti; thought you were a Hiisi, all covered in mud."

"Being alone is not so bad, Pirtto. If you tried it some time, you might find yourself with an audience that actually enjoys your stories."

"No, thank you. I prefer the company of others, even if they're dull. Your cousins are my favorites. Ah, the *Metsänaitoa*. The tree maidens aren't the brightest, mind you, but how lovely they are. I wonder that you could be away from them for so long. Then again, I understand. Being around such beauties all the time could make some feel inadequate."

"Rather like always being the shortest one in the *pirtti*?"

"I like being short. Better for avoiding trouble and slipping away unnoticed, like when old Väinämöinen is in his cups and throwing spells about. Besides, I can become tall anytime I wish."

Without a word, the gnome suddenly shot up three times his real height, turning into an ill-proportioned giant with a round, lolling head. It was only an illusion, but the Menninkaiset were masters of illusion and Pirtto, perhaps, the best of them all. The mortals were startled, nonetheless. The bobbing head winked at Ulla, but Tulikki snapped her fingers, and the gnome was instantly himself again.

"Best stick to your own size," she said. "Your pony's made for midgets, not monsters."

As they rounded Suurijärvi and approached the North Road from the southeast, Väinämöinen grew more cautious. He studied the sky, watching the clouds and stars. Twice he reached his mind out, using his *sight* to search the nearby lands. Ulla did the same. They saw nothing, only woods, marsh, and the wild animals that now had the north of High Länsimaa to themselves.

Ragnar often scouted ahead in the early morn or when they stopped at twilight. Though still summer, the days grew noticeably shorter. The

Itäläinen ranged about, searching for signs of his kinfolk or other servants of Löhi. Like the wizard, he came up empty. Apart from stacked, yellowed birchwood that might have been left by either Wardens or Easterners years before, no sign of camps could be found.

As a rule, Ragnar said little, and the others largely left him alone, except for Väinämöinen. Ilkka watched him with dark eyes. Ragnar avoided Tulikki and Pirtto, off put by the strange little gnome and by Tulikki, an Erilainen from an unknown *väki*, such as the Easterners feared. Ulla and Kaukomieli felt awkward around the lanky, long-haired Easterner. Sometimes Ulla caught him watching her, but he would quickly look away. After that, she dreamed about him, imagining him to be the man who had caught her in the woods on the day that Grankulta was burned. Yet the man treated Väinämöinen with a respect bordering on reverence and, to the surprise of all the others, Ragnar sometimes invoked Ukko, as if he had come to accept the beliefs of the Seven Clans and honored the Vanhalaiset.

One night they sat around a campfire. Birch logs sputtered yellow flame. The horses grazed nearby on long summer grass. The company feasted on dark rye bread from their packs and roast rabbits that Ulla and Tulikki had shot with their bows. Väinämöinen told them to enjoy the fire; he expected to reach the North Road the next day. Once on the road, they would light no fires, nor do anything to draw unwanted attention.

Ragnar sat a ways apart until Väinämöinen called to him to join them. Then the Itäläinen sat cross-legged by the popping, crackling blaze as twilight deepened. He took the meat Pirtto offered him—the little man was also their cook, when they needed one—and the old wizard spoke with him about their journey's next stage. This was why he had wanted Ragnar in the company. If they met any Itäläiset, Ragnar would talk their way out of trouble. Väinämöinen wished to reach the Marches and disappear from Löhi's sight into the Wastes by trickery, not battle.

Kaukomieli listened to the horseman describing the lands of the Easterners and suddenly asked him the question on all their minds.

"What exactly happened with your folk, Ragnar?" he said. "What made you realize Löhi is evil?"

The Easterner hesitated, reluctant to speak about himself.

"My people are dead," he replied at last. "The Witch is responsible."

"But how did they die? At Sumuvuori? And why did you follow her in the first place?"

Ragnar looked around. All eyes were on him. The man sighed.

"Löhi came among us long ago," he began. "I was only a child. I do not remember a time when her name was not upon all lips.

"Itäläiset you call us, Easterners. But there are many peoples and clans to the east of your lands. We are not all one folk. There was always warfare among us, never enough land for our families and herds. Löhi came to my clan and to others, promising to deliver these lands to us, to give us the room we need."

"By ruining *our* people?" said Ilkka, sharply. "Burning *our* villages, killing *our* children?"

Ragnar met the Warden's dark gaze.

"Nothing was done here that has not been done in our own lands," he said at last. "Such is life in the east. And these lands that you call home were ours in the beginning—or so our tales say. But Löhi came to us as a great spirit, a goddess. She told us that she had returned to this world to set it aright and that her servants would be richly rewarded. That those who fell in battle would find paradise.

"Well-nigh all my kinfolk followed her. When the time came and we were called, the warriors of my clan rode to Pohjola and then down into battle. My uncle, my cousins, my three brothers—all my clan, my *rodu*, the *Siniyerechnie Rodii*; the Blue River people, in your tongue. We answered the call."

"And you spread ruin," said Ilkka.

"I fought," answered Ragnar. "I do not deny it. Many raids, many battles. For four summers, I fought for the queen. And then came the great battle."

"Sumuvuori," said Ulla. "Where Egan died."

"Yes. The battle where your king fell. I did not see him. The Witch was determined to destroy him. 'He must be killed at all costs,' she said, or else all of us would perish from his black magic.

"Already, even before the battle, some among us grumbled. The queen's promises had not come true. She needed us to fight for her, but none had known that so great a war lay ahead, a war without end.

"After the battle...nothing was the same. My cousins and two brothers had died; our herd destroyed. My clan was in ruin. Two things came from the East that spring: news and men. The news was ill. Our homeland had been taken by other riders. My mother and grandmother were displaced from our village near the blue water and worked as serfs. The men who came, riders from strange clans far away, were just as bad. We wished to return home, those few of us still left, to help our folk, but Löhi forbade it.

"The Moonface came among us. He told us to lay aside our disputes. We were Löhi's subjects now. We took some farmland in the Elk country, hoping to send for our people later, but the newcomers came in greater numbers."

"In Deep Länsimaa," said Ilkka. "And what did you do to the Elk Folk who lived there? Enslave them?"

"The serfs worked for us," Ragnar replied, matter-of-factly. "It is no different in our own lands. I am sorry for their loss. I cannot change all that has happened. I wish that I had never come to the Far Northern Land. It is a cursed place."

"But what happened to your clan?" asked Kaukomieli. "Why did you come to us?"

"The newcomers," answered Ragnar. "They wanted our farms. The Moonface told us to work it out among ourselves. The chief of the incomers invited my uncle and brother to a meal, a feast, to eat, drink, and talk about our differences. After they drank, the newcomers attacked my people, killing them, *all* of them. The snow was red with blood. They rode on our farms then and slew everyone who remained.

"My uncle had left me behind at the farms, and I barely escaped with my life. I was an outlaw then. I rode to the Marches, pursued by riders and goblins. Then I came upon the elves. I thought that they would kill me, but they did not. They spared me. Spared my life."

Ragnar fell silent. Väinämöinen fed the crackling fire. Ilkka turned away, drawing his hood over his face.

"Löhi was the doom of my people," Ragnar said, suddenly. "I have nothing left. I will fight against her until my dying breath."

* * *

The road was dangerous, but they had no choice. The land was heavily wooded north of Gamla, sprinkled with lakes, pools, and stagnant meres, and it would take too long to pass through the marshland. Väinämöinen wished to ride hard and reach the North Marches swiftly. Pirtto, the illusionist, had prepared a special *loitsu* to trick any enemies.

Ragnar, clad in his red and black garb, rode next to Väinämöinen, ready to speak with any Easterners they encountered. The old man knew a little of the Itäläisen tongue, but not enough to talk their way out of trouble. Ragnar would take the lead there, while Pirtto's spell would make them all look like Itäläiset or serfs.

Väinämöinen would appear to be a clan chief, his long hair spilling onto Itäläisen leather armor. Kaukomieli and Ulla became young riders with Ulla's hood pulled over her face. Pirtto would make himself look like a tall Itäläisen horseman. Ilkka and Tulikki remained as they were, but with their weapons hidden, two slaves from the Bear Folk accompanying their masters.

Pirtto could not keep the spell up all day, every day. Such illusions were difficult, just like Tulikki's Cloak, the spell that Ulla had woven to steal into Työ's camp. However, the gnome was ready on a moment's notice to weave the illusion the instant they spotted anyone.

They traveled up the North Road, passing through the empty lands of the Karhulaiset where the Bear Folk once dwelt. The slash-and-burn rye farmers were gone; their villages and hamlets abandoned. White birch trees lined the way, marching into the distance as far as the eye could see. The weather held, fine and warm. Animals scurried away at the sound of their horses' hooves. At night, the lonely sound of wailing wolves carried on the gentle wind. With the people all gone, wolves had returned from the wastelands, reclaiming their old hunting trails. They did not bother the company, however. With plentiful game, they had no need to hunt mounted horsemen.

On their third day on the road, they encountered Itäläiset at last. An obviously well-used trail cut away from the road. As they approached it, they met a group of Easterners in a wagon, settlers from a nearby farm. Ragnar spoke briefly to them, but the Easterners asked few questions. They showed more interest in trade than the company's destination or its errand. Pirtto's spell held true and the Itäläiset clearly suspected nothing.

The next day, they met a similar group. Again, after a brief exchange with Ragnar, the Easterners moved on. It began to look like Väinämöinen's plan would work.

"If Löhi or one of her sorcerers isn't watching the road, we may escape," he said. "Luck or fate seems to be with us. Let's hope their *sight* is turned elsewhere!"

"Pshaw," said Pirtto. "It's my magic that's gotten us this far. My magic and Ragnar's golden tongue. These weak-minded mortals can't see through my spell."

"There is still a long way to go," said Tulikki. "Let's not become overconfident."

True to Tulikki's words, the next group of Easterners they met were not farmers, but a pack of a dozen horsemen, well-armed, heading south. They appeared suddenly round a bend in the road, and Pirtto had only just enough time to weave his illusion before they approached.

The leader, a middle-aged man with braided, salt-and-pepper hair and a mottled complexion, wore black leather greaves and arm bands wrapped around his red shirt, high boots, and gold bands in his drooping mustaches. He pulled up his horse, held his hand out in a gesture of both warning and greeting, and then looked Väinämöinen and his companions up and down.

"*Brivi, parni. Udevlinye javjastya, bolsoji udevlinye*," the man said in the harsh Itäläisen tongue. "Hail, lads. We did not expect to meet anyone so far north. Where you going with your *polucaii uduvolstii*?"

"Up the road," replied Ragnar in the Easterners' language. "To Severnosh."

"Severnosh?" The Easterner's tone change. "Severnosh is empty; has been since spring. Why are you going there?"

Ragnar shrugged.

"We were sent there."

The Easterner exchanged glances with the rider to his left, his look darkening.

"Sent? Who sent you? What's your *rodu*?"

"What is yours?" asked Väinämöinen, roughly, doing his best to imitate Ragnar's thick accent. The wizard spoke authoritatively, as a chieftain would, and reached out with his power to compel the horsemen.

"My name is Dagna, Dagna of the Crow Clan," the leader answered slowly.

"We heard the Crow Clan was up in the wasteland," said Ragnar.

"So we were, but we're riding back now. Who are you? Who sent you to Severnosh?"

"Lord Kuupää sent us," said Väinämöinen. "My name is Illik, of the Adder Alliance. My son, Borlia," he added, nodding toward Ragnar. The Itäläinen blinked in surprise.

"Kuupää?" the leader said. "He sent us north as well."

It was Väinämöinen's turn to be surprised.

"The Moonface sent you north?" asked Ragnar, cautiously. Behind him, Ulla and Kaukomieli discreetly gripped their staffs, disguised as spears by Pirtto's magic. Ilkka loosened his sword. They couldn't understand a word, but it seemed the encounter might go badly.

"He sent us up the road over a week ago," said the horseman. "Looking for spies. We're on our way back now to make our report. The *polucaii uduvolstii*—are these the spies Kuupää is searching for?"

"No," said Ragnar. "They belong to my father. Our errand is different, but no less urgent. Come, Father, let's be off. If Kuupää is waiting for you," he said to the Easterner, "you had better be off too. His mood is foul when he's left waiting, and it seems you are empty-handed."

Ragnar and Väinämöinen kicked their mounts, moving forward. The old wizard nodded a gesture of farewell. The Easterners made way, but eyed them suspiciously as they passed. Ulla felt them watching the company until they rounded the bend and disappeared from sight.

When they had passed out of range of the horsemen, Väinämöinen finally broke the silence.

"Slow, slow. Don't hurry, not yet," he said. "Not until we are sure they aren't following us. Then we must make haste and ride swiftly."

"I can't keep the spell up all day," said Pirtto.

"Just a little longer, until we are sure they are gone," said Väinämöinen.

Ragnar explained to the others what had been said.

Tulikki sighed. "Why did you tell them the Moonface sent us, Väinämöinen?"

"How could I have guessed he was in Lansimää? It seems we are hunted after all and have kept just ahead of the hounds. Still, it is better to know the danger behind us than be unaware of it. And if I read the Easterner's words rightly, the road ahead is clear. We must put many miles between us and the Moonface, wherever he may be lurking. Let's hope he's left these parts and it's days or weeks before this Dagna finds him."

"You did well, Ragnar," the old man added. "Very well. I could not have pulled that off. We never would have made it this far without you. Tapio has blessed our choice of you for a companion."

After a while, they stopped to let the horses graze. Ragnar rode back down the road alone. Ilkka went into the birchwood. Returning, they reported all was quiet; no one followed. They companions rode swiftly then, as swiftly as Pirtto's pony allowed, anxious to put as many miles between them and the Easterners as possible. If the Moonface learned of 'spies' on the road, the chase would be on.

The *tietäjää* put their power into all their horses, giving them strength to endure the hard ride north. They rode day and night. The countryside passed by, silent and unseen, brooding forest on either side. Here and there, long stretches of pine-crowned eskers lined the way. The road seemed sunken between them. As dawn broke, the shades of night gave way once more to a world of color, revealing white bark, green leaves, and blue sky. Ulla noticed the telltale signs of old trails branching off the road.

Ulla had been on the North Road only twice in the fifteen years since *karhu* left his Mark upon her shoulder, once when she had made her hunt and again on the long march with Egan to Sumuvuori. The dark-haired young woman was infinitely more powerful now. Kaukomieli could sense a change just since her return from Tuonela. Ulla had challenged Tuone and won. She bore Tuonetar's Arrow in her quiver. Her magic had grown so potent that Kaukomieli could feel it at times as he rode next to her, like a copper kettle filled with water right at the boiling point, threatening to spill over.

The company stopped to rest and graze their horses beside a little pool. Ulla led Midnight to a stand of thick grass, wandering a ways from the others. She stretched her sore legs. No breeze moved the still, warm air. She looked up. Silhouetted against the clear blue sky stood a tall drumlin. Shadowy trees crowned its height.

Her heart beat faster. Midnight's tail swished; Ulla brushed stinging flies from her eyes. She blinked. A path clearly marched up the gentle rise.

Head swimming, she steadied herself against the horse's flank. She felt delirious.

Väinämöinen was suddenly beside her. She took the old man's hand in hers.

"This is it," she stammered. "Here, this path; this is it."

"Yes, child," he answered. "So it is. I would not have stopped here had I realized it."

Midnight whinnied, sensing her excitement and surprise.

"You passed by this place once," Väinämöinen continued. "You did not wish to know then; you did not wish to see it. Do you now feel differently?"

Ulla closed her eyes. She took a deep breath, exhaling slowly. Power coursed through her.

"Yes," she answered at last. "Yes. I am not afraid now."

"Yes, you are," said Väinämöinen. "But that is not a bad thing."

Ulla turned to him. "I am going," she said. "It will not take long. Wait for me here."

"Oh, no," he said. "You are not going alone. Not there or anywhere else."

"Kaukomieli," he called.

As the young man approached them, Ulla realized the others were watching her. Her eyes met Ilkka's; the Warden's face showed pity.

"Come with us, Kaukomieli," said Väinämöinen. "There is something Ulla must do. Mount up."

The three *tietäjää* mounted their horses. Väinämöinen called back to the others.

"Rest the horses," he cried. "We will not be long."

They rode up the drumlin along a grassy path through a sparse birch wood. Tall white trees rose among juniper bushes. Squirrels scurried from tree to tree at their approach. The path led to a teardrop-shaped lake. Turning sharply, it continued on toward a green rise. Bilberry thickets and blueberry bushes clustered along the lakeside. Ulla's hair stood on end as they passed.

Gaining the rise, Midnight reared and snorted. Ulla reined the mare in.

Before them lay the village of Grankulta.

To the left of the path lay a field, clearly slashed and burned long ago. Tall grass and wildflowers grew upon what once, perhaps, was meadow. Stands of young birch sprang up unevenly, but the woods had not yet reclaimed the lost ground.

To the right lay another clearing, closer to the tree line. A ruined, stone-piled oven, now the abode of birds, sat alone amidst a sea of green sage. Grassy mounds like the tombs of old kings rose at regular intervals along the roadside. Smaller mounds lay scattered behind them.

Nine mounds, Ulla counted, nine. But the young woman knew that these were not tombs, but all that remained of the *pirttis* of her home village.

Ulla swung down from Midnight. Leaving Väinämöinen and Kaukomieli behind, she walked toward the second mound. Larger than the others, crowned with tiny white sage flowers, it held her gaze. Black timbers peeked out from the turf; stones mingled with the earth.

Ulla felt suddenly drawn, unwilling, by another power out of the waking world and into the colorless woods where spirits wandered. Her vision narrowed. A gust of cold wind broke the still air. Shaking, she realized that she was no longer herself, no longer the tall young wizard, staff in hand and sword on belt, who had challenged Löhi. She was a little girl again, a little girl with dark hair clad in a simple homespun shift.

The little girl with dark hair peered into the open door of the *pirtti*. It was twilight; the sun had already sunk behind the trees and a soft yellow glow filled the western sky. Pilkka, her shaggy dog, ran to greet her, almost knocking her down.

Ulla stepped across the threshold. Her bare, white feet softly patted on the earthen floor. Päivikki was sweeping with the birch broom. Meria sat beside the stone-piled hearth, stirring a large copper pot. Her aunt spotted her. Setting the broom against the wooden chest that Ulla's father, Big Janni, had made, Päivikki knelt before the little girl; she smiled.

"You look more like your mother every day," said Päivikki, laughing. She swept aside a stray lock of Ulla's unruly hair. "Did you find your uncle and cousins? Are they back from the lake yet?"

The little girl shook her head.

"I told you to find them," said Meria, sighing. "Now I'll have to do it myself."

"Let them be," said Päivikki. "Reiko won't come back until the baskets are filled with fish. The days are still long; it won't be dark yet for some time."

Päivikki went to the hearthside. "Come, Lumikki," she said, still smiling. As her aunt gathered her into her arms, she took a hot rye cake from the hearth, carefully handing it to the little girl. Meria took another. The dark rye cakes were drizzled with melted fat and butter—it had been a good year for the Bear Folk in the north of High Länsimaa.

"When your uncle returns," said Päivikki. "I want you to take all the husks in the threshing shed to the goats; there are three baskets full. Hebla's boy will help you. Take them away from the sheds, out past the last *maja*. Put the baskets back in the shed. Can you do that for me?"

Ulla nodded.

Laughing gently, kissing the girl atop her dark head, Päivikki returned to her cleaning, sweeping the one-room *pirtti's* floor free of the day's debris. Pilkka curled up beside the hearth, one eye on Meria as she tended the cakes and porridge.

Nibbling on the rye cake, Ulla watched her aunt. Clad in a simple, pale blue dress with a long white apron, her kerchief drawn tight over her flaxen hair, Päivikki moved swiftly and with purpose. Ulla noticed the slight swell of her aunt's belly.

A rustling outside of the *pirtti's* open doorway signaled Reiko's return. Pilkka leapt up and ran to meet him.

"Ulla!" called the man's voice from outside. "Ulla, come here!"

The little girl walked to the open door.

"Ulla!"

As she stepped across the threshold, she quickly looked back, meeting her aunt's blue eyes. Päivikki stood still, watching her, but the expression on her aunt's face had changed.

"Ulla!"

And then it was Väinämöinen beside her, Väinämöinen and Kaukomieli. Ulla trembled. Her staff fell to the ground. Midnight nuzzled against her.

Kaukomieli touched her shoulder, speaking a single word; the trembling stopped. She looked into his eyes, as blue as Päivikki's, and then at Väinämöinen.

"Are you all right?" asked the old man. "You left us."

"I... I can go back. I can go back, Väinämöinen. It is all still there, waiting for me."

The old man paused.

"I do not know what the vision was, though I can guess," he said. "But it is no more than that, a vision."

"No, this was different. It is there for me. I cannot explain it, Väinämöinen, but it is all still there."

"I do not think so, child," the old man said, gently. "Even for a spirit so strong as yours. But if such a thing was possible, if you could leave the waking world for a moment caught in time, it would not change what has happened here or alter the fate of those left behind to carry on the battle. Choose carefully, little one. Much may depend on it."

Ulla gazed toward the green mound, the only true home that she had ever known. Turning back to Väinämöinen, she buried her head against him, sobbing. Kaukomieli stroked her hair, tears welling in his own eyes; he could comprehend her loss all too well.

The horses reared up again, restless. A horn sounded in the distance. Kaukomieli suddenly recognized the sound of horses' hooves riding hard, galloping toward them from the direction whence they had come.

"Väinämöinen!"

Shaking off her tears, Ulla picked up the staff. They quickly mounted, trotting back to the road just as Pirtto appeared, flying as swiftly as his pony could muster.

"Hei!" cried the little man, pulling up-red faced and panting. "I thought

I'd never find you. Itäläiset, Itäläiset are here—lots of them. They attacked us on the road."

"Where are Ilkka and the others?" asked Väinämöinen. More horns sounded in the distance.

"I think they fled east, into the woods," gasped Pirtto, "But I cannot be sure. I came this way to warn you. They chased me. I thought they were right behind me."

"Well, we won't wait here for them to find us," said the wizard. "Let's go—not up the road, but through the woods!"

Kicking their horses, they raced past the green mounds and into the birch wood. Without another glance back at Grankulta, Ulla followed Väinämöinen into the trees. For the second time in her life, Easterners chased her through the forests of her homeland.

* * *

"Follow me!" cried Ilkka. The Warden's horse crashed through the trees. Ragnar and Tulikki trailed close behind. Horns sounded all around them. The Easterners' harsh voices echoed throughout the woods.

They had been waiting for Ulla to return when, without warning, Itäläisen riders appeared from both directions, charging with drawn swords. Pirtto spurred his pony up the path to Grankulta, weaving a glimmer to dazzle the riders' eyes. Ilkka, Ragnar, and Tulikki took the opposite course, plunging into the forest to the east.

It was hard going. The horses leapt over fallen logs and bramble, skirting pools, stones, and mossy turf. The Easterners gave chase. Less used to riding through the forest, the red and black garbed horsemen fell behind, sending their arrows whistling through the woods instead.

"They will maneuver around us," shouted Ragnar. "I know their ways."

"So do I," replied Ilkka. "They think to cut us off to the north. We must turn south, double back to the road. That is the only way to elude the Easterners without becoming lost. Then we must try to find Väinämöinen."

With Ilkka leading, they managed to distance themselves enough from the pursuit to try his plan. Striking a stream, they rode down its course. The horses slipped, but none fell.

"Tulikki," pleaded Ilkka. "Can you help us?"

"Not unless we stop," she answered. Her horse had been slashed by an Itäläisen sword and her own leg cut.

"I cannot hide all of us, but perhaps I can set phantoms chasing about the woods to confuse them. It is not a simple *loitsu* to weave."

"We cannot stop, not yet," said Ilkka. "Not until we gain the road."

He drew his horse in. His companions came up beside him, all three breathless, their horses fearful and skittish.

"Listen!" exclaimed Ilkka. Cries and shouts echoed back down the watercourse from whence they came, but dimmer now. The nearby woods were still.

"We've escaped them, at least for the moment. Now, cut back to the road. Keep the sun over your left shoulder!"

Weapons drawn, they left the stream and moved slowly toward where Ilkka guessed the road lay. The trees drew close. Great mulberry thickets barred their way. The turf grew firm. The woods suddenly opened onto a grassy clearing where fire had burned some years before. They cautiously left the cover of the trees.

"Are you sure the road lies this way?" asked Tulikki. "I am already confused."

"One thing a Warden knows is to never be sure of anything in the forests," said Ilkka. "The best scout can quickly become lost on a chase. What do you say, Ragnar? Straight across the field?"

"I do not have your craft," he replied. "But it does not matter. We must keep moving or they will find us. Hiding is useless."

Ilkka examined the yellow sun to get his bearings. He kicked his horse.

They trotted across the glade, approaching the tree line where thick birches again blocked their way.

Just then a shout rang out. Ilkka's horse reared, whinnying in surprise. Tulikki reined hard. Four horsemen emerged from the woods directly in front of them. The two on the outside gripped drawn bows with arrows nocked. Twisting round, Ilkka saw four more coming up from behind—two with bows at the ready and two clutching spears.

They were all Easterners except for the two riders in the middle. Before them in the flesh sat the Moonface and his lieutenant, a Dark Erilainen clad in black.

The sun blazed on the Moonface's silver mask, creating a riot of shifting color against his jet black armor and golden shield. No weapon lay in his black-gloved hand, yet a menacing magic wrapped all about him, a deadlier threat than any blade of mortal make. And his companion from Pohjola held an iron chain.

For a moment, all was silent. Ilkka and Tulikki hesitated, tense, poised to strike or flee. Ragnar sat a ways apart, his dark eyes hidden. The riders, at point-blank range, could not miss.

The Moonface broke the silence.

"Well met, daughter of Mielikki," he said, his voice both sinister and hollow. "Well met, indeed. Art thou so surprised that I know thee? I know thee and all thy deeds. I know all the days of thy life. And I have been waiting for thee; for thee and the ones who ride with thee. They are near, are they not? Ulla Karhulainen and Väinämöinen?"

Ilkka made a sudden movement as if to kick his horse, but Tulikki grasped his shoulder, restraining him. The Moonface laughed.

"A wise choice, *Metsävartija*," he said. "Little worth do I find in thee compared to thy mighty company—wizards, *tietäjää*, and Tulikki, daughter of Mielikki herself, the undying Lady of the Green Woods. What use couldst thou possibly be save as an encumbrance upon the way? Still, I may have more use for thee than thy friends do, and perhaps thou canst bargain for thy life. Tell me, why art thou, why art all of thee on this forsaken road to the Wastes? The queen may yet spare thee shouldst thou answer truthfully."

"You are brave, Kuupää, if you think that eight of you are a match for us," declared Tulikki. "Brave or foolish, for you claim to know all about me, yet seem not to understand your peril. I suggest you make way, until another time when you have more companions of your own kind about you. For, if you strike any blow here, it will be your last."

The Erilaisen woman seemed to grow, straight-backed and stern, her white power reaching out to contest the darkness; but the Moonface only laughed again, cocking his ghastly face to one side as if in mockery.

"Cloaks I have about me that thou cannot see," he replied. "Woven by the greatest magician in all the world. And there are far more than eight of us. But our chain shall suffice to bind thee, woman, and with us to Pohjola thou shalt return."

"No chain can bind me," proclaimed Tulikki, fiercely. "I am free!"

"So thought Turi," said the Moonface. "Or didst thou not know? And this chain has yet other companions. Only one more journey shall Väinämöinen make, and it shall be his last. Together with him shalt thou face Löhi's judgment, and even thy skulking mother shall be powerless to save thee."

"Be not so certain, mortal," she replied. "You may know my name, but I do not remember you or your magic, whether weak or strong. I think you are no Erilainen, nor do you comprehend our power; but it shall surely reach out to take you nevertheless."

"*Ka!*" cried Kuupää, in rising wrath. "Tuonela take thee!" Then, turning his scrutiny to Ilkka, he said, "Now, *Metsävartija*, consider carefully, for you will be the first to die, stuck like a pincushion. Tell me if Väinämöinen and Ulla are nearby or your next breath will be your last."

Before Ilkka could reply or Tulikki act in desperation, Ragnar called out. Ignored up to now by all save a single archer who covered him, the Easterner held his arm aloft, scimitar turned down, in the Itäläisen gesture of parley.

"Lord Kuupää," he exclaimed. "Spare me, Lord! This witch, this *biitsa*, she and the old man bewitched me. I am myself again now."

The Moonface swiftly turned his steed to face Ragnar.

"Who art thou?" he asked, coldly.

"I was a scout with Devgar's clan, my lord, when they took me captive not far from the Fence. I do not remember how long ago it was. The old man came to me first, then others. They bewitched me with their spells."

"Then I shall grant thee release from thy misery," said the Moonface, motioning to his rider to shoot.

"No, lord! I can take you to them!"

Even as the arrow flew, the Moonface shouted out the *kalma* to slow it, making a quick gesture to turn the dart aside. It whistled past Ragnar's head.

"Take me to whom?" asked Löhi's captain.

"To the old man, to Väinämöinen and the girl, the dark-haired witch with the Mark on her shoulder. They are not far."

The Moonface hesitated. Even though his face was hidden, Tulikki sensed his excitement.

"Thou knowest where?"

"Yes, lord," answered Ragnar. "I know where they are. I know the path. They went to the dark-haired witch's birthplace, to the old village where she lived. That is why they came here. There is some hidden magic in the place, perhaps."

"Ragnar!" screamed Ilkka, "Traitor! How dare you!" He shook with fury.

"*Ka*, enough scorn I've endured from you, *Metsävartija*," Ragnar answered derisively, bitterness welling in his voice. "I am among my own folk now. But it will be my pleasure to kill you first to prove my loyalty."

"Ragnar," Tulikki said, her arm still grasping Ilkka's shoulder to hold him back, her tone deadly serious. "Ragnar, listen to me. If you betray us, if you betray our friends, then your plight is hopeless. No forgiveness will you find, no solace. The darkness of oblivion will surely overtake you, oath-breaker. Your soul will be lost forever."

Ragnar moved his horse closer to the Moonface, narrowing his eyes. He spat on the ground before Tulikki.

The Moonface raised his rod.

"Enough," he cried, his power reaching out so that even Tulikki's voice stopped in her throat.

"Where is Ulla Karhulainen's birthplace?" His voice quivered. "What does she seek there?"

"I do not know what she seeks, but the place is not far. No more than a few miles. I can take you there."

The Moonface still hesitated. All seemed to waver on the sword's edge. The Easterners, tense, drew their bows even tighter.

"Lord?" said Kuupää's lieutenant.

"Bind the woman with the chain." he commanded at last. "We shall take her to Pohjola. And if thou shouldst resist, daughter of Mielikki, thy friend will die ere the words of thy spell form upon thy lips. But this Itäläinen shall bring me to Ulla. Thus will he purchase his life."

The Dark Erilainen brought the chain forward. Ilkka and Tulikki looked one another in the eye. Tulikki mouthed 'No,' but Ilkka raised his knees to kick his horse, regardless of the arrows trained upon him.

And at that moment, Ragnar sprang.

Slashing at Kuupää's rein hand and thigh, he gashed the horse's flank deeply on the upward stroke. Reins cut, the Moonface's panicked steed bolted, throwing him to the ground. Next, Ragnar struck the lieutenant across the face. He tumbled down beside his captain, the heavy chain on top of him.

The startled Easterners shot wildly, then dropped their bows and drew swords. Spurring his horse, trampling the Moonface underneath, Ragnar came to grips with the nearest rider. He cut him down with one swift stroke.

Ilkka, as shocked as the Itäläiset, struggled to master his horse. Tulikki had just enough wits about her to grasp what was happening and act upon it.

"*Tuli!*" she shouted. A white fireball blazed in her hand. She thrust it toward one of the riders. The man launched his spear, piercing her outstretched arm, but the next moment the fireball struck him. He ignited. Shrieking, his steed reared in terror. The Easterners' horses bolted. Tulikki just managed to calm their own mounts with a hastily uttered word. They reared, but did not dash off.

"Now for it!" yelled Tulikki. "Ragnar, Ilkka, follow me!"

They made for the woods, but as Ragnar rode past the Moonface, he staggered up, cursed, and cast a short, iron-tipped lance. Ragnar was hit; he doubled over, drew the dart out, and rode on.

With the Easterners scattered and Kuupää unhorsed, the three companions fled through the forest while the burning man's screams echoed behind them. They soon struck the road. Turning north, they galloped for a mile, then cut westward into the birch wood.

"Are you all right, Tulikki?" gasped Ilkka.

"I'm bleeding, but it's not bad," she replied.

Ilkka slowed until Ragnar caught up. "Don't ever do that again!" he cried. "I was about to run you through! Next time you plan to be so crafty, tell me about it first."

"Your blow would have never landed," said Ragnar. "They'd have put an arrow in your back before you drew your sword and you never would have learned your mistake."

Ilkka laughed.

"Maybe," he said. "But that was quite a trick you pulled. If not for that silver mask, I believe you would have done the Moonface in. No one has ever bested him from what I've heard."

"You are hurt, Ragnar," said Tulikki, noticing the Easterner's blood-stained shirt for the first time.

"A spear," he said. "No worse than your arm. But there is no time to tend to it now."

"No," said Ilkka. "We need to keep moving and find Väinämöinen."

"Do you think they know about the Easterners?" asked Tulikki.

"They must have heard the enemies' horns, whether Pirtto reached them or not," said Ilkka.

"Where would Väinämöinen have gone?" asked Tulikki.

"I do not know," said Ilkka. "Not back to the road. Perhaps they fled north. Our best hope may be to draw the Easterners after us and away from Ulla. So be it. Hers is the true errand; our task only to speed her on her way."

They turned north. Riding through the thinning birch wood, the ground turned marshy. Twice, Tulikki's horse became stuck in the boggy turf. Ilkka noticed many dead trees, their bark stripped. The farmers who once lived here had meant to fell them, burn the land, and plant rye. That was long ago. They were gone now, slain, captured, or else fled far away. Only the stripped trees remained.

Ragnar fell behind, then slumped over his saddle. The Easterner's long, lank hair covered his face.

"Hey there, Ragnar," called Ilkka. "Keep up! Are you all right?"

Ragnar straightened a little in the saddle, then waved them forward; they moved on. Once or twice they thought they heard horns and distant cries away southeast, but they saw no signs of the Itäläiset or any others of Löhi's servants. Most importantly, they did not meet the Moonface. Having no idea if Kuupää was badly hurt or not, they feared the sorcerer might ambush them again. The Warden looked doubtfully at every thick stand of trees or bushy hollow.

The sun sank. Twilight was upon them. They had put miles of wilderness between them and the site of the ambush. They halted beside the still water of a dark lake just as the setting sun cast a net of gold upon the glassy surface.

"Where in the Far Northern Land can Väinämöinen be?" Ilkka said, exasperatedly.

"For shame, for shame," said a deep voice. Turning around, Ilkka saw first Väinämöinen, then Ulla, Kaukomieli, and Pirtto emerge from the trees. Kaukomieli held his staff aloft. Ulla had an arrow trained on them.

"And the Lord Captain of the March Wardens to boot," said Väinämöinen. "Your woodcraft is failing you, Ilkka."

"Väinämöinen!" cried Ilkka. "Why am I not surprised? But you would be weary, too, if the Moonface had chased you all day."

"The Moonface?" asked Ulla. "You saw him?"

"We not only saw him; he captured us. Tulikki and Ragnar are both hurt, but Ragnar here saved us. I take back my angry words and beg his pardon; we'd be dead now, or worse, if not for his bravery."

"Captured you!" exclaimed Väinämöinen. "I can see there's quite a tale here, but maybe now is not the time to tell it. We were chased by the Easterners ourselves, but never saw the Moonface."

"And I hope to never see him again," said Ilkka. "He was deadly. It hurt my eyes even to look upon him. Ragnar attacked him, though; cut him with his scimitar. Almost killed him beneath his horse's hooves, I'd wager. That was a mighty deed; without it, we might not be alive."

"Tell us your tale, Ragnar, swiftly. We may have eluded our enemies for the moment, but we cannot linger in these parts."

As if called, Ragnar's horse trotted forward. The Itäläinen, hunched over, was silent.

"Ragnar?"

Ragnar swayed back and forth, then dropped to the ground with a dull thud.

"Ragnar!"

Kaukomieli leapt down first, cradling the Easterner in his arms. Ragnar's head rolled back, his face deathly pale. A thin spittle of blood stained his lips. His blue eyes were open, the pupils fixed and unmoving.

"He's dead!" cried Kaukomieli, noticing now for the first time the man's blood soaked shirt. "He's dead, he bled to death."

"That's impossible," said Ilkka, coming to his side. "A spear pierced his side, but he told us that the wound was not serious."

Väinämöinen quickly knelt beside them and took Ragnar's hand. Eyes closed, he took a long, deep breath. The old man trembled. After a minute, he opened his eyes again.

"It is too late," he said, shaking his head. "Too late. His spirit has passed across the river in the White Maiden's boat."

Kaukomieli smoothed back Ragnar's lank hair. He placed his hand on the man's eyes and gently closed them.

"I cannot believe it," said Ilkka. "If only we had known. He said nothing."

"There is nothing you could have done," said Väinämöinen, inspecting the wound, a small hole that nonetheless had torn through his vitals. "Not even a *tietäjää* might have saved him, not unless he had been succored in the first few moments, perhaps. Who can say? And if you had stopped to do so, to lay hands on him and pray to Ukko, you all might have been captured or slain in short order. No doubt he knew this."

They stood in silence as dusk descended. The weary horses grazed on marsh grass.

"Come," said Väinämöinen. "The hunt cannot be far behind, not if the Moonface lives. We must go."

"But we cannot leave Ragnar like this," cried Tulikki, passionately. "He saved our lives."

"I will not leave him to rot unburied or toss him into a shallow grave, his bones dishonored by wolves and wild beasts," said Ilkka.

Kaukomieli caught Väinämöinen's eye, then motioned with his head at the glassy mere.

"When folk died in the lowlands during flood time in Deep Länsimaa," said Kaukomieli, "It was hard to find solid ground in the forests. We cannot bury him easily or quickly, I think. But the lake will receive him."

Ilkka shook his head. "He deserves better."

"So he does," said Väinämöinen. "So do we all, but Kaukomieli is right. The pool is deep, the water still. It will receive him."

"Come, Ilkka, Tulikki. It is fitting that you help me."

Together they waded waist-deep into the water. Ulla, Kaukomieli, and Pirtto watched from the shore. Väinämöinen looked up into the sky. The last ray of yellow escaped through the trees, gilding the old man's face with pale light.

Mighty Ukko, fearless father,
Father of uncounted children,
Take our brother, faithful follower,
Welcome him into your kingdom.

Faithful follower of the Vanha,
Friend to those in need of comfort,
From the East he came unbidden,
Take him now into your kingdom.

They released Ragnar. For a moment, he floated on the surface. Then, slowly, the Easterner from far, far away disappeared beneath the dark water.

The yellow light faded. It was night. The Great Bear shown in the northern sky. Silently, they mounted. Leading Ragnar's horse, they set out through the wild. Wolves wailed mournfully in the distance, but they saw no sign of their enemies while the darkness lasted.

Chapter Eleven
The Maanalaiset

The nights grew noticeably cooler. Harvest season hastened in the southlands. The midnight sun had long since vanished; dusk fell earlier each day.

The six remaining members of the little band rode north from Grankulta. They journeyed through the wilderness, returning to the road just once for a mad gallop of several hours. Turning northwest, the companions picked their way across a land of little lakes and thin woods. No men had ever lived here except for wandering Karhulaiset. If any remained, they must have hidden themselves; the countryside seemed empty.

Väinämöinen feared pursuit. They made no fires. Each night, they took turns keeping watch. If the Moonface followed them, he did so stealthily. The company saw no sign of the Easterners.

At length they came to the North Marches, passing into the Wastes beyond.

"Now's the time, Ulla," said Väinämöinen. "We cannot take the horses any further into the Wastes. Starchaser and Midnight made the journey to Sumuvuori and back, the only horses to do so. They might go on a ways yet, but would not return. Now is the last chance for all our beasts to find their way back to Karelia."

"But our pursuit will be mounted," said Pirtto. "How can we escape on foot?"

"As ably as we can on horseback," answered the old man. "Maybe better. We can hide more easily without them, especially in the marsh."

"What about our packs?" asked Kaukomieli.

"Shoulder them," replied Väinämöinen. "We are wizards. We'll carry as much as we can and leave the rest. We won't starve, at least not until winter. There's game in the wild and fish in the waters."

They divided up their goods, taking only the essentials: food, weapons, and winter clothes. They buried the rest in a swamp along with their saddles.

Ulla had known they would let the horses go at some point. There was no possibility of riding them all the way to Pohjola. She loved Midnight like no other horse she had ever known. The thought of never seeing the black mare again brought tears to her eyes, even though she had sworn to herself to remain stoic.

To Sumuvuori and back, she thought. *And Egan rode beside us to Sumuvuori...and back.* Ulla whispered in Midnight's ear. The mare whinnied. She knew that Midnight trusted her and she felt guilty for abandoning her after all they had been through together.

Chanting the spell that he had prepared, a spell to help the horses find their way to Karelia, Väinämöinen sent them off. Enchanted, their steeds turned south, walking as if led on a line, Starchaser in front—all except Midnight. The mare stopped, turned, and walked back to Ulla. Despair swept over the young woman.

"No," she said firmly, through her tears. "Not this time. Lempi waits for you in the great forest. Wait for me there, *ystava*. I will call you when the time comes."

Väinämöinen gently put one big hand on the horse's muzzle and the other on Ulla's dark head.

"I will weave the spell again," he sighed. "Stronger this time. It is a hard thing, little one. *Love is like feeling the sun on both sides*. It's never easy to let go. That's as true of beasts as of people."

At last the deed was done. Midnight set out to catch up with Starchaser and the others. The horses were quickly lost to sight and hearing, leaving them alone, on foot, in the Wastes.

"Wonderful," said Pirtto. "My favorite pony too. Well, let's keep walking, if walk we must. I don't want to be caught by Löhi."

"Tulikki?" asked Väinämöinen, gesturing to her wounded arm. Kaukomieli had bound it and Ulla had sung a spell of healing, the same with which the old man had healed Ulla long ago after *karhu's* attack.

"I can manage. Pirtto's right for once. Let us go."

Väinämöinen planned to head due north, using Taivaantappi to guide them. It was not the most direct way to Pohjola, which lay hundreds of miles away northeast. They needed to disappear, however. With the Moonface pursuing them, the Witch would soon learn of their whereabouts and guess their intentions, even if she knew nothing of the Arrow of Tuonetar. Her servants and spies would spread throughout the wilderness, watching all the approaches to Pohjola. The element of surprise would be lost; Löhi would be on guard. The least likely, most difficult approach to Pohjola gave them their best chance.

Yet none of them, not even Väinämöinen, was familiar with such a route. It had been years, long years, since ever the old man had journeyed in those lands; all had been snow-covered and white in the time of Löhi's first dominion before ever the Kaamoslaiset came to the Far Northern Land. He remembered little; Pirtto recalled even less. Only Tulikki had been in the north since then, but she had never come near to Pohjola. They had little idea of what to expect, save that the journey would be a long one, and that winter, perhaps, would become their greatest enemy. If the snow began before they reached Pohjola, their lives were in peril. Even the Erilaiset might perish in the freezing, barren lands of the farthest north.

The days passed. They marched on. The wilderness seemed empty and abandoned. The landscape remained the same, a monotonous mix of birch and pinewood broken by outcroppings of grey boulders and little lakes. Marshland bordered the lakes. They were sometimes obliged to go out of their way to avoid the reeking fens, marching west for several miles until they found firm footholds again. For all that, Väinämöinen always found a true path and Ilkka helped guide them. They avoided becoming entangled in valleys. There were many of these, largely flat, yet serpentine, winding their way to boggy ends where travelers might be trapped or forced to retrace their steps.

Trudging along all day, stopping only for brief rests before Väinämöinen roused them, Ulla felt like a little girl again, tagging behind him on one of his journeys. At night, the company ate their cold meals in darkness unless the stars shone overhead. They marched in silence for the most part, tired and weary. Only Pirtto remain cheerful. The irrepressible Menninkainen delighted in needling Tulikki, or anyone else, for that matter. When the others slept or sat wrapped in their own dark thoughts, he would lie on his back in the woods, sending little colored lights chasing one another round the trees for his own amusement.

At last came a day when the company encountered a marsh so large, they could find no way around it. A particularly tall stone like a small, grey hill jutted above the fen. Väinämöinen and Ilkka climbed it while the others, weary, rested below.

"*Here marsh, there swamp, nowhere dry*," sighed Väinämöinen. "Hei, Ilkka! The land's so flat we can see for miles and miles. And I don't care for what I see!"

The swamp stretched north into the distance. Short bog trees grew here and there on mossy tufts. Apart from that, the land was featureless. To the south, the land from whence they came lay in a thick haze. With his wizardly *sight*, the old man could dimly guess where the Marches were and, beyond that, the Seven Lands.

"There lies Sumuvuori," he said, pointing southeastward. "We are north of it, north of any land that the men of the Seven Clans have ever walked in, except for adventurers. If only we could skirt this accursed swamp!"

"What is that away yonder?" asked Ilkka, peering northwest. The haze lay thickest in that direction, but a dark shape like a great, grey esker hovered on the edge of sight.

"Hard to tell," replied the wizard, shading his eyes. "Maybe nothing. Too bad Ulla no longer has the glass. It might be a ridge or range of hills. Turi told me about a long ridge, as long as the Wall of the Giants, far to the north. The dwarves' mountain, the Kääpiövuori, sits on its western end. We don't want to go that way, but at least we know that there's an end to the marshland."

Before he climbed down, the wizard turned round in a circle, surveying the land a final time. He noticed something away to the south. At first, he thought it was just a family of deer passing through one of the larger clearings. Focusing his *sight* and speaking a word of power, he realized his mistake.

"Ilkka! Look there!"

The Warden followed the wizard's gaze, noticing for the first time the tiny black shapes in the distance.

"I don't have your power, but I can see something moving, several things. What are they, Väinämöinen?"

"It's what I feared; it is the Moonface."

Indeed, distant but clear, the wizard plainly saw Kuupää riding a horse through the sparse woods. Several companions trailed behind him. For a moment, sunlight escaped the haze, glinting off the silver mask. The distant horseman stopped, seemingly facing them. Väinämöinen fell to the ground and Ilkka threw himself beside him.

"Foolish," he muttered. "Foolish, foolish. This stone can be seen from miles away and here we stand, silhouetted in the twilight. He can see us. I feared all along that we'd be followed, though how he tracked us, I can't say. *Kalma* of Löhi, most likely. But there he is, no more than a day behind, I'd wager, and on horseback to boot."

"Mounted!" said Ilkka, in surprise. "Pirtto was right. But even if they brought horses so far into the wilderness, how can they take them into the swamp?"

"They cannot," answered Väinämöinen. "Or at least not far. He will abandon the mounts when no longer useful. What does he care about their fate? At least we know now what to do."

Ilkka looked over his shoulder.

"The swamp?"

"Yes. We cannot march up and down its borders, the Moonface will swiftly find us. More of Löhi's servants may be nearby too. We must lose him and, above all, force him to abandon his horses. Into the swamp! We will make for the ridgeline and hope we've guessed right."

"If not, it will be a grim ending," said Ilkka.

"No worse than being spitted or dragged in chains to Pohjola," answered Väinämöinen.

Descending the grey stone, they roused their companions and explained what they had seen. Fear and excitement swept the group.

"I won't say I told you so," said Pirtto. "Then again, I really don't need to. If only we had our horses back."

"They would only perish, with us or without us," said Väinämöinen. "There is only one way to escape now; we must go into the marshland."

Hoisting their packs, the company set off. They soon reached soft, boggy ground. The swamp's reek filled the air. The marsh sat lower than the surrounding lands, limiting visibility. They could not see far in any direction.

Ilkka and Väinämöinen knew more about traveling through swampland than perhaps any others in all the Far Northern Land. Nonetheless, it was hard going. Their boots often sank in the sludge. Slimy green moss and swamp grass clung to their cloaks until they were filthy. The still air, coupled with the fen's reek, stifled them. They longed for a fresh breeze to drive away the fetid vapors. Mosquitoes and biting flies made it even worse.

The insects bit incessantly during the day, sometimes gathering in veritable clouds to torment them. They disappeared as evening fell, but this was small solace. It was cold and cheerless at night in the barren fens; even if they had found any dry wood for a fire, Väinämöinen would not have permitted it. Dim lights seemed to shimmer all about them, reminding Ulla of the Devil's Lights of Kurppajärvi that she had seen as a child. The Erilaiset were unphased by the dancing lights, but to Ulla, Kaukomieli, and Ilkka, they were most unsettling.

The company trudged along like this for five days, slowly but steadily working their way northward, hoping every day that the marshlands would suddenly end and drier ground appear. Once, Tulikki slipped into a slime-covered pool, pulling Kaukomieli headfirst after her. Had they been alone, without friends to fish them out, they might have come to grief. As it was, Kaukomieli lost his staff; only Ulla's patient spell found it again, drawing it to the surface like a snake wriggling up from the depths.

Finally, they reached a point where it was impossible to go further. The marsh had grown more close. Deep pools spread everywhere. No dry land was to be found. Only occasional mounds of mossy rock broke the fetid, green landscape. Some had dark holes in their south-facing side—the dens, perhaps, of some foul animals that inhabited the fenlands.

"Wonderful," sighed Pirtto. "You brought us to a dead end, Väinämöinen. No food, no clean water, no way forward, no way back. No ideas either, I suppose?"

"Only one," snapped Väinämöinen. "To work a change upon you and send you back to the Moonface and his friends. You can beg their help while we wait here."

Ulla, exhausted, slumped to the soft, spongy ground beside her pack. She pulled her hood tighter against the cold.

"We are in trouble, aren't we?" she asked, stretching her aching legs.

Väinämöinen and Ilkka looked one another in the eye.

"Five magic-users," he said at last. "And the wisest March Warden in the Far Northern Land. Trouble? Surely we have it. The road to Pohjola is beset with troubles. But we are no ordinary party.

"Let us sleep here tonight. It will soon be dark. Tomorrow, I will work a change and scout ahead as best I can. Perhaps I can find a path through this watery maze. Then we will decide what is to be done."

Wading through waist-deep water, they climbed on top of one of the rocky mounds and camped. Larger than any others, it had a dark hole almost as big as a doorway in its side. A warm vapor, like swamp gas, issued from within.

"What do you suppose lives in this beastly hole?" asked Kaukomieli. "It's as snake-like a place as I've ever seen and I lived on the edge of swampland as a child. Is it safe to sleep here?"

"Safe or not, where else is there?" answered Ilkka. "I've never seen such mounds and I cannot imagine what lies inside, if anything."

Pirtto peered inside the hole for a long time while the others doled out their meager supper. The twisted remnants of two dead bog-trees still clung to the mound.

"Help me, Tulikki," said Väinämöinen. "At least tonight, we'll have fire, come what may. I'm cold and want to warm up a bit."

They broke the dead wood into kindling and sparked it with a spell. The fire popped and spluttered while they gathered round its warmth.

"Here, Pirtto," called Väinämöinen. "What are you staring into that hole for? We can seal it up with a spell ere we sleep so you'll stop worrying."

The little man shook his head, his face unusually serious.

"I don't know what it is," he muttered, half to himself. "I feel something strange, and yet familiar, about this place. I do not like it."

The fire burned low; it went out. They kept watch in turns, sleeping uneasily, while the night passed.

Kaukomieli had the last watch. Lying quietly near Ulla, trying to stay awake, he watched the rise and fall of her shoulders as she slept. Her loose hair had slipped from her hood. Without thinking, he reached out to touch it, then swiftly drew back his hand.

She had changed since the journey to Tuonela; yes, she had changed. She was less grim, perhaps, and slower to speak harshly to him or any other. Her purpose had become even more singular, however; she would destroy Löhi or die in the attempt. She did not complain about any hardship or despair as things grew more hopeless. The Child of the Prophecy, she who bore the Mark of the Clan, she now did only what she must do, and that was enough.

In one way, Ulla seemed more distant. Perhaps she had grown beyond the reach of understanding of any mortal man. Yet, in another way, his bond with her had become more apparent and stronger than before. As they journeyed, he and Ulla were almost constantly together. She turned to him first, before any other. He loved her as desperately and deeply as ever, and if she needed only a last companion on her final journey, he would fulfill the role fate set before him.

Kaukomieli sighed. The morning song of the tiny waterfowl that lived in the fens struck his ears. He looked over Ulla's sleeping form, gazing into the grey-green haze all around them. Dawn was very near. The young man's frosty breath was visible in the murk. The bird call quickened; several fluttered past them, tiny wings beating rapidly.

The birds seemed startled—*startled.*

Curious, he sat up, blinking. Then he saw them.

A grey shape emerged from the mists on the largest mere. Another appeared beside it.

Kaukomieli twisted around. Behind the mound, another dim shape hovered on the edge of sight atop the water. *Boats!*

Rude dugouts navigated the water channels and, in the foremost, stood a dark figure with a gleaming silver mask—the Moonface.

"Väinämöinen!" cried Kaukomieli. "Ilkka, Ulla! We're caught!"

The old man jumped to his feet, grabbing his staff. The others did the same.

Across the water, the Moonface cursed. Surprise would have been complete if only the boy had not seen them.

The next moments were a blur. The Moonface cried out in a hateful voice. He flung a fiery ball from his iron staff straight at Väinämöinen. From at least half a dozen other canoes came similar fiery bolts mixed with arrows.

Shouting a counter-spell, Väinämöinen turned aside the fireball with his staff, sending his own flaming missile toward the Moonface. Ulla and Kaukomieli followed suit. Tulikki shot an arrow toward another boat; a grey figure screamed, falling heavily into the water.

A flurry of lightnings and fireballs thundered back and forth. Screams and cries filled the air. Tulikki was burned. Väinämöinen's cloak caught on fire. Ulla jerked convulsively as an electric bolt struck her legs, sending shocks throughout her body. Their enemies fared no better, several falling into the slimy pools from their unsteady perches, splashing about as they tried to regain their boats. But the company, clearly outnumbered, had no hope of escape.

"We're trapped, Väinämöinen!" cried Ilkka, dodging an arrow. "Take Ulla and go, however you can!"

"Wait!" yelled Pirtto, crouching by the mound's dark fissure. "There's a passage down here, a cave or tunnel. It's the only way!"

"No, we'll be trapped inside," said Kaukomieli.

"It is large," said the little man, "I can feel it. I don't know where it leads to, but it won't be *here*."

Väinämöinen hesitated for a moment. The canoes had momentarily drawn back, but he could hear Kuupää shouting orders. The sun broke the eastern horizon. Its first rays lit upon the Moonface's mask, bringing it horribly to life.

"Let's go!" cried the old man. "Grab your packs. Follow Pirtto!"

The wizard made a sweeping gesture with his staff; a shimmering wall like a curtain of golden sunlight sprang over the water, separating them from their enemies. Before it faded, one by one, they passed through the mound's dark entrance. Väinämöinen helped Ulla, who was still shaking. With a last glance back, taking her staff in hand as well as his own, he pulled her across the threshold and disappeared within.

Moments later, the dugouts hit the outcropping's mossy turf. Kuupää leapt to the ground, followed by a dozen Haltiatar, Dark Erilaiset of Pohjola sent by the Witch to pursue her enemies.

"They are inside," cried one of the elves. "Do you have the chains, Kullekki?"

The Haltiatar prepared to plunge into the opening.

"No," said the Moonface, blocking the others with his iron staff. The dark elves looked at him in wonder.

"But they will escape," said the elf. "Surely there is another way out. These mounds are set all about this filthy place. We must go in after them."

The Moonface knelt in front of the hole. He turned his head this way and that, as if considering.

"Perhaps they will find a way out," he said in his toneless voice. "Perhaps not."

* * *

Väinämöinen rubbed his head. A knot was already forming where he had hit the stony floor. Only a short way inside the hole, the slippery floor angled down sharply, like a natural stair. One after another, they had fallen down the steep corridor, unable to slow or stop their descent until they crashed together in a jumbled heap on level floor.

They found themselves in an underground cavern of some sort, far beneath the pools and bogs. Natural or not, it had clearly been altered by living hands, perhaps in the ancient past before the marsh had grown and swallowed up everything for miles around. Only the opening remained aboveground. Strangely, it remained unflooded, though dank and damp.

The old wizard immediately noticed two things. Although they had struck no light, the wet, rocky walls shone with a faint luminescence, casting a dim, bluish glow over all. More troubling, the old man's wizardly power was gone. He felt exhausted, as if he had woven spell after spell, day and night. The battle above could not account for that.

"Is everyone here?" asked Tulikki. They were.

"And is everyone all right? Ulla?"

"Yes and no," Ulla answered, slowly. "I'm recovered from the lightning, but...I cannot feel my power, my magic. I do not understand it."

"Nor I," said Kaukomieli. "I've never felt so drained since I won my staff."

"This place is evil," said Tulikki. "It is a *taikareikä*, a place where *loitsu* die and songs are useless. I found other such places during my journeys."

"A *taikareikä*," said Väinämöinen. "A spell-hole. I had forgotten such places existed. Long years has it been since ever I encountered one. I do not like this feeling."

"Such weaklings," said Pirtto. With a flourish, he waved his arm. Colored sparks buzzed about his head like a rainbow of fireflies.

"It does not affect you!" exclaimed Väinämöinen. "But how?"

"Now we know once and for all who the true wizard is," chuckled Pirtto. "My songs aren't affected by such rubbish."

Then, speaking seriously, he said, "Tulikki is right, though. This place is evil. I may have my power still, but I also have a terrible feeling. Perhaps we should not have come down here."

"What choice was there?" asked Ilkka. "We would have been overcome had we not. Listen!"

They fell silent, straining to hear what might be happening above ground.

"What do you hear?" asked Ulla.

"Nothing," replied Ilkka. "I thought our enemies would come after us, but so far, at least, they have not followed."

"I don't necessarily find that reassuring," said Väinämöinen. "Perhaps they're waiting to ambush us when we reemerge, or perhaps they fear this place and will not enter."

"Whatever the reason, here we are," said Ilkaa. "So, the question is, where do we go from here?"

Väinämöinen peered down the passageway. The bluish light faded into a soft glow, which made it impossible to see far.

"Well and good," he said at last. "What choice indeed, Ilkka? The Moonface sits on the doorstep and we have little food and less water. Magic or no, we can only go forward and hope to find a way out."

Despite their exhaustion, the company set out down the underground passageway. Though roughhewn, it was level, and damp, since the wet of the marshes about seeped through the stone. Väinämöinen and Ilkka had to stoop in most places, yet the passage was broad enough for several to walk abreast.

They encountered no one and felt nothing, no traces of any underground denizens or clues as to who or what had delved the tunnel in the first place.

On it went, seemingly for miles; they trudged along silently, stopping now and then to listen for any sound of pursuit from behind. Ulla, who hated enclosed spaces, soon felt as if the walls closed in around her. She struggled to fight off panic, remembering the first time that she ascended the Seer's mottled tower. Kaukomieli, none too comfortable himself, sensed her panic and walked with his hand on her shoulder to reassure her. At least the air felt fresh and, strangely, warmer than in the mere above despite the fact that they were deep underground.

"Who do you think dug this place?" asked Kaukomieli. "And why?"

"Maybe goblins," answered Tulikki. "We have come closer to Pohjola and are far from the Seven Lands. In ancient times, they were more numerous and dug for gold throughout the Far Northern Land, even in the wilderness. They still mine gold for Löhi near Sariola."

"This doesn't look like any goblin mine I've ever seen," said Pirtto. "And I see no gold or silver in this rock."

"And what about this light?" whispered Ulla. "And this—*taikareikä*. Do goblins make such places?"

"Who can say?" answered Väinämöinen. "But I don't think the Hiisia shaped these tunnels. Mountains and woods are their preference, not loathsome holes. This place feels old, very old. Maybe many different folk have lived here over the centuries. Pirtto, can you sense anything?"

"Yes," said the gnome. "Yes, I can. I do not know what it is, but it is aware of us."

Suddenly the passageway opened onto a round chamber with a high roof. The bluish luminescence was stronger here. In the middle of the room, water from above dripped onto the stony floor. Across the way, openings indicated multiple passageways leading from the chamber.

"By the vaulted heavens," muttered Väinämöinen. "We are in a maze; let us hope that we can find a way out."

Pirtto tasted the dripping water. "It is fresh," he said. "Fresh as any Karelian stream."

"I wonder," grumbled Väinämöinen. The old man tasted the water as well. His face brightened. Pointing to a little pool that had formed on the ground, he said, "If it is enchanted or poisoned, so be it. We will die of thirst soon enough without it. So drink your fill and fill your skins. We'll rest here for a while. We've come miles, it seems. I'm tired. Keep your swords unsheathed and packs ready. If the Moonface followed us in here, fight or flee, we will need both."

They set a watch. Tulikki drew the first turn. Despite their fear and anxiety, the others soon fell asleep, all except Pirtto. Though skilled with illusions, he had limited powers of *sight* and could not easily make an *etiänen*, a spirit-self. Still, he tried to reach his mind out through the dimly lit passageways to discover the tunnel's secrets. Try as he might, he found nothing.

After some hours—who could be sure in the underground maze?—they set out again, choosing a passage at random. They soon discovered that this part of the maze was very different. Side passages and branches, large and small, appeared at regular intervals. The sound of rushing water could frequently be heard echoing through the rock wall. They came upon several chambers similar to the first, although they discovered no more fresh water. It became clear that they had entered the heart of some vast web of caverns and tunnels; the original passage had been only a roadway of sorts leading to the outlet in the marsh above.

"This is no good, Väinämöinen," said Ilkka, as they walked along. "Taking one passage or another blindly, without trying others. We will never find our way out unless fortune favors us."

"Who says it won't?" replied the old man.

"Let us take only the left-hand passages when the tunnel splits," suggested the Warden. "This is what the Wardens teach if lost in a cave. By so doing, one may find a way out or work back with some certainty should the lead prove false."

"So be it," said Väinämöinen. "How many times has this worked for you?"

"Never," said Ilkka. "I have never been lost in a cave before. But it sounds wise, does it not?"

The old man laughed, a rich sound echoing down the passageway, multiplying as if a troop of Wardens were chortling while they explored the tunnels.

"Do you hear that, Ulla?" he asked the girl, who was just behind him with Kaukomieli. "At the next split ahead, we'll put Ilkka's wisdom to the test and—"

At that moment, as they passed two smaller openings on either side, a dreadful cacophony of shrieks and cries broke out. Hands grasped Ulla, knocking her to the ground, and pulled her away. The others grappled with their own attackers.

Struggling, Ulla kicked and writhed, trying to break free. She knocked one attacker back with her staff. From the corner of her eye, she glimpsed Kaukomieli do the same. An enemy landed on top of her, his hands reaching for her throat. She expected to see an elf or even the Moonface himself, Dark Erilaiset from the *väkis* of Pohjola, but it was no Haltia!

The ghastly, mottled, and misshapen face above her looked grey-blue in the cavern's eerie light. Slime dripped from its fangs and broken teeth. Though small, no larger than Pirtto, the creature was strong, terribly strong. Its claws tore her skin.

Ulla screamed. Terror filled her heart. Chaos raged all around her. She managed to bring her knees up and, pushing with all her might, kicked the creature back. She swept out her sword.

The creature charged again. Ulla stabbed upward. Run through, the ghastly thing fell shrieking, jerking violently and beating the ground with its arms and legs like a wounded spider. Ulla stabbed again and again until the creature lay still.

Looking around, she saw that her friends had slain several others. Väinämöinen stood over one dead monster, slime and dark blood dripping from his blade. Ilkka stooped atop another. The creatures broke off their attack, scrambling back up the side passages, wailing as they ran.

"What in the Far Northern Land are those things?" cried Kaukomieli, shaking with fear and excitement. The young man had beaten off his attacker with his staff.

"I understand now," said Pirtto, peering down a dark, unlit side passage. "Yes, I understand. The Maanalaiset! We have stumbled into the holes of the Maanalaiset. No wonder that your magic doesn't work here."

"What are the Maanalaiset?" asked Ulla and Kaukomieli together.

"The Earth People," answered Väinämöinen. "Evil gremlins that live under the ground. I didn't know any still lived in the Far Northern Land. It has been hundreds upon hundreds of years since last I encountered them."

"But who are they?" asked Ulla. "Are they goblins, servants of Löhi?"

"No," said Pirtto, grimly. "They serve no one but themselves. They are not relatives of the Hiisia—but rather of the Menninkaiset."

"What?" exclaimed Ulla. "These…things, they are part of your *väki*?"

"No!" said the little gnome. "Not any longer. But once they were, once long ago, before Löhi ever came back from her first sleep.

"They say it grew cold then, very cold. Snow and ice covered nearly all the lands. My folk left the North and went southward, to the great forests, with the other Erilaiset. Not so the ancestors of the Maanalaiset. There was a family among us back then, a great family, with dozens of aunts and uncles, nieces and nephews, and all types of cousins, all living together. Like unto its own clan it was—or so the tales say. It was long before my time.

"They became very powerful, but very strange. They turned away from the woods that the other Menninkaiset loved and delved into the ground, seeking shelter from the snow. And their magic changed. They crafted powerful *loitsu*, drawing upon the spirits they found imprisoned within the dark places of the earth. Rituals they had and strange practices. They sought to keep the *loitsu* and the knowledge it gave them secret. They had no more dealings with the other *väki*.

"Their magic changed and, in turn, changed them. Horrible deeds were done deep underground, far from light. Twisted souls gave birth to twisted bodies. Menninkaiset no more, they became a new thing, a terrible thing: the Earth People."

"Aye," said Väinämöinen. "So I, too, was taught. And I remember that their magic was strong, strong enough to make *tietäjää* powerless, as it is in this beastly hole. Yet you, Pirtto, are not affected."

"Does that surprise you?" said Pirtto. "The Menninkaiset and Maanalaiset are enemies, always will be. They hate us more than any other living thing—and they hate *all* living things, feeding upon whomever they can. But we are linked; we were the same in the beginning. Their magic will not work on me or any of my folk. I have seen them only once, long ago in my youth and very far from this place. I met but a few, yet the memory is very evil. I have never spoken about it outside my folk until today."

"So it is," said Tulikki. "Like Väinämöinen, I did not remember these things until now and had forgotten that they once lived among us. But enough of tales! Let us flee now while we can and leave these holes!"

"Which way?" asked Ilkka. "Back whence we came? It seems the prudent course, but perhaps the Moonface waits at the other end."

"Or perhaps he is trapped inside, too," said Ulla. "His magic must be just as useless here as ours is."

"Not back," said Pirtto, slowly. "No, I think not. I have been trying to sense the tunnels ever since we entered. There is a danger here, all around us. We must be nearly to the heart of the Earth People's dreadful den. But I can sense that the way ahead is shorter, much shorter, than the way behind. And I feel that there is another way out of the maze or several. We should not go back. They will follow us in any case. Let us go forward and leave these holes as swiftly as may be."

"Are you sure about this, Pirtto?" asked Väinämöinen. "Our lives may depend upon the choice."

"I'm sure of nothing in this dismal place, but my heart tells me the way ahead is our way."

"Then let us go, swiftly! Be wary, all of you. Here, Pirtto, walk up front with me."

Stepping over the dead Maanalaiset, Ulla set off behind Väinämöinen. Kaukomieli walked beside her and Ilkka, sword at the ready, brought up the rear.

The tunnels twisted this way and that. Side passages crisscrossed the main way or, at least, what they thought to be the main way. Soon they had little idea if they were walking in a circle or actually moving forward. From time to time, far-off cries echoed in distant passages, startling them. Ropes, chains, and sacks littered the corridors. Roughhewn chambers appeared more frequently. It grew warmer, noticeably warmer; they sweated beneath their heavy cloaks and hoods.

Ulla and Kaukomieli whispered together while they walked.

"I can't believe that these monsters, these Earth People, were once Menninkaiset," said Ulla. "They look like the shades I saw in Tuonela."

"Just our luck to have stumbled into their den. They may live in the ground, but they seem slimed with the foul mass of the swamps above."

"Perhaps they get food there. They have to eat and there cannot be many creatures in these parts."

"I wonder," said Kaukomieli. "I suspect we may not want to know where their food comes from; I certainly don't want to wind up a meal! But if we hadn't come down here, I don't know how we would've escaped the swamps ourselves."

The cries became more distant, fading away at last. The tunnel seemed to gradually climb. How many miles they had walked could not be guessed, but the side passages became less frequent. The deep parts of the caves had been dry, but now the rocky walls were wet again, glistening in the preternatural luminescence.

They paused for a while in a small alcove, drinking precious water and munching some of their dwindling stock of food. Their packs were already noticeably lighter.

When they started off again, the main passage sloped steeply upward. They were definitely climbing. The air felt cooler.

"Pirtto was right," said Kaukomieli. "We will soon be out of these holes and back again in fresh air and sunlight."

Chilling screams erupted on all sides. Strong hands grasped Ulla's legs; she fell. Ulla tried to draw Longleaf, but her arms were pinned. A Maanalainen was suddenly above her, its dripping fangs inches from her face. She cried out in terror. Something hit her head very hard. The world went black and she knew no more.

* * *

Upside down. She hung upside down when she came to. Everything was topsy-turvy in the deep subterranean lair.

Ulla's head throbbed. She tasted blood in her mouth. The dark-haired young woman gradually realized that she was caught in a type of net, suspended in the air. Her eyes blinked in the dim light. She tried to move, but was hopelessly tangled. With a start, Ulla realized that the hand next to her head was not her own. Twisting round, she saw Väinämöinen's face uncomfortably close; the old man glared.

"Väinämöinen—" she began, but at just that moment something snapped. The net dropped. Ulla fell to the ground, landing hard on a rocky floor many feet below.

From the jumble of bodies, four groaning figures emerged—Ulla, Väinämöinen, Kaukomieli, and Tulikki. Shaking off the roughly woven rope netting, they scrambled to their feet. Ilkka and Pirtto were nowhere to be seen.

The four companions found themselves in a round chamber with neither door nor opening, a great, deep hole of some sort whose depth could not be guessed. The strange luminescence had vanished. High above, suspended from chains, torches cast a yellow, smoky light. Their weapons had been taken, sword, staff, bow, and knife. Only their packs and water skins remained. With a start, Ulla reached for the arrow; it was still there, hidden next to her skin.

"What happened?" asked Kaukomieli, weakly. Blood streaked his pale face.

"We were ambushed," said Väinämöinen. "Taken by surprise and brought here, to this dungeon of the Maanalaiset, I suppose. I wonder what has happened to Ilkka and Pirtto."

Ulla looked around. Long shadows, their shadows, stretched across the floor, fading into the darkness. Round stones lay here and there upon the ground. Stooping, she reached out to touch one, then drew back with a muffled shriek. These were no stones.

"By the vaulted heavens!" she cried. "Skulls! There are skulls here!"

Scattered across the floor were a jumble of bones, including many skulls. Some looked like mortal skulls, others like the elongated skulls of goblins or elves, still others like animals'. Even in the dim light, they could see that some were weathered and yellow, while others seemed much newer. Dark eye sockets stared blindly above grinning teeth.

"Trapped!" cried Väinämöinen. "Like rats in a hole."

"Only rats can usually scurry out," said Tulikki, peering up into the unknown height. "Or dig. We can do neither."

Ulla kicked at the chamber wall: solid stone. She felt her aching head. Two large knots had sprouted where she had been hit. Another painful bump swelled on her forehead. She felt miserable.

"What are we to do, Väinämöinen?" asked Kaukomieli.

"What is there to do?" replied the old man.

"But why didn't they just kill us?" said Ulla. "Why bring us here? And why leave us our food and water?"

The old man laughed grimly. Catching Tulikki's eye in the murky light, he winked.

"Why indeed?" he said. "Tulikki can tell you, can't you, Tulikki?"

The Erilaisen woman smiled back, strangely, at the wizard.

"They were not ready for us, not yet," she said. "Perhaps they will not be for some time."

"So they made us prisoners?" mused Kaukomieli.

"No, we are not prisoners; we are food."

With a shock, Ulla realized they were not so much in a dungeon as in a pantry. The Maanalaiset planned to keep them fresh until their grisly plans were ripe. She looked at the skulls and scattered bones of mortal, Erilaisen, and beast. They had been victims of the Earth People.

"There's nothing to be done at present," sighed the old man. "We can only watch and wait." Casting his thick cloak on the ground, he lay down in the shadows.

"We must keep watch, two at a time. We can't be surprised again. How I hate this powerless feeling, this sense of my songs having left me. It is unnatural! But songs or no, these foul little demons have caught the wrong prey this time. After a rest, we'll see where things stand. At the very least, we will take many of them with us."

Ulla and Tulikki took the first watch, sitting side by side in the dark with their backs against the wall. They whispered together for a while, then fell silent. Ulla wondered if she had come to the end of her adventures. *After a rest, we'll see where things stand.* What was there to see? It was impossible to scale the walls. They could work no magic in the *taikareikä*. Panic seized her as she considered a slow death by thirst, alone in the dark, her own bones joining the others forever in the forgotten tunnels. Not even Löhi would know what had become of them.

A few times she thought she heard distant noises or rumor of commotion, but she could not tell for sure. After several hours, they woke up the men and switched off. So they took turns sleeping, exhausted from the terrible sensation of having no magic, power, or spells with which to save themselves.

Ulla's turn to watch came again. Despite the danger, the young woman dozed, too tired to stay awake in the dark. Snatches of dreams tempted her, weaving a patchwork over her consciousness of which she was only dimly aware. As she often did, she dreamed of Egan—Egan upon his white charger as she had last seen him, the blue and white banner of the Swan Folk in his gloved hand while he faced down the hordes of Pohjola. No fear was in his heart that day. Nothing deterred him from his purpose. The King of the Far Northern Land had died unwavering in his resolve to save his people.

Eyes fluttering, Ulla rose slowly to wakefulness. Something shimmered across the way. *Had Egan returned to save her?*

Tulikki gripped Ulla's arm. The dream vanished. The opposite wall lay just within the torchlight's reach and something had shifted there. A black hole appeared at the bottom of the wall as if a great stone had been rolled back.

Tulikki jumped to her feet. She tensed for the expected onslaught.

"Väinämöinen!" she cried. "*Saapanut!*"

A small figure popped out. It held a knife in one hand and a large sack in the other. It stepped into the torchlight, casting a long, undulating shadow across the ground, a grotesque, misshapen image.

Väinämöinen and the others scrambled up. "*Pysäyttää!*" the old man called instinctively, though his voice held no power now in the depths of the Earth People's labyrinth.

The little figure laughed.

"Pirtto!" they all shouted together.

"Who else?" laughed the gnome. "Expecting somebody different?"

"How did you find us?" asked Ulla, beyond surprise.

"We thought you were dead," said Kaukomieli.

"That I am not, luckily, for you," said Pirtto. "At least not yet. We'll see how things go from here."

"How did you escape? Where's Ilkka?" asked Tulikki.

"So many questions," answered Pirtto. "There's no time to swap tales now. Ilkka's waiting down the corridor. We had a hard time finding you, I can tell you.

"I've sent phantoms and illusions all throughout the maze; the Maanalaiset are still chasing them down. They believe that there are dozens of us. Monsters or not, they are no match for a Menninkainen! We've killed a few more of them too. The devils!"

Pirtto handed Ulla the knife.

"Here, my lady. This is Longleaf. I've got the rest of your weapons here in the bag. What's more, we found a way out, the main entrance, I gather. The hole we came down must be a seldom used passage, distant from the hovels they actually live in. We've got to be quick, though. My spells won't last forever and I'm getting very tired."

"Pirtto, you're an absolute marvel," said Väinämöinen. "We are all eternally in your debt. Lead on and let's get out of here. By Ukko's Hammer, if they want to chase us when we're above ground again, I'll give them a show the likes of which they have never seen."

Taking up their packs and weapons, they stooped low and followed Pirtto into the corridor. To one side sat the great cut stone that fit neatly into the opening in the wall, which the Earth People used to come and go from the chamber. After several minutes, they reached a cross passage and found Ilkka waiting for them. Two dead Maanalaiset lay nearby, just visible in the dim, bluish glow.

"It's about time," said Ilkka, clapping Kaukomieli on the shoulder. "Waiting alone in the dark with these monsters all about is not exactly my idea of fun. I have never been more anxious. Thank the Vanhalaiset that Pirtto found you, safe if not wholly sound."

"Not safe yet," said Väinämöinen. "Not until we escape the labyrinth. Keep moving!"

"Wait a moment," said Ilkka. Reaching down, he picked up several objects.

"Our staffs!" cried Ulla.

"Yes," answered Ilkka. "Seems they knew what they were; they kept them separate from the blades. These two here were handling them when we stumbled upon them. Take them back!"

Following Pirtto, they set off down the passage at a good pace, encouraged by the little gnome's report that the entrance lay nearby. The passage became wider and less close, the ceiling higher. Objects sat here and there: baskets, bags, and stacks of bog-wood. The air grew cool and damp. The maze was heated somehow, by magic or design, but, as they neared its gateway, the swamp's chill air flowed in like an invisible stream. Pools of water spread upon the rocky floor.

They rounded a corner and the passage suddenly opened into a large, cavernous room. Other passages led from the room in all directions. At the cavern's far end burned a light like a star, white-yellow, so radiantly bright it hurt their eyes.

"There it is!" cried Pirtto.

"The entrance," said Väinämöinen. "And it is bright daylight outside. Fortune has indeed smiled upon us, fortune and Akka's goodwill. These creatures may delve inside the earth, but they are no friends of hers. Let them try to trouble us once we leave this spell-hole!"

But the old wizard spoke too soon. The now familiar cries of the Maanalaiset erupted around them as, from a dozen passages, the corrupted imps poured forth, bent on preventing the companions' escape and avenging their losses.

Mottled faces and twisted mouths screamed in anger; slimy claws snapped feverishly as the gremlins approached. The largest of their foes, warriors summoned from the deepest dens to kill the sky-dwellers, no matter the cost, bore clubs and mattocks.

"Run!" yelled Väinämöinen.

Before they were halfway to the radiant light, the imps closed on them and a wild melee began. Tired as they were, the hope of escape energized them for a final battle.

Ulla cut down several with *Pohjanpiikki*, wheeling about madly. Kaukomieli did the same with *Runolaulaja*. Jumping atop a slippery stone, Tulikki sent arrows flying at their enemies, bringing down several of the club-wielders before they could attack. Yet Pirtto once again saved the day.

With a flash of lightning, he transformed into a gangling, troll-like giant, red eyes burning with flame. Roaring like a lion, he formed a fireball in his bare hand and cast it at the Maanalaiset. Several ignited, dancing about frantically as they burned. The rest momentarily drew back.

The company raced toward the sunlight, Pirtto loping along like a monster from Tuonela. Though only an illusion—he had worked no real change—it was terrifyingly effective just the same. The Earth People would not give up, however. Seeing them almost at the doorway, the Maanalaiset made a final, frenzied attack.

"Up the stairs!" gasped Pirtto. "Get out. I'll hold them back. But be ready to blast them when I emerge; they'll be at my heels!"

No!" cried Ulla, but Väinämöinen already had her in his grasp.

"Listen to him," he hissed, "Only Pirtto has the magic we need in here; outside, it's another matter. Run for it!" But the wizard stayed beside the gnome just the same while the others sprinted for the exit.

They reached the roughhewn stair that led to the opening through which the light poured. The Maanalaiset set upon them again. Ulla pushed one off the first step. A club came down on Ilkka's sword arm, but he turned the blow aside and ran the bearer through.

"Now!" cried Pirtto. Bellowing in the old speech, he swayed this way and that, his *loitsu* sending colored lightnings in all directions as the gremlins leapt upon him.

Pulling Ulla free from the monsters, Kaukomieli scurried up the stairs. The others followed close behind, all save Pirtto and Väinämöinen.

Stumbling into the open, the cold air hit them as they emerged from the rude hole. They climbed out onto a mound much larger than any other they had seen, the chief passageway to the Earth People's dismal underground lair. Swamp still surrounded them, but there was much more solid ground. Indeed, the mound sat in a clearing almost like an island in the marsh.

They blinked in the daylight, so bright it was to their eyes, though the day was actually overcast and the sun partially hidden by clouds.

And at once, they felt it. Tulikki, Ulla, Kaukomieli, even as they crossed the threshold, they felt it. Their wizardly power, the strength and magic of the *tietäjää*, coursed once more through their veins, setting their hair on end.

Swords drawn, staffs in hand, they backed away from the maze gate, ready to face whatever emerged and deal deadly blows.

"Steady," said Kaukomieli, breathing heavily. "Hit them with everything you have."

But nothing emerged. The rumor of distant cacophony faded.

Silence settled over the swamp.

"Where are they? Where's Pirtto and Väinämöinen?" cried Ulla. The others echoed her, shouting out their friends' names, though the gateway was empty and dark.

"I'm going after them," cried Ilkka, but before he could act, the old wizard shot out of the hole and collapsed on the ground with a dull thud. He quickly scrambled to his feet. Like the others, he felt his power surge within him.

"Where's Pirtto?" asked the Warden.

The old man started. "He was right beside me. We left a trail of dead enemies behind us."

They waited. The seconds passed like hours.

"Stay back," said Väinämöinen, motioning with his sword. He carefully crept to the maze gate. Peering inside, he stiffened, reaching out with his *sight* down into the dreadful hole. The others watched in suspense. Without a word, the wizard slipped inside the opening's shadow, disappearing from view. Ulla started forward, but Tulikki held her back.

"Wait!" said the Erilaisen woman sternly.

Väinämöinen was not gone long. He emerged from the shadows after only a minute, bent and crooked. Finally, the old wizard straightened. He turned to them. His sword hung slack and his staff dragged the ground.

He said nothing. The expression on the old man's face told all. Ilkka hung his head. Tulikki openly wept.

The day was short. The clouds grew thicker. The North Wind blew cold upon the bogs, rattling the reeds and hissing through the swamp grass.

Long after they had left that place, ere darkness fell, a mottled face emerged from the gateway, splotched and dripping slime. Looking around with bright eyes, scanning from left to right, it hissed, a sinister, sibilant sound atop the wind's voice.

Then the face disappeared within and the North Wind blew alone.

Chapter Twelve

Ajatar

"There's no way up," said Kaukomieli dejectedly, throwing his staff to the ground.

Picking it up, Ulla scolded him in the tone she had used so often in the past when frustrated with the young Hirvilainen.

"There is *always* a way for a wizard. You just have to find it. Did Pirtto despair in the maze of the Maanalaiset? Or Väinämöinen and I in Tuonela?"

Shaking her head in disgust, she turned away. Ilkka peered up toward where they guessed the mountaintop must be.

"Up or around," he muttered. "We chose up, up and over. Now the choice seems ill. What do you think, Väinämöinen? Is it time to go back?"

The old man, already gazing southward toward the now distant swamplands, ran his big hand through his long hair as he considered the Warden's question.

"Halfway up," he said. "More than halfway, I'd guess. Still, if we can't find a clear path or way to scale the wall, we might as well be back down at the bottom. Half measures won't get us to Pohjola before winter."

"Nor will empty stomachs," said Tulikki. "We've already eaten almost all the grouse that we caught in the marsh. No animals come here and little enough grows. I know how to live in the wilderness well enough, but you have to pick your place well or move on. This place is unwholesome. We cannot survive here."

"At least the North Wind cannot find us," said Ilkka. "That will change when we reach the top—if we reach the top."

The five members of the dwindling band of adventurers, the five who remained since Pirtto fell to the Earth People, stood in a shallow draw filled with bracken, running parallel to the ridgeline up above. After escaping the Maanalaiset, they found that the underground tunnels had brought them to the swamp's edge, just a few miles from the jumble of great stony hills that marked the mountain's foot.

And it *was* a mountain, part of a long grey mountain range, the same that they had glimpsed when fleeing from the Moonface into the marshland. Running nearly east-west, it cut right across their path. To the east, it bent back southward toward an even denser bog, spilling a broad river, too strong to ford, down a steep channel. To go that way seemed pointless, even if they managed to cross the river. To the west, the range ran on as far as they could see with naked eyes or wizardly *sight.* It might take weeks to go that way and skirt the mountains. In the end, they would be even farther away from Pohjola and the journey's end.

As Tulikki noted, their food had almost run out; they depended on what they could hunt, fish, or forage from now on. Väinämöinen had another worry, however. *Winter.*

They had left Karelia in the summer and spent most of the fall moving north. Autumn was passing and winter, true winter, would soon be upon them. Even so far north where the days were short and the sun appeared from strange directions, Väinämöinen knew the month, the season, and when the weather would likely turn well enough. He did not know how far they were from Pohjola or exactly where they must turn east to make for the Witch's Keep in Sariola, but he knew that they were still far from their goal.

If winter caught them in the pathless north, if heavy snow came while they wandered through the wilderness, the old man didn't care to consider their plight. The Erilaiset might perish in the frozen white wasteland as well as mortals. No spell was guarantee against nature's fury.

His other worry was that they were lost, truly lost. Already unfamiliar with these parts, he had been thrown off his reckoning by the unexpected detour through the marshlands. He did not remember the stony mountains. Tulikki was not much help. She had spied the range from afar when she returned to the Seven Lands, but had not passed near them. She had no idea how to cross them or where they stood in relation to Pohjola.

The old man sighed. Realizing that they were all watching him, he shook it off and put a brave face on their situation.

"Well, there's some good news at least," he said. "No sign of the Moonface or any other pursuit. Perhaps we finally lost them."

"Perhaps they returned to Pohjola, knowing that winter was coming and the lands unhospitable," said Tulikki.

"Maybe so. It would be another mistake on their part, because we will not give up so easily. Let us keep searching for a pass, at least until the food runs out. There must be a way up, as Ulla said. I can work a change if need be to scout around. If we still can't find it, we'll turn west. Tulikki knows those lands; they are more gentle. We can hunt elk, moose, and deer there, and won't starve. Maybe we will find some sign there to guide us."

So they continued searching for a way over the stony mountains, scrambling in and out of draws and deep channels, often retracing their steps for hours when they came to impassable places. Light rain fell. Dark clouds broke over the mountaintop, riding low in the sky. They tried using rope to hoist one another up, climbing from shelf to shelf, but it was dangerous and futile. Väinämöinen and Tulikki might have used their magic to work a change and so escape, but Ulla and Kaukomieli did not make such spells, nor would they leave Ilkka behind.

After two days, they ate the last of their food for breakfast, then decided to give it up. Water dripped from Väinämöinen's hood onto his red, potato-like nose. Ulla shivered in the damp wetness. Climbing down would not be easy; Ilkka and Kaukomieli lay flat, peering down into the gloom to chart out a path.

Tulikki cocked her head to one side. "Listen."

"What is it?" asked the others.

"Water. Can you hear it? Not far from here there's water rushing down, maybe a river or fall."

"And what of it?" said Väinämöinen. "Can we ride it back down to the swamp? In any case, it's probably just rain trickling down the mountainside."

Tulikki didn't answer, but went toward the half-guessed sound. The others wearily followed. Pushing through a thicket of scrub trees and bushes that clung to the hillside, they came out onto a broad shelf. The sound of rushing water grew louder. Now they saw the source, a water channel carved into the stone.

Years of rain and snow melt had carved a channel down the mountainside like a path delved by the hands of giants. Often dry, it ran now with fresh rainwater gathered from above, racing down to the lowlands where it fed the marshes. The water ran swiftly, but the channel was not so steep; its rocky walls were not so high. In some places the watercourse fell almost like a stair.

"Ilmatar's Tears!" exclaimed Väinämöinen. "This may be just what we're looking for. If it climbs like this all the way to the top, with no steep falls or chasms, we may be able to go right up the channel to the high ground."

Ulla peered at the cold, bubbly water. Though not snowmelt, it still looked icy.

"How can we climb through the rushing water? It's shallow, but far too cold and it's too dangerous to climb the steps through the flood."

"There is always a way for a wizard," said Kaukomieli, drawing a quick glance from the young woman. "We'll wait it out. Right, Väinämöinen?"

"Exactly, lad. The rain can't keep up forever. When it stops, the channel will run dry again soon enough. Now if our stomachs hold out, we may make it to the top yet."

The rain had already tapered off. During the night, it stopped completely. The clouds broke up and the morning dawned bright and cold. The rainwater stream had shrunk overnight; it now ran only as high as their ankles.

"Now for it," said the old man. "Cold it may be, but our boots are made to keep out the wet; moreover, Mielikki's *Metsänaitoa* made 'em, and whatever magic they possess went into it."

"Wading through cold streams is one thing," said Ilkka. "Climbing up a stair or fall like this is quite another. Mind that you don't slip, and don't let those staffs of yours become burdens!"

With Ilkka in front and the old wizard bringing up the rear, the company splashed into the watercourse and began to climb. It didn't take long for Ulla to feel the chill. The cold pierced her leather boots like a knife. After only a few minutes, she was freezing. Water seeped in despite the Tree Maidens' craftsmanship. Worse yet, once inside the channel, it was difficult to climb out. They found no bank or ridge to stop on for a moment's respite. The rocky walls rose high in some places. Their luck held, though, as the water did not rise again.

Ilkka had predicted their greatest difficulty. Numerous, short falls ran the channel's length, the water running swiftly down irregular protrusions like steps. They almost tumbled several times on the slippery steps. In some places, the water fell straight down like a curtain. Ilkka managed to climb the rocky walls like a spider, using the Wardens' technique, back against one wall, feet against the other. Then, throwing down a rope, he would haul up the others one by one.

It was tiring work. Soaked in cold water, empty stomachs growling, even the Erilaiset felt shaky. They made slow but steady progress, however. As the weak sun westered and the short day drew toward its close, they suddenly came to a wide shelf. It offered an excellent view of the lands all about. They now saw how much higher they had climbed. The distant swamplands lay far below, still shrouded in creeping mist. To the southeast, they could descry green woods and a broad river with many tributaries.

"The right choice after all," said Ilkka. "We must be near the top. Feel the cold air and listen to the wind blow against the north face! One more push should do it."

Deep twilight spread across the lowlands as they finally gained the top of the stair fall and crested the mountain. Although the ridgeline seemed to tower above everything around it, it did not actually rise that much higher than the Wall of the Giants. The Folk of the Far Northern Land were flatlanders, however. Ulla could not imagine how anything could be so tall. The mountains further north, in the Witch's realm, were only a distant rumor.

The company stood atop the ridge, stamping in the cold wind that blew from the North. It was night, but Ulla could see that the mountains fell very gently on their northern face; the land remained elevated. The moon and stars illuminated the world with a silvery glow. Owls hooted in a nearby wood.

"Well and good," said Väinämöinen. "I don't suppose the Moonface followed us, but even if he did, we're making fire tonight. I need it! My bones are cold. We can camp among all these stones. Ulla, Kaukomieli, see to a fire with Tulikki. Ilkka, come with me."

While the two mortal *tietäjää* gathered wet wood and Tulikki tried to spark it, the old wizard and the Warden headed for the nearest stand of woods, a sparse pinewood that nonetheless looked promising. The snowy owls eluded them, but it didn't take the companions long to catch their supper. Several black and white grouse appeared at Väinämöinen's call and Ilkka caught three rabbits.

Later, sheltered from the wind by a large boulder, the company sat around the popping, crackling fire, drying their feet and eating roasted meat.

"This isn't so bad," said Kaukomieli, stretching his legs out toward the fire. "Looks like woods, real woods, from here on. The hardest part of the journey may be over...except for the end, of course."

"We're a long way from Pohjola yet, lad," said Väinämöinen. "A long way. Let's just be thankful for at least one night of rest, food, and fire."

* * *

The rainclouds had passed away south and the morning dawned bright and sunny. The wind died down; it felt much warmer.

Ulla had taken the last watch. As the sun broke the horizon, she left the little camp and searched the nearby area. The unfamiliar landscape looked strange. A jumble of boulders stretched as far as the eye could see, some quite large and tall, forming narrow passages here and there where they came close together. Then the moraine dropped. Woods gleamed in the distance, sunlight sparkling off the evergreens.

Ulla strolled around the strange boulders. They did not appear to be seidi-stones, but held some secret nonetheless. Some glistened with tiny crystals; others looked plain and brown. She ran her bare hand over one smooth stone that climbed like a wall. Then she noticed markings inside a little cut that ran like a passageway between two great outcrops.

She examined the markings more closely. They seemed to be pictures in white, black, and brown. The primitive drawings, faded and worn by the weather, could still be recognized. Reindeer with large antlers ran through a wood. Stick-figure hunters chased them, spears flying through the air. The hunters brought down an elk. Two stick men prodded it with poles while another stood beside a fire. Then, on one side where a shaft of sunlight snuck through the rocks and illuminated a small patch of rock wall in a warm, yellow glow, she saw it. *Karhu!*

The bear, larger than any of the other figures, had been drawn in the midst of strange symbols. Upright on two legs, head back as if bellowing with rage, the great beast stood alone. No enemies were visible, as if *karhu* had chased them all off. The shock of recognition sent a chill down Ulla's spine.

"So you found them."

Ulla turned; it was Ilkka.

"What are they?"

"I don't know," answered Ilkka. "I've seen them elsewhere—along the Marches, in a cave north of the Birchwood in Deep Länsimaa. Wardens sometimes come across these drawings of people and beasts, painted on rocks and stones."

"Who do you think painted them?"

"I do not know. I asked Väinämöinen once. He said that long ago, in the most ancient of days before the Kaamoslaiset came to the Far Northern Land, other mortals dwelt here. Not even the Erilaiset knew them, not even Löhi. No more could he tell me. It may be that these folk drew the signs, but who can say? They are vanished now and the world is changed."

Ulla stared at the painted bear. She traced its outline with her finger.

"And, yes, *karhu* was with them," she said, slowly. "And he is still here, even after ages have passed."

The distant sound of honking filtered down from the sky. They looked up. High above, geese flew south, an uncertain arrowhead moving on the wind.

"Winter is just around the corner," said Ilkka.

"And still we have far to go," replied Ulla. "Too far, and we do not even know our way."

"Spring follows winter," said Ilkka. "Yet I wonder if it will always be so. Perhaps this is the year that no spring will come and the Witch's long season begins."

Ulla turned back to the image of *karhu*. The scars on her back drew tighter.

"Let us leave this place," she said.

Väinämöinen and the others were up and about when they returned. After a quick bite, they shouldered their packs and set off. All was still; the North Wind had ceased blowing. In the uncanny quiet, they could hear the woodland sounds for miles about.

The company set off to the north. Väinämöinen intended to follow the land as it fell until they found a hill or ridge to climb. Then they could survey the region again. He feared the land itself now more than being followed by enemies. Once it froze, they could cross lakes and slow-moving streams with ease. Until then, if they encountered chains of lakes or swift, unfordable rivers, it would be more difficult. As wizards, they could always sing up a boat or use other magical means to cross, but such things took time and strength; time was not on their side.

The days grew ever shorter. They walked now in perpetual twilight, save for a few hours each day. Väinämöinen knew that they must soon cut northeast, toward Pohjola and the Witch's Keep, but where exactly remained a mystery. Yet the wrong decision would almost certainly be deadly to them. The company would be lost in the wild as winter set in and likely freeze to death, be they wizards or not.

A path suggested itself, however, as paths often do. They kept the pine-wood to their left. To their right ran a river that grew narrower as they marched along, knowing it would be easier to ford upstream. They passed through mazes of tumbled grey boulders. Some seemed to have been fashioned to reveal a winding but true course, bending away from the line of the river. As the red sun sank toward the horizon, its gentle rays pierced the woods and countryside, bathing all the land in a saffron glow.

The boulders suddenly closed together in a rocky outcropping, rising on either side of what appeared to be a natural path across the tumbled plain, like a tunnel without a roof. As they approached it, they saw steps cut into the stone leading up and over.

"What do you make of that, Väinämöinen?" asked Ilkka. "Surely these were made on purpose."

"But for what purpose?" asked Kaukomieli. "And by whom?"

The old man considered the climbing stair, with its weathered steps and old stonecrop that shone in the golden light.

"*Many are the mysteries under the sun,*" he said at last. "Who can say? They were not put here for our purposes and their makers must have vanished long ago. We will use them now. This light won't last. It may already be dusk on the other side. I want to put some more miles behind us and the range back yonder. Then we can think about finding our dinner."

With Väinämöinen in the lead and Tulikki at the rear, they climbed single file up the short stair. After no more than fifty steps, the stony walls on either side fell away and they mounted a rocky crest. A flat field lay before them, bordered by the unlikeliest sight they might have imagined, an oak grove, its trees bare, with thick mould beneath.

"Look at this," muttered Ilkka, moving forward. "These trees should not be here so far north. I do not understand it."

But the others, all wizards, were concerned with more than just the trees. They felt a buzzing, electric energy—the energy of magic, of the *loitsu* that they wove. The strange place was alive with it.

"Väinämöinen," said Ulla. "What is this place? There is something wrong here."

Before the old man could answer, their eyes converged on a mound in the nearest grove, as if drawn to the spot by another will. Golden brown in the twilight, the mound was covered with leafy mould and, as they approached, they realized that serpents slithered in and out of the litter. A feeling of revulsion swept over them; even Väinämöinen shivered.

As they watched in a horrified wonder, unable to turn away, the mound shifted. It rose and fell as if some loathsome creature of the forest breathed heavily beneath the decaying filth and slime. Ilkka drew his sword. Then out of the mould a serpentine shape appeared, far greater than the lesser brood that crept about it. Mounting ever higher, the snake rose toward the treetops.

And then they perceived that this was no monstrous snake.

Wings emerged from the litter. Mighty legs were revealed. From the forest floor, the figure of a dragon appeared, burnt-orange scales gleaming in the twilight. Its terrible, crested head bobbed this way and that on a long, armored neck, leering, its forked tongue flickering. But the dragon's eyes sparkled like crystals, reflecting sunlight from a thousand facets that both blinded and enchanted.

"*Ajatar!*" cried Väinämöinen, flinging his staff up to ward off evil. A grinding, metallic laugh came from the dragon and echoed throughout the forest. Indeed, only Väinämöinen among them recognized the creature and knew her name, Ajatar, the serpent queen.

For the great, burnt-orange dragon was ancient, the most ancient of all *lohikäärme*. None could say from whence she came or her true nature. Some tales told that she was an evil spirit incarnate in a dragon's aspect, a shape-changer, able to transform at will. Others called her the Dragon-mother, the first and most powerful of all that deadly *väki*. Of old, she had allied with Löhi and fought against the Heroes, for she was filled with hatred for all living things and delighted in cruelty. And she desired gold and jewels and other such precious things that she might hoard, coveting her treasure and gloating over it in the darkness of her den.

Ajatar had fought Väinämöinen and Enkeli, though they escaped with their lives; and she had conquered many other Erilaiset besides. And she hated Väinämöinen beyond all of her foes, for she had not slain him and was humbled by her failure, having bragged among the Pohjolaiset that no wizard would ever elude her. The dragon had vowed revenge upon him, awaiting the day when she might challenge him anew. But she had fled after Löhi's first defeat, vanished, and passed into legend among the few who still remembered those times.

In what lairs she dwelt, what dens she slept, who could say? No living mortal or Erilainen had seen her since the days of Lemminkäinen. But Löhi, Queen of Pohjola, had gathered all evil things under her sway when she returned. The Witch found Ajatar and seduced her, giving her a great hoard of heavy gold and silver. And each year, the goblins came to her with more—gold from the River Kemi, and precious spoils from battle gathered by the Easterners, and all manner of jewels and amber. For only her greed for treasure exceeded her hatred of other living things.

In her wickedness, Ajatar would bargain with her victims at times, promising to spare them in exchange for treasures. Sometimes she honored her bargains and let them go, while other times she slew them cruelly when she had taken from them all that she could; for holding the power of life and death over others was her delight. And, in this, she resembled the Witch of Pohjola.

And so Löhi had set her to watch over the lonely pass so that all the approaches to the North might be covered; for Löhi was wise, her webs everywhere, leaving nothing to chance or ill fortune. And for many years now, Ajatar had haunted the mountains, and none passed without her knowing it.

Now Ajatar loomed above them, surveying each in turn. If her great jaws, filled with teeth like iron spikes, could have opened into a smile, they would have done so.

"Do not look into her eyes!" cried Väinämöinen, for the dragon's eyes might enchant any who gazed at them, binding them with a powerful magic that could ensnare even the mightiest singer. Other weapons she had, too. If Ajatar was not so large as the beast that Egan had slain, she was far deadlier. Her spiked tail lashed like a terrible whip; her claws cut like silver-steel. No fire burned in her belly, but in her dark heart's embers, a noxious poison brewed, blinding and choking all that breathed those ghastly fumes.

Vipers and serpents, her deadly minions, crawled about her feet. One slunk over Väinämöinen's yellow boot, striking as it passed. With a start, the old man kicked it away. Ajatar laughed again.

"Long has it been, Väinämöinen," said the dragon, her metallic voice sinister and menacing.

"Long has it been. Long years have passed since last I saw thee. Quick to flee, quick to leave thy friends in the lurch. Did I not last see thee flying, turning tail to save thine own skin while thy companions perished beneath my feet? Yet now, at last, I have thee and thy cowardice shall be displayed for all to see."

"Are you so sure? I do not recall you at the Great Battle, worm," the wizard answered. "Your own *väki* perished, yet you dared not take the field in their defense. I was there, Ajatar. I fought against your kin, as well you know. So did many Erilaiset. Strange that you availed yourself not of the opportunity, were you so eager to do battle. Indeed, I am surprised that the Witch trusts you to guard the approaches to her realm. More faithful servants she surely has, though perhaps less loathsome."

"Brag, brag, and pride, wizard. Such was ever thy way. Yet what hast thou ever accomplished but to save thyself at others' expense? Even now, thou leadest thy friends to death and ruin. A pity none warned them what to expect when Väinämöinen of the Erilaiset comes calling."

Ajatar's forked tongue flashed like a ribbon of red flame. Her eager gaze cast about from one traveler to another, but they avoided her crystalline eyes. Ulla felt the dragon's magic beating on her.

"Of course," continued the serpent, "Mayhap thy companions have other ideas and do not desire to share thy fate. Why are they silent? Wouldst thou not treat with me? For if thine offer pleases me, Ajatar may permit thee to pass unmolested and go whither thou wouldst."

"A fine guardian you are for your mistress," laughed Väinämöinen. "Say rather that perhaps you have little faith in her power or your own. You do not know your peril, worm. Five wizards stand before you, the most powerful in the Far Northern Land. Never have you faced such foes in all your days. Not even were Lemminkäinen here, who slew Löhi of old, would such strength be gathered against you. If you would not fight all of us at once, consider carefully. Our journey concerns you not and we are pleased to leave you to your vigil.

"Choose wisely, Ajatar! It may be the most important choice you ever make in all your long life."

All the while Väinämöinen spoke to the dragon, the others had fanned out on either side. Tulikki and Ilkka moved to Ajatar's left flank. Ulla and Kaukomieli, stepping over slithering vipers, sidled to the right, swords in hand. Ajatar shifted her scaly bulk, blocking any advance even as her leering, crested head bobbed from side to side.

"What is Löhi to me?" hissed the dragon. "Her star is ascendant; her power waxes and the time of snow and ice returns. Yet what is that to me? 'Tis thy land, the Seven Lands of Men and the wood of the Erilaiset that shall be troubled, not Ajatar the Great. I was here before and will be here after. No rival is left to me, wizard.

"Yet what of thy companions? Again, I ask—wilt thou not treat with me? Hast thou nothing to offer in exchange for thy lives? Surely Ulla Karhulainen, she who bears the Mark of the Clan, does not go empty-handed into the North? Wilt thou not treat with Ajatar, Ulla Karhulainen? Consider carefully thy choice, for it may be the most important thou shalt ever make."

The shock on their faces was obvious. Ajatar laughed, the grating sound echoing through the woods. She *knew*. The dragon knew Ulla, had been waiting for her. Truly, all paths to Pohjola were watched.

Ulla stared at the burnt-orange dragon in disbelief, eyes drawn against her will to the great spiked head. Into the dragon's sparkling eyes she gazed, and straightaway was caught in Ajatar's spell. *Pohjanpiikki* fell to the ground. The staff wobbled in her hand. Her mind swam.

The dragon's mocking voice came dimly to her ears.

"Dost thou think my eyes blind?" asked Ajatar. "Dost thou not know that Pohjola watches all the ways of thy feet? Foolish *tietäjää*! Deliver unto me now what treasure thou hast, else I will deliver thee to Löhi. If not, thou shalt die here beside Väinämöinen and thy spirit fly as escort with him to the gates of Tuonela."

"Ajatar!" cried Tulikki suddenly. She stood forth with raised staff.

"Consider carefully, dragon! You do not know me, but my mother knows you—and my mother is Mielikki, the Lady of the Woods."

The dragon hissed, as if the name of Mielikki angered her.

"Ulla bears the Mark of the Clan, indeed," Tulikki continued. "And my mother's prophecy, Mielikki's prophecy, shall surely be fulfilled. *Comes a Child into the Northland, all the Clans to bring together.*

"Do you not know those words, Ajatar? Have you not heard the prophecy? Consider carefully! No one, not even Ajatar, may hinder what is foreordained by Tapio. How else has this company come so far, through perils that you cannot imagine? Come not between Mielikki's words and their fulfillment. Or else you will not return to your forest slumber, but rather die here, this day, your last upon this earth."

For a moment, surprised by Tulikki's brash words, the dragon hesitated, as if pondering what truth might lie in them. Then, gathering herself like a snake as if to strike, she opened her mighty jaws.

But Väinämöinen had not been idle. The moment he saw Ajatar rise from the mould, he had begun preparing a spell, finishing it while Tulikki taunted the beast. Like unto Unaja's Wall it was, if not so strong, a shield of fire that might burn even a dragon—or buy them time to flee.

"*Kilpi!*" cried the wizard. A flaming yellow disc blossomed about the monster's head. The spell did not surprise Ajatar, however. Too wise she was, too old and wary, and expected no less from her greatest enemy.

Ilkka, sword raised, rushed toward the dragon's legs. He made a great stroke against her foreclaw, shearing its golden scales. Tulikki charged with drawn bow, hoping to shoot an arrow through the fiery halo into the dragon's eyes. Ajatar could not see them, but she had other senses; no enemy had ever caught her unawares yet. Even as Ilkka dodged beneath her outstretched wing, aiming a blow at its delicate joint, she struck.

Snapping her spiked tail, she lashed out at the Warden. It struck him like a whip. The air thundered with its crack, followed by a sickening crunch. Knocked to the ground like a sack of straw, the Warden cried out, then lay silent. Tulikki sent another arrow whistling through the flame, but it glanced off her lolling neck and fell to the ground.

Rising on her haunches, from her nostrils Ajatar issued a blast of noxious poison. A noisome cloud of deadly mist spread outward like billowing smoke. Gasping, blinded by the venomous spray, Tulikki fell over Ilkka's crumpled body, twitching like a fish out of water.

Ajatar sprang through Väinämöinen's Shield. Though scorched by the magical fire, she came straight at the old man before he cast his next missile. The spell wavered; the shield flared and went out. Using his crimson cloak to ward off the poison, the wizard brought *Jääpuikko* down across the dragon's outstretched neck. The winterfast blade scoured the creature's scaly hide, but the wound was shallow. Recoiling, Ajatar batted Väinämöinen violently to the ground. The old man did not rise again.

Terrified as he watched his friends fall one by one, only Kaukomieli remained in the fight. Then the yellow-haired wizard swallowed his fear and sprang into action. Putting himself between Ulla and the loathsome creature, with a word he gathered the light and energy around him into his hand. He cast the blazing blue ball at Ajatar. Lightnings flickered about her head, blinding her. He cast another.

Furious, shaking off the spell, the dragon blew a spray of poisonous fume at the young man. Her tail cracked again like a whip. Kaukomieli fell. Overcome with pain, he covered his burning eyes with his hands, frantically rolling about. Ajatar's clawed foot came down on him, trapping him beneath even as the blue lightning flickered out.

Ajatar bellowed in rage and pain. Slashed, scorched, and burned—seldom had enemies defied her like this. Not since the battle with Väinämöinen and Enkeli ages past had she been truly challenged. Since then, her enemies had fallen victim to her magic, enchanted by her crystalline gaze, or they had fled, only to be cut down, devoured. No matter.

The battle was over. The so-called *tietäjää* were defeated. The old man had scarcely put up a fight. If this was the best that the Erilaiset could do, perhaps she should have ravaged Karelia long ago, regardless of Mielikki and her magic. For now, she would have her revenge upon Väinämöinen. It would be sweet, very sweet. *Yes, it was time to end this.*

The dragon looked down upon Kaukomieli. Here was a young victim, tender, just enough to whet her appetite for first blood. The others would follow in turn, the old wizard last of all. She would let him recover just enough to understand what was happening while she tore him apart. Ajatar stooped to take Kaukomieli into her jaws.

And then she noticed something from the corner of her baleful eyes.

For Ulla no longer stood enchanted.

The dark-haired young woman had stood in silence while her companions battled the *lohikäärme*, sensing dimly, as if through a fog, all that transpired. She felt like a drowning woman, inches from the water's surface, unable to break through to light and freedom. But Ulla was no ordinary woman.

Fighting off the spell, battling through the mist that clouded mind and soul, her power awoke. Her eyes blinked. Strength returned to hand and limb. She saw the burnt-orange dragon poised to strike her friends; she knew what she had to do.

Even as they had mounted the stairs, Ulla had strung the short bow she carried, though she seldom used it. Unslinging it now from her shoulder, she reached for an arrow. It was no ordinary arrow she chose, however. No feather-fletched arrow, no sword forged by man, no spell by Väinämöinen himself could save them now and Ulla understood this. It was too late for magic or trickery, too late for the simple weapons of men.

But the Arrow of Tuonetar came from the Lord of the Dead himself.

Tearing the arrow from its hiding place beneath her cloak, she nocked it. She drew back the string.

Ajatar glared. Preparing to spring, the great dragon opened her mouth, screaming, "Karhulainen!"

Ulla loosed the arrow. Though made of stone, it sped to its target as true as any shaft of pine or fir. Ajatar shuddered as the arrow pierced her belly, disappearing deep within.

The monster looked down in disbelief. Then, stretching out her long neck, she launched herself at Ulla. Thundering with rage, she sought to crush Ulla, tear her from limb to limb. The Witch could moan all she wished, for she wanted Ulla alive, but the girl would die here, *die now.*

Ulla shifted her weight, ready to dodge. Before she could react, however, Ajatar stopped in her tracks, dropping heavily to the ground. Her serpentine neck undulating like a snake, jaws snapping open and shut, she began to change.

The dragon's orange legs turned a stony brown, anchored to the earth. The color spread upward—flanks, belly, scaly breast, all turned to stone. Straight up her neck it ran, freezing the beast in place, until only her spiky head remained alive.

Last of all, the dragon's crystalline eyes blazed; she glared at Ulla, her gaze so piercing and hate-filled that it seemed some last deadly blast might issue forth to destroy them all. Then slowly, imperceptibly at first, then quicker, the life ebbed away. Light faded. Crystal became dull rock.

Ajatar stood motionless, a rocky statue blindly staring into nothingness.

The young woman with dark hair toppled to the ground.

Chapter Thirteen

At the Fireside of Peiko's Cottage

It was her hearing that first returned. A voice hummed soft sounds. Wind whispered overhead. A cold thrill passed throughout her body.

"Ulla," said the voice. "Come back, Ulla."

Kaukomieli. She knew his voice.

She opened her eyes. Night had fallen, but it was bright. Stars shone in the clear sky. The silvery moon smiled down on the wild northern woods.

Kaukomieli stooped over her. Even in the dark, Ulla could see his torn, bruised face framed within loose yellow hair.

"Are you all right?"

The young woman sat up. Her body ached, but she was whole. The frozen, stony figure of Ajatar loomed against the dark sky.

Looking around, she tried to piece together what had happened.

Not far away, she saw Väinämöinen. The old wizard knelt beside two figures shrouded in shadow, Ilkka and Tulikki. The Erilaisen woman drew up her knees; she coughed, passing her hand across her eyes. Ilkka lay motionless, however.

"He is hurt," said Kaukomieli, gravely. "Badly hurt. Väinämöinen called him back from the colorless woods, but, to what end, I do not know."

Unsteadily, Ulla came to Väinämöinen's side. She knelt beside him. Blood from a deep gash on his forehead streaked the old wizard's face, but the Warden's face, ashen in the moonlight, worried her more. She touched his shattered arm, but he did not respond.

"I've done what I could, child," said the old man, gently. "I set the bones in his leg and sang over them; they are whole again. I stopped the blood from several wounds. We'll see what the morrow brings. Curse the dragon!

"But help me now with Tulikki, if you can. The worm's poison sickened her. She was blind, but her sight is slowly returning. Wash her eyes again and give her clean water to drink."

At the mention of Ajatar's poison, Ulla started; she looked about nervously.

"They are gone," said Kaukomieli, referring to the snakes that had crept about Ajatar's feet. "Vanished."

Ulla and Kaukomieli tended Tulikki while Väinämöinen kept watch over Ilkka. Tulikki was hurt less grievously than the Warden. Her eyes burned badly, but after Ulla washed them repeatedly with cold water as the old wizard instructed, she felt better. They wrapped her in furs, then Kaukomieli held her amidst the bracken beneath the trees. Soon Tulikki slept.

Ulla remained awake, however.

"You know what I did," she said at last. Väinämöinen lay stretched out, staring up at the stars. The Great Bear twinkled overhead.

"You know what I did, Väinämöinen," repeated Ulla. "I shot the arrow, Tuonetar's Arrow. I turned the monster to stone."

"So I guessed," said the wizard. "What else? No song that I know of could have done that, not to such a creature as Ajatar. It was a mighty shot."

"But the arrow is gone," said Ulla, flatly. "Gone. Without it, what hope have we against Löhi? It was all for nothing—Tuonela, the gem with Lovêatar trapped within. All for nothing. We cannot return to Tuonela, we have nothing with which to bargain. Here we are, in the middle of nowhere with winter coming on and, even if we somehow make it to Pohjola, we have no weapon. What are we to do?"

"Was there any other way to destroy the dragon?" asked Väinämöinen.

Ulla hesitated only for a moment. "No."

"Then you did what you had to, child. The creature would have killed us all. I certainly could not have defeated her. I remember nothing after she attacked me. Ulla, when I fell and the darkness closed around me, I never thought to open my eyes again."

The old man sighed heavily.

"With hope or without hope, we go on," he said, finally. "If we come to Pohjola, we shall see what we shall see."

"With hope or without," answered Ulla.

Kaukomieli woke them in the chilly dawn. Yellow streaked the sky. Tulikki felt ill, but was up and about again, tending a small fire. Ilkka remained feverish, however. From time to time, his eyes fluttered as he called out in his uneasy sleep.

They stayed in the grove three days and nights, resting from their injuries. The sky clouded over; cold rain began to fall. At last, on the morning of the fourth day since Ajatar's attack, the Warden awoke, weak and in pain. He drank water, but refused food and said little. Väinämöinen did not conceal his worry. That night, while Ilkka slept, the others sat around a sputtering pinewood fire. The wizard spoke to them.

"I have told you enough about the dragon by now to satisfy curiosity's need. Never would I have expected to find her here, find her anywhere. But this much is clear—the Witch knows we have taken to the trails. She knows we are making for Pohjola and she watches all roads. We have no hope to surprise her, no matter what happened to the Moonface in the Wastes.

"There is more. We have no weapon. Ulla did what was necessary and so slew Ajatar, saving all our lives. 'Twas a great deed! But now she speaks truthfully when she says that we no longer have the weapon that our hope depended on. Even if we reach Pohjola alive, how shall we slay Löhi, in the very heart of her dark realm?"

"So what are we to do, Väinämöinen?" asked Kaukomieli.

"We have but two choices: to go back and seek the Marches before winter closes in or to go forward, no matter the risk. When we reach Pohjola—*if* we reach Pohjola—we must improvise. Most likely, we would have done so, in any case."

No one said a word. The fire crackled. Finally, Ulla broke the silence.

"This time you are wrong, Väinämöinen. There is only one choice. What good is there in returning? Better to die in the wilderness if die we must."

"Well and good," said the old man. "But what of Ilkka?"

They turned and looked at their friend as he slept fitfully, wrapped in cloaks and furs against the cold.

"Ilkka is a survivor," said Väinämöinen. "Never have I known a mortal so tough in all my many years. But his body is broken. He came close to death. He may heal in time, but we do not have that time. We cannot continue the journey, yet we cannot stay here while he recovers—if he recovers. We would only die in the wilderness with him."

"I will not die," Tulikki said suddenly. "More experience have I in these barren lands than even you, Väinämöinen. I will stay with him."

The old man looked hard at Tulikki in the flame's red glare. Her eyes still stung from Ajatar's poison. She seemed small, small and weak, as if the journey and the dragon had shaken her last reserves of strength, Mielikki's daughter or not.

"If they are searching for us," said Kaukomieli, "They will come here soon, either the Witch's servants or Löhi herself. The dragon's death will not long remain secret. Löhi must sometimes turn her *sight* this way."

"I will not wait for them," answered Tulikki. "I will not stay here. I felt from the moment we came here that this place was unwholesome.

"But the first night we mounted the ridge, I turned my *sight* westward. Something about those hills seemed familiar. I glimpsed a valley not so far away, a valley enclosing a little lake with silver water. I believe I know it; I came that way during my search for the Shards of the Sampo. Winterberries grow there. Deer shelter in the deep fir wood. Fish swim in the lake. It is a gentle place compared to this desolate wasteland. I will take Ilkka there and stay with him through the snows; then we will return to the Seven Lands in spring—to peace, if you succeed, and to face the storm, if you do not."

The old man looked at her doubtfully.

"A gentle place? Not likely. No place is gentle in the wild. And Ilkka cannot travel. The bones in his leg may be whole, but that does not mean he can walk, at least not far."

"I will help him; I have strength enough for us both, for a while. If not, we will perish together. Either way, as Ulla says, what choice is there? Ulla must go on and you, Väinämöinen, must help her. Yet we cannot leave our friend to die in the wilderness. I am Mielikki's daughter, descended from Tapio, Lord of the Forest. The Vanhalaiset will not forsake me. And if they do, how could any of you fare better?"

The others had no answer to this, though they feared they were leaving both friends behind to die. Nonetheless, it was decided and they spoke about it no more.

Väinämöinen, Kaukomieli, and Ulla prepared to leave the next morning. Tightening their belts, they shouldered their share of meager supplies left to them. Ominous clouds loomed darkly in the sky above.

Ilkka woke before they set out. Sitting up weakly for the first time since the attack, he implored Tulikki to leave him, only relenting as his strength waned. The companions hastily said their farewells.

Kneeling beside the Warden, Ulla took his hand.

"Be strong, brother," she said, willing herself not to shed tears. "You are needed at home. And when our task is finished, I will return at once to find you."

Ilkka smiled. "My love goes with you, little one. Far removed are we now in time and distance from the little village where first we met. Take care! Child of the Prophecy you may be, but, to me, you will always be that little girl from the Marches."

Ulla kissed the Warden's forehead and rose. Suddenly, she turned back, saying gently, "Ilkka, if you return and we do not...see to Siria. An island in the archipelago, someplace else—wherever you deem best. Please do this for me."

Just as gravely, he replied, "Do not worry. I will do for her whatever needs to be done."

Embracing Tulikki, the three companions—all that remained of the desperate band—set out to the north. Just once, Ulla looked back. In the distance, she saw them. Tulikki stood, watching, next to Ilkka, who sat propped against the tree. With a start, she noticed something else even more distant. The head and neck of Ajatar rose up over the treetops, a silent, stony sentinel still guarding the pass through the woods.

The three wizards tramped on, staffs in hand. The land was full of trails made by elk, deer, and badger, and they made good time. They had come far north of the Marches now, hundreds of miles from Länsimaa and the Seven Lands. The third day out, after fording a waist-deep bubbling river, they stood shivering on a little height, stamping their boots to get dry. Väinämöinen stood still for a long time, turning his *sight* north and east. He sighed.

The sound of wailing wolves echoed in the lonely wastes.

Shaking his head, he said, "It is no use. I can see ahead a little way to the north; I see trails and trees. Wilderness. To the east, all goes dark. It is black there; I see nothing."

"What does that mean?" asked Kaukomieli.

"That we are on the right trail, at least. That way lies Pohjola. The Witch's power and thought lie upon it and all about it for miles and miles. No wizardly *sight* can pierce the shadows of her homeland, where her power is greatest. But, thanks be to Ukko, we are on the right trail after all."

"Let me try," said Ulla.

"No!" cried Väinämöinen, sharply. "Strong you are child but not that strong. And it is dangerous now that we are nearing Northland. Löhi can feel our *sight*, feel us probing for the right path. She waits for you. No, I may have risked it this once, but we must not use *sight* again unless our lives depend upon it and we must strengthen the spells that we have used to shield us from her observation. Those spells and no other. We must be wary of using magic as we near Pohjola. Through it, Löhi can feel our presence."

As the journey continued, two things changed. First, snowflakes fell several times, light flurries signaling winter's approach. The cold air felt electric with anticipation. Second, the land itself changed. Daughter of northern woods, Ulla was accustomed to soaring pines and tall, graceful white-skinned birch, to say nothing of the majestic trees of the Karelian Forest and Enchanted Valley.

The farther north they journeyed, the shorter the trees. Poor soil and little light during the long winter stunted all living things. In places they found whole stands of woods that looked like new growth over burned lands, but these trees were full grown, mature, and hardy enough to withstand the coldest weather.

Animals were on the move too. Northern elk and reindeer were migrating, moving in large herds toward their winter shelters. At times, the lumbering beasts crowded them off the trail. They stood aside and watched them pass. Shaggy pelts and antlers shambled by. Unafraid, the beasts paid them scant attention, secure in their large numbers. Only when groups of calves passed did the bucks display, snort angrily, and threaten to charge. Then, they moved deeper into the trees and away from the trail until the animals were gone. Once, they saw a black bear and her cub crossing a rocky stream that lay in their path. The scars on Ulla's leg tightened; the Mark on her shoulder burned hot.

"Stay still," said Väinämöinen, swiftly. "Let them pass. They will soon be entering their den for the winter. None knows better than you, Ulla, not to disturb a mother bear and her young."

Despite their exhaustion and hunger, they moved swiftly on the northern trails. A little more than two weeks after they had parted from Tulikki, they had journeyed many, many miles northward. The days grew shorter than any Ulla and Kaukomieli had ever known; the watery sun shone for only a few hours each day, when visible at all. Other times, they walked in darkness or lingering, yellow twilight. When the sky cleared and the stars came out, they appeared strange, unfamiliar.

"Taivaantappi is not where she should be," said Kaukomieli one night. "Nor the Evening Star. And the Morning Star has disappeared. But look at the Witch's Star! Red it burns, red and bright! It is almost directly above us."

"Only *karhu* looks the same," said Ulla. "But he, too, is on the move and not where he should be."

"All runs amiss in Northland," said Väinämöinen. "Even the stars in their courses. Once—only once—have I been this far north since the ancient days. I am out of my reckoning."

At last they came upon a trail so broad that it seemed almost a road. The old wizard was wary. Game trail or not, it looked the type of path the Witch's servants might use.

Kaukomieli turned round about, surveying the land. "It runs northeast, does it not? We can walk fast on such a trail."

"I wonder," growled Väinämöinen. "If we can, so can others. And I feel exposed. The game trails we've been on wound all about, hiding us. This one does not."

Flurries swirled around them. Väinämöinen stared at the two young wizards. Shivering, they stood side by side, their frosty breath forming misty clouds in the gloom. They looked haggard, half-starved; they could not last much longer.

"So be it," he said at last. "Let's take to the road! It is time for a final sprint. Stay alert. The trees here are sparse, shrubby. There's little cover if we need to hide quickly."

The snow let up. As they often did, they walked a ways apart, each wrapped in their own thought. Väinämöinen brooded on how to find the direct path to Pohjola. Ulla steeled herself to find some way, any way, to outwit Löhi now that the arrow was lost beyond recovery. Kaukomieli, in the lead, contemplated the strange trees along the trail.

He sensed them watching expectantly. Not in a menacing way, as if filled with malice toward the company, yet waiting for something nonetheless. He was just about to tell the others to halt while he reached out to a particularly odd, gnarled birch tree when he spied something from the corner of his eye; a rope hung from one of its twisted branches.

"Väinämöinen!" he called.

The old wizard and Ulla came stomping up hurriedly.

"What is it?" asked Väinämöinen. "And keep your voice down. Don't call my name so loudly in these parts."

"Look!" cried Kaukomieli, pointing to the hand-twisted rope. He pulled it. Frayed at the end, it held fast to the branch above.

"A snare or trap?" asked Ulla.

"Aye," said Väinämöinen. "And not too old, by the look of it. Leave it be!"

"Another one!" shouted Kaukomieli, running to a nearby tree from which a second rope dangled.

"Be careful, Kaukomieli," Ulla called out. "Don't touch it."

The young man pulled hard on the grey rope.

"Väinämöinen, it's—" With a *swoosh*, a net snare for large game emerged from the ground's thin cover of icy snow, sweeping Kaukomieli up. His staff fell to the earth; he was ten feet off the ground.

"By the vaulted heavens!" cried Väinämöinen. He and Ulla took off at a run toward their friend, but just as they passed a knotted pine—*swoosh, swoosh*. Two more staffs dropped onto the snow. Ulla and Väinämöinen dangled side by side.

"Blast it, Kaukomieli," Väinämöinen spluttered, his beard in his mouth, hopelessly tangled in a tightly woven hemp net, hanging perfectly upside down.

"Yet again! I'm getting tired of this. I'm too old to hang upside down all the time like a ham dangling from the rafters. The blood goes straight to my head and makes me wobbly.

"I can't reach my knife. Ulla?"

"I'm trying to get Longleaf out of my belt," she said. Also upside down, she twisted back and forth while struggling to draw the knife to cut herself loose. She grew giddy.

"I'm going to be sick," she said. The ground spun beneath her.

So they went on for several minutes, unable to draw their blades while the wind picked up.

"This is no good," said the old man. "It will be dark in another hour; we're freezing. We will have to sing our way out."

"You got us into this; you get us out," Ulla said sharply to Kaukomieli.

"We might break our necks in the fall," he answered.

"Then choose your spell carefully."

"Spell? *Loitsu*? Can't cut your way out, so you'll sing your way out? You're wizards, then; that's what the sticks'er for. Well, well."

The voice was deep, a resonant baritone. As Ulla spun, she glimpsed the speaker, a huge figure standing right beside her, so tall that its head was even with hers, though she hung high in the air.

All at once she fell to the ground with a crash. A moment later, Väinämöinen dropped on top of her. She felt battered and bruised, but had broken nothing. She stared up at the giant bending over her, hands on its knees.

The troll laughed, the sound booming through the woods, for a troll it was and a particularly enormous one at that.

Clad in fur, the troll's long, carrot-like nose stuck out from beneath its cap. Tiny eyes sparkled in the twilight. Thin and wiry, its arms displayed muscles betraying tremendous strength. Each of its heavy booted legs was as large as Ulla. The troll held a mallet in its left hand.

Kaukomieli, still caught in the net and struggling mightily, remembered the trolls' attack in Tavastia. Indeed, he remembered that most trolls seem little more than ravenous beasts, delighting in destruction, speaking little, if at all. Here and there, even in the deep dales of the Enchanted Valley, lived some that were not evil, but they were few.

The troll laughed again.

"Hold on," he said. "I'll cut you down soon enough. Aye, I will!"

"*Pysäyttää!*" cried Väinämöinen, still flat on his back, enmeshed. The troll straightened. For a moment, he stood perfectly still. Then, shaking his head violently, he recovered. Trolls were renowned not only for their size and strength, but their resistance to magic.

"Well, I'll be damned to the Pits of Tuonela," he said. "You *are* wizards. What's more, comin' up my trail by the looks of it, not comin' down from Pohjola. Been many a year since strange folk 'ave come up!

"Now listen up! You'll 'ave to do lots better'n that to slow me down, so if you don't want me to bash your skulls in right now, hold off. The choice is yours. But I'd rather 'ave a word with you than kill you, at least for the moment."

Väinämöinen opened his mouth. Thinking better of it, he quickly closed it again.

"Good," laughed the troll. "I'll 'ave to cut you out, methinks. You ruined my snares, but it can't be helped."

The troll drew a long, silver knife from his belt. He stooped over Ulla. She winced, half expecting to feel the knife's sting. The troll cut her loose. Next, he freed Väinämöinen, then lumbered over to Kaukomieli and cut him down, too. The companions scrambled to their feet. The troll had gathered their staffs into a pile. Väinämöinen unsheathed *Jääpuikko. Pohjanpiikki* shone in Ulla's hand. The tall creature tensed.

Frowning, he said, "If that's how it's going to go, 'ave at it. Maybe one of you will still be standing afterwards, maybe not."

"We have no quarrel with you or any other servant of Löhi," said Väinämöinen. "Our errand does not concern you. Leave us in peace and we shall do the same."

"Löhi!" exclaimed the troll. "That's rich! 'Aven't been no servant of Löhi's for, oh, four or five hundred years, I reckon. Wish she'd never come back. Those goblins of hers 'ave near ruined my game trails. Tried to burn me out one night! I had to start huntin' them. After I caught a dozen or two, they stopped comin' round here much."

Väinämöinen hesitated. He didn't know whether to trust the troll or not. A mistake could be fatal. Still, the troll could have killed them while they were snared.

The wizard slowly sheathed his sword. Ulla did the same.

"That's better! No reason to go to fightin' if you don't need to. Now then, first things first. Who are ya? And where are ya goin'? No one comes near these parts anymore but deer n' elks."

Väinämöinen cleared his throat.

"My name is Tietainen," he said. "And you're right; I am a wizard. These are my niece and nephew. We're going to the Kääpiövuori on business with the dwarves and only wish to be left alone. And who are you?"

"Peiko you can call me; that'll do well enough. That's what they called me when I was young, back in the old days. But yer goin' the wrong way if yer headed to the dwarf mountain. You should have taken the split trail back yonder."

"Perhaps you can show us the way," said Kaukomieli.

"Perhaps," said Peiko. "And perhaps you can tell me the truth. But wrong way or no, by the looks of ye, you'll not go far. You're fair starvin'.'"

Ulla glanced at her filthy clothes and realized what they looked like. The rich, fur-lined cloaks were warm, but stained with long use. Their hoods were tattered and their tunics torn. Indeed, they *were* starving and, had they not been singers, would have perished long before.

"See here, Tietainen," said Peiko, looking sidelong at Väinämöinen with his beady eyes. "It'll soon rain snow, it will. I can feel it. First big fall of the winter's a comin'. No cause to be standin' round outside. Let's trade! If you give me what I *want*, I'll give you what you *need*."

The old man's eyes narrowed suspiciously.

"And what's that?" he said carefully. They had little with which to satisfy any demand for a toll.

Peiko laughed. "What do you need? Food, for one. Fire, for another. I've a home not too far from here; I'm stayin' there at present while I walk the trails.

Now's the time to catch game, while the herds are movin'. I'll take you there and you can 'ave both."

"And what do you want in return?" asked Väinämöinen.

"Why, news, of course! It's not often other folk come by, 'cept them Hiisia and they don't tell nothin', even if you make 'em squeal. It's news I'm wantin'. What'er mortals doin'? And what's become of the Witch? Her armies all went south some time ago. I'll wager you know more about it than old Peiko—am I right? C'mon, let's trade! Whaddaya got to lose? You'll die soon enough in the snow!"

The three friends looked at one another. They were not sure whether to trust the troll and willingly go to its lair. In any other situation, to do so seemed utterly foolish. But Peiko was right. They were starving and, *tietäjää* or not, just about at the end of their strength.

"What will your folk say about bringing home so many visitors at once?"

Peiko grinned, revealing sharp white eyeteeth in his wide mouth. "Aren't no other folk 'cept me. 'Aven't been in many a year. C'mon now, let's trade!"

The old man sighed. "Very well. But we'll take our staffs back now."

"The 'ell you will. I'll keep 'em at present. I have to trust *you*, too, ya know."

Peiko set off down the trail; the others fell in line behind. The troll's shaggy coat swayed on his broad shoulders as his boots stomped up and down. He soon left the trail, motioning to Väinämöinen to follow. If there was a path to be found through the woods, the three wizards could see no sign of it, yet Peiko clearly knew exactly where he was going. He skillfully moved through the trees, weaving this way and that. As snow began to fall, the light faded, and they came to a great outcropping of grey stone. A thin line of white smoke rose into the air.

"Here we are!" said the troll. "Not a bad place to spend a cold night. Not that I don't have others, mind you, but I like to stay here when I'm walkin' these trails."

Peiko led them around the stones, where they saw a ramshackle *pirtti*, facing south and sheltered from the cold North Wind by the outcropping.

The *pirtti* was like none Ulla had ever seen. Built to a different scale, the cottage seemed almost a barn to mortal eyes. Whole tree trunks leaned one against another with earth and stone packed between. Roughly corner-timbered, a peaked roof of mossy turf covered by a white dusting backed against the stone wall.

The troll swung open the door.

"Let's get inside," he said. "It'll be coming down harder soon enough." He stooped and entered. After a quick exchange of nervous glances, the three companions followed.

Inside, the *pirtti* felt homelike enough to Ulla and Kaukomieli. Peiko lit a few tallow candles, which cast yellow light and long shadows across the dark, smoky cabin. A huge iron pot bubbled over a great central hearth of piled stones in the middle of the single room. A wonderful smell overwhelmed their senses. They almost swooned at the scent that filled the air, thick porridge with mushrooms and venison.

"By the vaulted heavens!" exclaimed Väinämöinen. "Peiko, I, uh—"

The big troll chuckled.

"Hungry? I can well believe it. Many a time I've been a' starvin', too, wanderin' here and there. Seen some lean times. But yer in luck and not for the pot yerselfs, as you feared! Pull up a stool and get warm. There's plenty for all!"

While Peiko spooned porridge into large wooden bowls, they shed their wet outer clothes and warmed themselves beside the fire. The rye porridge, mixed with wild onions, mushrooms, and meat, tasted delicious. Too famished to care anymore about tricks or deception, they finished two bowls and were deep into their third before the troll stopped his puttering and sat beside them.

He had told them he wanted news, but either had forgotten or was so starved for company that he did almost all the talking himself. They drowsed while the old troll told his tale.

He lived alone now, as he had for years beyond count, and only wished to be left alone, or, at least, unmolested. He had other cabins scattered among the northern woods and moved around as fancy took him. Mostly he hunted.

The trails nearby were rich with game. Deer, elk, badger, fox, hare, and many others roamed the forest. There were even bear close by, though he seldom hunted them. Peiko regarded bear as taboo, using names like honey paw and bee-wolf rather than *karhu* after the manner of folk of old. He had a bearskin coat, however, big enough to cover even his giant frame. He wore it when the weather turned really cold.

They soon learned where he came by his stocks, for the *pirtti* was filled with supplies and there was more where they came from: barley and rye (he baked his own bread), barrels of red lingonberries, dried winter fruits, and, most remarkable of all, dried apples. Peiko obtained all this and more from the dwarves. He met them several times a year. *What* he traded—for Peiko was indeed a trader and dwarves give nothing for free—he wouldn't say. But trade he did and the dwarves paid him handsomely in food and iron. The troll had everything he needed.

"But see here, Peiko," said Kaukomieli, becoming more comfortable around the troll, especially after Peiko tossed him several apples.

"I always thought, well—no offense—but I always thought trolls served the Witch or at least were friendly to her. And you are a troll, are you not?"

"That I am," said he. "The last of my *väki* and that's a fact. But what good is old Löhi to me? War, fightin', death—that's all I've seen 'er bring. I had enough of that long ago."

"But you said that you once served her," said Ulla.

Peiko sighed.

"So I did, so I did. Aye, it's true enough. I won't deny I've done my share a fightin'. Things 'ave changed since then and Peiko's changed with them."

Peiko then told them the story of the 'old days,' as he called it. How in his youth, he had lived far to the south in the lands that became Akkala. He lived with his family and kinfolk in a little village beside a lake. Mortals came near and there was strife. The trolls moved north, beside another lake; then moved again, to yet another.

"Always there was more men comin', settlin' everywhere. Blows were struck, aye, they were. Some of my folk were a bad lot, thieves and murderers—wouldn't trust 'em myself. Most just wanted to be left alone. When mortals came, it weren't possible. Slashin' here, burnin' there, and drivin' us out if they found us. Weren't no peace left in the world for the Erilaiset."

Then Löhi came among them.

"The Witch had returned around that time, or so we heard. Been sleepin' for Ukko knows how long. She showed up in our place one day with a bunch of elves and some o' them goblins. Ugly she was, all withered like an old hag. Told us she was our champion, our protector. She wanted to drive the mortals out, them and the rebel Erilaiset that had come in with them. Everything would be ours again and we'd have our *revenge*; I remember how she kept sayin' that.

"Well, it sounded good enough and so we went for soldiers then, almost all of us. She had strong iron, did Löhi in those days. I had a mace and chain, all winterfast, and a buckler too. Star o' the North was painted on it! We came in with this Haltia, Tyë, and joined his army. Lots o' bad folk about, but what's done is done."

"Tyë!" exclaimed Kaukomieli. "He was Löhi's captain."

"One of 'em," said Peiko. "A right unpleasant fellow, too. 'Ell of a sorcerer, though. You could feel his power 'alf a mile away."

Peiko fought in many battles. For a time, all seemed well. They defeated their enemies and thought the final victory was at hand. Then Tyë sent them south, singly or in pairs, to haunt the farmlands of the Eagle Folk and terrorize them.

"That was a black time and I'll admit I done some bad things." The troll shook his shaggy head and sighed.

"Killed some folk as shouldn't a' been killed. Hurt 'em real bad. And they hunted us. Shot my brother full of arrows and killed him dead, right in front of me. Barely got away myself."

Peiko returned north, rejoining the army, but most of his folk were slain by then. He had thought of slipping away, but it proved impossible.

Löhi was gathering all her forces for a final assault. The mighty host marched on Tavastia. He fought in the Great Battle, where the last of his *väki* were killed; only he survived. But the battle was lost, Löhi slain, and he escaped into the wild.

"That was that," the troll said, sadly. "I tried to find my kinfolk, my old auntie and such, but they were all gone. Never saw 'em again. I came up here, then. Lots of Löhi's old people did, them's that got away. I didn't have no use for 'em. What did the Witch ever do for me? Lots o' lies and all my people ruined. And her folk, those Pohjolaiset, they *like* killin'—it's a game to 'em. Never wanted to be like that and don't like no troll that does. And that's the story, wizards. Been here ever since. Just want to be left alone, though I do like tradin' and hearin' news now and then!"

When Peiko's tale came to an end, Väinämöinen tried to repay him by speaking of the Witch's return and the wars in the South. The troll seemed to know some of what had happened, though he was surprised to learn that Työ, his old captain, had both returned and been slain. He had even heard rumor of the great fight at the Easterners' camp where Egan perished. His knowledge ended there, however. For several years, he had heard nothing.

The old wizard chose his words carefully. After all, no matter how friendly he seemed, Peiko was a stranger and member of a fierce race. His belly full and the warm fire lulling him to sleep, the singer could no longer keep his eyes open. Ulla was nodding. Kaukomieli slumped against her. Väinämöinen sighed and soon fell fast asleep.

* * *

The three companions awoke together. The fire had burned low. It was dark outside the *pirtti.* Snow fell lightly, but at least a foot already covered the ground. Peiko was nowhere to be found. Their staffs leaned neatly against the wall.

Väinämöinen, still groggy, was unconcerned; Ulla felt otherwise.

"Should we not flee?" she asked, nervously. "This is all well and good, but can we really trust him? We have food now; we are rested. Let us go before he returns!"

The old man served himself another bowl of porridge.

"Well and good, you say; but if we flee, Ulla, where do we flee to? Into the wild after a snow? With no clear idea of where we are or which way to go?"

"I don't see why we should run," said Kaukomieli, upon whom the apples had made a great impression. "Peiko hasn't harmed us, despite having several chances. What do you fear, Ulla?"

"To be trapped in a *pirtti* with you," she snapped. "But if the troll kills us, at least I will be spared that ordeal. *Think*, Kaukomieli. Where has he gone? There's a price on our heads, on *my* head, and they are searching for us throughout the North. Perhaps he has gone to fetch the Witch's servants. We are worth more to him alive than dead."

"I wonder," said Väinämöinen. "Your point's well taken, but I don't have that sense, Ulla. I don't know that we would fare any better if we leave. We need more food and rest, and more information about where we are. And the snow must stop."

They debated for a long while, but in the end, they agreed to wait and see what happened next. It was hard to tell day from night. The cloudy sky glowed red beneath its southern canopy for a few hours, their only indication that the sun had risen. They ate, slept, and told tales to pass the time. And they explored the cottage.

The troll had barrels and chests galore, but none filled with treasure or plunder. Food, drinks, furs, boxes of iron goods, and other useful things—such was Peiko's hoard, at least in this cottage. Apart from knives, he seemed to have no weapons at all. Ulla shrieked when she opened one dusty chest.

"Tapio's beard!" she cried. "What are they?"

Inside the chest were skulls, not animal skulls, but mortal or Erilaisen skulls, the skulls of intelligent beings.

"Strangely shaped," muttered Väinämöinen. "But I know them. I've seen many in my day."

"What were they? Or *who* were they?" asked Kaukomieli.

"*Hiisia*," answered Väinämöinen. "Goblins."

"So they are!" laughed Peiko, standing in the open doorway. A young elk lay in the snow behind him.

"Gettin' anxious? No matter, curiosity gets the better a' me, too, sometimes. Didn't see no need to wake you, but I had to be off. My traps need tendin', winter's comin' on. Got this one here down by the frozen fall. I've three now. That might be enough for you all winter, but I can eat an elk in a week or two! I'll need about six or so to get me through the dark time comfortably."

"Who were they?" asked Ulla.

"Why, goblins, of course, just like your uncle said. I hang them around in the trees sometimes as a warning, keeps their friends from gettin' too close. Not that they come round much anymore, not after I started huntin' 'em, I reckon."

Peiko joined them, prattling on about his trails, traps, and journeys, then asking questions about life in the South. After that, even Ulla trusted him, and their fears subsided.

They stayed more than a week in the troll's cottage, swapping tales and dressing Peiko's game. He baked fresh loaves of rye in an oven behind the *pirtti*. From a snow-covered *maja*, he carried in a barrel of beer, to the old man's surprise and delight. They ate all that they could, yet there was always more to be had; the troll had no want of victuals.

The three friends washed their clothes with hot water and stones and mended tattered garments with bone needle and thread. Since the troll's fingers were too big to use these easily, Ulla stitched up holes in his great leather boots and fur coat, for which he couldn't stop thanking her. Several times he left them alone as he tramped through the woods to check his snares for game.

All this time Väinämöinen considered their next steps and, especially, whether to tell Peiko who they really were and what they were doing in the wilderness. He had come to trust the amiable giant, but that trust only went so far. If they revealed themselves, they would be utterly at his mercy and discretion; Löhi had many ways of obtaining information, no matter Peiko's goodwill or intention. The troll had questioned them no further about their quest; it hung over the cottage like an unseen cloud of uncertainty that all recognized yet none openly acknowledged.

They could not stay in the cottage forever, though. The wizard knew in his heart that delay meant disaster. Löhi might launch her final assault on the Seven Clans next spring. They might be tracked down and trapped in Peiko's *pirtti*. They might reach Pohjola only to find the Witch gone, leading her forces south. Since they had failed to reach Pohjola before the snows came, their only hope now, though slim, was to catch the Witch in her own home during wintertime, which she seldom left during the days of darkness. In that dark time, she crafted and cast her spells across all the Far Northern Land.

Ulla was against telling Peiko anymore; Kaukomieli favored seeking his help. The old wizard waited, contemplating all courses until one night when again they sat around the hearth.

Väinämöinen saw the troll watching him intently beneath his bushy hair; Peiko's carrot-like nose glowed red in the fire's harsh light. Suddenly, he decided.

"Peiko, my friend," said Väinämöinen. "Our trade has been unfair. Tales we have swapped and then some, but little else have we to give for such hospitality."

"What else do ya have?" answered Peiko. "Starvin' and wanderin' lost in the wild. But I'll admit it's been nice to 'ave company. Been long enough without it. You don't owe me nothin' else."

"One thing we have to give is truth; a precious gift all folk have to give, for good or ill."

Ulla sighed heavily, but Väinämöinen continued.

"My name is not Tietainen."

"You don't say," said the troll, wryly.

"These young ones are not my niece and nephew."

"Their eyes told me that first time I met you," said the troll. "You're Erilaisen; they're not."

"I am Väinämöinen, Väinämöinen of Karelia. We come from the Enchanted Valley."

Peiko stared blankly at first, then slapped his thigh.

"Väinämöinen!" he cried. "The Karelian wizard! So yer still alive! The Pits of Tuonela take me! I know you—I fought against you at the big battle. Heard lots o' things about you, I did."

"Did you, now?" said Väinämöinen, unabashedly pleased at the troll's flattery.

"Stole the Witch's Sampo, they said; sang Joukahainen into the swamp. Aye, I've heard all about you."

"This is Ulla of the Karhulaiset and Kaukomieli of the Hirvilaiset, the Last Wizard ever trained by the Erilaiset in Tavastia. Ulla is the Child of the Prophecy, the girl who bears the Mark of the Clan upon her shoulder. Have you heard of her, Peiko?"

The troll furrowed his mighty brow.

"I heard tell of a witch-child that Löhi was lookin' for, but that's been some years back."

"This is she," said Väinämöinen. "The witch-child, they say. She is a child no longer. She is the strongest *tietäjää* in the Far Northern Land, stronger even than I."

"I can believe it," replied the troll. "I can feel her power just sittin' here. I'm good at such things. Now then—old Väinämöinen, a young witch, and a young wizard, all miles and miles from home, with battles and war goin' on down south. There's a tale here, that's for sure. What is it?"

"We are going to Pohjola," said Ulla. "To kill the Witch."

Peiko laughed, shaking his big head.

"Kill old Löhi? Up there in her castle, at that Sariola? Come now, wizard or not, ain't no one with the power to do that. Why, they killed her once already, that Lemminkäinen fellow did, and she came back. Knows the way out of Tuonela, she does. How do you plan on killin' the queen? 'Ave a powerful magic, do ya?"

"We did have a powerful magic," said Ulla. "And we, too, know the way out of Tuonela, for we've been there. But we lost our weapon in battle with Ajatar, though we slew the dragon in the end."

"You killed Ajatar? So she was still down south, guarding that old pass, eh? I wondered about that. C'mon, tell me the story!"

They told Peiko all their tale then, from the journey through Tuonela to the fight with the Moonface in Länsimaa; from Pirtto's death in the tunnels of the Earth People to the battle with the burnt-orange dragon. The troll took it all in, looking at them with newfound admiration.

"Never heard anything like it," he said, when they had finished. "Maybe you can beat Löhi, after all. Don't know how you can sneak into Sariola, but don't know how you made it this far, neither."

"Neither do we," said Väinämöinen. "Yet we will make it to Sariola or perish in the attempt. The Witch must be stopped, Peiko, or else she will cover all the Far Northern Land again in ice and snow, killing or enslaving whoever remains. All peoples, all *väkis*, all will be slaves; no *choice* will remain, none of what makes us free."

"Will you help us, Peiko?" asked Kaukomieli. "Much you have done already, but we need more. Food for a journey. Your guidance and counsel. To walk blindly into the North is perilous, as we've discovered. We need your help."

The troll hesitated only a moment.

"You've got it," he said. "Never had no use for Löhi or Pohjola; wish she'd never come back. Just want to be left alone, and 'ave other folk left alone, too. Aye, I'll do what I can for ya. After all, we're *friends*, right? Been a long time since I had friends. Friends help one another, I've heard tell. You certainly need help if you're going to Pohjola."

They decided to remain one more night in Peiko's cottage, if night it could be called. Only the troll could tell the time with certainty in the gloom outside. The snow had stopped, however. A clean wind blew lightly from the North. Peiko said that he would help them prepare the next day and, what was more, escort them to the borders of his haunts and point them in the right direction—for Pohjola was closer now, much closer than they had realized. They had only to strike the right road.

Kaukomieli lay next to Ulla beside the fire. Väinämöinen snored nearby. Peiko slumbered in his fur-strewn bed piled against the *pirtti's* back wall. The young man watched Ulla as she slept by him, lying on her back in the darkling light. The girl's face was rounder, less drawn. Her clean hair shone. They had all put on weight during the stay in the troll's cottage and were the better for it.

Unconsciously, almost imperceptibly, Kaukomieli's hand reached out to the girl's sleeping figure. *The last stage,* he thought. *We have come so far. This is the final stage. I came to help her, to save her, in any way that I can. I came to die with her, if I can do nothing else. So I will. But if only—*

His trembling hand touched her shoulder. For a moment, he let it linger, tracing a path down the length of her arm. Ulla stirred. Kaukomieli quickly withdrew his hand. The girl turned over, facing the glowing fire.

Her open eyes reflected the firelight.

The next day, they started out early. Peiko provided new packs made of dark leather that fit tightly on their backs. He packed them full of food: cakes of blood bread, whole rye loaves, cured meat, deer sausages, and berries. To Kaukomieli, he gave a sack of dried apples, further cementing their friendship. The troll also gave them leather caps to wear beneath their hoods and birch snowshoes.

"Skis would be swifter and I've got some of those too—took 'em from some goblins as didn't need 'em no more. But you've too far to go fer skis and the ground's too rough in spots. The shoes will be better on rough ground, though slower. Anyways, yer not goin' to ski yer way into Sariola."

Tightening their belts, they set out through the dark woods. Peiko knew precisely where he was going and guided them well. The big troll shambled through the trees; they followed behind in single file. The eastern sky grew lighter after a while, and they knew the sun was up. They rested a while beside a copse of berry bushes. To Peiko's delight, Väinämöinen sparked a small fire with a word.

The little group kept at it for several more hours until the sky darkened again. Then the clouds broke, revealing a silvery moon and twinkling stars. At last, the troll halted. They had marched some fifteen or twenty miles through the snow. Except for Peiko, they were exhausted.

"That's the way," said the troll, pointing to a long, arrow-shaped lake in the distance. The moon reflected off its frozen surface.

"Now then, listen up.

"Skirt the lake to the right and keep on straight, due north. There's the Nail shinin' in the sky, see? The queen's star is chasing 'er. Keep 'er just to the east. If it clouds up, feel the wind on yer face and go toward it. After a few more marches, you'll come to a wood; close it is, but not so broad. The trees are smaller up there, like little candles. The Candlestick Forest, they call it."

"How many marches?" asked Väinämöinen.

"Don't rightly know. Don't come this way much, not for years an' years. A few for me. Maybe more for you all. When you find the forest, you either go straight north and through it or skirt again east, always east. There's a road up there, a good one. The dwarves made it."

"What for?" asked Kaukomieli.

"Tradin' with the Witch. It runs all the way to Sariola. Anyways, once you find the road, yer in Pohjola. "

"Pohjola!" exclaimed Väinämöinen. "Is it that close?"

"Don't know. Never used the road, never went there. Don't plan to. It may be only a few days or a week from the wood, maybe more. But that's the way to Pohjola, all right, at least, the only way I heard tell of. The dwarves told me all about it."

"What lies within the wood, Peiko? What else is on the road?" asked Väinämöinen. "Is it watched?"

"The Witch watches everything up there, or her folk do. She's not goin' to let you sneak up on her twice!"

He laughed, slapping Väinämöinen on the back and almost toppling him over. "But as fer what's on the road—far as I know, nothin'. Don't reckon many folk use it in winter. Maybe you'll get lucky."

Väinämöinen sighed.

"We'll need luck," he said. "Peiko, you have been a most excellent host, guide, and friend—the last not the least. We can never repay you, but we won't forget you. If we succeed in our quest, I'll bring you back your weight in gold."

"That's a deal!" said Peiko. "Don't expect to see you folk again, though, more's the pity. Not sure you know what you're gettin' into. But if anyone *can* kill old Löhi, I reckon it's Ulla here. Feel the magic burnin' off 'er like steam risin' into the air!

"Farewell! And if you do make it, come back and tell me the tale!"

"Farewell!" they cried. With Väinämöinen in the lead and Ulla and Kaukomieli following, the three companions set off, stamping through the thick snow in their birch snowshoes. After a ways, they looked back. Peiko was already lost in the gloaming.

Chapter Fourteen

The Candlestick Forest

Ulla watched in amazement. Standing on the shore of a little snow-covered lake with an unobstructed view to the east, she observed the sunrise. A huge red orb climbed slowly over the rim of the world, chasing the stars from the sky. The red sun climbed just above the horizon. Bathing the lake in a bloody glow, it described an odd path before sinking again without fully rising.

The dark-haired young woman had never seen such a thing before, though she had heard of it. In the farthest North, the winter days grew so short that eventually the sun disappeared altogether for weeks at a time. The Dark Time, men called it, though few had ever seen it. The companions had come so far north by now that they were on the very edge of complete winter darkness. Pohjola could not be far away.

"I remember," said Väinämöinen. "When the world was young and so was I. We often came here and walked beneath the stars. Löhi changed everything. Talvimaa, the White Kingdom, became Pohjola, the Dark Land. Only evil things and twisted made their home here.

"We must take care! The only way to tell time's passage is the moon's course; it's tough to follow. The darkness can do strange things to your mind and body."

"But who knows all its courses?" asked Kaukomieli. "The stars are not in the right places. The moon sails a course I've never seen. Can you tell time in the dark, Väinämöinen?"

"I could once. Now? We shall see, my lad."

Several marches and many miles further north, they had yet to reach the wood described by Peiko. The land was rough, as Peiko had predicted. During summer, when the sun never set for days on end, flowers, sage, and berry bushes bloomed among stony outcroppings and trickling streams. Short grasses grew in sheltered hollows. Peat fields defined crisscross patterns throughout the wilderness.

Not so in winter. Snow covered the land like a white blanket, save for sparse woods, the trees short and stunted. Moonlight and starshine bathed the northlands softly like gossamer. All was cold and dark, and it seemed both qualities were tangible things, the only permanent things in that barren land.

The snowshoes Peiko gave them proved invaluable. Crunching along over the snow, avoiding deep drifts as best they could, the three companions knew they would have faltered soon without them. Even so, the risk was great. A storm might blow from the North at any time, catching them in the wilderness without aid or shelter, even as Ulla's father had been caught so long ago. Yet, as it had so often, their luck held. Light snow fell, but the North Wind brought no blizzards.

When night fell—or so they guessed—they would make a small fire beside a stand of trees, both to mask the flames and shelter them from the wind. Väinämöinen sang the snow spell to clear the ground on which they sat, the only spell he allowed them. Miserable, they slept uneasily wrapped in cloaks, furs, and blankets.

The sun never broke the horizon now. The eastern sky glowed saffron and yellow for an hour or two to herald the dawn, but no more. Several times, bright lights flashed brilliantly overhead; green and red fingers flashed and withdrew in rapid succession like the lightnings from a wizard's staff. Almost directly above, the red Witch's star, Löhi's Star, burned beside Taivaantappi, as it strove to overtake the Nail of the Heavens and replace it. Neither Ulla nor Kaukomieli could keep their bearings beneath the strange sky. If not for the brief morning glow, when they could see it, they might have lost all sense of direction.

At last they mounted a low shelf set against a large snowdrift and glimpsed what they sought, a dense wood of short pines and firs. Beneath the moonlight, the snow-covered trees looked like rows of tallow candles marching onward into the night.

"The Candlestick Forest!" cried Kaukomieli, his voice muffled by his hood, cloak, and scarf, bound tightly against the cold.

"So it is," said Väinämöinen. "And none too soon. We haven't met a soul since parting from Peiko, but I feel exposed tramping through these desolate places all alone. Dark it may be, but Löhi's spirit haunts all this land. Feel it now! We have come to the borders of Pohjola."

Ulla climbed atop a grey rock, peering northward.

"Hard to tell how broad it is," she said. "Well, Peiko gave us two options, to go straight through the wood or go around it to the east. The road lies somewhere on the other side. If the wood is thin, it may be swifter and less tiring to strike a path straight through, provided we don't become lost. We will also have more shelter. I do not think the trees are close enough to block the stars."

"Perhaps," said Väinämöinen. "Yet even beneath an open sky, we had trouble keeping a straight path. It is easy to become lost in any wood, let alone this wood of Pohjola."

"We still have food, thanks to Peiko," answered Ulla. "But not for long. When it fails, what then? The time for hunting is past, if there are still beasts to hunt in this winter wilderness. How long will it take to go around the forest? Time is not on our side."

"*A winding road may lead to gold, but a straight path to ruin*," said Väinämöinen. "Shortcuts do not always pan out. Well, let us go down and see what we can see. The risk seems too great to me to walk into the woods with no idea how thick they are, and *sight* is useless here. We will find a way around, delay or no."

Ulla, staff in hand, slogged down the drift; the others followed. Twice, she toppled over in deep snow. They reached the forest's eaves, then bore to the right, which they guessed was due east. Even in darkness, the Candlestick Forest appeared beautiful. The poor, thin northern soil limited the trees' height, so some were no taller than a man. Their loveliness remained intact, however. Ulla found herself mesmerized by the forest, the very counterpoint of the great trees in Karelia if ever there was one.

Before long, Väinämöinen's plan went wrong. A river cut across their path. Issuing from some height hidden by the woods, it ran swiftly southward into the darkness; pieces of ice bobbed among the foam.

"Checked," said Ulla.

"So it seems," replied Väinämöinen sullenly. "Peiko said nothing about a river. It is not so wide, but wide enough. Too cold to swim, too swift for a boat in the dark."

"Then it's through the Candlestick Forest after all," said Kaukomieli.

"Very well," said the old man. "I'll not be sorry to disappear from spying eyes, but help me keep our way. If we become lost, we're done for. The weather will not hold much longer."

Using the North Star as their guide, they entered the woods. The trees seemed scattered unevenly. Some clustered together thickly. Others spread out with open spaces in between.

Soon the forest enveloped them, a black and white world of snow-covered pillars marching endlessly on. The sky clouded over. What Väinämöinen feared most happened: the moon and stars went out and deep night returned. They were at the mercy of their wizardly senses. No heavenly lights remained to show them the way.

They grew tired. Kaukomieli's legs felt leaden. Up and down, in and out, his staff plunged into the snow, digging little holes to mark their progress. *At least we may find them if we double back*, he thought. The snow cover was less inside the woods, quite thin in some places. New snow began to fall, however. He waved it away as the wind blew into his face.

What if we do make it through the woods? he thought. *What if we make it out the other side; then what? The road? Surely it will be watched, surely all roads are watched. Dark, cold, lifeless...this is no place for living men, only monsters and ghosts. Perhaps we're already dead. Perhaps we must haunt these woods forever. Should we not stop to rest now? What difference can it make to dead men? I know that I shall never leave this place alive.*

He shook himself back to lucidity, reining in his wandering spirit. Kaukomieli could feel a presence, many presences, all around them. The Witch's thought lay heavy over all this place, clouding his mind and tiring his body. The trees, though beautiful, were unwholesome. He sensed spirits locked within some of them—brooding, watching, waiting for a chance to give them away.

Kaukomieli was about to call out to Väinämöinen to halt when he heard a loud crack.

"*Pysäytää!*"

The harsh voice came from behind. They spun round. The snow fell more swiftly.

A dark figure stood before them, cloaked, booted, and on skis. It gripped a huge bow. Several others emerged at the edge of sight, also with bows drawn tight. Calls rang out in the woods on all sides. They were surrounded.

"Väinämöinen—" said Ulla softly; she was cut off by the sudden braying of dogs. A pack of white hounds with wolflike muzzles emerged from the gloom. Snarling, the dogs circled round with bared teeth. The three companions tried not to move.

Another figure, less tall, stepped out of the shadows. Uncovering a dark lantern, the figure shone bright light in their faces. They could make out her features in the glare.

The woman who stood there was a Haltia—of that, they had no doubt. She was shorter than the Haltiatar of the Enchanted Valley, but her long, narrow face, leaf-shaped ears, and fluted eyes betrayed her. The elf wore a long, fur-lined cape of midnight blue with cunning symbols like unto stars, snowflakes, and crescent moons along its hem. Her long, dark hair spilled from beneath a tall, peaked hat. Chains dangled from her neck and belt; bronze spirals glittered upon her robes. When she spoke, they felt her magical power.

"Do not move," she said in a thick accent. "You are at arrow point."

She used the Old Speech, but in a manner that Ulla barely understood.

"Who are you?" the elf asked, calm and cold. "Why are you in these woods? Answer truthfully or die."

Väinämöinen drew a deep breath. He considered his words carefully. Their lives and quest balanced on a knife's edge.

"We mean you no harm," he answered. "We are wayfarers and in these woods only by chance. Let us be and we will leave as swiftly as possible."

"Wayfarers? No wayfarers sojourn in the North," said the woman. "Least of all, *tietäjää.*"

She walked around them slowly while the dogs snarled. Peering into Kaukomieli's eyes, the elf nodded.

"Mortal," she said.

Then she turned to Ulla. The girl met the elf's steady gaze. Her heart pounded. *If this was the end, so be it,* she thought. Escape was impossible. The woman's magic radiated like warmth from a fire. *Best to be bold, come what may.*

"Who are you?" asked the elf again. Ulla replied not in the Old Speech, but in the tongue of the Seven Clans.

"Dost thou not know?"

Taken aback, the Haltia stiffened.

"Valkea," called out one of the others. "Take care!"

"Verily," said Ulla. "Take care, Valkea. If thou art a subject of the Witch, do what thou must. But few shall return to their homes. Decide!"

"All are the Queen of Pohjola's subjects now," replied Valkea, using the language of the Clans, though in a fashion scarcely more understandable to Ulla than the Old Speech. "But that does not mean all are her servants."

"If you are not her servant," said Väinämöinen, "Then let us go."

"Silence!" cried Valkea, sharply. Leaving them within the ring of hounds, the elvish woman conferred in whispered tones with several of her company. Kaukomieli, who saw keenly in the dark, marked others watching them from the shadows. Suddenly, Valkea barked out a command. The nearby elves lowered their bows. At another word, the dogs relaxed.

"You will come with us," said Valkea.

"Why?" asked Ulla.

"Press not thy good fortune. We do not permit strangers to wander through our forest unguarded. Pimentola, the largest of our villages, is nearby. There we may converse. We will decide swiftly what should be done."

With little choice but to follow the elf's instructions, they complied. The dark lantern was covered; Valkea climbed back onto her skis. The three companions trudged along on their snowshoes, aware of many elves about them in the dark wood. Snow continued falling.

They had not gone far before they reached a clearing where many sleds awaited. Reindeer nosed in the snow for moss. Exchanging words with another elf wearing a similar, peaked hat, the elvish woman gestured toward a sled.

"Get in."

The three friends approached the nearest sled, but Valkea stopped them.

"Not together," she said. "This one is for you," she added, signaling to Ulla. "That one for you, old man. The blue sled yonder for the young one."

They exchanged nervous glances.

"Do as you are asked. It is not wise to linger in the open. You are on the marches of Pohjola; even the Candlestick Forest cannot hide everything from the queen's sight. But be warned! If you betray our trust and attempt any trick, fair or foul, you will die. Do not think we lowered our guard along with our bows."

"Why ever would we think that?" asked Väinämöinen.

The elves loaded their skis, dogs, and other gear into the sleds and set off.

Valkea climbed in beside Ulla. One elf sat in front driving the sled, another sat on a high-backed seat just behind them. Väinämöinen and Kaukomieli, in separate sleds, were soon lost to Ulla's sight.

Valkea said nothing at first. Ulla felt the elf's bright eyes on her as they raced down the trail. Sleigh bells jingled softly in the dark. Trees slipped by like silent, snowy sentinels. Despite her caution, Ulla grew drowsy. Tired, exhausted, covered in warm furs, she fought the sleep that threatened to overwhelm her. The reindeer's haunches rose and fell. Väinämöinen's sled pulled even with them, then fell back. The old man's beard, half frozen, bristled from beneath his cape and hood.

"Is that really him?" asked Valkea, suddenly.

Ulla stirred.

"Yes," she answered. "Do you know him?"

"I was not born when he came to Pohjola and stole the Sampo. Yet some remain in Pimentola who still remember."

"They would do well not to hinder him."

"What do you now come to steal? What does Löhi have that makes you risk your life?"

"Such is not our errand—to steal. What could the Witch possess that we might possibly want?"

"Many are the secrets of Sariola. I do not pretend to know them all. You are the *tietäjää*, are you not? It must be a great magic you seek. But whatever your errand, it is hopeless. All paths to the Witch's Keep are watched. It is winter. The queen herself is in her tower, crafting spells and weaving *kalma* to send throughout the Far Northern Land. Löhi gazes with her unmatched *sight* at all that transpires in the South. She enters her enemies' dreams. Her power waxes. The Dark Time is hers. Your power will not avail you, Karhulainen."

"You know much of Löhi," said Ulla, hoping her voice suggested a confidence she did not really feel. "Have you often been to Sariola?"

Valkea laughed.

"What could there be in Sariola that I might possibly want? Never since Löhi's return have I been to Sariola. The Haltiatar of the Candlestick Forest wish only to be left alone, to live as we always have. I do not serve the queen."

"Then you have much in common with the Erilaiset of Taikalaakso and the Seven Clans; we also wish only to be left alone."

"No. You wish to defeat Löhi. Steal her magic. Destroy her, if only you could. You are foolish. Such is the difference between us. My *väki* will survive, as we always have. Yours will perish."

"Better to perish than live in thrall to evil."

The wind picked up; it whistled through the treetops.

"You are dangerous," said Valkea, lowering her voice so that Ulla could barely hear her. "Your coming to the North was not unlooked for."

"The wizard told you we mean no harm; he did not lie."

"Your very presence is dangerous," replied Valkea. "If the queen knew you were here, or thought we helped you, she would destroy us. Perhaps not at once. There are few folk in Sariola during the Dark Time save goblins, and most of those were killed in the battle far to the south. Only her most trusted servants dwell in Sariola. But in spring, when the days grow long and the red sun hangs over the Kipuvuori hours on end, many folk gather at the Keep— men from the East, elves from dark *väki*, and others.

"She will send them to the forest to destroy us; our bodies will hang from the trees. All who remain will be enslaved and taken to Sariola. But perhaps she will not wait, perhaps she will come herself. You are dangerous, Karhulainen. You cannot remain."

"I do not wish to remain," said Ulla. "Let us go on our way, if you will not help us. We will trouble you no longer."

"You will be caught; then you will trouble us greatly. You will betray us to the queen, willingly or no, and we will suffer. She is strong. Her red star rises; it will replace Taivaantappi one day. Why should we not deliver you up to her? Were we prudent, we would do so."

"It is your choice," answered Ulla. "To fight evil or abet it. But do not fool yourself that this is prudence. You are a singer, are you not? You know Ukko's path, the trail for singers. Do you fear Löhi's vengeance in this world more than Ukko's in the next? I could hide in the South, if I wished. I could hide in the deepest vales of the Enchanted Valley in Karelia, where none but the Erilaiset might find me, while the Witch conquered the Far Northern Land. Perhaps she might let me be. What then? I would have only doomed my own spirit to Tuonela's darkness."

"Tuonela? When Löhi catches you, you may wish you were in Tuonela."

"No, I do not think so." Ulla's eyes flashed in the gloom. "Have *you* walked in Tuonela, Valkea? No, I will not wish for that."

The elvish woman opened her mouth, a surprised look on her long, narrow face, but quickly closed it. Turning away from Ulla, she fell silent. The reindeer kept a steady pace through the forest.

A few hours later, they drove out of the deep wood into a large glade and slid to a stop. Lights twinkled here and there. *Pirttis* and low sheds clustered around reindeer pens. The air smelled of hearth fire and smoke. Several elves came forward to greet them.

"This is Pimentola," said Valkea. "Our chief village. Most of our folk dwell here or in the woods nearby."

Valkea gave instructions to her people. Then, with a nod, she left to take counsel with Pimentola's other leaders. The remaining elves busied themselves unpacking the sleds and unharnessing the reindeer, taking the tired beasts to their pens. Although they seemed to give little heed to the three strangers in their midst, Väinämöinen had no doubt they were closely watched. Stamping up and down in the cold, they had a chance to talk for the first time since meeting Valkea and her folk.

"What did she say to you, Ulla?" asked the old wizard.

"She is afraid. She fears us and fears the Witch. She wishes us to leave swiftly lest the Witch learn of our presence and take revenge upon them."

"I do not trust these elves," said Kaukomieli. "The wood feels unwholesome; this village is the heart of that unwholesomeness."

"I wonder," said Väinämöinen. "The Witch's power runs through all these trails; how I feel it! But Valkea could have slain us already if she wished. What did you tell her of our quest?"

"Nothing. She guesses close to the mark, but thinks that we plan to steal some talisman like the Sampo, as you did long ago. She wishes to know what this thing is."

"If we could convince them to help us," said Väinämöinen, "It would be a boon beyond measure. In their sleds, we might even reach Sariola unchallenged."

"I do not trust her," repeated Kaukomieli. "We should leave here as soon as possible, openly or by stealth. Väinämöinen, do you not know this place—Pimentola? Or this *väki*?"

"Many are the *väki* of the North. Many folk lived in Pohjola and the surrounding lands, though it may be hard for southerners from friendlier climes to believe it. Pimentola is known to me only as the name of an Erilaisen settlement in Old Talvimaa. Anything else, I have forgotten."

Valkea soon returned. Motioning toward some blue lights twinkling in the distance, she told them to follow her. The North Wind blew harder. A gale approached, flinging snow and freezing sleet upon all Pohjola and its marches. They wrapped their cloaks tightly against the cold and followed the elves' swinging lanterns, which cast yellow fingers across the ground. Reindeer bellowed in their pens.

Stopping near a scattering of cabins facing a high stone well and oven, Valkea addressed them. The wind nearly stole her voice.

"It is past midnight, though you may not know it. A storm is upon us. Best to shelter until it passes. The *pirtti* yonder is for men; this one at hand, for women. We will bring food and drink to satisfy your need. Fire already burns upon the hearth."

"Why can we not shelter together?" asked Kaukomieli.

"Men and women do not live in the same cabin, unless espoused," answered Valkea. "Are you husband and wife?"

About to answer affirmatively, Kaukomieli stopped when he saw Ulla's expression. Väinämöinen put his hand on the young wizard's shoulder.

"Such is the old custom among some *väki*," he said. "'Tis the same, too, in Tavastia and Etelamaa. We respect your custom, Valkea. Kaukomieli and I will sleep together. But come now! You have brought us to your village, plucked us from your wood. To what purpose? Are we prisoners, Valkea?"

The woman looked around, as if unfriendly ears might overhear.

"Remain inside the cabins," she said, in a voice so low it seemed almost a whisper. "Cast no spells, try no tricks. It is not safe to wander in the open, even amidst the storm. Ungracious hosts you may think us, but you do not appreciate the risk we take in dealing with you. When the storm blows over, we will take you to the forest's edge. Pimentola lies near the northern borders. From there, you must make your own way and not return. If you do, I am not responsible for the consequences. No more can I say to you."

A strong gust brought snow down upon them from the nearby trees.

"So be it," answered Väinämöinen.

"Pimekä will take you to your cabin," answered Valkea. "Do not betray our trust."

Turning to Ulla, the elvish woman said, "Come with me."

Ulla's long, low cabin had a sloped roof that coaxed snowfall to the ground, where it piled in drifts. Inside, it resembled the cabins of the Enchanted Valley. Left alone, Ulla took off her wet things and warmed herself beside the crackling fire in the stone-piled hearth.

Two beds stood against the wall. A small table, benches, and several stools made from tree stumps were the only furnishings. A single tallow lamp hung from the rafters and, above the doorway, hung a great pair of antlers; not reindeer antlers, but the horns of some mighty elk, bleached white and seemingly ancient.

Ulla stretched her feet out toward the yellow blaze. She felt exhausted. Warmth flowed over her tired body. Despite the day's stress and uncertainty, she wanted only to sleep now, to forget for a time her fear and pain. *What is meant to be, shall be.* Her hands looked red in the otherworldly light. She closed her eyes, but kept her staff by her side.

Sleep would have to wait, however.

Valkea entered with another elf, an even shorter woman dressed in the same fashion. The woman's dark hair was streaked with grey, her sharp nose defining a narrow face. She carried a steaming covered pot.

"This is my aunt, Hilja," said Valkea. The older woman came forward, handing Ulla her burden. Inside the pot, a rich porridge bubbled; blood sausage floated on top.

"Eat," said Valkea. "You are tired, famished. This may be the last night you can enjoy such comfort. Use well the time."

Taking a copper spoon, Ulla dove into the porridge. Its warmth filled her belly, spreading to her limbs. Hilja also bore a copper ewer filled with berry-water. Valkea watched Ulla as she ate. She removed her peaked hat, allowing her long, curly hair to fall upon her shoulders. Grey eyes, as grey as Väinämöinen's, sparkled above her rosy cheeks. Ulla often thought elvish women unattractive, their long features unsettling to mortal eyes. Valkea was beautiful.

"Do you wish to join me?" asked Ulla, uncomfortable with the silent woman standing motionless while she supped.

"We will not stay long," Valkea replied. "Much remains to be done ere we take our own meal and retire. But tell me, if you will. This much you owe me. What is your errand? What brings the Child of the Prophecy to Pohjola's doorstep?"

Ulla set down the spoon. "To kill Löhi; what else?"

A moment passed. Valkea pursed her lips.

"Show me the Mark, Ulla."

The young woman rose. Brushing aside her long, straight hair, she unclasped the brooch that held her garment. Turning slightly toward the elves, she bared her shoulder. The Mark shone black against her pale skin.

"By the Clan-Mark shall you know them," said Ulla.

Valkea threw back her head. The lamp flickered.

"Use well the time. When the snow stops, I will be back with my companions. We will not tarry."

Without another word, the Haltiatar left the cabin, leaving Ulla alone again.

The young woman sighed. The doubt seemed overwhelming. Nestling close to the fire, she felt lonely, as lonely as she had ever been. She wished the old wizard and Kaukomieli were with her. *Or Kirsikka, dear Kirsikka, so very far away. How I wish to see her again, if only once more before I die! Or Siria, beside the sea with your children, my blood. May Ukko keep you safe.*

Setting aside the porridge, Ulla settled back. Sleep overpowered her, more compelling this time. She felt tired, tired and hopeless. Her eyes fluttered. Her mind fled away. She wished only to drift off to a deep slumber of forgetfulness and lay aside her many cares for just one night.

But the sleep of a wizard is not like the sleep of others; strange dreams and visions come unbidden to trouble them. Ulla drifted through a darkling dreamscape. Tiny lights twinkled in the gloom, fireflies beckoning like heralds of a miniature kingdom. Ulla fell slowly through thick cloud. Into a deep well she fell, enveloped by water that chilled her heart, yet she felt no fear, no choking death; peace and rest awaited at the bottom. Slowly, she slipped away.

"Not yet, Ulla."

The girl with dark hair looked up. She knew the voice well. Egan stood above her. Even through the water, Ulla saw him clearly, without filter.

Egan knelt, poised atop a grey stone. The young king's blue eyes glittered. His tousled, sandy hair framed his fair face, still fair despite the white scar that cut through his beard where the dragon had struck. Egan looked just as he had the last time Ulla saw him on the field of Sumuvuori. A gentle smile spread across his lips.

"Come back, lass," he said. "It's not your time yet. There's still much to be done."

Ulla's heart beat swiftly. She tried to raise her arms, to reach out to him, but could not.

"That's all right," said Egan, softly. "Here, Ulla, take my hand. I won't let you go."

The embroidered collar of his simple white shirt brushed the wave tops as Egan reached in. The young man's hand touched hers. Its warmth coursed throughout her body.

"Help me now, little one!"

Bracing his boot against the stone, Egan grasped her arm. Pushing off with his leg, he wrenched Ulla from the deep well. Straightaway through the clouds she raced, straightaway through the lamps and shimmering lights. Straightaway like an arrow she flew through the misty dreamscape and back into the waking world, leaving Egan and all else far behind.

Ulla opened her eyes. Hazy smoke filled the dark room. She lay on the bed next to the wall. Across the stony hearth, Valkea and another elf rummaged through her things. Ulla had been enchanted. They had cast a spell upon her; well she knew the feeling. But Ulla was no normal mortal or common sorcerer, she was the most powerful wizard in the Far Northern Land.

She realized that her hands and feet were bound. Ulla closed her eyes. She imagined a snake, a tiny viper, coiling and uncoiling itself in knots, wriggling inside its den. The snake was smooth and slippery. Remembering the words Turi had taught her long ago, she softly whispered the magic spell. The rope around her wrists wriggled just like the snake. The cords about her legs loosened. Kicking them off, she slid the rope from her hands and was free.

At that moment, Valkea spun around. The elf-woman's face twisted with anger.

"*Ka!*" she snarled. "*Suka!*"

Ulla knew she had only a moment. *Pohjanpiikki* sat propped against the fireside where the elves had set it. Ulla jumped to her knees, leapt, and rolled across the floor. Grasping the sword's hilt, she braced herself against the stones. Valkea's companion, a male elf, loomed over her with a long knife in his hand. He struck, but too late. Still on her back, Ulla stabbed upward, piercing her enemy's chest. Blood spurting from his mouth, the elf crashed into the fire. Sparks scattered everywhere.

Ulla sprang to her feet. Valkea raised her hand, crying, "*Pysäytää!*" But, though Valkea's magic was strong among her own folk, she was no match for Ulla. No hastily uttered holding spell could bind Ulla when her own wrath and power were roused.

"Thou fool!" cried Valkea, slipping into the formal language and prosody of the Erilaiset in her anger. "I might have delivered thee alive to Löhi; perhaps thou couldst have bargained for thy life. But thy worth to me dead is as great as thy worth alive, and still we will be done with thee and spared the Witch's anger. Thinkest not that I can slay thee?"

"Traitor!" cried Ulla. "To thy guest and to thyself. The Pits of Tuonela shall be thy home, oblivion thy reward!"

Valkea, sword drawn, closed on Ulla. Nimbly leaping over the legs of her dead companion, she dealt a swift blow with her scimitar. Ulla parried with her heavy sword. They traded blows across the room, cutting and thrusting, neither gaining an advantage. Ulla realized at once that Valkea was an expert swordsman. Seldom had the young woman faced a foe with such skill. She pressed the elf, but in such close quarters, she could not make the sweeping final stroke she needed. She had no time to weave the sword-spell. Valkea struck in turn, twice slashing Ulla's sword arm. Blood dripped to the ground.

In pain, Ulla stumbled back beside the hearth. She landed on her back; her hold on *Pohjanpiikki* loosened. Valkea's eyes flashed bright blue. Sensing an opening, she lunged. But Ulla was too fast. She kicked with all her might, catching Valkea in the stomach before her sword stroke fell. The elf toppled backwards, tumbled over a bench, and struck the hearth stones with a cracking sound.

Gripping *Pohjanpiikki* tightly, Ulla rose. Valkea did not. Ulla stooped over the elf, who lay flat on her back. Valkea's eyes opened wide, then rolled up into her head, and looked as white as a goblin's. Blood trickled from her mouth and left temple. Her leg twitched. Dead, dying, or senseless, Ulla did not know, but she had no time to lose.

The young wizard half expected enemies to rush into the cabin due to the commotion. However, the North Wind's bluster had masked all noise. Ulla searched frantically for her staff, but could not find it. Hastily she gathered her other things into her badger-skin pack—Valkea had been fingering the twin wooden figures and *karhu's* remaining tooth—and strapped her boots and belt on. Sheathing *Pohjanpiikki*, she glanced around the room a final time. The dead male elf smoldered on the hearth. Valkea lay unmoving. Then Ulla noticed the elf woman's fur-lined hat and midnight blue cape on the floor.

With a twinge of regret, she cast off her own cloak and wrapped Valkea's rich garment about herself. Donning the hat, Ulla closed her eyes, took a deep breath, and left the *pirtti*.

The North Wind whined. Heavy snow swirled in the darkness. The storm's full fury raged. Amidst the flurries, Ulla spied two elves standing beneath the cabin's lee.

Her power blossomed as she approached them, raising her hand. She pulled back the hood, staring them in the eyes. One of the elves opened his mouth, but the words died on his lips. The other went slack; his arms fell to his side.

"*Pysykää!*" said Ulla, softly. "*Pysykää ja Nukkukaa!* Stay here and sleep."

The young woman unclasped the elves' cloaks, which resembled Valkea's. *Let them freeze*, she thought. *Let them die. I must find Väinämöinen and Kaukomieli.*

Taking the cloaks under her arm, she tramped through the snow. Lights flickered in the distance. Voices sounded on the wind. Panic nearly overcame her. *Where are they? What has happened to them? Where am I to go in this murk if I can't find them?*

Suddenly, she stumbled toward what she sought, a *pirtti* with three elves shivering outside its door. The Haltiatar huddled together in the bitter night, stamping their feet, pacing up and down to stay warm. They carried ashen spears tipped with black iron.

Ulla pulled the peaked hat down. As she approached the elves, she worked her best illusion. Using the Old Speech, she asked, "Are they still here?"

"Of course," answered one of the guards. "We have done as you bid, lady."

"Good. The mortal witch has been dealt with. I shall now deal with the other two. Go back to your homes, the night is evil."

"Do you not need us?" asked another. "Where is Kumo?"

"Go back to your cabins. I need you not. Kumo will come presently."

Ulla spoke with great compulsion, but the elves made no sign. Her hand strayed to her sword hilt.

"Very well, Valkea. *Ka*, 'tis ill this eve. The queen's wrath blows from the mountaintops."

The guards disappeared into the night. Ulla entered the cabin. Red embers glowed on the hearth. Empty bowls sat on the ledge. Väinämöinen slept in a corner, wrapped in his cloak. Kaukomieli was slumped over, propped against the hearthstones, his eyes half open. He started as the cold wind swept inside.

"Get up!" cried Ulla. "Let's go—now! There is no time to waste."

They sprang to their feet. Väinämöinen, still groggy, nearly toppled over. Kaukomieli stumbled, knocking an empty bowl into the fire.

"Ulla, is that you? What has happened?" he said.

"No time to explain," she answered. "Has Valkea been here?"

"No. Another elf brought us food. What's going on?"

"Valkea tried to kill me. I've bought some time, but we have to flee. Now!"

Ulla noticed two staffs set against the wall. "Strange," she muttered. "But no time for mysteries. Gather your things swiftly. They will kill us if they catch us!"

Shaking off sleep, they quickly packed, girt their weapons, and grabbed their staffs.

"Where is yours, Ulla?" asked the old man.

"I don't know. Wait; put these on." She handed them the midnight blue cloaks. Väinämöinen hesitated. Weather-stained, battered, and rent though it was, the old man was still reluctant to part with his mink coat, crafted by his kin in the Enchanted Valley.

"Väinämöinen! Take your old coat with you if you must, but put this on now."

He wrapped the new garment around his shoulders.

"Too small," he grumbled. "But first things first. What are we to do? Flee blindly into the storm?"

"No," answered Kaukomieli. "I thought it might come to this. To the sleds! That's our only hope for escape unless we work a change."

"I do not work such magic," said Ulla. "And neither do you."

"Then let's find a sled. If our luck holds, and if whatever you've done to Valkea lasts, we may get away in this blizzard."

Venturing out into the storm, they guessed at the direction of the reindeer pens. The animals sheltered in half-open enclosures. The elves of Pimentola were not true reindeer herders, but kept a good stock of hearty beasts for draught and, at times, to slaughter for meat. The reindeer survived the cold with little difficulty, well protected by thick hides and shaggy fur.

Riding sleds were scattered everywhere, some smaller, some larger for hauling heavy burdens through thick snow. The nearby cabins lay mostly dark. Pimentola slept through the storm.

"We need at least two beasts," said Väinämöinen. "Hei, Kaukomieli, this sled will do. Find reindeer while I fetch the harnesses. Ulla, stand guard. Let's hurry!"

The old man rummaged through traps, ropes, and chains while Kaukomieli tried to coax the nearest reindeer, a bull with huge antlers, out of the pen. Speaking softly, he pulled gently on its neck halter. It refused to budge. He pulled harder. The bull snorted, moving backwards. He tried again. The bull pulled away, braying loudly. Ulla suddenly saw an elf emerge from a *pirtti's* doorway. The elf peered through the driving snow, then vanished inside the cabin.

"Kaukomieli," she hissed, "Hurry!"

"Hurry yourself," he shot back. "I'm trying! These deer don't know us; they're stubborn." He pulled again with all his might, but the bull charged, tossing him backward into the snow.

"For the love of Akka," groaned Ulla. The girl and old man rushed to help him. Then Ulla saw it. Just within the enclosure waited a *reiki* with a single bull harnessed at the runners.

"Are you blind?" she cried, exasperatedly. "Look! This one is harnessed; it's ready."

Brushing off snow, Kaukomieli answered, "How could I see in the dark? And if your eyes are better, why didn't you say something sooner?"

"Enough!" cried the old man. "This beast wasn't left here idly, all strapped with gear and ready to go. It's here a'purpose, waiting, and not for us. I've half a mind to sing all these beasts to sleep, put 'em out for a while. But that would take time and strength; we have neither. Haste is best. Climb in!"

They jumped into the sled, tossing out skis and other gear. With Väinämöinen at the reins, he called, "*Menkaa!*" The bull jumped. Trotting out of the pen, the old man circled the clearing, trying to decide which way to go. Sleighbells jingled in the wind.

"Valkea said that Pimentola is on the Candlestick Forest's northern border; the road must lie that way," he muttered. "But which way is north? The storm blows from all sides and my reckoning is off."

Guessing more by sense than sight, Väinämöinen shook the reins and chose a trail, broad and well-travelled. Passing several cabins, they slipped into the night. Pimentola's scattered lights were soon lost in the gloom.

The *reiki* raced through the snow. Its curved runners, carved from bone and hand-fitted, slid smoothly along the frozen tundra. Candlestick trees, even shorter than those in the forest's southern eaves, marched beside them.

The reindeer's strong legs and broad hooves beat a steady rhythm. Snow and freezing rain came down harder.

Kaukomieli pulled his hood over his face. His skin burned. Clutching his staff in one hand and Ulla in the other, he peered backwards. He saw nothing, nothing but night and darkness. Blackness swallowed everything the moment they raced past it. He still felt uneasy. The feeling he had had since they entered the strange wood, a feeling of brooding, anticipatory evil—that feeling lingered.

We must leave these woods, he thought. *We must leave them now.*

They drove down the trail for almost an hour. Väinämöinen put his strength into the beast, but three people on a *reiki* made a heavy load for even a mighty reindeer. The wizard knew that he had to be careful; if he ran the reindeer to death, they would be stranded. The trees suddenly grew sparse and scattered. The forest's end approached. Just a little farther and they would be free, out of the woods' grasp for good or ill.

"Hei," cried the old man, "There's a lake here, a big one, or I'm no Karelian. See how the snow drifts? The woods end here and the other side looks open. Let's cross! It may be Pohjola, but it's better than what lies behind. We'll rest our friend a bit and decide what to do next. We need more shelter than a sled!"

He cracked his whip, but at that moment a horn blew in the distance, rising above the wind. Others answered close by. Braying dogs emerged from the shadows, giving chase. Sleds suddenly shot onto the ice on either side, aiming to cut them off. The elves of Pimentola had caught them.

"Väinämöinen!" cried Kaukomieli.

"Hold on!" yelled the old man, driving the reindeer as hard as possible. "Kaukomieli, the dogs, the dogs!"

Several white wolfhounds ran beside them. The frightened bull careened madly about. Two dogs leapt onto the sled. Kaukomieli knocked them senseless with his staff. Another dog jumped at Ulla, snarling. She cut off its head with *Pohjanpiikki*. A fourth leapt at Väinämöinen, savagely biting his rein-hand. Still clutching the reins, the old man shouted a word of power and the hound fell to the snow, writhing in pain.

Arrows whined through the air. At least a dozen sleds skated across the frozen lake. Drawn by several reindeer, these swifter sleds had the advantage. Väinämöinen pulled this way and that, seeking a path through their foes. Ulla cut down another hound with her sword.

Kaukomieli heard a dull, smacking sound over the wind. Ulla fell forward, nearly toppling out. Kaukomieli wrenched her back into the sled, then saw the source of the smacking sound—an arrow had pierced Ulla's right shoulder, the tip driving straight through. A sled pulled directly behind them, an elf with a drawn bow standing beside its driver. It was Valkea! She notched another arrow.

"I'm all right," said Ulla, steadying herself, but the pain was excruciating. "Kaukomieli, watch out!"

Valkea launched her arrow. It narrowly missed the young man's head, saved only by the sled's jerky movements. Ulla met Valkea's eyes. The Haltia glared back, her white face still streaked with blood.

Then the world turned upside down. Väinämöinen pulled back on the reins sharply to avoid a sled passing in front of them. Their reindeer—already maddened by the dogs—stumbled and fell. The *reiki* crashed on its side, flinging the three companions out violently.

Jumping to his feet, Kaukomieli grabbed his staff. The Haltiatar closed in from all sides. Ulla stumbled up, dripping blood, still grasping *Pohjanpiikki* with her good arm. The old wizard, half-dazed, helped support her.

"Work a change!" screamed Kaukomieli. "Ulla, go—go! Work a change, work a change, now!"

Turning toward their foes, the young wizard swiftly described a semicircle with his staff, as if warding off the flying snow. Cape billowing in the wind, he cried aloud three times. Electric blue light crackled all around them. Kaukomieli wove the light into a pattern, a checkered cocoon of energy to protect them. Slowly, he bent the blue wall back to make a circle.

But Valkea stood before him. The bright blue light illuminated all the lake. Her target clear, Valkea drew her mighty bow. The missile sped true. With the spell unset, incomplete, the arrow found its mark; the shaft plunged into Kaukomieli's chest.

"Kaukomieli!" screamed Ulla. "Kaukomieli, no!"

The young man fell backwards, arms outspread. No voice was left to him, no song in his shattered breast, but, with his dying breath, he silently mouthed a single word, releasing his life-force into the spell. *Sulataa. Melt.*

At once, thunder boomed across the lake. Great cracks rippled through the ice. Shaking off his horror, Väinämöinen grabbed Ulla by the hair. "Sing with me, Ulla. Now! Work the change!"

"No!" she screamed, lunging toward Kaukomieli's fallen body.

With a rush, the ice collapsed, swallowing up sleds. Valkea's final shot, aimed at Väinämöinen, flew wide as the ice beneath her feet opened. Grasping wildly at her sled, she tottered for a moment, then disappeared beneath the freezing water with a short, muffled cry. All over the lake screams rang out as the elves, dogs, and reindeer fell into the lake. A white mist rose immediately, blinding all who remained.

Another crack rent the ice at Ulla's feet; her leg plunged into the icy water. The old man hauled her up, desperate. Chanting in the Old Speech, eyes closed, he worked a change. Never in all his long life had old Väinämöinen worked a change on both himself and another; never had any Erilainen done such a thing, not even Turi. He poured all his love for Ulla, the dark-haired girl from the Marches whom he loved as no other, into that song. Distilled into the purest magic, the old man cast a spell more powerful than any he had ever cast before—he, Väinämöinen, the legendary Hero whose deeds were sung in every corner of the Far Northern Land.

With a flash, the two wizards transformed into birds, great black and white birds of the North. They took wing even as the ice beneath them collapsed. The struggling reindeer, the sled, Kaukomieli—all disappeared into the black water. Mounting higher, the birds flew north while the cries faded below.

The storm beat upon them. Gusts buffeted the lonely pair from side to side. It was difficult to stay aloft in such conditions. They skimmed the tree-tops, unable to rise higher. A lake passed by, then another. They flew over stands of short, stumpy trees, forlorn outliers of the larger wood. Then the trees failed. There was nothing, nothing but a white moonscape devoid of life. The frozen plains of Pohjola stretched before them.

All the while, one bird, lame of wing, dripped a tell-tale trail of blood onto the snow below. The crimson patch beneath its right wing grew ever larger, its troubled flight ever more labored.

They had flown only a few miles, perhaps, when the bird with the crimson wing gave up. It fell to the ground. Its companion followed, the magic spent.

Väinämöinen, on his hands and knees, gasped for breath. Ulla lay face down in the snow, still grasping her sword. The old man looked frantically for his staff, but it was gone. The spell that transformed them had consumed it.

Väinämöinen turned Ulla onto her back. Delirious, she muttered, "Kaukomieli, oh Kaukomieli."

The arrow protruded just above her breast. Blood drenched her garments, staining the snow. She was rapidly bleeding to death.

Gathering Ulla into his arms, Väinämöinen rocked back and forth. Despair swept over him. Alone amidst the snowy wastes, far from help or hope, he knew not what to do. Staring up into the darkling sky, he cried aloud in a great voice, "*Ukko! Ukko Kakki-Isä! Älä hylkää minua! Anna minulle voimaa pelastaa tämän lapsen kuolemasta!*"

In his sorrow, he cried from his heart, "Ukko! Ukko All-Father! Forsake me not! Give me the strength to save this child from death!"

But Väinämöinen was in Pohjola, the land of the Witch. Löhi's evil will lay over all that realm. Snow, wind, ice, and storm all obeyed her command and furthered her dark design. No answer came to the wizard's plaintive wail, no respite from his sorrow.

The old man took a breath. With his long knife, he cut off the arrow-head. Cradling Ulla in his left arm, with his right, he drew out the shaft in one swift pull. She cried out in pain. Fresh blood broke through the frozen red crystals. Passing his hand over the wound, Väinämöinen began to chant in a strange, sonorous tone, putting all the power that remained to him into this final attempt. The spell he wove was the same he had cast near the Marches long ago when the little girl with dark hair had been hurt by *karhu*.

Flesh be made whole,
  stop the red flood.
Rents knit anew,
staunch the bright blood.
Dam the river,
stem the tide.
Choke the fall the arrow's tip has carved

Utterly spent, the wizard slumped against Ulla. The arrow wound was closed front and back, but no power remained to Väinämöinen. He was naked as any mortal, helpless. Snow piled around them. The old man's hands and feet tingled with sudden warmth. He was freezing to death.

Rising, he lifted Ulla into his arms and carried her as best he could through the black, featureless landscape. He could see nothing. The storm blew harder. Each step was agony. Often he fell, rising painfully, collecting Ulla, and tramping on. Väinämöinen had no idea which way he walked or where he might find shelter. The old man drifted in and out of wakefulness and, whether the voices on the wailing wind were real or part of some dimly realized nightmare, he never knew.

At last, stumbling on his feet, Väinämöinen threw himself to the ground. He crawled to Ulla and uncovered her. Her lips were blue, her eyelashes sealed with ice. The old man was exhausted, his wits scattered, his hope all but lost. Red-faced, beard white and frozen, he sat on his knees staring blankly into the darkness.

He thought he saw something in the corner of his eye, a flash of movement and flickering light. Suddenly a herd of reindeer rushed past. Bells jingled as a sleigh approached. Fumbling at his sword hilt, he tried and failed to draw the blade from its sheath. The sleigh appeared, its great curved runners stopping only a few feet away. Mumbling an empty incantation, bereft of wizardly power, Väinämöinen toppled over. Figures jumped from the sleigh, racing toward him. A dark lantern was uncovered.

But these were no Haltiatar from Pimentola. They were men, mortals, thickly clad in leather and fur with tall, colorful caps and pointed boots that curled up at the toes.

Väinämöinen raised his head to look at them. Blackness took him.

Chapter Fifteen

Sariola

The boy watched the dark-haired woman as she slept. He knew by her fluttering eyes that she would awaken soon.

His mother had given him instructions. First, give the woman water and a cupful of cloudberry porridge. Next, come to the neighboring *viessu* to tell the adults. The boy had been tempted by the cloudberries. Picked in summer, then mixed with water, fat, and milk, the golden berries were doled out sparingly during the long darkness. All he had to satisfy the pangs of hunger were strips of dried reindeer meat, the standard fare during winter journeys.

He resisted temptation. All of eight years old, the boy understood responsibility well enough to be trusted. Life was not easy among the reindeer herders. Margins were slim in the farthest north. Obeying the simplest instruction might be the difference between survival or death. For as long as he could remember, the boy had worked alongside the adults, tanning skins, twining sinew, guarding the herd from wolves and bears. He could be trusted.

The woman awoke. She lay flat on her back, unmoving, for a long time. Gingerly, she felt her heavily bandaged right shoulder. The boy considered her carefully. Strange, she was. He had never seen another mortal like her. She had black hair, like an elf's; freckles dotted her pale, narrow face. When they had washed her, he had seen that her body was scarred and torn. A witch among the southerners, he heard his uncle say. Her speech was alien, incomprehensible.

Three days she had slept, ever since they found her dying in the snow. Three days, she had spoken in her fevered dreams. He could understand nothing save one thing: a name, a strange name that she called out again and again.

A tear welled from the woman's eye. It traced a path down her cheek. Then she turned, noticing the boy for the first time.

Taking the wooden cup, he knelt beside her. His reindeer leather boot, covered in white fur, brushed her face. He fed the cloudberries to her with a spoon made of bone.

"*Eat this*," he said, in a tongue as incomprehensible to her as her speech was to him. "*We picked them on the taiga in summer*." The woman ate the porridge, gazing intently at the tow-haired little boy with ice blue eyes.

"*I will tell my mother that you are awake now*."

When she finished the cloudberries, the child placed a skin of warm water beside her. Glancing back a final time, he left through a flap in the *viessu's* skins.

Ulla drank some water, then lay still. Her shoulder felt stiff, painful. She knew better than to move suddenly or strain the damaged joint. She wondered if her arm would remain lame forever.

The young woman remembered nothing after Kaukomieli's death. Everything afterward was a blank, a jumble of confused, hazy impressions. She had dreamed for days, dreamed of Kaukomieli's sacrifice and Valkea's sinister face. Waking seemed stranger than dreaming. Ulla did not know where she was or how she got there. She did not know what had become of Väinämöinen. Balanced between despair and indifference, her eyes reflexively scanned the environs for want of anything else to do.

She lay within a simple shelter, reminiscent of the *majas* of the Karelialaiset, but more primitive. Narrow pine logs formed a framework covered by reindeer skins stitched together with sinew. Smoke issued from a hole in the top of the cone-shaped *viessu*. Turf smoldered in the fire pit, along with something else, something that Ulla could smell but not identify.

Apart from reindeer pelts strewn on the ground and an odd collection of small items, the lodging was warm and empty inside.

Still balancing her emotions like an unsteady juggler, she drifted into a half-sleep for a while, until someone entered the *viessu* from outside. The woman, shorter than the women of the Seven Clans, looked more like Taika and other Erilaisen women, though clearly mortal. The woman wore a colorful red and blue leather garment with a long skirt. The garment's high, stiff collar was banded, embroidered with encircling metal thread. Tin chains and rings dangled from her neck and belt. Fur boots stuck out beneath her skirt. The little boy lingered behind her.

As red-cheeked and white-haired as her son, the woman knelt beside Ulla, speaking quietly. She stroked Ulla's forehead. After inspecting her wounded shoulder and feeling her pulse, the strange woman poured something from a leather flagon into a cup, offering it to her. Ulla took the cup and drank. She had tasted the thick, yellow drink only a few times before, in Karelia. It was reindeer milk, soured and stored in the frozen earth during the winter.

She drank more. The red-cheeked woman put a hand over the cup, speaking softly, yet sternly. Ulla did not understand her language, but took the meaning well enough. The milk was exceedingly rich. *Do not drink so swiftly.*

"Thank you," said Ulla. "But please, can you tell me where my companion is—my friend? How did I get here? Where am I?"

"Your companion is here," said a deep voice. Väinämöinen stood just within the *viessu's* entrance. "And you are in Pohjola, in the shelters of the Saami, the reindeer herders. As to how you came here, I can tell you that too. Or at least what I remember because I do not remember everything myself."

The Saami woman nodded, rose, and retreated to a corner of the lodge with the little boy. Picking up a needle made of reindeer bone, she began to sew, taking no more notice of them. Väinämöinen sat down cross-legged next to Ulla. He still wore his tattered Karelian garb, but with the addition of a new, brightly colored leather poncho decorated with strange symbols. The old man's face and long nose were brown and peeling from frostbite, but his beard was combed and forked.

Väinämöinen stroked Ulla's hair. "How is your shoulder?"

"It hurts, but I can move it. It is very stiff."

"You must not let it freeze in place. The arrow wound was clean, though you lost much blood. Alas, I can stop the blood, but I cannot heal all the hurt within. You may never wield a sword or draw a bow with that arm again."

"Then it is good that I know the sword *loitsu* and can wield *Pohjanpiikki*, and Longleaf, too, with one hand. Only one more fight remains, in any case."

The old man nodded.

"It was no dream, was it? Kaukomieli, I mean."

"No. He is gone. The Last Wizard of Laulavalaakso. If not for him, the Haltiatar would have slain us all."

"We are the last, aren't we? The others are dead—Ilkka, Tulikki—they are all dead, are they not?"

"I do not know, Ulla. Perhaps. *Better a bitter truth than a sweet lie.* In any case, the end approaches. Do not despair."

"When have I ever despaired?"

Ulla suddenly sat up. Despite her injury, she felt power blossoming again within. *What have I left to fear, after all?*

"Let us make an end of it, then. *Will shall be the sterner, heart the bolder, spirit the greater as our strength lessens.*"

"So be it," answered Väinämöinen.

Ulla lay back while Väinämöinen told her about their escape from Pimentola. "We made a change, you and I. Like two birds, we flew away as the ice melted beneath us."

"What of Valkea? Did she die?"

"Aye. I saw her fall into the lake. No one could survive that."

"Good," answered Ulla. "But how did we find the herders?"

"We did not; they found us. We were lost on the frozen plains of Pohjola amidst the storm. I was dying and so were you, child. Chance or fate favored us then, for usually the Saami would already be far south of here, where their herd winters. But this group came north to retrieve animals stranded in a little valley, to save them from the storm. They found us and took us in, but I remember very little of it."

"Are they to be trusted?" asked Ulla, glancing at the Saami woman sewing in the corner. After her experience with the elves of the Candlestick Forest, Ulla expected the worst.

"The Saami do not serve Löhi," answered Väinämöinen. "They never have. They are free, wild and free. They know no boundaries, no borders save the trails of their reindeer, which they follow.

"All they need, they take from their reindeer: meat, fur, skin, bone. All that you see within this lodging comes from the beasts. The Saami live in harmony with nature, fighting no wars, troubling no others. They wish only to be as they always have been, alone and free in the North.

"Mortals they are, though not reckoned among the Seven Clans of the Far Northern Land. Few men in the South have ever met them. No, they do not serve Löhi, but fear her. She deems them of little account, though they set a tribute of furs along the road each year for passage through her kingdom—so much dealing they have with her. But do not fear to trust them. There are sorcerers among them, *noaidi*, who follow the Old Ways of the Vanhalaiset after their fashion. They are good folk; they will not betray us to Löhi."

Ulla's eyes fluttered. The Saami woman, as if summoned, rose and said something in her own tongue to Väinämöinen. The old man nodded.

"Sleep now, little one. You still need much rest, though we have little time for it. Sleep and rest your mind on the trail for singers."

They remained seven days with the Saami, so far as they could reckon in perpetual darkness. The Saami, however, knew well the passage of time. Ulla healed swiftly, each day sufficing for a week to other mortals. *Tietäjää* that she was, the dark-haired woman's wizardly power returned quickly, speeding her recovery. Still, her hurt could not be wholly cured. She could no longer raise her right arm above her head or place it easily behind her back. Thick, rubbery scars marked the spots where the arrow had entered and exited. Yet, nourished by the Saami's food and Väinämöinen's spell, she soon regained her old energy.

Not so with old Väinämöinen. The singer wasn't wounded, but his wizardly fires burned low. They were in Pohjola, the Black Land of Löhi, where all her dark sorcery found its source. His magic, the magic of Karelia, shone dimly. The Great Oak of Väinölä was far, far away. Not so quickly did he recover, not so swiftly did his strength return. Above all, he felt the Witch's thought over everything, a pall of dark cloud overshadowing mind and body.

The dozen or so Saami in the little camp had been no more troubled by the blizzard than Ulla might have been by a heavy rain when she lived in Grankulta. They carried logs, skins, and fuel with them for such eventualities, ready to make a lager at need and ride out the storm inside their *viessus*. Indeed, the Saami handled the cold better than Löhi's goblins, which they hated and feared. Covered by snow, with only small turf fires burning inside, the unremarkable *viessus* blended into the snowy wastes so well that even the Witch's *sight* might miss them. Only the reindeer, patiently nosing in the ice for buried moss, gave any indication that mortals camped nearby.

When Ulla had recovered sufficiently, the Saami leader told Väinämöinen that they must move. He was a shaman, powerful among his folk, and had recognized Väinämöinen and Ulla at once as wizards. He even knew Väinämöinen's name, as well as bits and pieces of old legends. Of Ulla, he knew nothing. He did not understand their quest, but he agreed to do what he could to help them. The old wizard remembered enough of the reindeer herders' language to communicate with some difficulty.

"We cannot remain here any longer," said the shaman. "Close we are to Sariola. We sleep now almost beneath the shadow of the Witch's mountain. If she sees us and learns that we have helped her enemies, she will kill us and enslave our children. Times are bad since Löhi returned to Pohjola.

"We will take you to the road. From there, you must make your own trail. You must be careful. The storm has passed south. It rains snow far away in places where the sun still sails across the sky. The air tells us that it will be clear in northland for many days. The stars will be bright and the eyes of Sariola see far. Strong *noaidi* you are, especially the girl. Löhi is stronger. You must outwit her if you wish to fulfill your quest, whatever that may be."

They thanked the short, stout herder many times for, without the Saami's mercy and kindness, they would already have perished. That night, Väinämöinen sat with the shaman and his brother, chanting and joiking. The Saami produced small leather drums, beating them in time to the men's slow cadence. Yet Väinämöinen worked no magic and taught no *loitsu*. This close to Sariola, he feared he would bring the Witch's wrath down upon them unawares.

The next morning, so the Saami told them, they prepared to set out. The reindeer herders stood in the snow to wish them farewell. Some were already breaking down their lodgings. The Saami harnessed two sleds with four animals apiece. The shaman and another man would accompany them to the road, driving the sleds. The Saami gave them reindeer meat and cloudberries, enough for a short journey. They wore new, fur-lined mittens and warm leggings. No other garments would fit them, however, nor would the herders give away their long, fur coats in any case, though they were the warmest coats Ulla had ever known. With a whoosh, they set off across the taiga. The herders' dogs gave chase for a while, then they were on their own.

Navigating by the stars, the Saami drove the sleds northeast. It was bright; the waxing moon rode high, its light filling the winter sky. Taivaantappi, the Nail of the Heavens, rested almost directly overhead. The red star, the Witch's Star, had now come so close to Taivaantappi that it seemed the brighter, inching ever closer toward overtaking the North Star and supplanting it as the center of the sky.

Ulla sat behind the driver, watching the featureless plain roll by. No trees grew here, nothing but snow, broken only by the occasional boulder peeking from beneath its white cover. She could see for miles in the bright starlight, but had no sense of depth or distance. She grew giddy. Without any point to focus on, it seemed they were not moving; the horizon was unchanging, the stars fixed in place. Ulla dozed as the white reindeer, fairer and smaller than the reindeer of Karelia, pumped their strong legs, pulling the sleds across the barren wastes.

After many hours, the sleds pulled east, stopping at an outcrop of grey stone. Even in the endless night, the Saami knew their way.

They dismounted. The shaman, dressed all in fur with a red, four-cornered hat, motioned eastward.

"Yonder lies the road," he said. "We dare not go further. You will find it easily enough by the stars. Few folk use the road in winter, for Sariola is nearly empty during the darkness, they say, except for the Witch's ghosts and the demons that never sleep. The truth of it I do not know.

"My brother came here while you first slept, while we waited to see if you would live or die. Many people moved up and down the road then, goblins and other evil things; that is strange. Perhaps they searched for you. You must be careful, Väinämöinen, even you whose name is old as the stones themselves. My heart tells me that your coming to Pohjola is not unlooked for."

"Thank you again for your hospitality," answered Väinämöinen. "We can never repay you. In the South, when one man saves another's life, a great gift or great service is owed—the Life Debt. It is one of the Seven Laws that governed the world of men on a time. I once saved Ulla's life when she was young and so she came with me as prentice in return.

"We have nothing with which to pay the Life Debt we owe you. No service can we perform that you need and we have no treasure to give save one. Accept this, then, as a token of our gratitude and friendship. Remember us, come what may!"

Väinämöinen reached inside his shirt. From around his neck, he drew the golden talisman that hung there. Always he had kept it with him, for years uncounted, and it had been made by Ilmarinen in ages past. He handed it to the Saami shaman.

The man's broad, flat face reddened. He smiled, showing his white, regular teeth.

Without another word, the reindeer herdsmen mounted their sleds and shook the reins. Turning their beasts, they headed back down the trail they had just made. Ulla and Väinämöinen watched them for a long time. The sleds remained visible for a while, dark, dwindling specks against a billowy white sea bathed in moonlight. Then they disappeared, swallowed by some fold of land. Ulla and Väinämöinen were completely, utterly alone.

* * *

The Saami had given them a final gift of snowshoes. Not the birch shoes Peiko used, but bone shoes, finely-carved, with tough, sinewy rawhide webbing. Wrapping the elves' midnight blue cloaks tight, they set out for the road.

"The shoes are good, but a sled would have been better," said Ulla.

"So it would," answered Väinämöinen. "But they could not spare one, nor would it serve us well with its great, curved runners and distinctive look. A Saami reindeer sledge driving straight to Sariola! That would be a strange sight indeed. No, remember what the shaman told us. We must outwit Löhi. He was right."

The old man sighed. "I need your help now, Ulla. I feel very weak; my songs are all off."

Ulla wondered at this. Despite her wound, she brimmed with power and excitement.

"Can you feel her?" the wizard asked, meaning Löhi.

"Yes," answered Ulla. "She is there, to the east. I need no other guide now."

"She can feel us, too. Especially me. I am going to do all I can to hide us. I wove a spell, the Wizard's Cloak, long ago when Lemminkäinen, Ilmarinen, and I came to Pohjola to steal the Sampo. It is not like Tulikki's Cloak; it will not make us invisible, but it can mask our power for a while so that Löhi cannot sense us precisely. It will take all my strength to keep it up. You must do the rest."

"Should we not weave Tulikki's Cloak as well? Both of us? Then we can slip into Sariola unseen."

"No! Some spells may confuse the wizardly sense of a powerful sorcerer. Others excite it. Tulikki's Cloak may hide one from unfriendly eyes, but it creates ripples that the Witch can feel. We are in Pohjola. Löhi would feel us at once if we cast such a spell in her own realm. It would also exhaust us, as you know better than anyone. You must save all you have for the final confrontation. Besides, it is useless with Löhi; her eyes can see through it."

After an hour or two of trudging through the snow, they found the road. Called the Dwarves' Road, it ran from Pohjola all the way to the Kääpiövuori, hundreds of miles to the west. There, the dwarves still lived beneath their mountain, mining, delving, and hammering at their forges. They used the road for their trade with the Witch. For long stretches, it was little more than a cart path through the wilderness. But here in Pohjola, it became a raised highway with a curb on one side and a high bank to the north to deflect the blowing snow.

Väinämöinen and Ulla climbed the curb. Standing on the icy road, they gazed eastward toward Sariola.

"Should we not stay below?" asked Ulla. "We are exposed here."

"I wonder," answered Väinämöinen. "But the going will be much slower. If we encounter anyone—or anything—we can try to hide. But if Löhi or her sorcerers turn their sight this way, best they see two elves from Pimentola on the road than stragglers in its shadow."

"Surely the elves of the Candlestick Forest have told her that we are coming."

"Maybe," said the old man. "If so, our garb may be the worst possible disguise. Not all of our attackers died in the lake, however. I saw some below as we flew away, standing on the lakeshore. The survivors cannot know for certain what happened or that we escaped in the confusion. They may have searched a long time for us, wondering if we perished along with Valkea, Kaukomieli, and their kinfolk. Perhaps they fear to warn the Witch, guessing her displeasure and anger when she learns of their failure. Who can say? They may be paralyzed with doubt, at least for a while. That is what I hope."

They took to the road. Väinämöinen chanted softly as they walked. Ulla remained alert, all weariness gone. The wind was mild. Cold it was, but not so cold as when the storm had blown. Bright stars lit the path ahead. Gradually, Ulla realized that the dark spot just above the eastern horizon was no cloud or mist, but mountains, a tumbled, stony range spilling down from the North: the Mountains of Pohjola.

Now this was the fashion of Pohjola in those days.

To the west lay a vast expanse of wilderness, snow-covered during winter. Stands of sparse wood dotted the plain, but further north, all trees failed. To the east lay a range of mountains shaped like a drawn bow. At their northern end, they were mere hills, rocky and barren save for bushes hidden in their stony folds. Dropping down from the north, they grew in height. But at the southern end, a great mountain reared, its rocky spire rising high into the sky: the Kipuvuori, the Mountain of Pain.

High atop that spire sat Löhi's throne. From it, she gazed out upon the Far Northern Land, casting her evil spells. Spirits and unclean things she gathered there upon the summit, holding concourse, and it was the source of her wizardry, the black *kalma* of Pohjola. Inaccessible was that height, unscaled by mortal or Erilainen, and whether Löhi went there incarnate, in spirit-form, or changed into bird or beast, none knew. Few were those she ever took with her.

Far below that height, the Kipuvuori threw out a great spur. There the Witch had made her capital, dismal Sariola. On its western side lay Hiitola, Goblin Town, where the Hiisia bored a thousand holes into the mountainside to dwell in. But nestled beneath, in a vale below Goblin Town, was a strip of enchanted land that Löhi had made perpetually fertile. Her slaves dwelt there, folk of the Seven Clans taken in Löhi's wars. Chattel they were, working the land for rye, barley, and other needful things. And their lives were hopeless, for there was no escape from Pohjola save death.

On the spur's eastern shoulder was built the Witch's Keep. There stood the dwellings for her servants and the roundhouses for the Easterners who gathered at Sariola in spring and summer. But on the mountain itself, above these dwellings, stood Löhi's castle. Dark and brooding were those walls and towers, the abode of evil things. And within abode Löhi of Pohjola.

Such was the realm of Pohjola, though Väinämöinen knew little of these things and Ulla nothing. The old wizard had been to Sariola only once, hundreds of years earlier when he had rescued the Sampo from the Witch's clutches. He had not entered the Keep then, hearing only whispers of its dark secrets.

The old man and the girl walked on, dreading the rumor of Löhi's servants on the frozen road. Sled tracks marked the highway in some places; the road had been used recently. Ulla wondered where they would sleep when their strength failed. No stone, tree, or bush marred the white winter wasteland. Green lights appeared in the northern sky, streaking across the heavens and bathing everything below in their glow.

The girl watched the lights advance and retreat. Beautiful they were, yet the harbinger of ill things, or so Ulla thought. She hoped only to reach Sariola, to make it that far. The thought gripped her that she would never see sunlight again or feel its warmth. She could not remember the last time she had seen the sun. It had not seemed important then and was now just another moment lost in time.

Ulla suddenly descried something in the distance, a flicker of light like a will o' the wisp dancing above the snow.

"Väinämöinen!" she cried, pointing. The old man saw it too.

They leapt over the curb, pressing into the snowbank. The light continued to flicker, but came no closer. They crept forward silently. As they approached, they realized the flickering light spilled from a dwelling of sorts built against the high bank on the road's northern side and made of grey stone with a covered animal pen beside it. Coming within a stone's throw, they peeked over the curb.

The stone house was a way station for travelers journeying to and from Sariola. Smoke rose from the chimney. Shaggy ponies stamped in the shelter. Three large sledges sat side by side. Figures moved among them.

"Dwarves!" whispered Ulla. "They are dwarves!"

Ulla had never met a dwarf. As secretive as they were, they had never come to the Seven Lands for many lives of men. She had no doubt, however. The short figures, only slightly taller than the Menninkaiset, had forked and plaited beards. High caps trailing long tassels sat atop their heads. The dwarves had apparently just arrived and were settling their ponies.

"So they are!" said Väinämöinen, softly. "Traders from the Kääpiövuori."

"Are they evil? I know little of such creatures."

"Some are; some aren't. Same as could be said for most peoples. An entire army of them fought for Löhi in the first war; most died, including their king. Some fought with our side, too. Brave warriors. Afterward, those that remained took to their mountain and never came south again."

"What do they trade for?"

"Gold," whispered Väinämöinen. "Gold from the Kemi, the great lake and river of Pohjola. The purest yellow, the softest touch, the brightest sheen—the most treasured gold in the Far Northern Land. Their smiths work it into shapes wondrous and beautiful. From it, they can make thread, paint, and all manner of art. The goblins mine gold from the Kemi. The dwarves forge weapons of iron and steel for the Witch in return. The dwarves' lust for gold from Pohjola is great."

Väinämöinen and Ulla watched as the dwarves finished their tasks, trudging back inside the cottage's warmth. They waited. For a long time, speech and laughter could be heard within. Ulla tried, but could not understand the strange tongue. She began to slip into sleep. Images drifted through her mind. Suddenly, the old man poked her. She snapped awake.

"Ulla, it's time. Let's go."

"Should we stay below the curb?"

"No. We are not walking. I want a sled! The Saami's would not do, but these are different."

They hurried across the highway. Crouching in the darkness among the sleds and gear, they listened carefully. All was silent. Only a thin trail of smoke rose from the chimney. Väinämöinen rummaged through the baggage.

"See here, Ulla!" he whispered, excitedly. Rocks lay inside two sleds, looking for all the world like bloodrock to Ulla. Moon sheen glinted off a shiny nugget.

"Gold!" said Ulla.

"Yes. Such was their reward from Löhi."

The third sled held no gold, but a rough wooden box containing weapons: twelve pikestaffs with steel heads, beautifully crafted with silver bands wrapped round the polished shafts.

"I don't understand," said Ulla. "Gold and steel; are they coming or going?"

Väinämöinen thought for a moment.

"Both, I guess. Two groups met here, one returning from Sariola, one still on its way. Perhaps the gold bearers mean to wait for their companions ere they return together to the Kääpiövuori.

"Now listen, Ulla. We're going to steal this sled, the one with the weapons. I want you to choose two ponies; you're good with animals. Use just enough power to calm them, no more. If the dwarves awaken, we'll have a fight on our hands."

Ulla did as the old man instructed. Speaking soft words to the shaggy beasts, she chose the two largest, a piebald and a grey, then led them from the pen. Meanwhile, Väinämöinen drew his long, bone-handled knife. Going to each of the other sleds in turn, he cut the leather harnesses left there, rendering them useless. Then he took all the coiled ropes from the other sleds and tossed them into their own.

"There," he whispered. "So far, so good. Let them try to catch us on foot. We will have several hours on them, at least. That is all we need."

"Should we sing the other beasts to sleep?"

"I wonder," answered Väinämöinen. "Had we done so in Pimentola, much evil might have been averted. But no, I think not. It is too risky. They will not be going anywhere swiftly, in any case. We have made a puzzle for them to boot. Let them figure it out! Come now, help harness the ponies to our sled and let's be off."

They worked swiftly. The green lights streaked across the sky as they set out. Luckily, the dwarves' harness and riggings had no bells. The ponies snorted, their iron-shod hooves slapping against the ice, but no dwarves emerged to challenge them.

Väinämöinen drove the ponies, his boots pressed against the runners. Ulla perched between the old wizard and the pikestaffs. She gazed back at the way station until it disappeared from sight. They had escaped unnoticed.

The shaggy ponies were strong, bred for draught and well-suited for running in the snow. The old man set a good pace. Straight down the road they raced, straight toward Sariola, and always the Kipuvuori loomed larger. Snow and ice flew in Ulla's face. Cold air sharpened her senses. Power simmered inside her. Before her lay a dreadful presence, drawing her like a lodestone: Löhi, the Queen of Pohjola. Ulla felt the Witch's presence keenly now. Did Löhi feel hers just the same?

"Väinämöinen," she said in the wizard's ear. "What will we do when we reach Sariola? Long has it been since we spoke of it. The quest was to reach Pohjola. That we have done. The task at hand now is to kill the Witch."

"That is up to you, Ulla," he answered. "My power wanes, child. Yours waxes. If I can hide us long enough to give you a chance...that is all I can do."

"When you stole the Sampo, you sang Sariola to sleep."

"Lemminkäinen and Ilmarinen were with me then and the spell long prepared. And it was not all of Sariola, only the goblins who guarded the Sampo where Löhi had hidden it. She was away then, returning just in time to chase us. That song will not avail us, even if I could weave it again."

Ulla thought for a while.

"We must surprise her," she said at last. "Always the Witch schemes, always she lays her plans far in advance. She fears the unexpected. Is that not how Lemminkäinen defeated her?"

"Aye," said the old man. "If we can catch her unawares, you have a chance. Löhi often sends her *etianen* into the world. She enters the dreams of others. Her spirit lies in wait in the wood without color as she prowls the borders of Tuonela. If we can catch her at such a time, she will be vulnerable. Perhaps you can destroy her."

A full moon sailed high over Pohjola. Stars shone in the heaven like diamonds. The sled's runners cut the ice like knives, carving delicate patterns in their wake. The Mountain of Pain rose so high now it obscured all the eastern sky. Three hours, four hours, on they drove. Twinkling lights appeared to the northeast. First one, then another, then dozens caught flame. Tiny yellow lights flickered like fireflies, chasing one another in a mad dance as the sled rocked back and forth. Väinämöinen pulled hard on the reins. The sled skidded to a stop. Snow flew everywhere.

The quiet of Pohjola fell upon them. The sled rested at a crossroad.

"Behold Sariola!" said Väinämöinen, pointing to the yellow fireflies. "Yonder lies Hiitola, that the Men of the Seven Clans name Goblin Town. See how their lanterns blaze!"

The road north led upward toward the mountainside and Goblin Town. Hundreds of lights shone from their stony dwellings. The road south sloped downward, disappearing round a bend.

"And the downward road?" asked Ulla.

"That way is our way; it leads to the Witch's Keep and Löhi's castle. I wonder that we have yet to meet anyone. But surely we will not come to the castle unchallenged."

The old man laughed grimly. "Two elves from Pimentola on a dwarvish sled. And are we to drive openly into the Keep for all to see?"

Ulla rose. She stood in the crossroad, surveying their path. A fierce courage welled within her heart.

"Yes, two elves from Pimentola," she said. "Mask us but a little longer, Väinämöinen. I will weave the illusion to gain entry."

"No!" said the old man. "That illusion may be worst of all. And working magic is treacherous now, deadly. Can you not feel the Witch's thought all around us?"

"We must risk it," she replied, steadily. "It is the only way. Trust me, *Isani*. If we fail, we fail together. Let us take the long road to Ukko hand in hand, knowing we chose rightly."

The old man smiled.

"Daughter of my adoption, kinswoman of my heart, lead us now, come what may."

Returning to the sled, Ulla put on Valkea's tall hat. She arrayed her dark hair like the elf's, wrapping the cloak—still encrusted with her own blood—tightly around herself. For the last time, they set off.

The downward road hugged the dark base of the Kipuvuori. The lights of Goblin Town were soon lost to sight. Round the bend they drove, going slower now. To their right, a sheer cliff fell to a snow-covered lake far below. Väinämöinen pointed it out, for that lake was the Kemi, upon which he had sailed long ago on his quest to steal the Sampo. Silver moonlight reflected from its untroubled surface. Colder it grew; the lonely pass was dark. No wind blew, all was still and silent, yet a heavy weight descended, oppressing their very souls.

They had travelled only a few miles when the road ended abruptly, opening into a broad valley. They had reached the Witch's Keep. Lamps flickered in the gloaming. Here stood the roundhouses of the Itäläiset. The dwellings of Löhi's servants had been built on the white, rocky plain, along with sheds and smithies, forges and fires, all that the foul folk of Sariola needed.

Small figures, white-eyed goblins in the livery of Pohjola, dragged a sledge from a *kota*. Others moved about in the murk. They took no notice of the two Haltiatar riding into their village. Indeed, Sariola seemed almost deserted. In spring and summer, companies of Easterners gathered there, and Dark Erilaiset from throughout the North. Dwarvish traders and mortals from faraway lands trafficked on the plain while the red sun never set.

Not now. Now was the Dark Time. Cold, snow, and ice held sway. The

Witch wove her spells in solitude. The goblins remained in Hiitola on the mountain's western face. Men and elves wintered elsewhere or were far to the south fighting Löhi's wars. Only the queen's most faithful servants dwelt in the Keep during the Dark Time, and of those, only the most trusted gained entry to her castle.

Fascinated, Ulla gazed upon the heart of Löhi's realm—and then she saw it. Before her eyes stood Löhi's castle, built onto the mountainside. Below it, she saw the entrance to a narrow path, which climbed to the castle from an iron gate bounded on each side by stone towers. No other way was there to the Witch's abode.

The watch tower on the left, built of black stone, was crowned with a parapet of jagged teeth. Above the parapet stood a great bronze dish with spindly rays fanning out in all directions. And that tower was called the Tower of the Sun.

The watch tower on the right was built of white stone, streaked red as if with blood. A silver diamond stood atop its crest with four arms tapering to deadly points. And that tower was called the Tower of the Star.

Ancient were those towers, raised in ages past to guard the narrow approach lest Löhi be assaulted; and they were named after the sun that never set on Pohjola during summer and after the stars that twinkled continually throughout winter's dark. Within their circuit lay an open pit filled with red light blazing in the endless night. The iron gate stood open now, swung wide in pride or folly, for none had ever dared challenge Löhi's might in her own kingdom. But within it and about the towers, the Witch's servants gathered, the guardians of her dreadful rule; and now they saw the sled, wondering what it might mean.

Väinämöinen checked the ponies, but Ulla laid her hand upon his shoulder.

"No," she said. "They have already seen us. Drive straightaway to the gate. And if this be the end, wait for me by the Dark River and guide me again through Tuonela."

Ulla sang a spell as the piebald pony led its companion toward the gate. It was the first real magic that she had worked in Pohjola. And the tower guards saw not a frightened young woman wrapped in bloody garments driven by a red-eyed old man, but two long-faced elves from the Candlestick Forest. The sled stopped before the open gate and the guards came forward: goblins, misshapen creatures, and Dark Erilaiset who had long served the Witch.

But from the shadows stepped a huge figure, taller than Väinämöinen, dressed all in mail with a breastplate of black steel. He held in his hand a long spear, its bitter tip painted red. A scimitar hung from his belt. Upon his head sat a helm, the visor fashioned like the pointed beak of some terrible bird of prey in a feverish nightmare. Red were his eyes, and red the harsh glare from the blazing pit, bathing everything in a somber, bloody glow. And the token upon his breast was the North Star of Pohjola.

No giant was this, no Erilainen of the North, but a mortal man. For ever and anon, Löhi would take the strongest children from among her slaves and raise them to her service. She cast a spell upon them, binding them to her evil will; and they grew strong and fell beneath her shadow. Such was the man who challenged Ulla, the Captain of the Guard of the Towers. And it is remembered that, in the tongue of Pohjola, he was named Enkko.

Ulla and Väinämöinen rose from the sled. The shaggy ponies shied from the flames. Enkko looked down upon them.

"Who art thou?" he said, his strangely high-pitched voice echoing from the iron beak of his helm. "What is thy errand to the gate of Sariola?"

Enkko spoke in the Old Speech, recognizing them as Haltiatar. Ulla did her best to imitate the thick accent of Pimentola.

"We have come from the forest at thy mistress's bidding," she answered.

"What are thy names?"

"Ilta am I," said Väinämöinen. "And this is my daughter, Aamu. Summoned we were by the queen and so we are here. She is eager to hear our report."

The giant man considered them carefully. He motioned and goblin guards inspected the sled, uncovering the pikestaffs.

"No word from the castle have I to betoken thy coming. Thy names are unknown here. Ungird thy weapons; lay them upon the ground. Thou shalt deliver thy report unto me."

Väinämöinen and Ulla exchanged a nervous glance.

"Such were not our instructions," said Väinämöinen. "May we not pass within? The queen would hear our report directly."

"Word shall be sent," answered Enkko, his tone darker. "Meanwhile, thou shalt deliver thy report unto me. No man, mortal or Erilainen, passes the Towers without the queen's consent. Now place thy weapons upon the ground." He shifted the spear in his hand.

Then it seemed that things would go ill, as both Väinämöinen and Ulla had expected. The old wizard scanned the gate, marking their enemies. His placed his hand on *Jääpuikko's* hilt.

With sudden inspiration, Ulla turned to the sled. She selected one of the ornate pikestaffs.

"These weapons are yours, Lord Captain," she said. "We only agreed to bring them to you at the dwarves' request. One of their number took hurt in the storm. They wished to return to the Kääpiövuori."

She opened the box. Several goblins came forward, grasping and fingering the pikestaffs.

"From the gold owed to the dwarves, set aside one-tenth," continued Ulla. "Such was the bargain we struck. We shall take it with us. Do with the sled and ponies what you will, for our kinsmen will soon reach Sariola and we shall return to the forest with them."

Ulla snatched a pikestaff away from a goblin. The white-eyed creature drew back, hissing.

"No one passes the Towers without the queen's consent," repeated Enkko.

"The queen's consent we have; for her *etianen* came to us, instructing us to hasten to Sariola. We obeyed. Have you not heard rumor of disquiet in Pohjola and death of our kinsmen? Even Valkea was slain, my cousin, and others of my clan."

Enkko laughed.

"Valkea? What is Valkea to me but the name of a wild Haltia in the woods far away and of little importance? But now thou art in Sariola, at the Tower Gates where I am Captain. And here thou shalt stay until word comes from the queen that thou may pass. Do not press thy case, elf, else I shall take you to the castle in chains. But first thou shalt deliver thy report unto me so that I may better decide in this matter."

Ulla narrowed her eyes.

"We are bid to deliver our report to Löhi and to Löhi alone. Do you dare to defy the will of the queen? Who are you to question her commands?"

Enkko's eyes flickered within the pointed visor as if made of flame.

"Dost thou dare to teach me my place? Who art thou to question my mandate? For the last time, place thy weapons on the ground and do obeisance unto me. Thy insolence shall no longer be tolerated."

He swiftly drew his scimitar; the fine blade glittered red in the firelight.

Ulla did not flinch.

"And for the last time, let us hasten on our way. We do not wish to incur the queen's wrath at this delay. Doubtless she already knows that we have arrived. I will not be responsible for what may follow."

Ulla looked Enkko in the eye, regarding him intently. She held his gaze. For the second time she risked a spell, a *loitsu* of persuasion, compelling the man to agree, convincing him that he served Löhi best by so doing. But such spells were treacherous; what worked on one might fail with another. And Enkko's guards stood close by, watching every move.

They strove with one another for a moment, perfectly balanced, until at last Ulla's will mastered his.

"Pass through," said Enkko, heavily. "These spears are not unlooked for. Only two days it is since the dwarves departed from Sariola. But, as for thy reward, I know nothing. Thou must await the queen's pleasure for that."

Ulla bowed her head. Leaving their gear in the sled, she and Väinämöinen walked past the guards, gates, and towers. The gaze of Löhi's servants followed them. Past the gate, the path began to climb immediately.

The *tietäjää* continued straight ahead. Just before the path veered out of sight of the towers, Ulla risked a quick backwards glance. The goblins had unpacked the sled, passing the finely crafted weapons among themselves with delight. However, Enkko stood watching them, the firelight reflecting off his armor like a hellish sentinel of evil.

Seven steps, and the Towers of the Sun and Star were lost to view.

"Do you think he will follow us?" asked Ulla in a muffled tone.

"Who can say?" answered Väinämöinen. "But what does it matter?"

The old man looked up at the castle above.

"Where we go is more dangerous than what we leave behind. Let him follow if he will."

The path wound across the mountain face like a sunken road. To the left, black ice hung on the sheer wall like a frozen waterfall. To the right, the wall was shorter, a crumbling ruin. As they climbed higher, the fall from its jagged, uncertain edge grew steeper. The slick path threatened to send them tumbling to their deaths. Cool stars shone above, a narrow ribbon of sky all they could see. Darkness obscured all else.

Step by step, they trudged up the icy path. Väinämöinen stumbled, bent over like an aged man with faltering feet. Ulla caught him.

"Would that I had my staff," he muttered. "I am growing very weary, Ulla."

"Let us rest here a moment," she said.

"No," he said, "No, we must not stop here."

Yet several minutes passed before he straightened.

"I am better now."

They continued upward.

Gibbets, suspended from iron bolts driven into the stone, appeared at unequal intervals. The first few they passed were empty. Then, with a start, Ulla realized that the next gibbet dangling directly over the path held a body. A frozen skeleton leered at them, its lichen-like beard clinging to the rotting skull like dripping icicles. Bony fingers reached out through iron bars.

So Löhi warned her folk, displaying the price of disobedience or disappointment. Rebellious slave or ineffective captain, none were immune from her ungentle discipline. And the Witch delighted in torturing the innocent, engrossed in the arts of pain and categorizing the types of suffering she might inflict.

Up the icy path they walked. Väinämöinen moved ever more slowly, as if burdened with some heavy load. Ulla realized that when they found their enemy—if they found their enemy—all would be up to her. The old man had spent his strength to get them this far.

Three times round the road turned on itself, crisscrossing the Kipuvuori like stitches. They passed a final gibbet with another frozen corpse within. The path ended. The rock walls fell away and a wide space opened up. The castle lay before them.

The wizards quickly dodged into the shadows.

Ulla stared up at the black stone walls. The ramparts of Löhi's castle rose almost a hundred feet high, built of granite and hard rock; silver crystal therein glittered in the pale moonlight, reflecting its sheen like tiny candles dancing in the dark. Strange and ghastly shapes like the twisted faces of leering demons peered down from irregular battlements. Behind the walls loomed the castle's ancient buildings and towers, grey, with no windows or embrasure to be seen.

One tower reared above the others, reaching upwards toward the black sky, a red light burning within a deep alcove. A parapet sat above all, open to the wind and stars. No banners flew from that parapet, no device fair or foul hung from those dark walls. But spells of ward and doom wrapped dismal Sariola, the Witch's Keep of Löhi of Pohjola. Ulla felt the Witch's power all around her.

An iron bell suspended high within a hidden belfry tolled a single note, its harsh clang echoing throughout the Keep. Starkly colored black and white birds flew up, croaking with unnatural voices before settling down again upon the massive walls. Then, in the gloaming ahead, Ulla spied the gateway.

An iron gate, black as night and crowned with deadly spikes like a thicket of spears, rose high along the wall beneath an archway of glistening stone. The gate was winterfast, made of bloodrock mined from Lake Suurijärvi in ages past and fashioned by the dwarves in their great smithy beneath the Kääpiövuori.

Before it lay a pit filled with sharp rocks, crossed by a narrow bridge without a curb. The great gate itself was shut. As Ulla's eyes adjusted to the murk, she discerned a smaller doorway cut into the gate, a miniature of the huge iron barrier. The small door stood ajar so that the Witch's servants might come and go as needed. Light flickered just within.

The girl with dark hair closed her eyes, drawing a deep breath.

"Come, *Isani!*"

Taking his hand, they fled the shadows, across the narrow bridge, and to the door. No call rang out to challenge them. It seemed the castle slept throughout the long, dark night.

They drew their swords. Without another word, they slipped through the doorway and inside the gate. They had breached the castle.

The two companions found themselves in a large rectangular courtyard scraped clear of ice. Only a light dusting of snow covered the irregular cobblestones. Sleds, barrels, boxes, and troughs sat scattered about the stone-piled ovens and low, half-ruined walls. Doors leading into the castle's many passageways and buildings opened from all sides, save the wall with the gate.

"What do we do now?" whispered Ulla. "Which way should we take?"

"That way," answered Väinämöinen, motioning deeper into the courtyard's interior. "Perhaps we will find a sign."

Shuffling silently like thieves, they crept along the wall. Ulla peered upward, trying to determine what entrance led to the tall tower they had seen while climbing the path, which she guessed must be Löhi's own. Shouts suddenly rang out. They shrank back into the shadows, holding their breath.

A door opened. White wolves ran into the courtyard, howling with excitement. Ulla braced for the attack. The wolves ran past them, however, as goblins issued from another door.

"*Ka*, get back!" they shouted, in the tongue of Pohjola. "Get back, damn you!"

While the wolves leapt about, the goblins tossed great slabs of meat to them from a wooden locker. Ulla shuddered. The beasts attacked their meal like prey, rending, tearing, and devouring it in a frightful frenzy. She remembered the poor captives at Sumuvuori.

Still cursing, the Hiisia returned inside.

"*That* door," hissed Väinämöinen. "The one from which the wolves came—it must be right. See! The tower looms directly overhead. That way, Ulla."

They crept toward the open door, from which a little yellow light spilled, trying to escape the wolves' attention. With the beasts intent on their food, it looked like they would make it inside the doorway unseen.

Just then, Väinämöinen tripped over something hidden in the snow. One of the wolves looked up, no more than a few dozen feet away. Its eyes gleamed red. It snarled, baring bloody fangs.

Ulla raised her hand. She met the white wolf's gaze.

"*Sokeaksi!*" she said.

The animal shook its great white head, seeming disoriented.

They didn't wait to see what happened next. Sprinting into the doorway, they ran down a short, narrow corridor, then took a side passage to the left. Panting, they readied their weapons, but neither wolf nor goblin followed. Cold sweat dripped from Ulla's forehead.

"We have to find the stairs," she whispered. "Löhi must be in the top of the tower."

"Lead on," said Väinämöinen, weakly. "But be careful!"

The castle's passages were much like those of the Keep in the Stone City of Etelamaa where Egan had lived, but no mirth or laughter echoed there. Cold it was and always would be. No warmth would those dark halls ever know. Time did not pass there, memories remained uncollected. Regret was Sariola's banner, despair its coin. Endless and byzantine were the countless corridors running throughout the castle. Brooding silence flowed down hallways opening onto nothingness. Ulla's mind wandered.

"I'm confused," she muttered, coming to a scullery they had already passed through. "I cannot think straight, Väinämöinen. Where are we?"

"Stairs," the old man answered. "Stairs climbing upward. Must find them, Ulla."

"Yes," she replied.

They continued down the dank stone corridors, lit here and there by sputtering pine torches soaked in tar. The pungent smell overwhelmed their senses. Some of the chambers they passed through appeared empty. Others contained chests, barrels, and tools. One chamber seemed a guardroom of sorts, with spears, shields, and helmets resting in wooden racks. The remains of a half-eaten meal sat on a table. Chips glowed red in the hearth.

Still, they encountered no one.

Up short stairs and down others they went, but they could not find what they searched for, a passage to the tower's upper reaches. Ulla had lost all sense of direction, all sense of how long they had roamed the tower's hallways, or even her sense of whether they had passed into another of the castle buildings.

She began to despair. *It would be easy to end it all*, she thought. *This task is hopeless. Easy to shout until our enemies discover us. Or, if no enemies come, easy to take our own lives, to hasten the inevitable journey. Why should we suffer longer?*

In the torchlight, Ulla suddenly saw movement crossing the passage some ways ahead. Three wolves passed before them, vanishing on the other side. Ulla focused.

"Now!" she hissed.

They hurried forward to where the passages intersected. Ulla peeked round the corner, just in time to see the last wolf's shaggy haunches and tail disappear. She saw a stairway there, clearly a tall stair built against a rounded interior wall. Ulla set foot on the first step, then motioned to Väinämöinen. The old man nodded, doing his best to shake off his fugue. Cupping her hand to her ear, Ulla listened. The pitter-patter of the wolves' paws on the granite steps faded away above.

"This is it," said Ulla. She began to climb. Väinämöinen followed. The stair climbed slowly in a great circuit, as if it circled the tower all the way to the stop. Twice they came to broad landings. Torches burned there, filling the narrow stair with acrid smoke. Ulla's eyes burned. She felt like a child again, climbing the Seer's tower at Kyöpelinvuori for the first time.

The walls closed in. The familiar feeling of panic gripped her.

The old wizard put his hand on her wounded shoulder.

"All right, little one. It is all right. We are almost there. If Löhi is in her chamber, do not hesitate. Strike. Leave the rest to me, no matter what you see."

In less than twenty steps, they reached the top. Iron doors stood open. Dim light shone within.

Ulla and Väinämöinen stepped inside. Across the large round room a throne of ice glimmered a pale, translucent blue. Beside the throne stood a tall figure wrapped in shadow. A high diadem crowned her head. Unmoving, gazing out a tower window as if lost in a trance, stood Löhi, the Queen of Pohjola.

Väinämöinen swiftly moved to the left. Ulla went right. Carefully they crept toward the ice throne, trying to avoid unseen objects in the dark. *We have her*, thought Ulla. *Her spirit is wandering elsewhere. We have her!*

Suddenly, the throne room blazed with light. Great lamps ignited overhead. Löhi spun around, her black robes rippling.

"*Sulkea!*" cried Löhi. The iron doors slammed shut.

The Moonface stepped forward, his silver mask gleaming in the lamplight. Three white wolves sat at Löhi's feet. Vepsa, Captain of the Haltiatar of Pohjola, and two other elves faced them with drawn swords. Several goblins moved in behind them with long spears.

They were ambushed.

Red were Löhi's lips, raven her long hair spilling from beneath her crown. No imperfection marred her beauty. Against her flawless skin, white as snow,

Löhi's blue eyes burned like sapphires, compelling all to surrender to her eager will. In her hand lay a staff of iron. Tall and reverent she appeared, a goddess unto mortals and Erilaiset.

"Welcome, Ulla," said the queen. "Didst thou think the eyes of Pohjola blind? Didst thou think to catch me unawares, Karhulainen? I have watched thee from the moment thou didst set foot on the Dwarves' Road. No secret remains hidden from me. For I am Löhi of Pohjola, Queen and ruler of the Far Northern Land!"

Overcoming her initial shock, Ulla acted swiftly. She made straight for Löhi, leaping over a bejeweled chest and sending a goblin sprawling. The wolves sprang. Unable to grasp her blade in both hands, Ulla cried aloud the sword-spell. Pivoting more quickly than any other living mortal, she dealt a deadly blow to the first wolf as it passed by. Another leapt at her. With one stroke, Ulla beheaded the beast. Blood flew everywhere. The third wolf shrank in terror as Ulla screamed a word of power.

And all the while Löhi laughed like a madwoman.

Väinämöinen acted just as swiftly. He had prepared a spell for the final conflict, a *loitsu* learned from Lemminkäinen long ago. That spell would draw other magics to it, distracting sorcerers and redirecting their power. If it worked long enough, if it distracted Löhi, it just might give Ulla the moment necessary to launch her assault.

The old wizard was weary, however. He had no staff. He had spent all his strength in the futile effort to hide from the Witch's *sight*. Little was left for battle. He cried aloud and raised his arms, sword in hand. Silver sparks glittered about his head as he wove the spell.

The Moonface was on him in an instant. He brought down his black sword. Väinämöinen parried, but his enemy struck again, slashing his sword arm. The wizard dropped *Jääpuikko* as a goblin's spear pierced his leg.

As Väinämöinen stumbled forward, Kuupää cried, "*Pysäyttää!*"

The binding spell coiled around the old man like a snake. He struggled, raging against the spell, then suddenly went limp. He fell to his knees, entirely in the Moonface's power.

Across the room, Ulla charged. The young woman's power crackled like lightning, for in that moment she was become the strongest *tietäjää* the Far Northern Land had ever known. Dispatching another goblin like a leaf blown in a gale, Ulla struck. Löhi dodged the blow, quicker than any living creature could possibly be.

Ulla attacked again and again. Darting like a ghost, the Witch eluded her. Lashing out with her iron staff, Löhi finally struck Ulla's wounded shoulder. Then the Witch closed in, their faces only inches apart.

And lo! No more did they duel with blade and staff, but with magic.

Screaming like a banshee released from Tuonela, Ulla gathered all that remained to her—pain, rage, and the loss of all she had ever loved. Images flashed before her: Päivikki, Kaukomieli, *Egan*. She wove the greatest enchantment ever known, born of that loss and the lament of all men for what should be and yet never will.

The spell Ulla wove sought to bind the Witch and cripple her, the forfeiture of hope set against the very instrument of its loss. And it is said that never had Löhi known such a challenge, not even when Lemminkäinen assailed her.

But that was long ago and far away. In Pohjola, Löhi was queen. Here in Sariola sprang the fountains of the Witch's black magic. Here atop the Kipuvuori beat the dark heart of Löhi's *kalma*, the poisonous incantations that flowed throughout all the world. Here was Löhi's power greatest, in the depths of winter, like unto even that of the Vanhalaiset. And she was evil.

Not even the strength of Tapio's chosen, the girl who bore the Mark of the Clan, could defeat the Witch, not in the heart of her own dismal domain. They strove like that, each seeking to subdue the other. And though Ulla's will be adamant, Löhi slowly gained the mastery. Unseen cords constricted Ulla's body. An icy grip seized upon her soul. Feeling her power deserting her, imprisoned within, Ulla threw back her head, crying, "No!"

Before her, the Witch's aspect shifted—from the flawless snow queen, to the gap-toothed crone, to a loathsome monster, and then back again. And all the while, the Witch cackled in her madness.

Then Ulla's magic ran dry. Her song fell silent. The sword slipped from her hand, ringing dully on the stony floor. Tears fell from her hazel-green eyes.

Löhi had defeated her.

The Witch stepped back. Breathing heavily, eyes sparkling, she cried out in triumph. The great lamps danced above. The goblins howled with glee.

"Thinkest thou couldst ever destroy me, Karhulainen?" she gasped, slowly collecting herself. "Think again! For I and I alone, Löhi of Pohjola, am Queen of the World!"

But Ulla answered nothing.

Turning her attention to Väinämöinen for the first time, Löhi stepped over the wolves' carcasses, gore staining her sable robes. At a sign from the Witch, Vepsa hauled the old man to his feet.

"Pay proper respect to thy mistress," mocked the Moonface. "Or else I shall prepare thy torment with special care. What hast thou to say now, conjuror? Hast thou no song?"

When Väinämöinen said nothing, Kuupää slapped his face.

"Patience, Lord Kuupää," said Löhi. "After all, Väinämöinen is a guest in Sariola and knows not our ways.

"Foolish Väinämöinen. Though thou deserves some credit—I am not too proud to admit that thy wandering feet eluded my *sight* at times and Lord Kuupää's pursuit, as well. Where didst thou hide, I wonder? And tell me, how didst thou defeat Ajatar? What spell didst thou cast? Turned to stone, my servants report. Still and silent as a statue, she appears when I gaze upon her. No small deed was that.

"Tell me, what spell didst thou cast?"

Väinämöinen met the Witch's gaze, but said nothing. The Moonface slapped him violently.

"No matter," continued the Witch. "Here it ends, Väinämöinen. And what other ending could there be? What hast thou ever achieved but failure? What boon hast thou ever brought thy friends save ruin? Lemminkäinen, Enkeli, all thy friends of yore. Where is Lúven of the Haltiatar, Väinämöinen? Or Egan, he who would be king? Nothing didst thou achieve save to send him to his death.

"And now, again, thy crooked path leaves only a trail of broken lives in thy wake. Where is Mielikki's daughter, Väinämöinen? Or the boy thou raised to be *tietäjää*? Do I not guess rightly that he wanders the plains of Tuonela? Thou hast achieved nothing, old man, save to bring Ulla directly to me!"

"Shall we not show the conjuror his gift?" said the Moonface. "Long has been its preparation."

At a word from Kuupää, goblins emerged from a side door, dragging with them a man bound in chains. Clad in filthy rags, the wizened figure stumbled forward, weak and frail. His beard had been shorn and he had been blinded. The man's mouth writhed, but he spoke no words; his voice was stopped with spells. And Väinämöinen and Ulla watched in dismay, for they knew him.

"Turi!" cried Väinämöinen. "Turi!"

The Moonface struck the wizard's wounded leg. Väinämöinen sagged to the ground.

"Silence," commanded the Moonface. "Dost thou not like what thou seest?"

The Witch laughed, a hideous sound trailing off into a cackle. Excited, the goblins danced about.

"Turi the Changer," said Löhi, full of malicious merriment. "Or at least, it was once. Now he is just another slave awaiting his turn in the gibbet. Yet I spared him for thee, Väinämöinen. Dost thou not wish to thank me? Now thee may wait together for a time; and thou may be reminded each time thou layest eyes upon him of all thy friends led to destruction by Väinämöinen the Failure."

Väinämöinen hung his head, his old face a study in agony. Still laughing, Löhi turned back to Ulla.

The girl, though no less horrified by the sight of Turi broken, stoically awaited the end. She would give the Witch no pleasure in her sadism.

Löhi came before her now, reaching out to touch Ulla's long, dark hair.

"Little did I expect from Väinämöinen," said Löhi. "But thee, Ulla? I am very disappointed in thee. Thy life need not have ended thus. So much potential lost. Search her!"

Coming forward, the Moonface tore the elves' midnight blue cloak from her shoulders. Reaching for the badger-skin pack that still hung on her belt, he pulled out a small bundle.

"No!" cried Ulla, attempting to stay his hand. The bundle fell to the ground.

The Moonface swept it up, stepping back. He unwrapped the colored cloth, expecting to find some talisman or magic weapon that Ulla might use to assault them. But in his hand lay two carved wooden figures, a little boy and a little girl. Cocking his head, the Moonface considered them for several moments, as if troubled by an old memory or sudden doubt.

But the Witch looked upon the figures with wicked delight.

"How touching," she said. "Two children. Handiwork of the Bear Folk, are they not? Thee and thy brother?"

"Give them back!" cried Ulla, feeling the searing pain of Löhi's compulsion in her very mind.

"We know that story, do we not, Lord Kuupää? The foolish father taking his children into the wilderness. But thou dost not know the whole story, Ulla. It was I, Ulla, who came into your father's dreams. I who made him restless. *Comes a child into the Northland, all the Clans to bring together.*

"My servants waited along the Marches for the father and Child of the Prophecy. And indeed, they brought me a child. Come, Lord Kuupää; now is the time. Take off thy mask. Show Ulla what gift my servants brought back to me. Tell her the end of the story."

The Moonface stared at the wooden figures in his hand. Then, slowly, he removed the silver mask, revealing his pale face. His long, dark hair fell to his shoulders. Freckles dotted his nose and cheeks. His face so perfectly reflected hers that Ulla might have been looking into a mirror.

"Janni," she said incredulously. "Oh, Janni, it is *you*."

"Oh, Ulla," mocked the Moonface. "Hast thou recognized me now?"

Ulla swayed, mumbling, "My...brother. Child of my father, of my..."

"No brother hast thou," said the Moonface. "No father, no family. No sister art thou to me, Karhulainen, scatterling of the North Marches. Lord and Master am I to thee and Death, even as I was to Egan."

And with a word, the Moonface crushed the carven figures into dust.

The Witch cackled with glee.

"No mark was on the shoulder of the child delivered unto me, but no matter. He has grown great, my most loyal friend and servant. Well has he served me."

The Moonface stepped forward. He raised his sword to Ulla's throat.

"Shall I end this?"

But the Witch crossed his blade with her iron staff.

"Not yet," said Löhi sternly. "Still one thing remains that I wish to show her; one thing to complete her failure. Guard Väinämöinen and await my return. Let none molest her form, on pain of death. I shall not be long away."

Baring its fangs, the remaining white wolf sat by Löhi's side. The Witch's aspect changed, her skin turning as translucent as ice, for she had worked the spell that protected her body when her spirit wandered.

Löhi took Ulla's hand. The girl trembled.

"Come with me now to the Kipuvuori. There thou shalt understand thy doom."

A jolt like a thunderbolt rocked Ulla's mind and body. In an instant, she was transported to the spire of the Kipuvuori, leaving Sariola far below. In spirit form she stood by Löhi among the high places of the world. Cold mists parted, revealing a long pier of rock. Upon the precipice sat a stony throne. Countless stars twinkled in the heavens. The great saucer of the moon, waxing full, hung in the northern sky, casting silvery light over everything. And from the north, a bitter wind blew upon the mountaintop.

Tall was the Queen of Pohjola, and tall her lofty crown. And lo! Löhi raised her long, white hand and, within her palm, a jewel burned like a red star.

"Here upon the Mountain of Pain is the font of my wizardry," said Löhi. "Here is the heart of my realm. And here shall be the heart of my new realm, which is all the world. For I am its Queen, and a goddess unto mortals and Erilaiset.

"Here thou mayst be reborn, Ulla. Verily, thou art the Child of the Prophecy, she who bears the Mark of the Clan. Believe not the rumors spread by Mielikki—and where is she now, when thou needest her most? Thou wert born to unite all the Seven Clans under *my* banner, Ulla! Thou needest not die today. Today may be the day of thy rebirth."

"I will never serve you!" cried Ulla. "You destroyed my people, killed my family. You enslaved my brother. I will never serve you. Use him for your dark designs, if you will. But for me, I choose death."

And tears fell from Ulla's eyes upon the Kipuvuori.

Lightnings flickered in the sky. The Witch raised her voice above the gathering storm.

"Strong is thy brother, but *thou* hast the Mark of the Clan. Ten times more powerful art thou, as thou knowest. It is thy destiny to become my handmaiden. I can give thee a magic the world has never seen. The *kalma* of Pohjola will unleash all that power trapped within thee. Listen to me, Ulla! Thou shalt be stronger than Väinämöinen, stronger than Lemminkäinen, stronger than any mortal or Erilainen who has ever lived.

"A spell I have prepared, Ulla; a spell to bind us together as one. My power will quicken within thee. My time comes; I will return to the Far Northern Land itself. The ice and snow shall carry my essence to every corner of the land. And *you* shall be my sentinel, my herald unto all the world.

"Bend thy knee and accept me as thy mistress! And all of this will surely come to be."

And the words of Löhi were true. For only of Ulla's free will might the spell work and Löhi's design come to pass.

Tall stood the Witch, silhouetted by the rising moon behind her. But still Ulla defied her.

"I will never serve you! Do with me what you will. But I will not be a pawn of Pohjola, whatever may betide. I am a *tietäjää* of the Far Northern Land."

Then Löhi took Ulla by the hand, leading her onto the pier of rock. And from that vantage point, beside the throne, Ulla beheld all of the Far Northern Land. She saw the banners of the Swan snap in the breeze along the battlements in the Stone City of Etelamaa. Snow covered Tapiola's Seven Hills in winter's dark. Trapped at Siinesaare amidst the frozen lake, Teemu and the Elk Folk contested their enemies. The longships of Langvika sat on rollers while the lords of the Eagle Folk warred among themselves.

And Löhi pointed to the South.

"Worship me," she said. "And all the kingdoms of the world shall be yours. Look upon the Far Northern Land, Ulla. The woods, the lakes, the rivers—all these things will be yours to command in my name. A Queen you shall be, my vehicle upon this earth. The Vanhalaiset are vanished; I alone remain. But as I journey into regions unknown to mortal kind, you will remain my trusted servant and order all things as you see fit."

And Ulla lifted up her eyes to Löhi, and said, "No."

And Löhi pointed to the East.

"Worship me," she said. "And you shall never die. Erilainen I will make you. Immortality will be yours, life everlasting. No dark journey through Tuonela will you ever know, no failing body and fading strength. Years uncounted will you enjoy to savor howsoever you would. Death will be a stranger to you, and you will live forever."

And for the second time, Ulla lifted up her eyes to Löhi, and said, "No."

And Löhi pointed to the West.

"Worship me," she said. "And you shall never be alone. All those whom you have loved and lost shall be returned to you. Your mother, whom you never knew. Your father, who protected you. Egan, thy love, and all of your friends and kinfolk. And Väinämöinen will be spared and dwell with you. I will deliver from death all you have ever loved, Ulla. Never will you be alone, never again."

And for the third time, Ulla lifted up her eyes to Löhi, and said, "No."

Then Löhi turned cold and sullen. Long she gazed on Ulla in silence while the wind fanned her raven hair. And then a change began, a horrible change, as her aspect shifted once more. The fair form of the snow queen vanished, transformed into a hideous, gap-toothed crone. But so horrible was her visage, so awful the monstrous face, that no evil ever seen in the waking world has been so terrifying.

Ulla recoiled as if struck by a blow.

"Then thou shalt die!" cried the queen. "And curse the day that ever thou wast born. Here, atop the Kipuvuori, thy spirit will be destroyed and thy body will rot within a gibbet. And all who remain of thy folk shall be crushed beneath my rod. Thy red-haired friend in Etelamaa, thy cousin in the South—thinkest thou I know them not or cannot find them? Thou hast chosen death, Karhulainen, and death shall be thy lasting reward."

The Witch raised her hand. A shimmering orb of crackling flame wove golden about the web of her fingers. Chanting in the tongue of Pohjola, she sang the final spell. Ulla shrank against the foot of the stony throne, terrified.

Out of habit, her hand strayed to her pouch. She grasped something—a single object that had come with her into the spirit world, all but forgotten: *karhu's tooth*. It was the last of the three, never needed until that moment. Ulla drew it forth now. The bear tooth gleamed in the moonlight. Ulla raised it in her small, trembling hand.

"*Karhu, karhu, KARHU!*" she cried.

Even as the Witch moved to strike, she hesitated. A deafening roar shook the mountaintop. Wheeling round, she found *karhu* looming over her.

For Ulla's call had summoned him, brought the spirit-bear at last to the one place in all the world he had never come. Safe was Löhi atop the Kipuvuori, safe to weave her spells, and safe to let her spirit wander, entering the dreams of her enemies, losing herself in the wind, snow, and ice.

Karhu could not come there.

The black magic of that evil place had defied the spirit-animal. But the Witch herself had brought Ulla's spirit to that dreadful summit, with the bear tooth taken in her hunt. No other power could have summoned the bear in Löhi's despite.

Karhu grew huge, feeding off the mountain's magic. He towered over all the world.

"*Pysäyttää!*" cried the Witch, flinging the flaming orb at the shaggy giant, but to no avail. Straightaway, he leapt full upon her, raking Löhi with his deadly claws.

Screaming in terror, she sought to flee *karhu's* grasp, but the bear's awesome strength was too great. His leap brought them to the brink of the rocky pier. Together, they tumbled over.

Lightning struck the mountaintop. The northern lights raced crazily overhead. Hail rained down on the Kipuvuori. The North Wind blew like a gale. And even as Ulla clung desperately to the throne lest she fall, she heard the wail of Löhi's screams mingled with *karhu's* mighty roar as together they plunged into the darkness.

At last the wind dropped. Ulla regained her feet, peering from the brink into the gloom. And with her wizardly *sight*, Ulla glimpsed Löhi along the banks of the pale river in the colorless woods.

No crone now, no wizened monster corrupt from years of wickedness, she was young—young as a sapling in springtime, young as winter's first frost, young as a lithe, fair maiden of the Far Northern Land in the dawn of the world long ago. As Ukko had made her at the beginning of time, Löhi appeared now. But she was naked, confused, and blind, groping her way through the dark reeds and rushes, desperately searching for a way of escape.

Then a shape emerged from the creeping mists, a little boat upon the sad, still waters. Within stood a figure suffused in white. Slowly she came to where Löhi struggled.

And Pain Girl stepped down, a chain in her white hands. When Löhi saw her, she rose, straightened, and, with frantic gestures, sought to weave a spell. But no power remained to her, no strength of magic or wizardry. She was dead and the dead carry no magic with them. No cloak or garment, no mask or shield can protect the dead in Tuonela. They must face their fate alone, their true soul bare before Ukko to account for what they have done with the time allotted them.

So, though Löhi fought and struggled, pled and bargained, the girl with the broken face did not falter. She coiled the iron chain about Löhi, she who would be goddess unto all the Seven Clans. And she cast the Witch in ruin to the ground.

"Each link in this chain thou hast forged," said Pain Girl. "Each ring made fast by thy evil. Long was its making, for years on end; patiently have we awaited thy coming.

"Now it will bind thee and lead thee into my father's kingdom. And so bound shalt thou remain forever, even unto the ending of the world."

Then Pain Girl dragged Löhi through the mire into the little boat. As her long pole dipped in and out of the darkling water, Löhi's cries echoed up to heaven. Even to mortal ears they came, here and there in the waking world. But Ulla's *sight* grew dark, the vision faded, and never did she see nor hear the Witch of the North ever again.

Cold wind blew on Ulla's face. Her mind swam. When her vision cleared, she stood in Sariola, in the Witch's throne room, with all eyes in the room upon her.

For when Löhi died, her *kalma* died with her. The dark webs that she wove throughout Pohjola, her spells of despair, a thousand incantations and enchantments—all vanished. Throughout the Far Northern Land, her servants perceived her absence as a blow to their hearts. And the ground shook beneath all of Sariola as a storm raged in fury.

But Ulla's power kindled like a newborn star. Golden light shone all about her. Her strength grew beyond the world's measure, all weariness and pain banished. If all of Sariola had been marshalled against her, no blade, dart, or spell could have harmed her.

And Löhi's body, bereft of spirit, changed a final time. Her mantle fell away; her lofty crown dropped to the ground. All of ice she became now, a frozen sculpture, utterly transparent. No substance remained within her.

Ulla breathed upon the form—and lo! Into a thousand pieces Löhi shattered, scattered across the stony floor. The Witch was no more.

The goblins screamed in terror, running wildly from the room; the white wolf followed. And from Hiitola, the Goblin Town, arose a wailing so loud it could be heard even within the castle's walls. But Löhi's slaves broke into joyous song, though they knew not why sudden hope welled within their hearts.

Ulla picked up her sword. Väinämöinen, drawing strength from Ulla despite his hurts, did the same, while the Moonface and Haltiatar stood transfixed, disbelieving their eyes.

"It's impossible," muttered Kuupää, the silver mask falling from his shaking hand. "Impossible. The Queen cannot die. The Queen can never die!"

"Dead she is," said Ulla. "And you are vanquished. It is over."

"No," said the Moonface. He whirled about in his madness, looking frantically from face to face. "No! I am the Lord of Pohjola! I am the Heir of Löhi and of Lemminkäinen! I am the King of the World!"

Springing forward, the Moonface shouted a word of power, aiming to deal Ulla a deadly blow. But he was diminished, the font of his magic dry, and Ulla had come into her own.

With a swift stroke, Ulla cut off his sword arm, plunging *Pohjanpiikki* straight through his breast and out the other side. Blood gushed from the sorcerer's mouth.

Their faces only inches apart, the Moonface gazed into Ulla's hazel-green eyes, the eyes that mirrored his own.

"Sister...my sister..."

But Ulla raised her leg, thrusting him back with a savage kick. Slipping off the sword, the Moonface fell dead at her feet.

"I have no brother," said Ulla.

Turning to the elves, Ulla raised her sword. Väinämöinen rushed forward to help Turi. But Vepsa held his hand up in gesture of parley and submission.

"The Witch is dead," said Vepsa. "You have destroyed her, she who was deathless and invincible. And I do not doubt that I have seen the hand of Ukko at work. Who am I to defy the will of Ukko made manifest? Never have I felt such power."

He knelt before her, his companions beside him, holding out their sword hilts.

"As Löhi's last captain, I surrender Sariola unto you. You are the Queen of Pohjola."

Ulla stared at them, unmoving. Väinämöinen came to her side.

"Rise, Vepsa," he said. "Gather all the folk left to you who will still obey. For the story is not over. There is still much work to be done."

Chapter Sixteen

The Departure of Väinämöinen

The little boy dug his boot into the snow. Brushing back his flaxen hair, he pulled his cap down. It was warm. The yellow sun shone bright in the cloudless blue sky. Though still winter, the snow was already melting.

The boy's name was Janni, a common enough name among the Tavastialaiset. For all his seven years he had lived with his parents in a little village not far from the sea. His father farmed rye and greens in the nearby fields. When his mother wasn't helping in the fields, she tended goats or kept house in their tiny *pirtti*. There had been another child—a girl—but she had died when Janni was still very young. He did not remember her.

Janni's uncle had also died, in the very same year that the boy was born. Janni's grandmother told him a story about a great battle far away. His uncle had marched off to war with the king and never returned. Janni's grandmother grew sad when she told the story.

The boy had another uncle, too, this one even younger than his father. He fished the lake in a little boat, dragging woven nets behind him. Now his young uncle was also gone—called to Tapiola to fight for the new queen who ruled the Hare Folk. Janni had never been to Tapiola, but his mother had. She had once lived nearby, one of the *maaorjat* in a serf village. Tapiola was beautiful, she said, filled with tall white towers and fountains made of gold. Janni hoped to see the towers someday, but mostly the little boy just hoped that his uncle would come home.

He kicked the ground again. Beneath the snow divot, he found another one—wet, green shoots beginning to blossom. All over the field it was the same. Seeds and chaff from last year's crops were sprouting up before it was even spring. This was not supposed to happen.

Janni ran home to tell his father. The big, grey-bearded man sat by the hearth stirring thin porridge in a black pot. Little enough remained from their winter stores.

"More of them?" asked the man, who hadn't placed much stock in his son's tale the first time. Janni was a truthful lad, but children were children, after all.

"Green shoots in the ground? All right, I'll put my boots back on and take a look. The day's fair enough for a walk. But if you're lying, I'll have to beat you, boy. *A false tongue begs the rod.*"

Janni was not beaten.

From southern Tavastia to the woods of old Länsimaa, people noticed two things that year. Spring came early, unusually early—earlier, in fact, than ever before, even in the years before the Witch returned. Snow melted, plants bloomed, and it seemed a fair growing season had come at last.

Second, the red star disappeared.

The Witch's Star had shone ever brighter as it approached the Nail of the Heavens. Then, one night in midwinter, a great storm descended from the north. Thunder boomed, ice rained down, and strange voices wailed on the wind. The sky remained overcast for many days afterward. When the clouds finally broke, the red star had faded. It appeared weak, low in the northern sky as if running away. One night it failed to rise and people wondered what that might portend.

For several years, the Itäläiset had grown ever bolder, raiding the Marches of Tavastia and Etelamaa as soon as the water opened. Now, despite the fair spring, they withdrew behind the Wall of the Giants. The soldiers of the Hare and Swan Folk waited for attacks that never came.

In Deep Länsimaa, something even more unexpected occurred. One morning, Teemu's scouts returned to Siinesaare where the Elk Folk still endured the siege. Their report was as shocking as it was welcome. The goblins were gone, the camps of their enemies deserted. The Easterners had apparently fled north, leaving stores of food and even animals behind. Fearing a trap, Teemu hesitated, but his people were starving.

He led them from the isle, crossing the lake in hundreds of boats and marching toward Linnavuori in a long, straggling line. The Tavastialaiset met the refugees there, bringing food, medicine, and supplies. The Elk Folk's long nightmare was over; it seemed their enemies had given up the fight.

The Folk of the Seven Clans eventually learned what had happened. Elves appeared, sent by Mielikki in the Enchanted Valley. They carried news to Tapiola, Langvika, Seppälä, Kotanrannta, and all the villages and towns in between. Janus himself, Lord of the Haltiatar of Taikalaakso, rode to the Stone City with an escort of ten companions. Standing in the square beside the great swan, clad in white robes bordered with scarlet, his herald blew a silver horn three times.

Then Janus proclaimed the news to the gathered folk, bringing great joy that spring to everyone in the Far Northern Land. For he proclaimed that Ulla had defeated Löhi; the realm of Pohjola was no more.

People rejoiced at the news. Across the Far Northern Land, folk made songs praising Ulla, calling her the hero and savior of the Seven Lands. Many expected her to become their ruler, a High Queen set above all the other lords and monarchs. Though still feared in some places as much as she was loved, none doubted her strength, perseverance, and majesty. The tale of her last battle with Löhi atop the Kipuvuori spread among the common folk of the Seven Clans, especially the men-at arms. Her name became a rallying cry. Not since Egan marched to Sumuvuori had any mortal been so popular.

None knew the time and manner of Ulla's return. Much remained to be done. Famine was everywhere. The lives of thousands depended upon the harvest. Juvari took all the men that he had gathered to build the great towers and set them to work in the fields. They dug rocks, felled trees, burned fields, and planted seed. All across the Far Northern Land, it was the same. Scouts reported that the Easterners north of the Wall withdrew into their holds or else gathered at Keskimaa, fearing that they would now be attacked in turn.

Spring ran on toward summer. More news arrived. Mielikki sent messages to all of the surviving *tietäjää*, saying Väinämöinen and Ulla were returning. She summoned all the lords of the Far Northern Land to Kotanrannta to receive them on Midsummer's Day. None refused that summons. So from Akkala to Karelia, companies set out for Etelamaa and Ulla's homecoming.

Väinämöinen and Ulla passed into the old lands of the Bear Folk at the head of a great company. They had freed Löhi's slaves, both the descendants of prisoners taken in ancient times and new captives alike. Sariola was abandoned, save for the goblins hiding in their holes. The Dark Erilaiset who refused Vepsa's call to surrender had fled into the wilderness.

Since Sariola was stocked with large stores of goods, the freed men, women, and children were left well-provisioned and outfitted. Following Ulla, the host drove straight down the road from Pohjola to Karelia, crossing the Jouksi just north of the forest.

They marched east of Suurijärvi, through those very lands where Ulla had wandered as a scatterling from the Marches. Karhulaisen fugitives, hiding in the marshes from the Easterners, joined them. Few Itäläiset lived in those parts, but those who did dared not molest the company. Ulla's people were armed, many of them bowmen, and wore mail taken from Löhi's armories. Moreover, Ulla was there. Wherever she went, her power passed into the lands nearby, strengthening friends and frightening enemies. Not even an entire army would attack her, for fear of her magic.

From all corners of the Far Northern Land, they came to Kotanrannta: Osmo from Karelia, Snurri from Langvika, Vara from Tavastia, and many others. Kirsikka and Marjatta rode north from the Stone City, the red-haired woman anxious to see her friend. Teemu came from his people's camp at Linnavuori, accompanied by Ilkka and Tulikki, for, indeed, they had survived and returned.

After Ulla, Väinämöinen, and Kaukomieli had left them in the snowy wilderness, Tulikki had built a shelter to weather the harsh winter, catching fish through holes in the ice and luring small animals from their dens. It was touch and go, but slowly Ilkka had healed. When spring came, they had journeyed south together, slipping silently through the Easterners' lands about Valkeakosk until they reached Linnavuori. Though starving and exhausted by then, they had now recovered and wished to see Ulla at once. Leaving Teemu to wait at Kotanrannta, Ilkka and Tulikki rode ahead, going north to greet their friends.

At last came the day all had waited for. Guards reported that Ulla approached from the north. The sun shone golden in a clear blue sky, a shade of blue only seen at Midsummer when the heavens opened like a field of morning glories after a dewy dawn. A gentle breeze moved the grasses. Arrayed on the field were the lords of the Seven Clans, with Juvari at their head amidst a picked escort of Swan Knights in full regalia. And Mielikki stood among them.

The Lady of the Forest had come from the Enchanted Valley with a dozen Metsänaiset, her handmaidens. The people were amazed, for they had never seen the tree maidens that tales spoke of, let alone the daughter of Tapio. Mielikki, dressed in a green gown studded with sapphires, wore her long hair loose upon her bare white shoulders, and men murmured that they had not known such beauty was possible.

Väinämöinen and Ulla rode into sight, their folk following in well-ordered companies. The former chattel of Pohjola drew up in formation like soldiers. The people of the Seven Clans wondered what this might mean. Had Ulla come to claim the queenship of all the Seven Lands? Ilkka and Tulikki rode with them and, beside them, rode Turi the Changer. Though his eyes would never again see the world, his wizardly *sight* could and did.

Turi bore a great horn upon his lap. Setting it to his lips, the wizard blew a long note, rising and falling, echoing over all the nearby lands.

Then Väinämöinen and Ulla rode out from the ranks. Ulla rode upon Midnight and the old wizard on Starchaser, for the Karelialaiset had rescued the horses in winter.

Väinämöinen looked resplendent in a crimson tunic bordered with yellow trim and bronze thread, with gold bands in his snow-white beard. *Jääpuikko* hung from his silver belt. He held a staff of yew in his hand.

Beside him sat Ulla in her black mail, her long, dark hair spilling out from a visored helm. Clasped by a red garnet stone at her throat, her white cloak draped gracefully over Midnight's back. Ulla's weapons remained in their sheaths on her saddle; in her left hand she grasped an iron spear, from which a flawless argent flag flew, snapping in the breeze.

Mielikki stepped forward to greet them. Bowing low, she swung round to face the gathered folk, her green gown swaying magically about her.

"Folk of the Seven Clans!" cried Mielikki. "Receive now thy savior! For Ulla Karhulainen, Tapio's chosen who bears the Mark of the Clan, returns! Ulla, who journeyed to Pohjola and back. Ulla, who battled Löhi atop the Mountain of Pain and slew her. Ulla, who delivered us all, mortal and immortal alike, from the cold hand of the Witch even as it reached out to destroy us. All praise and glory be given to her! For she is the greatest singer that the world has ever known and all shall honor her."

Then Ulla removed the black helm. And lo! The people perceived that her hazel eyes were fluted like those of the Erilaiset, shining beneath the noonday sun.

But Väinämöinen raised his staff, crying out in a great voice, "Hear me, o ye people! True are Mielikki's words. Ulla is the mightiest *tietäjää* of all, mightier even than Lemminkäinen of legend. Yet she makes no claim to rule you."

"Nay," said Mielikki. "For Ulla's heart is true. Not for power, spoils, or revenge did she endure the quest of Pohjola. For duty alone did she fight the long battle, as did we all; for duty, responsibility, and *to do what must be done.*

"Listen now to the Prophecy of Mielikki. Listen, for this is the last vision given unto me by my father and the last prophecy concerning the Seven Lands of mortal men that ever I shall make. No claim does Ulla make upon the Seven Clans, but you may make claim upon her. The Far Northern Land still teeters on the edge of ruin. Famine, illness, enemies, and woe beset all your Folk. Löhi's evil cannot so easily be remedied despite her demise. If you will take Ulla, willingly, to be your leader through this time of uncertainty, the lands will prosper. Peace shall return and, through her power, many ills made right again. Yet if you do not, if division and jealousy rule your hearts, the Clans will still know strife and many sacrifices will have been in vain.

"For your people, your land, and your magic, in unity lies your hope. Choose now, ye lords and ladies, and choose well. *Comes a child into the Northland, all the Clans to bring together.* This is the Prophecy of Mielikki. Choose well!"

They chose well and swiftly.

Here and there among the crowd folk cried, "We will have her, we will have her!" Others joined in, then still more, and soon all the gathered folk called out Ulla's name in praise.

Lifting high the spear in her left hand, Ulla rode slowly from one end of the line to the other. She said nothing, looking sternly upon the folk who knelt in obeisance or offered their sword hilts in gesture of fealty.

Juvari of Etelamaa, who had lost a leg at Sumuvuori, offered his sword to Ulla, saying, "Command me, my lady," as she passed him. Toiva Merikainen and the lords of the Stone City knelt before her. Teemu of Deep Länsimaa and the rulers of the exiled Bear Folk offered their swords to her. Ikämä, the Lord Captain of the March Wardens in Ilkka's absence, pledged his fealty. Even Vara, the cold Queen of the Hare Folk, bowed her head.

Grave and somber Ulla appeared, a woman of proud mien and bearing whose power could be felt by all.

But at the end of the line stood a red-haired woman regally dressed who suddenly ran forward.

"Lumikki, oh Lumikki!" cried Kirsikka.

Hopping off Midnight, Ulla let fall the argent flag and embraced her friend.

"Oh, Kirsikka," she cried.

Tears flowed from them both, for truly they were sisters at heart.

Then the people came together, mingled, and, led by Väinämöinen, returned to Kotanrannta where the Lady Annika had organized a great feast. Thus did Ulla return to her Folk, acknowledged by all as the Ruler of the Far Northern Land.

After the feasting ended, Ulla took counsel with the leaders ere they departed for their own lands. Then she made ready to ride south with the Swan Folk to the Stone City. The people rescued from Pohjola remained in a great camp close to Kotanrannta, however. And Ulla said to them, "Wait here for me. Labor with the Etelalaiset in the fields, but do not despair. I promise that I shall return to thee within a season or two and I shall lead thee to Akkala, even to the lands once held by the Susilaiset. For you shall become the new Wolf Folk and the Lost Clan shall be renewed."

And Ulla said that the name of their first town and capital would be called Unajala in memory of her friend.

At that time, Turi, Mielikki, and the Erilaiset said their good-byes, for they would now return to the Enchanted Valley.

"Farewell, little one," said Turi, with a sad smile on his kindly face. "Never did I doubt you, even during the darkest hours of torment in Sariola. Greatly did Löhi wish me to deny you; it angered her when I would not! My thought and love will always be with you, most precious Ulla."

Ulla and Mielikki spent one night together upon the Luntamäki, the Snow Hill outside of Kotanrannta where Väinämöinen had once waited for both Lemminkäinen and Egan. They talked of many things and Mielikki instructed her concerning the time to come when her word would be as law to the struggling people.

"But will you not always be there to counsel me?" asked Ulla.

"Perhaps," answered the beautiful woman. "Yet you perceive even more sharply than I that the winds of the world are changing. The Erilaiset have dwindled to a small folk now. Our paths run in different directions."

"Good-bye, my daughter," said Mielikki, kissing Ulla upon her white brow. "It may be long ere we see one another again. You have done very well, Ulla. Yes, you have done well with the great light set within you. Neither greed nor revenge, neither pride nor despair did you let turn you from the path appointed. No temptation overcame you; thus did you save your people. Let the wisdom you have learned guide you all the days of your life. And know that one day, you, too, shall find peace."

Väinämöinen did not say good-bye, however. He travelled with Ulla to the Stone City to help her in her labor. Standing atop the Keep, overlooking the glassy bay, she wove the magic of Akka with spells of increase, fertility, and health to chase away winter's sicknesses. Even as Löhi had poisoned the Seven Lands with her dark *kalma*, so Ulla now healed them, her power flowing over lake and field.

The harvest that fall was bountiful. Some still suffered, but for the most part the Kaamoslaiset had food to eat and store against the oncoming winter. They cared for the homeless as well as they could, building shelter for thousands across all the lands. Exhausted from her labors, Ulla felt happy nonetheless, for she knew now that the Seven Clans would survive.

She faced other, more difficult choices. Juvari and Teemu wished to attack the Itäläiset in Länsimaa and so free the Elk and Bear Folk still oppressed as thralls. Thousands of Easterners remained in the Far Northern Land despite Löhi's fall. Not readily would they abandon the lands for which they had shed so much blood.

Long did Ulla and Väinämöinen consider the wisest course, but, in the end, despite her grief for those still enslaved, she rejected Juvari's counsel.

"We are too weak," she said. "We came to the edge of ruin and the northern parts of Tavastia and Etelamaa are still in disarray. Countless are the refugees among us. The Easterners will fight fiercely, the outcome uncertain.

They may cross the Marches to strike at us unawares even as we march on Keskimaa. And moreover, not only will soldiers die, but many common folk, too, who might otherwise be saved from hunger and want. Whatever we may do later, let us first repair our house and regain our strength."

To this they assented, for they recognized Ulla's wisdom in a difficult choice. And even as they debated, Ilkka was hard at work. He enlarged the March Wardens, sending hundreds to the borders of Tavastia and Etelamaa to strengthen their defenses and guard against any unexpected foray.

So passed the summer and fall. Throughout the mild winter, Ulla rested in the Stone City with Kirsikka. The Swan Folk gave her Egan's chamber to dwell in and old Orvo looked after her. Ulla and Kirsikka spent long hours together, speaking of all that they had seen and done since childhood. The high station to which Ulla had come meant nothing between them. With Kirsikka, Ulla could almost be that little girl from the Marches again.

In her heart of hearts, Ulla yearned for nothing less. Now that the war was over and the fear of famine receding, Ulla's thoughts turned to the little islands she had seen from Langvika's shores. *It would be quiet on those islands,* she thought. *Calm and peaceful, with nothing except the sea, wind, sun, and stars.* Ulla secretly longed to be alone in just such a place, away from the cares and responsibilities that defined her. Had she not done enough for her people? Had she not earned a measure of peace, as Mielikki had said? But that time was not yet come, so she put away her secret thought and carried on.

* * *

When the first blush of spring returned to the Far Northern Land, Ulla, Kirsikka, and Marjatta rode to a wood not far from Nummela. A cabin used by the royal family stood there next to a blue lake. The three young women passed several pleasant days in the bright wood, walking the trails and watching the stars at night. One afternoon, they wandered together through the forest, picking their way through scattered trees. Black, red, and yellow, their heads bobbed this way and that. They appeared for all the world like three simple village girls out looking for berries.

It was too early yet for berries; the fat, plump blueberries came at high summer with the black crowberries in the marshes. In late summer, red lingonberries would cover their little bushes on the forest floor for the poor folk of the villages to pack in barrels of cold water to last throughout the winter. Cranberries would ripen by the lakeside. Now it was even too early for strawberries to hide in their thickets and bushes, growing huge in the long days and summer sun.

A flash of scarlet and gold caught Marjatta's eye. She spied a patch of tiny green buds aglow in a beam of sunlight. Among the buds, a single ripe, red berry shone like a gift from the heavens, a strawberry, two months too soon, ripe and ready. The yellow-haired girl stooped, plucked the berry, and popped it into her mouth.

"Marjatta!" cried Ulla.

An ominous shadow descended upon them suddenly from above. A strange presence filled the wood. Ulla spun round, a spell on the tip of her tongue, but found nothing there. The dark cloud passed slowly overhead.

By the time the three women returned to the Keep in the Stone City, Marjatta felt ill. She burned with fever. Aarva, the Master Healer, sat by her bedside. Ulla and Väinämöinen tried to divine the nature of her illness. They feared she might die and dreaded the need to tell Vendla that her last child had perished.

All the while, an amazing change came over Marjatta. Dream after vivid dream colored her sleep. A sense of expectant wonder grew within her. She no longer felt ill, but more full with life than ever she had felt before.

Soon it appeared to everyone that she was with child. Each day seemed to count for a month. None could explain it, for Marjatta, unmarried, had never been with any man. Ulla told the Swan Folk about the berry in the woods, but it was old Väinämöinen who finally discerned what had happened.

One night, the old wizard suffered strange dreams and visions. The next morning, he called Ulla, Toiva, Juvari, Aarva, and others to the Hall of the Swan. Beneath the great blue and white token of the Etelalaiset, he told them his tale.

"Verily, as we have guessed, Marjatta carries a child. Ilmatar the Vanha, Mistress of the Clouds, came to me with this wisdom, for, in the days of old, I was her first servant. Listen! The child that grows now within Marjatta will be a boy and he shall be called Egan III, after his uncle. He comes to the Far Northern Land to heal its ills and unite the Seven Clans as High King, fulfilling his uncle's promise. Ulla will serve as his regent, instructing and guiding him until he comes to manhood. And, if the Seven Clans embrace him, a golden age will dawn upon all the lands."

Marjatta's child, born a few days later, was the very image of Egan as a baby, save that he had golden brown eyes, not blue. After Marjatta recovered, Väinämöinen and the Erilaiset sent messages throughout the Seven Lands proclaiming the child's birth and Ulla's regency. If some of the leaders among the other Clans murmured at a prince of the Swan Folk, born under strange circumstances, becoming Lemminkäinen's heir, none dared gainsay the prophecy; for the common folk revered Ulla so greatly, they would follow whatsoever she instructed no matter their own lords.

The summer turned golden. Folk labored to bring in a bountiful harvest. Ulla prepared to journey west; she would finally see Siria again and her niece and nephew. She intended to go north after that, to Tapiola, then on to the Neck of Tavastia where Teemu and thousands of Hirvilaiset still lived in makeshift camps. She also thought to send scouts into Akkala to search for the lands that would become the home of the Wolf Folk.

Saying her good-byes to Kirsikka, Marjatta, and Väinämöinen, Ulla set out with only a small escort. She rode along the coast, greeted by cheering crowds in every village and town along the way. She would always be the wizard who bore the Mark of the Clan and who had killed the Witch.

Väinämöinen had busied himself with many tasks in Etelamaa, especially the organization of those *tietäjää* who remained. His own secret thought and counsel he revealed to none, however. Ever since he returned to the Seven Lands, a feeling had been growing inside him.

The Erilaiset of the Valley had suffered much during the war. They had dwindled to a small folk now. Wild Erilaiset still dwelt here and there, but they, too, were few, for Löhi had hunted down many of them in her days of power and others had fled far away. In the utmost north, Löhi's servants were scattered throughout the wilderness and wished nothing to do with the mortals away south.

The old man could feel the change happening everywhere in the Far Northern Land. It ran through the cold rivers as they rushed down to the lakes and sea. It ran through the forests as green leaves opened beneath the gentle sun. The wind sang a new song, a song the Vanhalaiset prepared for the newcomers. Ulla would sing that song, and little Egan when he came to manhood, but not old Väinämöinen. A new age had come to the North, an age that the Erilaiset could never fully know.

His own home called. The Great Oak beckoned. Turi, Mielikki, and the remnant of his people dwelt deep within Karelia, awaiting his return.

He did not have the heart to tell Ulla these things before she departed. Dissembling, the old man wished her well, holding little Egan as he stood beside Marjatta and Kirsikka when Ulla rode away. Yet he had already made up his mind. Saying farewell to only a few, he slipped away at night, as was his wont. Starchaser clattered across the bridge while the red sun hung on the horizon. Turning north, Väinämöinen made for the Karelian Forest.

But the old man reckoned without Ulla. She had not yet reached Harmaaniemi when a strange mood came upon her. The premonition was strong—so strong, in fact, that she reached out her mind to Väinämöinen that very night and found all dark. Her wizardly *sight* was blind to the old man's whereabouts. Ulla turned around at once, racing back to the Stone City.

Väinämöinen had only been gone three days when she reached the Keep. Ulla did not hesitate. She followed after him immediately.

Alone upon Midnight, Ulla chased the wizard across the Plain of Etelamaa. She rode day and night, stopping only during the few hours of darkness to rest her horse. She felt angry at first, angry that he would leave her yet again without even so much as a good-bye. But her mood cooled as the miles sped past. She grew sad, even melancholy, for she rightly guessed the old man's mind and what his flight might portend.

She caught up with him in the Green Vales, not far from the eaves of the Karelian Forest. A long field of tall, green grass ran down toward a narrow defile, a pass through the kettle lakes to the woodlands beyond. Väinämöinen stood beside Starchaser while the horse grazed. The grass swayed in the wind. The old man smiled as Ulla rode up, her black mail and white cloak gleaming in the summer sun.

He was expecting her.

"Well met, child," said Väinämöinen. "It's no use trying to give you the slip. I should have learned that long ago."

"I should be angry with you," Ulla replied. "Leaving me, without a word of farewell. Whatever has gotten into you? Why did you leave, Väinämöinen? Where are you going?"

"You know well enough, child. I'm going to the Enchanted Valley. I didn't have the heart to say good-bye; I'm sorry. I thought that it would be better so. Not the first time I've been wrong and it won't be the last."

"I shall go with you."

"No, Ulla. Not this time. My *väki* await me. We are a small folk now and they need me, even as your folk need you. You belong to the Far Northern Land now, to its people, and they belong to you. They will need you for some time, Ulla. My time of doing is over now. It is time to be."

"But what will you do, Väinämöinen?" she asked, brushing the tears from her eyes.

"I do not know for certain. My kantale is waiting and my songs. Maybe journeys into realms where you cannot follow, not yet. The world is changing, Ulla. I feel it in the earth. I see it in the stars. The wind brings wisdom to those who listen. The time of the Erilaiset draws to an end. But your time is at hand, Ulla. And all the days of your life will be blessed as reward for your mighty labor."

Ulla felt her heart breaking.

"Am I never to see you again? Will you not be at Väinölä if I come there?"

"I do not know what the future holds, little one. But I think this will not be the end for us. My most precious daughter, my love will always be with you, beyond any love I could ever have for another soul. Always remember this."

Then Ulla dismounted, embracing the old man. He held her close for a long time, and they talked for a while of all their experiences together throughout the wide world. But when the bright sun passed into the western sky, beginning its slow descent, Väinämöinen kissed her.

Hopping upon Starchaser, he bade Ulla farewell and made to leave.

"Väinämöinen!" she cried. "That day in the woods near Grankulta; did you know that you would find me there? Were you searching for me?"

The old man looked upon her kindly. He broke into a smile.

"Who can say, child?"

Without another word, he spoke to Starchaser, riding hard for the defile and the great Karelian Forest far away.

But Ulla stood watching him, her eyes clouded with tears. She watched him dwindle into the distance until the sunlight glinted one last time off his copper-shod staff. Then he was gone.

Still she stood silent, stern and unmoving. The westering sun softened.

At last Ulla mounted, turning Midnight back toward the south. Slowly she rode across the grassy plain, then faster. At last she burst into a gallop, sitting tall and erect, dark hair flying in the breeze. Like an eagle she sped across the lands, the lands of the mortal Kaamoslaiset, *her* land, Finland, the Land of the Seven Clans.

The warm, early summer sun shone down on the green trees and blue waters. The south wind blew in measured, gentle gusts as the flickering aspen leaves shimmered and seemed to change color with each breath. The woods glowed with summer's blush of life. Summer in the Far Northern Land brought long days and short nights. Everything hurried to live, to grow, to bloom and thrive before the seasons turned again—for if the days were long, summer was not, and winter always waited just around the corner.

FINIS

What does an author stand to gain by asking for reader feedback? A lot. In fact, it's so important in the publishing world that they've coined a catchy name for it: "social proof." And without social proof, an author may as well be invisible in this age of digital media sharing.

So if you've enjoyed *The Far Northern Land Saga*, please consider giving it some visibility by reviewing it on the sales platform of your choice. Your honest opinion could help potential readers decide whether or not they would enjoy this book, too.